Critical acclaim for A BITTER PEACE

"Bradley Marshall, an American diplomat, is getting flak from all directions: his younger son, Chris, announces that he's gay and doesn't like how Dad handles the news; Bradley's older son, Ryan, a prisoner of war in Vietnam long considered dead, just might be alive; and Bradley's daughter, Sarah, thinks her father is the incarnation of a foreign policy gone insane. As if all that weren't bad enough, a fanatical Central Intelligence Agency operative . . . now wants to kill him. . . . Mr. Peterson has mastered the formula."

—Keith Dixon, *New York Times Book Review*

"Peterson seems to be trying to do for recent U.S. history what Alexandre Dumas did for the history of France—to ennoble and illuminate it throught a dramatic secret history that portrays the truth behind the facts. It's a mission he performs well."

—*Publishers Weekly*

"There is action aplenty, ample suspense, and clear description. This is a thoughtful and highly readable novel."

—Bill Roach, *Florida Times-Union* (Jacksonville, FL)

Praise for Michael Peterson's
A TIME OF WAR

"Powerful."

—Donovan Fitzpatrick, *The New York Times Book Review*

"The Vietnam War was unlike any conflict previously fought in history, and Peterson has managed to capture its unique mixture of horror and bravery on a large scale."

—Digby Diehl, *Playboy*

"Peterson . . . takes his far-flung cast of larger-than-life characters and cooks up a clever . . . fast-paced, thrillerlike plot. There's lots of snappy dialogue and a healthy sprinkling of sex."

—Mark Leepson, *Chicago Tribune*

"*A Time of War* . . . may well become a classic, on a par with *All Quiet on the Western Front* and *From Here to Eternity*. . . . a story of lasting significance, a novel that tugs at all our emotions."

—Tony Weissgarber, *San Antonio Express-News*

"Peterson adroitly evokes embassy intrigue, and his battle scenes are immediate and compelling. . . . an elaborate, absorbing, and viscerally affecting narrative."

—*Publishers Weekly*

"A highly readable, smart, balanced war novel."

—*Kirkus Reviews*

"Big, rambunctious . . . *A Time of War* pulses with bombast and melodrama. . . . likable and never, ever dull. . . . This intelligent lyricism—plus ribald wit and deft, complex structure—set *A Time of War* well above the generic war yarn."

—Judith Wynn, *Boston Herald*

Books by Michael Peterson

A Bitter Peace*
A Time of War*
The Immortal Dragon

*Published by POCKET BOOKS

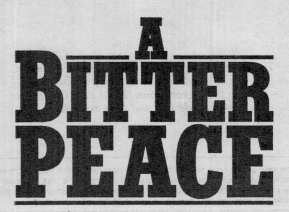

A BITTER PEACE

MICHAEL PETERSON

POCKET STAR BOOKS
New York London Toronto Sydney Tokyo Singapore

To my parents, Eleanor and Eugene Peterson,
who made life and love possible,
and to their grandsons, Todd and Clayton,
who made life and love complete

A Pocket Star Book published by
POCKET BOOKS, a division of Simon & Schuster Inc.
1230 Avenue of the Americas, New York, NY 10020

ISBN: 0-671-72696-X

First Pocket Books paperback printing December 1997

10 9 8 7 6 5 4 3 2 1

POCKET STAR BOOKS and colophon are registered trademarks of Simon & Schuster Inc.

Printed in the U.S.A.

Acknowledgments

To Bill Grose, who helped me more than he can know, and for more than I can express.

I would especially like to thank Dudley Frasier. And Al Zuckerman, whom I don't even view as an agent—but a good friend. And Fred Feldman too.

Let the word go forth from this time and place, to friend and foe alike, that the torch has been passed to a new generation of Americans—born in this century, tempered by war, disciplined by a hard and bitter peace, proud of our ancient heritage—and unwilling to witness the slow undoing of those human rights to which this nation has always been committed, and to which we are committed today at home and around the world.

—*John F. Kennedy*
Inaugural Address

Part I

PEACE

CHAPTER 1

Washington, D.C., 1972

Bradley Marshall's limousine left through the White House gates and turned onto Pennsylvania Avenue as angry bystanders on the sidewalk, bundled against the cold, their breath frosting in the crisp March air, shook their fists and waved antiwar placards.

He looked into the furious faces, then raised his gaze and saw the spiked fence around the White House. His eyes blurred the row of spikes into tiny crosses, and framed against the cloudless sky above the shouts and fury of the crowd he saw a cemetery that stretched to the horizon.

A young woman spat on his window.

"Sorry, sir," the Secret Service agent in the front seat said.

Marshall watched the sputum slide down the bulletproof glass, then closed his eyes and rubbed his forehead, thinking that this was just the first *minute* of his mission for the President.

Probably he deserved it, he realized, though his intentions were the best; yet even if he could explain to the angry woman on the sidewalk, she would not understand. He was just a diplomat, part of the charade and illusion of Government—politics—but in reality only another gravedigger who worked in the cemetery, this particular one where lay all the corpses from Vietnam.

The woman would never understand; indeed, he probably wouldn't be able to explain this to his own wife. Catherine wouldn't spit on him, but she was not going to accept his argument that he had no choice when the President of the United States asked him to undertake a mission to find a "just and honorable" peace in Vietnam and help bring back the POWs.

He might be a diplomat nonpareil who had served as envoy for three presidents, sat at tables with premiers, kings, and dictators, listened to the world's foremost liars and lied with the best of them, but he would not get anywhere convincing Catherine of the merits of working for Richard Nixon and Henry Kissinger.

He turned to look out the other window as the car sped away, blurring the people into a little streak of color against the gray buildings and blue sky, and he smiled—she might spit on him after all. She'd certainly have spat on Nixon and Kissinger had she been in the Oval Office a few minutes ago.

The setting had been as awesomely impressive as always, the room as huge as he remembered, the hushed silence throbbing with an undercurrent of power so vibrant that the air seemed electric, yet even so the scene had been discordant, for Richard Nixon could never get anything right, Marshall thought.

The President had stood framed in the French doors of the Oval Office, hands folded piously, shoulders hunched under the heavy burden of the world's sorrows, head bowed, face etched in anguish. Behind him, sunlight streaming through the glass, reflecting off the snow in the Rose Garden, broke over his shoulders in a dazzling aureole. Having maneuvered to the window to catch the light, Nixon held the pose for a long minute, but it was all wrong: the effect was not that of rapture and miracle, but of a deranged Botticelli.

Finally when he stepped forward, breaking the fresco pose, he had said in his portentous television voice, jowls waggling as if to add even more import as well as resonance to the words, "Peace is in your hands," then he took the momentous hands and pressed firmly. "Godspeed."

Jesus, Marshall thought, but only nodded as the short, pudgy man beside him said basso profoundo in German-accented English, "Perhaps *this* time you will succeed."

Marshall had smiled. "Henry, you and I know it doesn't make any difference."

"Oh, no; this is a mission of great importance," Nixon said ponderously. "Peace for the free world rests on the success of this mission. An honorable peace. That is your mission—to convince the South Vietnamese of our honorable intentions."

Kissinger nodded. "Of course, but it's the *honorable* that tops Brad's agenda."

"As well it should," Nixon intoned pontifically. "As it does my own agenda."

The three men, a startling contrast of bodies and manners, had stood in awkward silence. Marshall, trim and athletic, about the same age as the national security adviser but a head taller, radiated physical power; beside Nixon, a decade older, he conveyed health, assurance, and confidence.

He, a liberal Democrat who had served John F. Kennedy and Lyndon Johnson, understood why he was here—to sell South Vietnam a peace treaty it considered a betrayal, but he had his own reason for going, one he hoped Catherine would accept.

Four years ago Nixon had been elected with a "secret" plan to end the war, but there was no plan and the Paris peace talks continued interminably, with an entire year spent negotiating the shape of the table. American patience was exhausted, and Nixon knew his fate in the upcoming election would be the same as Johnson's if he did not end the war immediately, even if that meant sacrificing South Vietnam's best interests.

Marshall was going to prevent that.

"Convince them that this peace is just and honorable," Nixon told Marshall. "Assure them of our continued support."

The three—Nixon, Kissinger, and Marshall—had sat together in the Oval Office, Nixon as stiff and awkward as he appeared on television, forced and uncomfortable, fidgeting nervously in his chair, handling the elephant figurines on his desk like a spastic puppet, while Marshall sat relaxed and comfortable. For him the room was as natural a setting as it had been for John F. Kennedy, who had brought him into government service twelve years ago.

A patrician's patrician, descendant of John Marshall—tall, handsome, assured—Bradley Lawrence Marshall first saw government service as assistant chief of protocol for Kennedy; then he had served Johnson as special envoy, troubleshooting the Mideast, Latin America, and finally Vietnam, trying to end the war four years ago. He had returned to law practice in 1968, for there had been no end. Instead, there had been the Tet Offensive, his son's death as a Green Beret on a night ambush near the Laotian border on June 17, 1968—Ryan's body was never recovered—then Nixon's election.

The intervening years had brought Marshall personal success, a thriving law practice and greater wealth, but the war and his son's loss had burdened every aspect of his life, yet now he had another chance in Vietnam.

Looking into Nixon's eyes, Marshall asked, "What assurances can I give the South Vietnamese that we will support them if the North violates the treaty?"

"You can give President Thieu my word," Nixon said.

Kissinger broke in quickly, "Thieu and Ky trust you; you will be a vital link in the resolution of the war, and the return of the POWs."

There were many reasons not to go—his distrust of Nixon and Kissinger, his disbelief in the "just and honorable" peace—but if there was any hope to end the war, of course he would go. Catherine *had* to understand that.

Too many had died, including Ryan, too much suffering for America to walk away from without thought or penitence. There had to be a conscience: he would be that conscience.

Honor mattered. Ryan had gone to war for the most honorable reason: he could not bear some one's going in his place.

"I couldn't live with myself if some one died because of me," he had said.

A noble sentiment. Honorable. And because of it, he's been dead four years, Marshall thought, while those who fled or joined the Reserves and National Guard, who were not so honorable, survived.

Honor and principle and glory—slogans for marble monuments that had left his son rotting on a jungle trail. Yet the

slogans were not meaningless. Honor was what men died for. It was Ryan's life, and his death. It is what survived him and all who lay beneath the crosses. Honor *did* matter to the dead—what else did they have?

This time he would succeed—he *would* bring about peace and make the world better. He would make a just and honorable peace for the living *and* the dead. He would salvage honor out of this war yet. He would prove America had decency and integrity and conscience. He was going to shut off the faucet-flow of blood and ensure that the dead had not died in vain.

After Nixon released his grip, Marshall left the room without a word and got into his waiting limousine.

"Su esposa no es aquí," said a maid when he returned to his large brick home in McLean. He had never seen her before and was sure she was an illegal alien.

"Thank you," he said, then added, fearing she knew no English, *"Gracias."*

Where does Catherine get these people? he wondered as he went upstairs to change. Last week there had been a woman from Bangladesh; before, ones from Thailand, Burma, and the Fiji Islands. "What is this, a third-world pit stop?" he had asked his wife of the seemingly endless stream of non–English-speaking help.

"These people are in desperate need of assistance; our inconvenience at their lack of English and brief employ is of no consequence."

As with most every thing she said, this was true, though not germane. What was germane, he felt, was that he couldn't find anything in his closets or drawers.

Now he couldn't find his sweat pants. He was in his bedroom, searching under the bed, wearing only a jockstrap. He had come home to run, to excise his meeting with Nixon and Kissinger, because running had been his catharsis after Ryan's death, and now he ran five miles a day regardless of the weather.

"You look ridiculous," Catherine said, entering the room with folded laundry.

"She said you were gone," he said, getting off his knees.

"Who?"

"The new maid. What happened to the Fiji Islander? And my sweat pants?"

"Consuela washed them. She must be a reincarnated German, she washes every thing."

"She didn't wash my jock."

"I'm sure she didn't want to touch the damn thing; or maybe she thought it was a toy."

She tossed his sweat pants at him, then sat on the bed. "All right, let's hear about it—am I going to have to divorce you?"

He pulled on his sweat pants. "If you divorced me, you'd have to settle for half of what I have—you couldn't live on half, Catherine."

"I have my own money."

"Yes, but you'd have to give half of that to me in the settlement."

She turned to the mirror and brushed at her hair, gray-streaked and fashionably coiffed. "You're going, aren't you?"

He finished lacing his shoes and looked up at her, a tall, formidably intelligent woman of forty-six to whom he'd been married for twenty-five years and loved as much today as when he came back from the Pacific after World War II. "Are you going to divorce me because I'm working for Richard Nixon and Henry Kissinger?"

"I'm sure those are grounds for divorce in *any* court in the land."

He sighed. "Catherine, they *are* the President of the United States, and the national security adviser."

"They're war criminals! They make my skin crawl. Can you imagine going to bed with them, lying beside them? Touching them?"

He stared at her. "I've never thought about that, Catherine; I don't contemplate the sex lives of public figures. I didn't know you did."

"It's how I judge people. If you wouldn't go to bed with them, why would you entrust lives to them? The country? Thousands and thousands died in Vietnam, Brad—our own son. How can you be a party to what is happening there now?"

"I'm going to prevent a betrayal, to ensure they didn't die in vain, Catherine."

She turned from the mirror angrily. "They *did* die in vain, Brad. Ryan died for *nothing*. Isn't it bad enough that you and Johnson and McNamara and Nixon, all those old men, killed young boys and women and children, but now you want to pretend it was for something meaningful?"

"What would you have me do, Catherine, let the war go on, let more die? Which is better—a bad war or a bad peace?"

"That is such a *stupid* rationalization—you're not going to end the war, you're just being used by Nixon and Kissinger. You're like Agamemnon tricked into sailing off to Troy—a stupid war of no meaning or consequence. He sacrificed his own daughter for good weather, but he died, Brad, and lost everything. Now you tell me you are going to Vietnam. For what? Undo the murders? You can't. Ryan is dead, like thousands of others. Let them be. We have two other children; don't cheat Sarah and Chris by hanging on to Ryan."

He bowed his head. "I can't let go of Ryan. And *because* I failed last time and the war went on, I have to try again. Someone has to protect the interests of South Vietnam; someone has to care for them."

"It won't do any good, Brad. You can't make a difference."

"Men *can* make a difference, Catherine."

She shook her head. "All you do is kill others for those 'differences'—they're called religion or truth or nationality. You are a good and kind and decent man, Brad, but you are a colossal fool to trust in man's good nature." Then she patted his head as she might a child's. "Don't go, Brad. Don't play with those bad boys—you'll get in trouble."

He looked up at her with a smile. "If I go, like 'poor Agamemnon,' are you going to take up with some one else, then murder me like Clytemnestra?"

"There's an idea," she said. "I could find some young gardener . . ."

"He wouldn't stay; none of your illegal aliens do."

"This one would."

He took her in his arms. "Don't run off with the gardener, Catherine."

"I'll bet *he* wouldn't leave me to go out and jog."

Marshall laughed, then eased her down on the bed, working to get his shoes off, struggling out of his sweat pants.

That night he called his children at college.

"Sarah!" Marshall said in surprise when she answered the phone in her off-campus apartment. A junior at Oberlin, she was seldom at home, but instead on a barricade protesting the war. Outspokenly political, every thing an issue, she was a stark contrast to her brother Chris, a freshman at Stanford.

"Dad? What's wrong? What happened?"

"Nothing is wrong, Sarah; I called to say good-bye; I'm leaving for Vietnam in a few days."

"Aren't you a little too old for the draft, Dad?"

"I'm going as an envoy for Nixon."

"Jesus!"

He smiled; she was consistent if nothing else.

"I'm going to see what I can do to end the war."

There was silence on the line.

"Maybe I can do something. What if Chris was drafted, or if he disappeared with the Moonies or the Scientologists—wouldn't you want me to do something for him?"

"No! It'd be a step in the right direction for him."

"He doesn't have any direction, Sarah."

"Exactly. How *did* he get into Stanford? His wardrobe? All those tassel loafers?"

"I think it was baseball—he's a terrific first baseman."

"Dad, Stanford doesn't care about athletics. Maybe it was just a mistake."

There was a slight pause, then she asked, "You haven't talked to him, have you?"

"I was going to call him next. Why?"

"Nothing," she said quickly.

"Wait a minute. What's the matter? What happened?"

"Forget it, Dad. It was an innocent question."

"You never ask innocent questions. Something terrible has happened—what?"

She laughed. "Nothing terrible has happened; I promise.

So how long are you going to be gone, and is this going to be in the papers? Am I going to be publicly humiliated—my father, the flunky for Tricky Dick?"

"Yes, it'll be in the papers, and I don't know how long I'll be gone—maybe a month. So tell me about school, and your personal life."

"You really want to know?"

"Of course, unless you've found some one worse than Bosco. Bosco, for God's sake! I still haven't gotten over him."

"Actually Brent is a lot like Bosco, just smarter."

"He couldn't be *dumber*, unless you have to water him."

"Bosco is a nice guy. So's Brent—we're living together. Want to talk with him?"

"No," he said quickly. "But tell me about school. You still majoring in women's warfare?"

"Feminist studies, Dad. Yes, and I'm working part-time at a clinic for battered women."

They chatted for another twenty minutes about school and political issues, then said good-bye.

He was not successful in reaching Chris. He left several messages at his dorm, but Chris never returned the calls and he went to bed.

The next day he was driven to the CIA's cloistered headquarters at Langley for a working lunch with the director and his senior staff.

He enjoyed Langley—it was like going on a safari in suburban Virginia and finding a lost culture, Aztecs in business suits, an isolated life-form hidden away.

It *was* a visit to another civilization, Marshall thought, a closed brotherhood with secret codes and rites, a highly intelligent culture of advanced knowledge and technology, yet frighteningly barbaric.

The setting was serene, contrasting starkly to the butt-tight tension of the FBI building, the chaos of the Pentagon, and the gelatinous soup of the State Department. Here every thing was calm, assured, controlled. The priests who determined the sacrifices and pulled out the beating hearts of live victims had window offices and read the *Washington*

Post; they had been to good schools and spoke in complex sentences with good grammar.

His background briefings were surprisingly upbeat—the military outlook for the South Vietnamese was not hopeless and the political situation had stabilized.

"Just when we're pulling out," Marshall said.

"Umm," the senior analyst said noncommittally, lighting his pipe.

"Could they survive an attack from the North without our assistance?"

"The North is too strong, their army's superior, their generals better."

"Then an American pullout dooms them."

The man, tweed-coated, professorial, smiled. "I said the South couldn't survive an attack without our assistance. I did not say the North would launch an attack, or that we wouldn't assist the South."

The lunch was so civilized, the talk so reasoned and soothing, that he felt he could have been in a faculty lounge discussing abstruse philosophy, not in the inner sanctum of the cabal where wars and assassinations were plotted.

His last stop was to see Andrew Maynard, an old friend with whom he had served in the Marines during the Korean War.

Even fatter and more out of shape than when he'd last seen him, Maynard was in an upper-echelon policy-making job, chafing to get back to fieldwork.

"I've come for kind words, sage advice, and to have you cut through all the horseshit I've just heard."

Maynard clutched his heart. "Horseshit? Here?"

"Tell me about my mission, Andy—something not scripted by the White House."

"They're counting on your 'gift' of bullshit to stick it to Thieu and Ky. The South Vietnamese are stonewalling because they know they're going to take it up the ass if this treaty is signed."

"They're not buying Nixon's promise to back them?"

"You ever met a gook that dumb? For Christ's sake, South Vietnam is in the toilet, and we're asking *them* to pull the chain. Of course if they don't, we'll do it for them, but your job is to get them to flush themselves away."

When Marshall didn't respond, Maynard smiled sympathetically. "You didn't have any delusions about this, did you? How can you be an idealist after all these years? After what you've seen—Guadalcanal, Chosin, Vietnam?"

"Mortality, Andy. You have to keep believing. There has to be an ideal—what's the point otherwise?"

"Aw shucks," Maynard said, putting his thumbs in imaginary overalls. "Now you're talking pretty—philosophy and art." He spat on the rug. "Let's get back in orbit. You know what this is about? POWs. Americans are suckers for the weak and helpless—prisoners, hostages, those good American boys languishing in prison camps. We want our babies back! Every other sensible people would say fuck 'em, but not us. It makes us vulnerable. Someday we're going to be handed our ass on a platter of hostages, but this time it's the South Vietnamese who'll get shafted because of prisoners."

Maynard pulled an imaginary toilet chain. "Bye, gooks."

"I'm not interested in the POWs, Andy. I'm going to protect the best interests of South Vietnam. I'm trying to salvage some honor out of this war."

"Is there some liberal cue card you read this shit off of?" Maynard asked in disgust. "This peace treaty is about Nixon's reelection and that means the POWs—he's going to get them back and to hell with every thing else."

"I tell you, I'm going to represent the best interests of South Vietnam, and see to it that those who died, including Ryan, aren't betrayed by this peace treaty."

Maynard contemplated him a long minute, then reached under his desk blotter for a manila envelope and emptied the contents on the desk before Marshall—two black-and-white photographs and a military dog tag.

The photographs were grainy and out of focus but portrayed a young man, thin and looking unwell, unshaven, his hair closely cropped. In his hand was a dog tag, held up for the camera. Marshall studied the photos, scrutinized them from every angle, then he picked up the dog tag; it was dirty, caked with mud, but the name was clearly identifiable: Marshall, Ryan S, an identification number, the date of birth, and religious preference.

Marshall clutched the dog tag in his fist. "Ryan?"

Maynard opened his desk drawer and pulled out a candy

bar. He unwrapped it, then popped half of it in his mouth. "Looks like him, doesn't it?"

The dog tag cut into Marshall's hand, but he didn't feel it for the pain squeezing his heart. His son was dead; accepting that had been the most difficult thing in his life. Now some one had dug up the corpse and dragged it back into his life, thrown it before him muddy and rotted.

Munching the rest of the candy bar, Maynard pointed to the photos and dog tag. "They were turned over to a negotiator in Paris a week ago. We've done every thing we can to authenticate them, but can't."

"This can't be," Marshall cried. "He's dead." He closed his eyes against the crippling pain, then he dropped the dog tag onto the desk and pushed it away. "What are you doing, Andy? Why wasn't I told before? Why didn't Nixon or Kissinger tell me?"

Maynard shrugged. "Would you have believed them? The White House was afraid you'd think this was a trick, and they didn't want you to get your hopes up for nothing, so they turned this over to me, knowing we were friends, but I have no idea if Ryan's alive, if it is a trick, if you're being set up, or if I'm being used to con you. All I'm doing is giving you what we have. I think they have you by the nuts, Brad."

Marshall couldn't breathe; he felt a knife twisting in his gut, and he turned so Maynard couldn't see his agony. Then he said in a whispered choke, "Help me, Andy; you're my best friend. We're talking about my son."

Maynard shook his head. "I'm talking about two out-of-focus pictures of some one who looks like Ryan if he'd been starved and sick for a couple years. And a dog tag that could have turned up on a trail long ago. *You're* talking about Ryan."

Marshall gripped the table and started to rise. "My God, maybe he is alive."

Maynard crumpled the candy wrapper and tossed it into the trash can. "POWs. I told you that's what this was all about. You help the South Vietnamese stall on the treaty and the POWs don't come back. It's different now that Ryan might be one of them, right?"

But Marshall wasn't listening; all he could think of was

that Ryan might be alive. Hope surged. All the horror and pain of Ryan's death could be canceled. He put the photos and dog tag back in the envelope and dropped it in his briefcase.

"Maybe you shouldn't go," Maynard said. "Maybe they're just using you."

Marshall shook his head. "No. I *have* to go, especially now if Ryan is alive."

Maynard sat back in his chair. "The chances of that are as good as you saving Vietnam. Don't count on him being a prisoner, Brad, and don't count on succeeding on this mission. It's not your fault South Vietnam is going to sink into the sewer of history, it's a foregone conclusion—fate. Jesus Christ working tag team with the Buddha couldn't save Vietnam." He shrugged. "But who knows, maybe you can do something . . . oh, what? Decent? Honorable? Maybe you can hold their hands as they're being flushed away. Just make sure to let go at the last minute."

He watched Marshall's reaction, then said compassionately, "Maybe Ryan is alive; maybe you can get him back. But I wouldn't mention this to Catherine, Brad. Don't get her hopes up for nothing—that would be too cruel." He pointed a warning finger. "And don't discount the possibility that you're being used."

Marshall looked dazed. "Any other advice?"

"Yes. Remember Wilson Abbot Lord?"

"The bastard tried to kill me the last time I was in Saigon."

"Well, we forgive bunglers—the building would be empty otherwise—he's back on station. He doesn't make many mistakes, and never the same one twice. Be careful, Brad, he believes as ever."

Marshall sank back in the chair. He thought he had destroyed Lord's career four years ago after an aborted assassination attempt. Believing passionately in the war, Lord had viewed Marshall's mission for Johnson as the single greatest threat to victory. He would see Marshall's current mission the same way and do every thing to thwart him as he had last time. Marshall's jaw set. "I'll nail his ass this time."

Maynard nodded. "I'm sure that's what he's thinking too."

Marshall stood. At the door, he flashed the peace sign.

Maynard responded by pulling an imaginary toilet chain: "Whoosh."

Driving back in the limousine, the briefcase in his lap, Marshall resisted all temptation to look at the photos again.

Ryan couldn't be alive, he thought; it had to be a trick.

He put the briefcase on the floorboard to stare out the window. Snow covered the ground and the trees were bare, and suddenly on the inner lids of his eyes came images of his son, the time-lapse camera of his mind reeling through the years: the drooling baby, cap askew, his first bicycle, his first car, the grown boy going to college, that awful day Ryan told him he had dropped out of college to join the army.

Nineteen, so young and vulnerable, so idealistic and decent, he had come home on a cold winter day just like this four years ago to tell his father that the war would end only when families such as theirs were touched by it.

"I can't let some one go in my place," Ryan had said. "Anybody with money or connections can get out of going. Everyone at college is laughing at how only the dummies have to go—the dummies and blacks, the dregs. That's wrong, Dad, and you know it, and I couldn't live with myself if I thought some one died in my place."

He had begged his son, reasoned and pleaded with him, but to no avail. Finally he had shouted, for he knew what would happen, as if he were the Sibyl prophesying the death of his own child, "You'll die, Ryan. You'll get killed. You're just the type. People like you don't make it. Ryan! Ryan!"

And Ryan had stormed out, angry and unbelieving that anything could happen to him as he, Marshall, watched helplessly, knowing his fate, powerless to prevent it.

Then there was the last time, at the airport, so proud and strong in his uniform, saying good-bye to his father, and Marshall's heart was breaking, knowing he would never see his son again, wanting to grab on to him and never let him go, seeing the tragedy unfold, its final scene playing out before him.

Finally that awful day at the cemetery, burying an empty coffin, standing mute and bereft as the curtain closed on his son's life.

But what if it *was* true? What if it had never happened?

What if it had been a monstrous trick, and his son was alive? He felt his heart bursting. "Ryan, Ryan," he whispered. Oh, God, he wanted it to be true so badly.

He glanced at the briefcase. He would do *anything* to get him back.

"Take me home," he said to the driver.

When he let himself into the house, it was quiet and dark. Catherine was gone, he remembered, at a board meeting for the National Gallery, or perhaps it was Greenpeace—she had immersed herself in charities after Ryan's death—and she wouldn't be back until late. Probably the maid had decamped too, he thought, but he was thankful for that and dropped exhausted and overwhelmed into a chair in the living room.

"It looks like I didn't pick a good time," a voice said.

Marshall whirled, then jumped up. "Chris!"

A tall youth, disheveled and worn, his face anxious, a can of beer in his hand, stood in the doorway.

"What's wrong? What are you doing home? Why aren't you in school! My God, you look awful." Marshall went to hug his son, but Chris drew back.

"What happened? I knew something was wrong. Your sister . . . God damn her!"

Chris finally smiled. "Nothing's wrong, Dad. I look like shit because I took the midnight flight from San Francisco. I went standby, got bumped in Chicago, and just got in; I haven't slept."

"*Why* did you take the midnight flight? What's wrong?"

Chris laughed. "You always get so hysterical. You're supposed to be this world-class diplomat nothing bothers, but every time you see us, you go to pieces."

"That should give you some idea of the effect you and Sarah have on me—wars and assassinations, dictators and mass murderers, I can handle, but not you and Sarah. Are you in trouble? Thrown out of school? Are the police on their way?"

Chris drained the beer and crumpled the can in his fist. At eighteen, he was taller than his father, a blond, muscular youth in chinos and loafers who looked the collegiate all-

American—out of place in a psychedelic era of beards and beads. "Where's Mom?" he asked.

"Saving trees or whales. She won't be back till late."

"I came to talk to you both." Chris turned toward the kitchen. "I need another beer."

Marshall grabbed his arm. "You do not need another beer. You need to talk to me. You can talk to your mother later."

Chris considered a moment, then nodded. "Okay. But maybe you'll need a beer."

Marshall recoiled, then his heart clamped. So the time had come; he had hoped it never would, that they could ease their way around this without ever having to confront it.

Marshall stared at his son, then shook his head. "No, I don't need a drink. You don't either. Come on, let's go in my den." He picked up the briefcase and together they went into a book-lined, comfortable room with leather chairs and a sofa.

As he placed the briefcase on his desk, the manila envelope slid out. Marshall ignored it and said casually, "I called last night to tell you I was going to Vietnam for Nixon. Your mother doesn't approve; neither does your sister. Want to jump on my case too?"

Chris shook his head. "I'm sure you've thought it out."

"So tell me about school. Your sister still wonders how you got into Stanford."

"I assume you paid big bucks and pulled lots of strings."

"Are you doing all right?"

"I'm hanging in with a two point oh, and that's all I need to stay on the team and get into a fraternity."

Marshall nodded solemnly. "Well, that's every thing, isn't it?"

Chris smiled. "I'll settle for it. The coach thinks I might make the All Coast team, and only one other freshman has done that. I'm batting .348 and lead the team in fielding."

"Terrific, but you didn't catch the red-eye special to tell me this."

Chris took a deep breath. "No." He sat nervously in a chair and looked about, then seemed to gather his courage and faced his father. "Are you going to Vietnam because of Ryan? He's dead, Dad. Why don't you leave it alone—just let it go."

"It doesn't work that way, Chris. I might be able to do something. If there's any hope, you hope. Even when there's none, you still hope."

"You still hoping I'm going to turn out normal, marry some cute girl, and have sweet little children so you and Mom can be loving grandparents?"

Marshall felt the air leave his lungs; he didn't say anything for a moment, then he opened his hands. "Let's get this over with."

"I'm queer, Dad."

He said it levelly, his eyes full on his father, his voice controlled.

"I thought there were other terms for it these days."

"They're euphemisms. I'm queer. I don't like girls; I like guys."

So there it was, as he had known all along, of course, but he was still unprepared and did not know what to say. All he could manage was a feeble, "Does it bother you?"

"Of course it fucking bothers me!"

Marshall felt as if he'd been hit, not by the words, but by his son's pain. He crossed the room and crouched beside him, his hand on his arm. "I don't care, Chris."

"Oh, for Christ's sake! Don't pretend this isn't anything to you, Dad. You don't want a queer son, you want a normal one. You want Ryan back."

Marshall just stared at him.

"Of course you care. *I* care! But I can't hide it anymore; I can't pretend anymore."

"You never had to."

"Oh, sure," Chris said bitterly. "The world's ready for guys to announce they like other guys. 'Hey, great, Chris—want to suck my dick?' Oh, yeah, the guys in high school would have been real supportive. My coaches would have loved it. What fucking planet are you on, Dad? If I'd been a music major or wanted to dance ballet, it'd been different, but I was a jock. Ryan was the smart one, the sensitive one, but he joined the Green Berets and got killed. I was the dumb jock—dumb and queer, and it *doesn't* work. Then there's the guilt. My brother's dead. *I'm* the son, the only son, but that's not the bad news, the bad news isn't that you have one dead son, Dad, but that the other one is queer. And you want to feed me some bullshit about how it doesn't matter to you? You want to give me one of your fucking liberal lines about how it's okay? Can it, Dad."

Chris shook his head. "There was no wall between you and Ryan, but there was one between us. You never had a problem with Ryan. He was your first son, normal—you know you liked him better. You still do. That's why you're chasing after him in Vietnam. You don't want a queer son—you're still hoping the normal one isn't dead."

"That's not true," Marshall shouted.

"It is true, Dad, and you'd admit it if you were honest." Chris let out his breath and said sadly, "You know, you never came to my games in high school—you never even played catch with me when I was a kid. I busted my ass trying to get your attention, but I never did. Every thing was always Ryan. Even after he died when I needed someone because suddenly I was the only son—queer—it was Ryan. It *still* is Ryan. I've agonized for years over this, afraid to tell you because then you'd love me even less, and now finally when I get the courage to bring it out, you pretend it doesn't make any difference."

"It doesn't! I *don't* care. Do you want me to? Would it make you feel better if I disowned you? Slashed my wrists?"

Chris stood. "No, and I don't want you to forget Ryan. I just want you to see *me.*"

Marshall reached out for him.

Chris shook his hand off and headed for the door. "I needed to get this out, thanks for listening. I gotta be going now; I got classes tomorrow."

"What! You come in here, toss a grenade, then leave? That was it—the bomb, and then out the door?"

Chris nodded. "This is all I came for—I said what I had to. I had to tell you face-to-face, and I didn't want to put it off any longer. Let's consider this a start between us; maybe things will work out later. Say hi to Mom for me."

Marshall, overcome with inadequacy, just stared at him.

At the door Chris turned. "I have one question though. What do you think is the cause? About me, I mean. You being a powerful man? Mom a strong woman? Genes? Whose fault is it?"

"God's," Marshall said.

Chris nodded. "I was afraid you'd say that, Dad. The correct answer is: there's no fault because there's nothing wrong." He turned away. "Have a good trip, Dad. Maybe when you come back, when you let go of Ryan, then you and *I* can play father and son."

Marshall heard the front door shut and he remained standing in the middle of the room long after Chris was gone.

He went to his desk and dropped into the chair. Before him lay the envelope. He opened it and let the photographs spill out.

Chris was right, he *did* care. He didn't want a homosexual son. The wall *was* there because he didn't want Chris this way. He wanted a normal son. He wanted Ryan back. Jesus, Jesus, Marshall thought.

He closed his eyes and clutched the dog tag in his hand. He didn't want Ryan dead. He didn't want Chris the way he was.

He swiveled in his chair to look out on the garden, winter bare and stripped.

Then he braced himself and stood. Every thing would be all right, he said to himself. He could handle all of this.

He would wrest justice and honor out of this war yet. He would find out about Ryan, and if he was alive, he'd get him out. Then he'd take care of Chris's problem.

Yes, he thought, confidence flowing into him, every thing would be all right.

But then, staring out on the cold garden, he realized that nothing had ever gone right about Vietnam.

CHAPTER 2

Driving with slow determination, eyes intense on the road as if it might disappear, Sung Le Vinh gripped the wheel tightly, feeling as awkward as she looked in the large, battered Buick. She had never driven a car before last year; she had lived in America for two years before Ron finally insisted she learn.

"I'm not having my wife walk home from the Piggly Wiggly—even the dumbest, sorriest redneck drives."

"I don't mind. I like to walk; I like to be outside."

"No," he had said, one of the few times he had forced a decision on her, and he bought her a car he felt she'd be safe in. "I'd buy you a tank if they had one in the surplus store. The way you drive, you need *heavy* plating."

A tentative driver, she took it seriously; driving was not a pleasure for her.

Today's journey of twenty miles was the longest she had made.

Ron's car was in for repairs, so he had asked her to pick him up after work.

"I'll make it easy for you," he said. *"Don't* come into town for me—just meet me at the Texaco station on Highway 38. I'll get one of the guys to drop me off there. Five o'clock. That's about twenty miles from the house. It don't mean you gotta leave two hours early—thirty minutes is plenty. Okay, Sung?"

"I will be there," she said grimly; she had given herself an hour in any case.

He wouldn't be mad if she was late; he was never angry with her. Not once in four years had he even raised his voice at her. When he had taken her from the brothel in Saigon, he had promised he would never hurt her. He never had.

He wouldn't be angry, he would be worried, and he had been so good to her that she never wanted to cause him anxiety. Especially now with things bad.

Life had not been easy for Ron Mead after Vietnam. She thought he might stay in the Marines, but after his enlistment, he got out and returned home. He put his uniform and medals in his seabag, tossed it into the back of the closet, and tried to do the same with his memories, but that closet would not stay shut.

"You won't like Arkansas," he told Sung. "You won't like anything about it, except my mom. My dad is an asshole. I hate him, and Arkansas, but it's all I got."

"I will be fine," she said.

She was, but he wasn't; the war had harmed him more than it had her. He had left Arkansas to join the Marines because there was nothing for him there; he did not want to be a sharecropper like his father. But the war had been just blood and horror, and endless carnage.

After he had been transferred to Saigon from the battlefield and found her in the brothel, he told her sorrowfully one night, "You know what I done since I been here? Kill people, that's all. I'm an animal, just like the bastards who killed your family, a dumb animal who kills people. And I can't stand it anymore."

When he returned to Arkansas, there was still nothing for him, only now it was worse: he was older, twenty-three, back from a war no one wanted to talk about, with a Vietnamese wife, and there were dreams—nightmares that wrested him from sleep, dripping with sweat, bolt upright in bed, gasping for breath. The dreams grew worse over the years; now he dreaded sleep.

Because of his veteran's preference, he got a job with the county working on the roads, hard manual labor that paid moderately well and provided an outlet for his physical intensity. A big, powerful man, six feet three, two hundred ten pounds, he became even more massive and fit, but budget cuts by the county forced him to transfer to "sanitation engineering."

"A fucking garbageman; I might as well have stayed in the Marines."

Because of debts, payments on two cars and their house trailer, Sung got a job as a clerk in a convenience store—"Only until I get back on the roads," he said.

She was coming from her job to pick him up when the warning light on the gasoline gauge blinked on.

She panicked, then remembered this had happened many times when they were short of money, but the car went for miles. Close to the gas station now, she knew she would make it, but she gripped the wheel even tighter and held her breath.

She would fill the tank herself; that would please Ron. She had enough money and had watched him fill the tank often enough so that she knew how.

She eased the car off the highway toward the gas pumps as if landing a jumbo jet.

Only after she had come to a stop before the pumps did she notice the men slouching on the rickety steps that led into the cabin that was an old Texaco station.

She steeled herself, blocking the men from her mind. She had learned to do that long ago, starting with the men who had murdered her family and beat and raped her, and later with the men in the brothel.

Vietnam had taught her to bear anything—deaths, suffering, and pain beyond imagination. Men could no longer hurt her.

She got out of the car and went to the pump.

The day was overcast, chilly and grim, late afternoon of an out-of-sorts day. It reminded her of monsoon weather when she had watched the clouds sweep from the mountains, touching the top of the jungle in Ban Me Thuot.

"Hey, look," a voice called from the steps. "A gook. We got us a gook."

"I'd like to see *her* in some little black pajamas."

"I'd like to see her out of them."

She opened the gas tank.

Sung Le Vinh was twenty-one, nearly five feet seven, tall

for a Vietnamese, and she still wore her black hair long and drawn back from her face, which had the exquisite beauty of a porcelain figurine.

Born into a wealthy family in the Central Highlands province of Darlac, near the hunting preserves of the former emperors, to whom her mother was distantly related, she was a grandniece of the last emperor, Bao Dai, and had twice visited the court in Hue to see the old dowager empress.

The Vietcong killed her mother and father and brothers in front of her eyes after they beat and raped her. With nowhere to go, she joined the endless stream of refugees heading to Saigon, but there found no help or hope.

"Go to the Chinaman," she was told. "There are worse things to be than a whore."

She had been in the brothel five months, addicted to heroin the Chinaman gave her, when Ron Mead, a Marine embassy guard, stumbled into the whorehouse late one night, wild on dope, trying to drive out the demon dead who pursued him even then.

Later he took her from the Chinaman; then he fell in love with her and asked her to marry him. But life in America had been harder than she'd expected.

Alone they were fine, except for his dreams, which were becoming more frequent, and their sadness over her inability to have children.

The doctor in Little Rock told them there must have been some trauma in the past.

"Yeah," Ron said bitterly. "Maybe it was the rifle barrel they jammed up her when they raped her."

She pulled the nozzle from the pump.

"Cute gook too. Think she's a VC?" a voice from the steps called.

"Could be, and hell, we're unarmed. I forgot my gook and squirrel rifle."

"*I'm* armed—packing a *heavy* piece. Maybe we better interrogate her. She might have some valuable information."

She fitted the nozzle into the gas tank and stared to the sky. She remembered the land as a green ocean of jungle and rain forest, a jade canvas of rice fields and rubber plantations, the nights a symphony of cicadas and birds, with the wind rustling the reeds.

"Think she's got any money?"

"They don't use money—they use their mouths."

"A fill-up for a blow job. How about that, bitch?"

She pulled on the handle and gasoline pumped into the car.

The journey to the palace in Hue had been wondrous; she had seen monkeys swinging through jungle vines, and a black leopard in a mountain pass, but best was the dowager empress, with fingernails like knives, and a camphor trunk filled with dolls.

"Maybe she needs some oil and a lube job."

"I think we better check under her hood."

Once she went with the dowager to the River of Perfumes to pray to the spirits of the river. They drove in an old black limousine with a chauffeur dressed in yellow, the imperial color, and three ladies in attendance. At the riverbank, the empress got out to pray. Though old and frail, she allowed no one to help her. She told Sung that the warriors of the old emperors used to do this to drive away evil.

"I'd like to shove it up her exhaust. That'd be tighter than her cunt."

"You could probably drive the Buick up that."

"What are we waiting for?"

In back of the house was a small temple for the ancestors. She loved to go there. She could feel their spirits wafting in the still air that smelled of incense and fruit blossoms. And the moon at night was sometimes like a huge pearl on black velvet.

"I say she didn't pay."

"Yeah, just like a gook, trying to get something for nothing."

"We better straighten her out so she won't try something like this again."

"C'mon, bitch, you got what we want."

Their hands were on her, pulling her away from the car toward the cabin.

She did not resist. There was no resisting men; she had learned that too.

They had her to the steps, pulling and pushing her, when there was a squeal of brakes and a rush behind them.

Mead grabbed the first man. He kicked him in the back of the knees, buckling him, then pulled him by his collar from the stairs. The man fell on his back, and Mead stomped his chest, crushing ribs.

Another rushed him, diving from the stairs, but Mead brought back his fists as if swinging a baseball bat and struck him full in the face. The man crumpled to the ground—jaw, cheekbone, and nose broken.

The third man hesitated, then let go of Sung and charged. Mead caught him with a boot to his groin, and as he doubled over, Mead butted his face with his head, splintering bone. As the man collapsed to his knees, holding both face and crotch, Mead kicked him on the ear, bursting the drum.

The fourth man held Sung, too afraid to move. Then he let go and pushed her toward Mead. "Hey, man, we were just funning. Nothing happened." He started to back up the stairs, holding up his hands.

Mead stalked him, brushing Sung aside, never taking his eyes off the man.

At the top, the man cowered. Mead grabbed him by the neck and squeezed with both hands at the same time he slammed his head against the door. The man's eyes bulged. Mead stared into them with murderous fury and beat his head against the door.

"Ron! Ron! Stop it, Ron! Let him go."

Sung pulled on his arms. "Ron! Let go, Ron! Please, please, Ron."

Then the man who had come in the car with Mead started pulling. "Mead! Jesus, Ron, let him go." He struggled until Mead finally broke his grip.

Mead turned and looked blankly at him, then to Sung. "You all right?" he asked in a faraway voice.

"Get out of here," his friend said. "Take off."

"Yes, Ron." Then she tugged on his hands. "Come with me, Ron."

She led him down the stairs, past the bodies on the ground. He followed quietly.

"I'll drive," she said nonchalantly when they reached the car. He got in the passenger side obediently. She put the car in gear and, with both hands intense on the wheel, taxied the Buick out of the station.

"I filled the car with gas," she said chattily. "All by myself." Then she looked over at him and smiled. "But I may not do that again."

He nodded as he rubbed his knuckles. "No, better not," he said.

"You know, I have never seen you angry before. Long ago in Saigon, I was told you were dangerous, and no one, even the other Marines, would fight you. They said everyone was afraid. I never understood that. Before today."

"I'd never hurt you. You know that."

"Yes." She smiled. "Even so, I think I will not make you angry."

He moved close beside her, putting one hand around her, and the other on the wheel, gently nudging her foot off the accelerator with his own.

"I love you," he said. Then he kissed her on top of the head and stepped on the gas. "But you still gotta learn how to drive faster."

When they got back to the trailer, he dropped her off and said he'd be back in an hour for dinner—he wanted to stop by his parents' house.

"I want to talk to my dad," he said.

She knew the animosity Ron and his father bore each other. "Don't fight," she said. "It only hurts your mother. Be nice, Ron."

"I'm just gonna talk. I need to do that."

"Well, if it ain't America's foremost combat hero," sneered his father when Mead entered the four-room, tin-roofed, dilapidated shack his parents lived in.

The cabin was down an unpaved road miles out of town, set in the trees and surrounded by a yard littered with trash, discarded tools, and farm implements, and where three rusting pickup trucks rested on concrete blocks, and a pack of dogs yelped loudly.

His mother, a worn, gray-haired woman, came from the kitchen, wiping her hands on an apron. She met him at the door and hugged him to her, whispering, "Shhhhh," as she nodded toward the man slouched in a worn overstuffed chair before a television. Crumpled, empty beer cans were strewn on the pinewood floor.

"You had dinner yet?" his mother asked. "Can you stay to eat?"

"Thanks, Ma, but I gotta get back to Sung. She's cooking supper now."

"What?" his father called from the chair without turning from the TV. "Fish heads and rice?"

"Randy!" the woman said. "Sung's a good cook, you know that."

"You too fucked up to talk?" Mead asked from the doorway.

"I *gotta* be fucked up to talk to you. What do you want?"

Mead walked over to his father, kicking beer cans out of the way. "You live like a pig," he said, standing over him.

The older man looked up at him, then down to the floor. "Yep," he said slowly. "I gotta get me a gook to clean this place up. Why don't you go back to Vietnam and bring me back one too."

Mead caught his breath.

His father gazed at him coldly. "I had my chance in Korea, but we were fighting a real war then. We didn't have time to court gooks. We just fucked them and left them."

Mead shook his head. "God, you're a sorry bastard."

The older man stood. Though nearly fifty, he looked powerful and mean. As tall as his son, his craggy face and hard eyes were threatening. "No one comes into my house and calls me names. Especially a dickhead like you."

Mead sighed. "Pa, I already had my fight for the day. I came over to ask you if you wanted to go duck hunting."

"Wouldn't that be nice," his mother said anxiously from the doorway. "Remember how you two used to go out before? Oh, Randy, that'd be so nice. Just like the old days."

Randy Mead eyed his son carefully. "There ain't no ducks this time of year."

"Just as well, you couldn't hit one anyway."

The old man grinned evilly. "When?"

"Tomorrow morning. Think you can sober up by then? I'll be here at four. Better go get some sleep, old man."

At the door, Mead kissed his mother on the forehead.

"Say hi to Sung for me, honey. Tell her to come visit."

"Bye, Ma," he said, closing the door of the shack.

He stood on the porch, taking a deep breath of night air and woods. He had grown up here, spent a thousand nights in this shack with his drunken father, and had left as soon as he could, going to a war, finding a place even worse than this. Now he was back.

Was this going to be the rest of his life?

"For fish heads, they're not bad," Mead said as he and Sung sat at the dining table in the trailer.

Sung looked at his plate. "That's salmon; what's the matter with you?"

"Pa thinks you only cook fish heads and rice."

She shook her head. "Your father is a very unhappy man."

"My father is a drunken, mean, worthless cocksucker."

She made clicking noises. "Don't talk about your father that way."

He sat hunched over the table in the trailer, looking like a bear in a cage; then he spooned peas into his mouth and said slowly, "You gonna tell me about it now?"

"There is nothing to say, Ron. They were bad men, just like those in Vietnam who killed my family."

"Weren't you afraid?"

"Now I am. You hurt them; they might come for you. We should go away."

"Run? You mean run away?" he asked incredulously.

"You're not happy here."

"I sure as shit wouldn't be happy running away."

She put a finger to his lips. "Listen to me. What do you want to do?"

He loved it when she was serious; her brow would furrow and she would talk to him as if he were three years old. He leaned across the table and said solemnly, "I'd like to fuck. I'd really, really like to do that."

He started to stand, but she pulled him down.

"You don't like living here. And you don't like your job. Life shouldn't be unhappy, Ron. Especially if you can do something about it."

"Where should I go? What should I do?"

"You should go to college, Ron."

He laughed. "Yeah. Maybe I could be an astronaut too." He shook his head in mirth. "Sung, you married a dummy. I mean, serious dumb. The only reason I passed PE in high school was because I was on the football team; I didn't pass much else. I'm not a college person. I'm a fucking garbageman."

"Ron," she said angrily, "you can be what you want. I did not marry a dumb man, or a garbageman. And I do not want to go to bed with one."

She snatched the plates off the table and stomped into the kitchen.

He stared at her in surprise, then grinned. "You mean I'm not gonna get laid till I go to college?"

"Not in this trailer," she said, turning on the faucet, clattering dishes in the sink.

And she didn't sleep with him that night or in the morning when he reached over for her. She turned away and pulled the covers over her.

"You'll be late for the ducks," she murmured, twisting away.

He dressed in the dark, putting on his old jungle boots and camouflage fatigues, and was at his parents' house by four A.M. His father was waiting for him on the front porch, his rifle across his knees. He pointed to a large box beside him.

"Your mother spent the night cooking. *You* carry it, if you want it. All I want is the thermos of coffee."

Mead grabbed the box. "You want to take my car or your pickup?"

The older man didn't answer, just went to his truck. Mead put the box and his rifle in the bed, then jumped in the cab, kicking aside empty beer bottles and cans.

"I had those arranged carefully," Randy Mead grumped.

They drove in silence along dark, deserted back roads.

"Why are we doing this?" the old man finally asked. "There ain't no ducks—they're still wintering in Florida with the Jews."

"It's called quality time between father and son."

"Shit."

"You know, we haven't talked since I came back from Vietnam."

"I don't remember talking before you went."

"We didn't."

"Then why are we starting now?"

Mead didn't say anything. His father hadn't frightened him since he was sixteen, big enough to take care of himself, but he was still vulnerable to the older man.

"I just wanted to talk, Pa. I thought maybe if we went hunting . . . Those were the best times I ever had. We never spent a whole lot of time together, not without fighting anyway, but remember when I was a kid and you'd take me duck hunting? I loved that, just you and me and we'd freeze our asses." Mead shook his head in memory. "It'd be so cold, and wet, and I'd shiver for hours. Remember, Pa?"

The old man looked over at his son. "Sure." Then he grinned. "Why'd we do it?"

Mead sighed. "I guess it's just something men have to do. Like war."

His father nodded. "And women, and fucking, and babies." He shook his head. "And people wonder why I drink."

"Sung can't have kids."

Randy Mead cast his son a sidelong glance.

"The doctor said she'd never have a baby 'cause of what happened in Vietnam." Mead drew a deep breath. "I kinda wanted kids, Pa. I sorta dreamed of taking my own boy duck hunting someday. I thought it'd be . . . nice."

The old man stared ahead, both hands on the wheel. "It was."

Mead leaned his head against the window as the truck bounced down the dirt road. "My life's kinda fucked up, Pa."

Randy Mead grinned. "You sure you're coming to the right place for advice? Or you figure I'm the expert on a fucked-up life?"

He parked the truck off the road and grabbed his rifle and the thermos. "Let's go freeze our asses."

Mead got his rifle and followed after his father.

It was dark and cold, no different from his memories of years ago. His boots sank into the marsh and he had trouble keeping up with his father, just as when he was younger.

The older man moved with surprising agility; he was sure-footed and fast.

Most of his life Mead had hated his father, but he had liked being with his father in the woods and marsh. The older man was serenely confident in the woods, and he had passed that on to his son, which had probably saved his life often in Vietnam.

His father had grown up in the woods; his own father had been a bootlegger who had been killed when Randy was eleven. He had scraped his way through life, joined the Marines to fight in Korea, and came home bitter and violent.

Mead had never heard his father talk about war, nor did he say anything when his son went off to Vietnam, nor had he asked him anything when he returned.

They reached the lake an hour before dawn. With unerring instinct, Randy Mead found a perfect site on the water's edge, recessed in the reeds. They settled in, scrunching together for warmth. The older man took a sip from the thermos and handed it to Mead, who drank, then rested it between his legs.

He took a deep breath of clean morning air, then closed his eyes to concentrate on the smells and sounds. At first, his boyhood came back to him, the lake's wonderful crisp air, fish splashing on the water's surface, frogs and crickets, and he was lulled by happy memories.

Then the memories darkened; danger, and the hint of death, crept in, coloring the vision like a sepia print.

He frowned as other images stole into his mind, and his father felt him twitch beside him.

Suddenly he was not at the lake, but in the jungle; the air became heavier, more suffocating, and the sounds hushed.

He was in an ambush, the enemy approaching.

Now he could smell blood, the awful rancid smell of it on his hands, caked between his fingers, the blood of the man he had strangled in the tunnel, half his face blown away by a grenade. Then more blood, a river of it flowing from gaping wounds and severed limbs, seeping into the earth, now rising above him, a lake of it, and floating on the surface were mangled, bloated corpses.

He began to shake, but he was not asleep, yet he could not open his eyes.

Then he saw Sung and the men, and they were pulling her away from him. He couldn't help her; he was drowning in the lake of blood. She called to him; she was crying. The men were tearing at her clothes. He struggled in the blood, but was drawn down deeper into it. He could not breathe. He sank and, eyes open, all was red.

A hand was on him. He wrestled away and yelled.

It was first light, not blood, and Sung wasn't there; it was his father.

"Son. It's all right. You fell asleep; you were dreaming."

Mead took a deep breath. "Jesus."

"I used to have terrible dreams after Korea," Randy Mead said.

"You saw a lot there, didn't you, Pa?"

Randy Mead looked at his son. "Yeah. You did too."

Mead closed his eyes. "Yes."

Then suddenly on the horizon, flying lower over the trees, came a formation of ducks, a massive flock winging toward the lake.

"God damn," Randy Mead said.

They both raised their rifles as the ducks approached, wings flapping in long, graceful strokes.

The ducks dipped toward the water, skimming its surface, flying directly toward them, then they started to lift, a slow rise, peeling to the right.

Mead had them in his sights. They were only fifty meters away, an easy target. He watched them in the faint mist rising from the lake, necks outstretched, muscles straining, lifting higher, almost directly above him.

His finger began to pull on the trigger.

He saw them as they were about to die, straining for life, reaching for the sky, beginning to soar.

And he was in the ambush again, the bead of his rifle on the heart of a man, and in a second he would kill the man, explode his heart, and there would be blood, all red again, and then as his finger continued to pull on the trigger, he saw himself in the dark, on a trail, the fourth man in the line, all walking unaware into an ambush, and he knew there must have been a bead on his own heart, a man watching him, ready to explode his heart.

The ducks were so beautiful.

They all had been, all who had died. Perez and Donnadio, Davidson, Page, and Peterson, Snags and Miller, Landis and Dutton. So many, like the ducks straining to lift, lifting into life, beginning to soar.

Like those he had killed. And Sung's family. All the innocent dead.

The ducks rose higher, started a slow circle, soaring above him, and then they streamed away, a long banner trailing in the sky.

He lowered his rifle.

His father was watching him. Mead dropped his head and he was crying.

"You know," the older man said softly, "I wasn't worth anything after I came back."

Mead looked up at his father. "What am I gonna do, Pa?"

"Get out. Go."

"Where?"

His father pointed to the sky where the ducks were disappearing on the horizon. "It don't make a difference. Some one with a rifle will get them sooner or later. Or they'll drop someday and drown. The idea is to keep moving as long as you can. That was my mistake—I just dropped. Don't do it too."

Then the older man stood. He stretched and shook his legs. "C'mon, Son, my butt is froze."

Mead looked up at him. "You know, I don't remember you ever calling me 'son' before today. You did it twice."

Randy Mead smiled. "Maybe I never felt like a father before today."

Mead stood before his father, then he put his arms around him and rested his head on his shoulder. The older man stood stiffly a moment, then he patted his son's back and hugged him closer. Then Randy Mead grabbed his rifle and started back, not so agilely this time. "Good thing your ma packed all that food. We'd starve like Ethiopians if we tried to live on what you hunted."

When they got to the truck, Randy Mead reached into the glove compartment and pulled out a letter. "This came a while back," he said, handing the envelope to Mead.

Mead studied the pencil scrawl on the VA-hospital envelope, and the return address—Leslie Frizzell, Ward C, St. Louis, Missouri.

"We were in Vietnam together," Mead said.

"I know. He called once, asking for your address, then he sent this."

Randy Mead reached under his seat and pulled out a beer. He popped the tab and took a long swallow, wiping his mouth on his sleeve. "He was fucked up bad."

"Why didn't you give me this before?"

"You didn't need it in your life."

"Why you giving it to me now?"

"You need it now."

"You think that's where I oughta go?"

"Yep." He handed the beer to Mead. "But you better drink a lot of beer and get real mellow before you see him."

When Mead got back to the trailer, Sung was in the kitchen.

"Have I ever hurt you?" he asked, pulling her to him.

She shook her head.

He drew her tighter. "Oh, God, I love you. More than anything. You're all I have, Sung. I'm nothing without you."

"What's the matter, Ron?"

"I don't know what to do about my life. I'm not happy, but what can I do? I'm stupid. The dreams won't go away, they're getting worse, and I'm not a college person," he said mournfully. "I can't stand it if you hate me because I'm dumb."

She pulled away. "Stop that. You are acting foolish."

"It's true. You're too good for me; you don't have anything here with me, and you never will." He pushed past her.

The screen slammed behind him. He got in his car, the letter beside him.

CHAPTER 3

Saigon, 1972

Unable to sleep, Father Dourmant, seventy-six, thin and gaunt, shuffled from the rectory across a barren patch of ground to the church a hundred feet away. The small, unadorned church of crumbling plaster, looking like a child's clay replica of a medieval basilica, pockmarked by decay, neglect, and war, dominated a little square in the middle of Cholon, the old Chinese district of Saigon. In back, behind a metal rail with an unhinged gate down the worn path Father Dourmant had trod for decades, was the dilapidated rectory where the old priest lived alone.

He slept little these nights; the noise from the bars and brothels didn't disturb him, nor the suffocating humidity and stench of the city, nor was his bladder to blame for his restlessness. It wasn't voices or God, either.

Well, perhaps it was God, he thought, mounting the back stairs of the church without holding on to the rail for fear it would fall off and he would tumble into the Void; or rather His elusiveness. Somehow, somewhere, and he couldn't remember when, God disappeared—not in a blinding revelation or in sudden anger, but in forgetfulness, as if He were unused keys that had been misplaced and not missed until suddenly one sought to enter a long-locked door, uncertain what was within, but the key was gone.

Surely he still believed in God, he told himself; he was, after all, one of His priests, but he felt like an ear-tattered, nearly blind old mule who had tilled a field so long and rotely that he was not even sure he was still harnessed, or that anyone stood behind him.

Indeed, he thought, pushing on the sacristy door he had forgotten to lock and crossing to the altar, he had tilled the soil so long that he had no idea if it were God's vineyard he was plowing or just a bog. He had come to Vietnam fifty years ago to convert the heathens, charged with zeal, seeing the world in stark blacks and whites, but now, after so many years, the freshness, zeal, and contrasts had all been overcome; it was almost as if the intense heat and brilliant sun had rendered them insignificant. His Western ideas and thoughts had lost all definition in the corona of the Vietnamese sun.

Now after fifty years of toiling the Lord's rice paddies, as he called it, he saw that he had not been particularly suited to be a missionary, nor were the Vietnamese particularly suited to be Catholics. What, after all, was wrong with ancestor worship? And how did it significantly differ from the belief in saints and miracles? Why not honor the graves of forebears rather than erect Gothic charnel houses over the bones and relics of martyrs?

The church was damp and smelled of incense and mildew. It was nearly midnight, long past the military curfew, and the front door to Saint Francis Xavier had been locked hours ago, but even in the dim candlelight that reflected dull shadows off the soiled paintings and stations of the cross, and with his blurred vision, he caught the furtive movement at the back of the church.

Now what? the old priest thought. Am I to be murdered in the cathedral like Becket, though Saint Francis Xavier was certainly no cathedral, and he no Becket.

But why not murder a priest? he wondered. The church had seen every thing else, including bullets, births, and bombs. Ten years ago the Diem brothers had been dragged from sanctuary here. True, they hadn't been shot in the church; that had been accomplished in the military van parked in back, but the soldiers would have shot them on the altar if he hadn't threatened them with eternal damnation. Perhaps the soldiers thought that murdering them in the van wouldn't jeopardize their souls. Which might be true, he decided—shooting the Diems probably was not a mortal sin.

He squinted in the darkness, cleaned his glasses on his cassock, but still he couldn't see who was at the back of the church.

He wasn't afraid, fear being the only emotion he no longer felt. Anger, rage, fury—those coursed daily, as did compassion, sorrow, and pity. Fifty years in Vietnam—first as a missionary in the French colony during the decadent years of the Nguyen dynasty, living under Japanese occupation, enduring the French Indochina War, and now the Americans—had left him polarized between rage and sorrow, and in between was an immense weariness.

Father Dourmant had no fear because death did not frighten him; he was old and tired and he had no explanations for the atrocities and outrages he had seen in this world, and the answers his church gave him did not suffice. He no longer looked to God for solace or solutions because he was not sure there was a God who had any answers.

"Who's there?" he called out in Vietnamese.

Some one dropped behind one of the pews.

The priest sighed; it was probably a terrified woman, beaten and raped, or pregnant, cast out by her family or a brothel keeper. Or a child. They had nowhere else to go. All he could do was bring them to Teresa Hawthorne's clinic a block away, but that was so crowded, with so few supplies, that they were hardly worse off in the streets. He couldn't bring anyone else to Teresa. She wouldn't refuse anyone, but unlike horror, charity had its limits, and that was human endurance; Teresa Hawthorne had reached the end of hers. She was a saint; a heathen, but nevertheless a saint, he thought.

"Come out," he said softly. "I will help you if I can." When there was no answer, he walked toward the back of the church.

He reached the pew where a figure crouched. When the figure stood, Father Dourmant was surprised to see a well-dressed middle-aged Vietnamese man.

They appraised one another, then the man said in frightened, hushed French, "I thought the church would be deserted for the night."

"I often come at this hour," Father Dourmant said. "God needs many reminders."

The man looked at him with intelligent interest, then smiled. "Does He listen?"

The priest shrugged. "Perhaps it's perversity, or maybe incompetence, that prevents Him from doing what I suggest. But what are you doing here? Hiding I see, not that it will do you any good. The Diems tried that, but soldiers dragged them out and shot them."

The man glanced toward the door nervously.

"Is some one likely to drag you out too? Though these days they probably won't bother, they'd just shoot us both right here."

The man looked about in alarm. Father Dourmant saw that he was older than he first thought, fifty at least, and too afraid for jesting.

The priest sat in the pew and motioned for the man to sit beside him. Father Dourmant took off his glasses and rubbed his brow, then folded his palsied hands in his lap and waited.

"You really haven't changed at all, Father; you always frightened me."

Father Dourmant turned in surprise to examine the man.

"I was a little boy when you last saw me, Father, a terrified altar boy who couldn't keep the bells still. They shook in my hands so badly that you told me you were going to hit me over the head with them. I believed you. It was many years ago. You were a young missionary and always seemed angry. You came to our village near Hanoi every few months to give mass, and I would be the altar boy and tremble every minute."

"Oh, my, that *was* a long time ago," Father Dourmant said. "Nearly fifty years."

"My name is Pran Ba Trung, and I have come to you for help. I need sanctuary. Can you grant it to me?"

Father Dourmant considered, then nodded. "Yes, but no one would honor it."

The Vietnamese man said anxiously, "And I must make a confession."

"Now?"

"Are there special hours for it?"

"As a matter of fact, there are." Then the priest sighed. "Of course I will hear your confession. Is it going to take a long time?"

Trung bowed his head. "I have not been to church in many years. I have committed many sins. I am very frightened, Father."

"For your soul or life?"

"Both."

The priest nodded. "There is probably nothing I can do for your life, but maybe I can help your soul. What have you done that makes you afraid in God's house?"

"I renounced Him. I jeered His name. I mocked the Church."

The priest sighed. "You are a communist."

"I was."

Father Dourmant shook his head. "I *should* have hit you with the bells."

The man looked directly into the priest's eyes. "No longer."

"Is that why you are hiding?"

"Yes. They will kill me if they find me."

There was loud pounding at the door. The man cried out and jumped up, but the priest restrained him. "It is nothing; a prank; a drunken soldier; some one angry with God."

The man listened timorously; when there was no further disturbance, he perched back on the edge of the pew.

"I left the Church years ago, after you stopped coming to the village. I went to the university in Hanoi. I became a lawyer, then I joined the Communist Party. I thought it was the only way to save my country. I thought I was fighting for freedom, and I was—against the French, then the Japanese, then the Americans. I rose high in the Party. I am . . . I was in the politburo in Hanoi. I came to Saigon to meet with government leaders for talks about the cease-fire."

The priest closed his eyes.

"But there won't be a cease-fire; not one which will last."

Father Dourmant yawned; he was uninterested in politics—he had seen too much, and it was all bad: people suffered no matter the government or ruler. "Perhaps we can talk in the morning. I could hear your confession then. I'm sure the confession of a politburo member is going to take a long time."

The man grabbed his arm urgently. "No. Please, listen to me. No politics. I must make a confession tonight." He let go, then took a deep breath. "I am going to die; I know that. I knew it when I left the delegation this morning. I came here because I knew the church might be the only place where I would be safe. I hid before you locked the doors tonight. I can not go back. There is nowhere I can go."

"You could defect to the South Vietnamese. A politburo member would be a great triumph for them."

Trung shook his head. "I would die during interrogation. The South's Special Branch is filled with our people; I wouldn't last a night. You see, I have information they would kill me for—General Giap's battle plans for the invasion once the treaty is signed."

"Then go to the Americans—they would give you asylum."

Trung smiled sadly. "You are a priest. You understand God, not politics."

"I don't understand God at all."

"I can't go to the Americans because they want the war ended." Trung put up his hands like blinders. "They don't want anything that would interfere with the peace talks." He sighed. "That is why I am not asking you to hide me, but only to hear my confession."

The priest shook his head. "You don't need me, you can talk directly to God. It is not I who would forgive you—I am merely His instrument."

"I know it's only a formality, but I was raised Catholic—I want a priest to absolve me. Surely you understand."

Father Dourmant nodded, then he closed his eyes and inclined his head as he did in the confessional.

"I have done terrible things," the man began. "I lied, I cheated . . ."

"What is the worst thing you have done?" Father Dourmant interrupted.

Trung dropped his head and didn't speak for a long time, then said softly, "Denied God. Vanity. Thinking that *I* mattered."

The old priest nodded. "Go on."

Trung started a long litany of sins, venal and mortal, but there was nothing Father Dourmant had not heard before—a pathetic catalog of human weaknesses and failures of the mind, body, and spirit.

When Trung finished, he wept in the pew as Father Dourmant chanted the ancient Latin supplications, then took Trung's hand. "Come. You can stay in my room." The priest glanced at the altar reproachfully. "Maybe God will have figured out a way to help you by morning."

Before seven, after a sleepless night in his stuffy, cluttered room, with Trung thrashing on the makeshift bed beside him, the old priest was out of the rectory, shuffling toward Teresa Hawthorne's clinic. He entered the trash-littered alley, passing a long line of children, women, and cripples waiting for whatever meager food would be handed out after those within were fed.

Inside, he stopped, overwhelmed by the noise of shrieking children and wailing women and the squalor of hundreds of human beings cramped together without proper sanitation. The walls were gray and grimy, the floors slick with vomit, urine, and sputum, and though he came every day, he was stunned each time.

Years ago, the clinic had been a hospice run by French nuns. The white stucco, two-story building, once set in a quiet neighborhood, was now a crumbling ruin in a slum of tenements on a noisy side street in Cholon, crammed between whorehouses where drug dealers and money changers catered to the foreign soldiers.

Cots were so jammed together that there was no walking space through the barracks-length ward. The clinic had over four hundred patients in a space meant for a hundred. Blankets and straw pallets were strewn everywhere, and the stench from clogged toilets was overpowering, but worst was the noise, a cacophony of crying babies and sobbing women who pulled at his arms, holding up sick and deformed infants.

In the center of the chaos he touched the shoulder of a woman bent over the cot of a writhing pregnant girl. The woman turned and smiled warmly. Though only forty-five, thin and haggard, Teresa Hawthorne looked years older.

Her hair was gray, her simple dress drab and tattered, yet there was ethereal beauty about her, and when she smiled, the deep lines in her face were not those of age but of caring.

"Good morning, Father," she said in a light voice. "You look tired."

"I didn't sleep ten minutes," he said, then nodded toward the girl on the cot. "Is she in labor?"

"Not yet. She came in last night. She was able to hide the pregnancy until yesterday, then the brothel keeper threw her out."

"Dear God. How old is she?"

"Maybe fourteen." Teresa shook her head. "She's a heroin addict. I don't see any hope for the baby. Even if it lives, it'll be brain damaged and deformed."

Father Dourmant closed his eyes to pray, then he stopped. "What's the use?" he asked sorrowfully.

Leading him away gently, Teresa said lightly, "You're up early. Why couldn't you sleep? It was very hot last night. We could use a good rain."

He gripped her arm tightly. "Shut up, Teresa. I'd rather hear the din than blather."

They reached the stairwell that led to an equally congested ward on the second floor, but Father Dourmant dropped down on a stair to rest. "This has got to end," he said.

"What haven't we tried, Father? I even prayed last night."

"Don't mock me, Teresa. I'm an old, sick man."

She sat beside him. "I'm not mocking you; I *did* pray. I couldn't sleep either so I said prayers like I did back in the order. Then, whenever I couldn't sleep, I used to say Hail Marys until I fell asleep. Prayer is wonderfully numbing."

He reached into his cassock and handed her a few soiled piaster notes he'd taken from the poor box. Except for a small contribution from the Pearl S. Buck Foundation, it was the clinic's only income. Despite repeated requests to the U.S. embassy, Teresa received no money from the Americans, though most of the children in the clinic were the illegitimate children of American GIs.

Teresa and four women staffed the hospice and lived in curtained-off cubicles in an old supply room. This was her fifth year in the hospice, and her eighth in Saigon. Before that she had been a nun in Taiwan and the Philippines, but had left the Church when the demands of religion became too great—ritual and obedience detracted too much; God and His church got in the way of the simple good she sought to accomplish. She did not need mystery and transubstantiation: the desire to help others was enough.

After leaving the church, she went to work for the Pearl S. Buck Foundation, helping the illegitimate children of Asian women and Western soldiers. Through this, she met Father Dourmant and took over the hospice that had once been associated with Saint Francis Xavier.

"I couldn't sleep last night because there was a man in my room." Then he told her about Trung. "I need advice, Teresa."

She smiled. "Go to France, Father. Take a vacation in Nice or Cannes. Eat foie gras. Drink sauternes."

"I'll go if you'll come with me."

"Maybe next year."

"Maybe sooner. As soon as the Americans leave, the communists will throw us out. At *best* they'll throw us out."

"What will happen to these women and children then? What hope would they have?"

The priest edged close and whispered. "Maybe that's where Trung comes in. Perhaps he can help us; maybe he can be useful."

"I don't understand. You're a Jesuit; I'm just a poor defrocked nun, no match for your intrigues."

"Maybe we can get money out of this. What's wrong with that?"

"Using another poor soul? Exploiting him? I'm sure the Church has some stand on this."

"Nonsense; the Church would be first to exploit him. The wretched man has information," he said in exasperation. "He doesn't need money, *we* do. Perhaps we can help him, and he could help us."

"Sell the information."

"Yes, damn it, sell the information. There, I've said it. Are you happy now that you've humiliated me?"

She smiled. "To whom would we sell the information?"

"That's why I've come to you. How can we take advantage of this?"

She shook her head. "I'm afraid this is all beyond me, Father. I wish I could help, but I have no idea where to go with your information."

"What about that friend of yours, that ambassador, the man here four years ago, Bradley Marshall? He was in love with you. You should have married him, Teresa."

She blushed. Those few months when he had entered her life were her happiest. But that was long ago and there had been no contact in the intervening years. "He was already married, Father. Besides, he didn't ask me."

They sat in the sea of sorrow listening to the shrieks and cries, then Teresa turned to him. "Perhaps you could talk with Mr. Huong. He owns this building and every thing on the block. I told him we couldn't pay any rent, and he's never asked for any. He was very gracious. I liked him."

"The Chinaman! Of course," Father Dourmant said enthusiastically. "He knows everybody. His family used to deal with the imperial mandarinate and the French. He could help us. Yes," he said to himself, "Huong doesn't want the communists to win, he'd lose every thing. He'd help for greed and self-preservation."

Father Dourmant rubbed his hands together. "Oh, wonderful, Teresa, if anyone could find advantage in this, it's that Chinaman." He jumped up. "Come with me. He would give us money."

She shook her head. "I have work here." Then she smiled. "You're looking much better, Father."

He brushed at his cassock. "I'm feeling much better. I'll go see him right away," and he rushed out without another word.

Teresa watched him go. Oh, dear, she thought, a wistful memory of happier days, that brief moment of love and Bradley Marshall passing through her mind. She fingered her gray hair and touched the frayed cloth of her dress, then she sighed and went back to the cot where the girl lay, stroking her hand gently.

"You're going to have a lovely child," she said soothingly. "It will be beautiful, like you are. And we will take care of it."

* * *

Father Dourmant rang the bell outside the gate for so long that he thought it must be broken like every thing else in the city, though the house's location in the exclusive residential area and its high protective walls inspired confidence. Perhaps the Chinaman had moved, he thought, or fled or died, but as he was about to give up, the gate opened and a young, armed Vietnamese stared at him harshly.

"Does Mr. Huong live here?" Father Dourmant asked.

When the guard did not answer, the priest said sternly, "Tell him that Father Dourmant would like to see him."

The gate shut on his face, but within minutes it reopened and the guard politely stepped aside, ushering him in.

Behind the wall was an intricate garden bursting with color. A pond was in the center, and slate footsteps led through raked gravel to a large villa. Standing on the wooden veranda of a freshly painted white mansion was a tall, middle-aged Chinese man, stocky and well dressed, radiating power, affluence, and great intelligence.

When Father Dourmant reached the bottom stair, Chien Lin Huong bowed, then said in excellent French, "I was just sitting down to breakfast. Would you join me?"

Actually he was finishing breakfast, but out of politeness, and knowing how sparingly the priest would have eaten, he had had the table reset.

Father Dourmant mounted the steps ponderously, already exhausted from the day's exertions. Huong led the priest around the veranda to a table overlooking a garden blossoming with orchids, bougainvillea, and peonies. The scent from fruit trees wafted through the garden, masking the city's pollution.

The priest eased gratefully into a white wicker chair. "Exquisite. I may not leave."

Huong motioned a servant to pour coffee.

Just then a little girl ran from the house calling gleefully in Chinese, but when she saw the black-cassocked priest, she stopped and brought her hands to her mouth in fear.

"My daughter," Huong said, beckoning the child, who approached cautiously. He patted his lap and the child sat on it, but without taking her eyes from Father Dourmant.

"Say good-morning," Mr. Huong said to his child, but she

only mumbled a few words then slipped off his lap and ran back into the house.

"She leads a sheltered life; we rarely have company," Huong explained.

"She's beautiful. Four years old?"

"Five," Huong said proudly. "Our only child. My wife and I would like more; alas, it is impossible. Strange, isn't it, the hospitals and orphanages are filled with unwanted children while those who want children can't have them."

"They could have those in the hospitals and orphanages," Father Dourmant said, then bit his tongue; he was here to curry the man's favor, not antagonize him.

Huong nodded. "True, but how many are like that American, Miss Hawthorne?"

"Not many. Not enough."

"I have often thought of her. She seems a most selfless woman." Huong bowed slightly. "And I know of your good works too."

Father Dourmant waved a dismissive hand.

"No," Huong continued, "I have contemplated the nature of charity ever since I learned of you both. You see, Orientals have a sense of duty and honor, but love and charity are not essential to our societies. I do not think that the American woman and you are driven by duty or reward. That leaves charity and love."

He gestured toward his house. "I love my wife and child more than anything, but I have wondered if this love is not a Western concept. You see, not long ago our women's feet were bound, and love did not figure in our marriages. A child's duty was to honor a parent; duty was every thing, love never mentioned. I wonder if you missionaries aren't partly responsible for introducing love into our cultures. Do you think we have you priests and women like the American to thank for that?"

Father Dourmant pocketed a banana in his cassock. "I'm sure you do. Christianity took the idea of duty and softened it into love—it works better to have people do things out of love rather than duty—it's more palatable." He smiled faintly. "Of course we also use the stick along with the carrot. Actually it's more a bludgeon—damnation and eternal suffering for malingerers and malefactors."

Huong nodded appreciatively. "It's a clever cosmology; introducing love was brilliant, especially all that imagery with the heart."

"Yes—bleeding, pierced, sacred, quite clever indeed. I'll congratulate God on that should I encounter him in the church tonight."

"Is it charity that brings you here today? Did you come for money for the American woman and the orphans?"

"Would you give us money?" the priest asked in surprise.

"Of course. Why haven't you come before? Is it because I am a . . ." and he whispered, "pagan."

"Pagans have all the money. I never came because it never occurred to me that you would help."

Huong smiled. "What currency would you prefer?"

"Dollars. We can exchange them on the black market."

"Very sensible. I shall send money once a month from now on so that it will not be necessary for you to feel embarrassed to approach me again."

"Charity does not embarrass me."

"Nor does wealth embarrass me. However, it does obligate one."

"I hadn't noticed that among the few wealthy people I've known."

"They were probably Christians," Huong said with a smile. He offered a basket of fruit to the priest, then poured him more coffee. "If it wasn't money, what brings you? Not fear for my soul, I hope."

Father Dourmant slipped an apple and an orange into his cassock. "Business."

"Ah," Huong said, opening his hands encouragingly.

"I have some information to sell, and I need a buyer."

Huong shook his head sadly. "Information rarely commands much of a price; there is so little worth knowing—atomic secrets, a cure for cancer, would bring a large sum, but not much else."

"The information I have is valuable."

Huong sat back to listen.

"The end is near," Father Dourmant began.

"Metaphysically? The end of the world?"

"The end of Vietnam. When the Americans leave, the communists will take over."

Huong smiled indulgently.

"As soon as the peace treaty is signed, America will abandon us."

"Why would the Americans abandon South Vietnam?" Huong asked.

The answer was so obvious—treachery, duplicity, self-interest—that Father Dourmant sat back dumbfounded.

Huong lectured with slight admonition, "The United States has sworn to defend South Vietnam. They have invested billions of dollars and sacrificed thousands of their soldiers. They are a reliable ally. Look at World War Two. The Marshall Plan. Chiang Kai-shek in China, Korea. As a Frenchman, you need no reminder of Normandy and the liberation of Paris. The Americans have always acted honorably."

Father Dourmant studied the Chinese man's face for sign of jest or irony, but he appeared sincere. The priest was stunned—that anyone would believe in national honor or integrity was preposterous, but Chien Lin Huong was a shrewd businessman who had navigated the shoals of Vietnamese politics for years. "I thought it was commonly accepted that the Americans were leaving," he ventured.

"They are withdrawing, but that doesn't mean abandonment. You judge them too harshly; they will not let the communists overrun the South."

This is like talking to a Jew in the boxcar on its way to Dachau, discussing accommodations and the food, Father Dourmant thought.

"I trust the Americans," Huong said.

"Is it because you have so much? There is a story in the Old Testament about a man blessed with wealth, health, and happiness. He believed in God. His name was Job. As a test of his belief and devotion, he lost every thing."

"Did he still believe?" Huong asked politely.

"Yes, but in *God,* not the Americans."

"I have a great deal and am many times blessed: I have a wonderful wife and a beautiful child. My mother is well, living here with me. I know how fortunate I am, but my belief is based on practicality, not devotion; I don't worship the Americans."

"Well. . . . Well."

"My family has been in Vietnam for hundreds of years. Long before the French came we were scholars and merchants, and I am an honest businessman. People whisper that I am a crime overlord, but it is not so. Perhaps I am sympathetic to the Americans because we are both falsely accused of base motives."

Father Dourmant sat back in consternation. In distraction, he reached for yet another banana and stuffed it into his cassock. "A man's life is at stake. I knew him long ago when he was a boy. He has come to me for help. He needs protection. He is being pursued by the communists, and he doesn't trust the South Vietnamese or the Americans."

"He has narrowed his options. Who is left?"

"He needs safe passage out of Saigon."

Huong smiled. "I see. I have businesses in Hong Kong—I am to get him there. But you said this was business; so far we are only talking favors."

"The man has valuable information."

"What is it?"

Father Dourmant debated. Could he trust the Chinese man? There were so many uncertainties in the world; he wished he were younger, his mind more agile. It had been a fine instrument once. He had been so quick, even called clever in the seminary by Jesuits notorious for brilliance and intrigue. But now he felt his mind a dull blade, not much more than a simple tool. Age and the Orient had blunted its sharpness, anvils on which a thousand blows had been struck—a thousand thoughts deflected, a thousand dreams futilely hoped. Age and the Orient were bogs within bogs, pulling all down, erasing every thing, constantly resmoothing the surface. He had trudged the bogs now for fifty years—looking back, there was not even a footprint to be seen.

Now his mind struggled with another step. "If you are right, if the Americans are not going to abandon South Vietnam, they should be interested in a battle plan the North has for an invasion once the peace treaty is signed. I have this information."

Huong rested his hands on the table, then nodded. "And for it, the man wants safe passage to Hong Kong, and you want money."

The priest sighed. "Yes. But for the children, for the women and orphans."

"You can produce the man and the information?"

"Yes."

Huong stood. "I shall make inquiries." He offered the basket of fruit. "Please." Then he bowed. "I will contact you as soon as I hear something."

Father Dourmant returned the bow and walked off with the basket, his cassock bulging with fruit. Behind him he heard scurrying feet and, looking back, saw the little girl rush into her father's arms. Then a beautiful, elegant woman in Chinese dress led an elderly woman onto the terrace, and all four sat at the table.

It did look like a blessed family, Father Dourmant thought, but then he frowned, thinking of Job.

CHAPTER 4

Standing alone at the top of Gio Linh, a rocky crag looming like a medieval fortress, the most forward outpost on the battlefield, Luke Bishop surveyed the dark plain that stretched a mile north to the Demilitarized Zone. A mile to the east lay the ocean. To the west were the mountains surrounding Con Tien and Khe Sanh.

Bishop watched the last sunlight swallowed by the mountains. Almost immediately a cold wind blew across no-man's-land, once a lush green jungle and rain forest that a thousand air strikes and napalm had left a shell-pocked, defoliated waste.

Bishop picked up the starlight scope, aiming to the ridge along the coast where the enemy would soon start to move; they won't wait tonight, he thought—they'll come before the moon rises.

He shivered, but not from cold. Some one was going to die; he could always tell.

He glanced at his watch; in thirty minutes he would enter the arena of combat and death; it was animal and primal, a challenge to the god of war, and he loved it. Pleasure rippled through him; he could hardly wait to go out there.

Luke Bishop was twenty-six, a poster Marine, six feet, lean and muscular, with clean, sharp features, but beneath the smooth surface was a *Guernica* of tortured distortion.

The genie of war had been unjarred in him and become

his master. Once a woman, seeing Bishop's intensity at the moment of orgasm, a riptide of emotions breaking in his eyes, had recoiled. Later she asked him what he had been feeling. "It just felt great," he said. "So good it hurt."

But later he tried to remember what he had felt or thought at the mad moment of ejaculation. Nothing, he decided, exactly as in combat—it was all ganglia, every nerve alive, a crescendo of heightened awareness and being without sentient thought. Orgasm was like the spasms of excitement rippling through him in combat.

Now, looking out on the plain, his body was as alive as during sex, and the enemy waiting in the dark as compelling as a woman beckoning from the bedroom door.

This plain had drawn him back after four years and over ten thousand miles. Two thousand years ago he would have been a Roman legionnaire. He had been born a centurion; war was in his blood.

A starting halfback at Oklahoma but not good enough for the pros, he joined the Marines when he graduated because where he came from love of country was not acquired behavior but genetic. The Marines had been foreordained, war an extension of the football field; he had merely changed uniforms, shed padding to don flak jacket.

Many people talked a good cause yet managed to duck the fight—they were willing to *send* the Marines, but not join them; Bishop was not that way: he spoiled to fight.

When he returned from Vietnam, he had four rows of battle ribbons, including the Navy Cross, the nation's second-highest medal for valor.

He was offered an honorable discharge, but as an athlete needs a stadium, a soldier needs a battlefield, and having tasted combat, how could he sell shoes after the jungle? How could he return to Main Street after Elysium? Nothing else appealed to him; he didn't want to sell shoes and felt he could not go back to college and sit among students protesting nonunion lettuce and a war where his friends still were.

The first day back from the war while he was passing through the Los Angeles terminal in uniform, a young woman crossed the corridor and spat in his face. "Baby killer. Murderer," she said, spitting again.

He wiped the spit from his face, then almost reeled into a lounge bar to wait for his flight. He sat at the bar sheepishly, head down, but the man beside him slapped him on the back: "Let me buy you a drink, Marine." The man called to the bartender, but the bartender wouldn't take his money: "It's on the house."

When Bishop got on the plane, he felt schizoid, and ever after he was never sure if the next person was going to spit on him or buy him a drink; he felt at home only with those like himself in uniform.

He was stationed in California, where he learned what every real soldier and sailor had learned, that the mouth of the cannon and the maw of the sea are easier to bear than the boredom and routine of life in garrison.

Worse, dreams and the dead came back to wake him every night, so he tried to drown them in drink and outrace them by driving too fast and forget them with women, scoring them like ribbons on his uniform. But he still woke, and the dead would not stay buried, yet he was a hero, so every thing he did was overlooked until he crashed his Corvette on the San Diego freeway.

His commanding officer said, "I thought I was doing you a favor by ignoring your behavior, but I wasn't. I was your age when I came back from Korea. My CO, who'd made a hundred landings in the Pacific, set me straight. Now I'm going to pass on the advice to you—either harness what's inside or get out of the Corps."

The colonel touched the ribbons on his own uniform and pointed to Bishop's. "We're killers, Luke. The Marines did a good job on us, but we had the instinct. We're like thoroughbred horses—if we never see the racetrack, we'd pull a plow the rest of our lives. But once we've felt the track, you can't put us back in the fields. We're blooded, Luke, we've tasted the kill and we're dangerous."

The colonel smiled. "My daughter has a poodle that would run from a gerbil; I hate that dog. When I was a kid, I had a terrier that would chase grizzlies. I cried for a week when it died—a raccoon drowned it in a lake, but something was going to get him sooner or later—hell, it would have attacked a motorboat or a shark. That dog was doomed.

"Some men are like that, Luke; you're one. You went to

war and liked it. Well, we're in the war business. Marines kill people; it's our job. I can't say it's a high calling, but it's a living. We're warriors, paid to be brave, get wet, freeze, stink, eat shit food, risk our lives. In return we get excitement and glory, a never-ending hard-on. But like for a good watchdog, there are rules—you gotta stay alert, can't attack women and children, or bite the owner on the ass. And, Luke, you been chewing on our butt for months now. Either stop or we're gonna put you down."

He took the colonel's advice, was promoted to captain and sent back to Vietnam. The day he got back to war, the dreams stopped and the dead did not return, as if they too had come home and found rest at last.

He was assigned as adviser to a South Vietnamese regiment—three thousand men garrisoned on an exposed rock on the DMZ. His troops were young, inexperienced, poorly trained, badly led, facing a vastly superior enemy.

Bishop lived in a small sandbagged, underground bunker by himself and slept well every night. His platoon sergeant, Chi Phan, seven years older than Bishop and a father of three, had been a schoolteacher. He taught Bishop about Vietnam—the thousand years of Chinese domination, the French invasion, the Japanese occupation, and the origins of Ho Chi Minh's fight against foreigners.

"This is a complex country," Phan explained. "There are Buddhists, Catholics, communists, scholars, peasants, and two different people of the North and South who were united by the Emperor Gia Long long after your own country found independence. There really is no 'Vietnam.' "

"But there's going to be," Bishop promised.

"You really believe? You really care?"

"Yes. People should be free, and there's nothing better I can do with my life than help them. It sure beats selling insurance or used cars."

But Bishop knew there was not going to be a "free" Vietnam if the U.S. pulled out, or if Gen. Vo Thien Lam commanded Gio Linh much longer.

A stocky, blustering man of fifty, General Lam was a political appointee, a personal friend of President Thieu's who talked a great fight, but he had canceled all offensive operations, and none of Bishop's warnings about enemy infiltration or a massive buildup could persuade him to send out patrols.

Bishop knew the NVA was preparing an attack, but the only way to prove it was to go into the DMZ and bring back evidence, yet to take these men into the enemy's lair was not to challenge the god of war but to mock him.

He looked down on the plain. The enemy was out there; he could feel and smell them, and some one was going to die tonight—he could feel and smell that too.

He stared into the black night. Who? Them or him?

He listened to the murmurs and whispers of the war god on the dark plain.

Them, he heard. Yet he knew the war god's treachery; he often lied.

Fifteen minutes later when Phan had gathered seven men, Bishop motioned him aside. "Who's the new one? He looks like he's twelve."

"Private Thien. He's seventeen. He begged me to go out. He says everyone is making fun of him because he's never been on a patrol; he says he has to prove himself."

Bishop motioned the others around and sat in the middle, drawing the new soldier next to him. "We're going to make contact tonight. If the enemy sees you first, they'll kill you. If you make noise or do anything stupid, you'll die. But remember, it's just as dark out there for them, and they are just as afraid. All right, let's go."

There was no moon and the sky was cloudy.

Bishop switched off his rifle safety as he stepped through the wire into the arena, and his face transformed—the muscles tightened around his mouth and eyes to form a cold, intense mask at the same time his body loosened, merging with the darkness.

He moved effortlessly across the plain, leading the patrol east, toward the ocean, for the enemy would not expect them to come up the coast along an exposed beach.

A mile out they found a trail with deep footprints indicating the enemy was carrying heavy matériel. When he started forward again, his men hesitated. None had been this far north, nor ever engaged the enemy. Phan prodded them, and they moved inland up the ridgeline, but Bishop saw they were about to bolt.

A hundred meters beyond, they encountered freshly dug bunkers around an artillery position. His men crouched in the brush as Bishop checked it, but when he motioned them forward, they balked; the enemy's presence was too great. He was asking too much of them, he knew, so he set them in two-man firing teams and motioned Phan and Thien to follow him; he needed Phan, and Thien was too frightened to leave behind.

Another hundred meters up the ridge, they heard voices. Fearing Thien would run, Bishop forced him down. "Don't move," he commanded. "We'll be right back."

Edging closer, Bishop and Phan walked into two men. "You're late," one said in Vietnamese.

"You get lost?" the other asked, laughing.

Bishop's heart clamped, but Phan said easily, "Yes, it's darker than my mother-in-law's heart. You can go now."

They started away, but there was commotion behind them, breaking brush and a furious voice, then a man dragged Thien by his neck into the clearing.

"Look what I caught," the man gloated. "A scared little rabbit. Let's skin him."

The two men moving away looked at each other in confusion, then brought up their rifles, but Bishop pulled the trigger on his M16. A burst of automatic fire slammed them backward, nearly cutting them in half.

Before the man holding Thien could react, Bishop drew his bayonet and threw himself on them both, driving the blade into the North Vietnamese soldier's throat. He pulled it out and slashed again.

The North Vietnamese soldier lay motionless. Thien whimpered but offered no resistance when Bishop pulled him up and dragged him off, his hands slick from blood, its smell wild in his nostrils.

Voices shouted from everywhere and automatic fire erupted. Frantic commanders called for flares, but by the time one illuminated the area, Bishop and his patrol were racing toward the beach. As they crossed the desert toward Gio Linh, a massive artillery barrage was unleashed on the fortress from the ridge. Huge shells pounded the position for twenty minutes, leaving it smoldering by the time Bishop and his men entered the wire, picking their way through the ruin like shadows in a fog.

When Bishop reported to the underground command post, General Lam turned from his maps in rage. "You disobeyed orders! You went into the DMZ. You caused this attack! You're under arrest," he screamed.

"I'm an American officer, you can't arrest me. My patrol got lost. I never would have disobeyed an order."

"Liar! You went into the DMZ deliberately. You ruined the agreement."

"What agreement?"

Lam's eyes blazed, then hooded, and he asked levelly, "What did your patrol find, Captain?"

Bishop pointed on the map to the ridge. "I took out a patrol to give the men experience. I thought it would be safe because you told me the enemy wasn't there, but we found new bunkers. We were on our way back to report them to you when the enemy opened fire. A huge force is up there; they're preparing an attack."

General Lam contemplated him a long minute. "I will include your 'findings' in the after-action report. In the meantime, do not take out any more patrols; your sense of direction, or lack of it, makes me worry about your safety. You are dismissed, Captain."

There would be no mention of the patrol, the enemy buildup, or the artillery attack, Bishop thought as he went back to his bunker. Lam would cover it up. But why? Was he in collusion with the North, or just trying to loot the army, embezzle and steal as much as he could?

Whatever the cause, there was going to be a massacre at Gio Linh when the enemy attacked and he was trapped—he couldn't get away; he was going to die.

Then, staring out over the dark plain came the awful realization that it made no difference to anyone. No one would miss him except his parents—no woman, no children.

There had been a woman once, but Anne had left him; the one woman he loved could not accept him for what he was. Patting his head as if he were a Doberman, she'd said, "You're a Marine—a societally approved, licensed, paid killer. You have balls for brains, or maybe your brains are in your balls. I like you, Luke. Deep down you're a good man, and if I lived in a cave, I'd want you as my caveman—you'd save me from mammoths and saber-tooth tigers, but it's not the Stone Age, Luke. I want to live in La Jolla and listen to music. That's not you—you need a cavewoman or a cheerleader."

Anne was right; he *didn't* want to live in La Jolla. He preferred sleeping bags to sofas, C rations to candlelight dinners, the barracks to the beach, jungle camouflage to a jacket. Now he saw his mistake. Anne had gone on to some one else; she would have love and laughter and children, while he was here alone, about to die. He had made all the wrong choices—Corvette, the Marines, war.

He continued back to his bunker.

Then it occurred to him: what if Gio Linh was meant to fall as part of a larger plan? Perhaps the South Vietnamese were willing to sacrifice Gio Linh to shock America. If Gio Linh was overrun and everyone killed, the Americans might rethink their withdrawal.

Was he merely a pawn, insignificant, inconsequential, sacrificed by politicians and diplomats for a policy he couldn't even understand?

He looked back toward the underground headquarters.

The politicians and diplomats were worse than the god of war, he thought. The god took interest in the conflict and honored courage. He might be fickle, but he watched with an appraising eye and rewarded the brave—he sent them to Elysium.

Luke Bishop believed in Elysium. He was a warrior, proud to be a centurion, and he believed in honor and courage.

Fuck the politics, he said to himself. And fuck Anne Tavernise too. Let her live in La Jolla with some one else. He hadn't made a mistake. There were worse things than dying—being a coward and living a boring life.

And he hadn't made a mistake about his Corvette—he had just made that wrong turn on the freeway; and he hadn't made a mistake about the Marines or this war either.

And God damn it, he wasn't going to die—he was going to get out of this. The god of war wouldn't let him die. Those bastards in Washington would, and Anne Tavernise might kiss his ass good-bye, but the war god . . . he was on Bishop's side; Bishop knew it.

He went to his bunker to set up the radio to send a coded message to Military Assistance Command, Vietnam, in Saigon. Somebody at MACV would pick it up.

Some one there would be as honorable and courageous as he.

Surely.

CHAPTER 5

Wilson Abbot Lord sat motionless at his desk on the third floor of the U.S. embassy in Saigon, watching a small green gecko. Its flicking tongue was the only motion in the austere room devoid of personal mementos.

Neither Lord nor the gecko had moved since the gecko's last darting move had brought it close to Lord's hand ten minutes ago.

Lord, a tall, thin, severe man of forty-six with languorous movements, was senior CIA agent on station. Dubbed the Phantom by the Marine guard because he almost never spoke and usually worked at night, coming and going in the loneliest hours, he cast a chilling aura.

Suddenly the gecko edged toward Lord's hand. Sensing warmth, it climbed tentatively up a finger, then crouched on his wrist. Lord could feel the reptile's tension, but in a moment it eased into his flesh. Still Lord did not move.

Spread on his desk were three reports he had spent the day reading. All required attention, and each was troubling.

Bradley Lawrence Marshall posed the greatest danger; he was arriving in a few hours as Nixon's special envoy to convince the South Vietnamese to sign the peace treaty.

For twenty years, Wilson Lord had fought communism, and he bore the scars. Only one man knew the pain in his legs and back from the torture he suffered in Korea. He had been captured just before the Inchon invasion, and though he knew its plan, nothing they did made him talk.

Born into a once prominent New England family that managed to keep its name and pride but not much else during the Depression, Lord worked hard to meet expenses at Harvard and had neither time nor funds to socialize. Though there at the same time as Bradley Marshall, he did not know him and never mingled in his stratum—he waited tables, never sat at them, and developed a loathing for the scions of wealth and privilege. He hated their condescension and effete manners—they had never worked and knew nothing of the suffering in the world—they *pretended* to feel, but did not have feelings.

After graduation, at the beginning of the Cold War, he got a job in the CIA and became the coldest warrior of them all, but he soon discovered that his worst enemy was not the KGB, but good and decent men of misguided principles like Bradley Marshall—those liberal effetes from Harvard he had waited on in the dining halls, who would cede to communism what it could not otherwise win.

Lord had been in Vietnam when Marshall came as Johnson's envoy to find an end to the war in 1968. He did every thing in his power then to prevent Marshall from succeeding, but now Marshall was back, preparing Vietnam for burial—except Vietnam wasn't dead, but growing stronger daily, emerging as a stable nation able to stand on its own. Yet now, after all the blood and deaths, America was abandoning the fledgling country with a peace treaty that would destroy its last hope for freedom.

The gecko tensed at the fury racing through Lord, but he suppressed it and the creature gradually relaxed.

The White House had decreed a treaty would be signed and, in a brilliant stroke, Lord thought, had sent Bradley Marshall to convince South Vietnam to sign its own death warrant because Thieu and Ky would listen to him.

He *had* to stop him, yet when he sought to plant an informant on Marshall's staff, he learned an aide had already arrived from Washington—Lt. Col. Paul Jaeger, a career army officer with two previous tours in Vietnam, a highly decorated paratrooper sent from the Joint Chiefs in Washington. That disturbed Lord, and the fact that Jaeger had brought a young officer—Capt. Kurt Seidel—as his own aide was even more ominous. They sounded like a pair of clones of the Prussians who ran the White House, and Lord's concern intensified when he was not able to get either of their files—they were unavailable, he was told.

Marshall threatened Vietnam's survival, but Jaeger could prove as dangerous—he obviously was working for some one at the highest echelon in Washington to ensure the treaty was signed.

Yet this could wait—he would find out more about this colonel later, but now he turned to the second report on his desk, a more immediate threat. Last night Lord had intercepted a message to MACV from the U.S. military adviser at Gio Linh, who claimed that personal reconnaissance had uncovered a large enemy force massed on the DMZ.

But MACV had dismissed the report when Lord called them this morning. "A young captain up there got hysterical—it happens all the time; we call it cabin fever. They want action so badly they start hallucinating about it. We give the report no credence."

But Lord had the captain's file, and Lucas M. Bishop, a Marine with a Navy Cross, Silver Star, and three Purple Hearts, was not the hysterical type. Moreover, General Lam, the commander at Gio Linh, was untrustworthy, cowardly, and corrupt. Other signs also pointed to an NVA offensive—increased infiltration, arms and rice caches, and a disquieting lack of enemy contact: the expected enemy attack at Tet had not occurred.

Lord agreed with the young captain—an attack was imminent and the enemy would overrun Gio Linh, sweep south, and take Hue, sealing Vietnam's fate by reinforcing American public opinion against the South's ineptness and the military's stupidity.

The gecko tensed at Lord's aggravation, so great that only through incredible self-control was he able to relax enough to pacify the lizard.

He admired that captain on the DMZ—a man like that should be saved, Lord thought.

Suddenly he tossed his arm. The gecko flew into the air. With a precise snap he grabbed the reptile as it fell and held it by its tail.

The gecko hung limply.

Lord considered the motionless lizard. If it struggled, it had a chance to get away, but what was the purpose of going slack? How did freezing still protect the rabbit? Playing dead save the possum? Or ceding freedom to aggressors serve democracy?

He released the gecko's tail. It crashed headfirst to the floor, twitched once, then lay still. Lord tossed it in the trash can beside his desk.

He would save that captain at Gio Linh; he could use him: he needed a reliable, trustworthy subordinate. He alone was working to save Vietnam; everyone else was following the directive to disengage as quickly as possible, with MACV jumping ship first. The White House had made it clear that Vietnam was going to be abandoned, so everyone was racing to the lifeboats.

MACV didn't believe Bishop's report because they didn't care if Gio Linh fell, nor did anyone at the embassy. Careers were at stake: the scramble was on as the lifeboats were being lowered, and it was going to be officers and bureaucrats first. On this sinking ship, no women and children would be saved.

Only he, Lord, was not jumping off. He was willing to go down with the ship, but he thought there was still a chance to save the vessel itself—perhaps the third report on his desk.

He picked it up, freed his mind of preconceptions, and let the words strike as though for the first time.

Pran Ba Trung had disappeared. The North Vietnamese did not admit Trung's disappearance—a "sudden seizure" was their explanation for the absence of their chief negotiator at yesterday's secret talks between the North and the South, but the flurry of cryptic messages to and from Hanoi indicated something else affected him.

Though defection was possible, MACV and the CIA discounted it, but Lord knew that was like Gio Linh. The marching orders were to lockstep toward withdrawal—a defector would create such immense problems that they would drop him even if he leapt into their arms.

But Wilson Abbot Lord did not make decisions with career in mind.

Pran Ba Trung had not had a seizure, nor was he a poisoned pawn—there wasn't need for one in a game the North was winning without having to sacrifice a single piece. If Trung was gone, he was either lost, had amnesia, was drunk and holed up in a brothel, or he had defected. With those alternatives, defection didn't look so unrealistic to Lord.

But *where* had he gone? He had to find him.

Suddenly there was a rustling in the trash can; Lord looked down to see the gecko streak across the room, then disappear out the window.

Lord smiled in admiration. That explained the instinct: playing dead was a useful dodge—as long as one took the precaution not to be really dead.

Lord pushed himself from the desk and stood, but his leg buckled and he leaned on the desk for support. Since he was alone, he gave in to the pain. He massaged the battered limb, broken in eleven places, and limped a few steps, but when he opened the door and started down the corridor, his stride was powerful and sure.

He had time to handle Bradley Marshall. The defector was a more immediate problem; still, there was time—but the captain at Gio Linh was out of time.

He would solve that problem first—Luke Bishop could prove useful.

When he let himself into his house, a light blue, two-story, stucco dwelling of former French colonials on a quiet residential street not far from the embassy, his wife, Anh, came from the kitchen with a concerned look.

"What is wrong, Wilson? You are never home early."

"I missed you," he said, taking her in his arms.

She was fifteen years younger than he, a small woman with long black hair and piercingly intelligent eyes.

"You're going on a trip," she said, pulling away. "You came home to pack."

He pressed his body against her. "Just for tonight."

"Lance," she said, trying to wriggle free.

"It's time he learned about these things."

"Wilson, he is *five* years old."

"Daddy?" asked the boy, coming from the kitchen; he wore a baseball cap, and though dark-haired and lithe, he strongly resembled his father—his face was angular and his nose sharply defined.

"Who else would be kissing your mother?" Lord asked, holding out his arms for the child to run into, tossing him into the air as the boy squealed happily.

Lord's first marriage had been destroyed by his work. The stresses became too much, and when he was posted to Vietnam ten years ago, his wife told him to choose between her and his work.

Lord had found Anh seven years ago at the French embassy when he was working with Sûreté. She came from a prominent family out of favor with the Diems, and he wooed her for six months before she would go out with him. A sheltered, chaste girl, she nevertheless fell in love with the austere American. When she conceived, he tried to persuade her to have an abortion, but she would not listen to his objections—racially mixed parentage, his age, the hazards of his work.

Now he was grateful, for he loved Lance above all other things. Watching his son grow was a daily wonder for him, and he felt reborn with Anh, so that now determination to save Vietnam was rooted not just in politics, but love—his wife and son would be free, no matter what he had to do.

"I haven't started dinner," she said.

"I didn't come home for dinner."

She studied his eyes, but he shook his head, for he never discussed his work. "Don't worry. This is a good trip. I'll be back for dinner tomorrow."

Lance took off his cap and hit his father on the leg with it. "You promised you'd play baseball," he said in disappointment. "You *promised*, Dad. I been waiting all day."

"I know, but I can't tonight, Son. Tomorrow. I promise tomorrow. Play with your mother tonight."

Lance rolled his eyes. "She can't catch," he said in disgust. "Or throw."

"Well, teach her."

"Dad, she's a *girl*," he said disdainfully.

Anh rapped him on the head.

The boy looked so crestfallen that Lord laughed. "All right, but only for a few minutes. A plane's waiting—I've got to get to Da Nang before dark."

Lance slapped the cap back on his head, grabbed a baseball and two mitts from the sofa, and headed for the door. As Lord followed, Anh said, "You didn't pack."

He paused; the smile on his face turned serious. "I can't take the only two things I really need." He took her in his arms, kissed her, but as he did, Lance pulled him away. "C'mon, Dad."

As soon as they got outside, Lance thrust a mitt into Lord's hand and pounded his own professionally.

Inside the house, the boy spoke Vietnamese, but outside with his father, he switched to English. "You know why I like to play ball with you?" Lance asked, tugging on his cap.

"Why?"

"Because you're the only one who can."

Lord smiled at the backhanded compliment. "Don't any of your friends play?"

"No one else has a mitt. Trinh said they cost a thousand dollars." Lance drew back and threw the ball at his father. "Is that a lot of money, Dad?"

"Yes," Lord said, tossing the ball back in a soft underhand.

"That's a terrible throw, Dad. Do we have a thousand dollars?"

Lord caught the return pitch and threw it back overhanded. "Yes, but not for a baseball glove. Do you think I should buy gloves for all your friends?"

Lance crouched in a pitcher's stance; he glanced to imaginary bases, then hurled the ball, much harder than Lord had expected. "That wouldn't be right," Lance said.

"Why?"

"Because that would be showing off. You shouldn't ever do that. Come on, Dad, throw it harder this time. *Mom* could throw it harder."

Lord drew back and hurled a strong pitch that Lance caught without difficulty.

"Maybe we could give mitts to your friends without showing off."

Lance considered a moment, then shook his head. "They'd feel bad because we gave them something and they couldn't give us anything back. You can't make people feel bad, Dad. Trinh wouldn't want to play with me anymore. Okay, get ready for this one, then toss some grounders."

He heaved a terrific pitch that sailed high and wild. Lord jumped and caught it, but when he landed back on his feet stiffly, he felt his age.

"What should I do if I don't buy them gloves?" he asked, suppressing a grimace.

"You should play with me more. And buy me a bat. Do they cost a thousand dollars too?"

Lord smiled. "I think I can get one cheaper than that."

"Can you get me one, Dad? Really?"

Lord nodded.

"That'd be *great,* Dad." Then Lance frowned. "But I wouldn't tell anyone. We'd just play together with it, just you and me. No one would know."

They tossed the ball far longer than five minutes, until Lord could no longer put off leaving.

It hurt so much to leave now, even for a day. Before, he had loved ideas, principles, his country, but not until Anh and Lance had he truly loved. Yet strangely, his love for his wife and child deepened and personalized his love for those ideas and principles and for his country. Now when he thought of freedom, it was not abstract, but *people* being free, and poverty and hunger were women and children suffering and in need.

He threw a final pitch to his son, then handed him the glove and crouched beside him. "Lance, do me a favor."

The boy pushed his cap back and said easily, "Sure, Dad."

"If I ever tell you I don't have time to play ball with you, I want you to say, 'Yes, you do, Dad.' Okay?"

The boy nodded.

Lord hugged him and stood. "I've got to go now. I don't have time to play any longer."

Lance smiled. "Yes, you do, Dad."

Lord laughed, bending to kiss his son's head. "Nice try."

"Don't forget the bat," Lance called as Lord crossed the tree-lined street to his car. As he was about to unlock it, a man stepped out of a dark, chauffeur-driven sedan parked in back of his.

Chien Lin Huong bowed politely. "What a lovely boy you

have; he seems about the age of my daughter. It was a joy to watch you, but what is that game you were playing?"

"Baseball," Lord said, bowing in return.

Huong looked perplexed. "But what is the point of the game? It seemed just to catch the sphere. Is there a reward for catching it? A punishment if it is dropped?"

Lord smiled. "Reward is mastery of the sphere; punishment is disappointment."

"Ah, a game of life," Huong said approvingly, then he linked arms with Lord and steered him away from the car. "I tried to reach you at work but was told you might not be back for a while. May we talk?"

"Unfortunately, I am in a rush to catch an airplane."

"Why don't I drive you to the airport. We could chat on the way."

Lord did not hesitate. Chien Lin Huong did not have idle chats or make social calls; he was one of the wealthiest, most powerful men in the country, and Lord considered him a rare and authentic ally. Over the years they had had numerous dealings, interceding on each other's behalf for favors—Lord had power, Huong information and contacts: their currencies were linked, and their accounts even.

When Lord got into the car, Huong came directly to the point. "An individual has approached me for a favor."

As the car started up the street, he said, "I am disposed to help because one never knows when a favor might be needed in return. The man has a problem. I considered who might best be able to help him and be helped in return. I believe you are the individual."

The automobile entered a boulevard clogged with pedicabs, bicycles, and dilapidated small cars billowing exhaust. Looking out, Lord saw cripples, beggars, and amputees, but Huong drew the curtains on them, shutting out the city.

Lord said matter-of-factly to the black cloth, "You know the whereabouts of Pran Ba Trung." It was an intuitive stab, for if anyone would have such knowledge, it would be Huong. He was the logical man to go to for help—either to flee, to make contacts, or to remain in hiding.

Huong smiled in appreciative acknowledgment. "I knew I had come to the right person; he has information you may find useful. But we need to work out details."

This was going to cost money, Lord knew, a *lot* of money, but there was no hope of getting any, for the U.S. did not want Trung even for free, though Lord could hardly tell Huong that. "I would be interested in talking with him," Lord said casually, betraying no excitement. "Perhaps we can discuss this after my return."

"When will that be?" Huong asked.

"In three days," Lord lied, hoping to gain time; by then he should be able to track down the defector on his own.

"I will contact you then," Huong said, opening the curtains, signaling the end of the discussion. "Your wife is well?"

"Yes, thank you. And yours?"

"Very well. We are blessed men, are we not? Health, happiness, loving wives, beautiful children—we are like Job."

"Mmmm," Lord murmured as the car pulled up to the main gate of Ton Son Nhut. "Thank you for the ride," he said, bowing as he got out.

He stared after Huong's disappearing car. Job, he thought. What a curious analogy for a Chinese man.

After the flight to Da Nang, Lord transferred to a helicopter for the short trip to Gio Linh on Air America, the CIA's private airline; for some one of Lord's position, a plane was always available.

The chopper touched down on the rocky fortress just before sunset, landing on the helipad beside General Lam's chopper. After giving instructions to his pilot, Lord made a quick survey of the hill, noting the recent artillery shelling.

Uncertain of Lord's mission or position, knowing only that he was from the U.S. embassy in Saigon, Lam greeted him in his underground headquarters with supercilious indifference.

"You didn't report enemy contact," Lord said, crouching in the bunker because of his height.

"A few artillery shells don't qualify as 'enemy contact,' Mr. Lord. We don't get excited when the NVA lob a few shells at us."

"They're going to lob a great many more, General. I've come to warn you that the enemy is preparing a major offensive, possibly tonight."

"I have received no warning from MACV or American intelligence."

"*I* am American intelligence; consider *this* a warning."

"Perhaps we should call MACV to verify your prediction."

"Please do so; I would like my warning on record. However, MACV doesn't share my concern." Lord smiled with no warmth whatsoever. "But they are often wrong. My record is *much* better, General."

"Thank you for the warning," Lam said curtly. "I will call MACV immediately. Did your visit have any other purpose, *Mister* Lord?"

"Yes. I am here to relieve the American adviser."

Lam nodded. "Good, it will save me the trouble."

When shown to Bishop's bunker on the far side of the hill looking over the darkening plain, Lord found the young officer in his skivvies, writing a letter by candlelight.

Bishop looked up with curiosity at the older man dressed in slacks and sport shirt.

"Captain Bishop? Wilson Lord. I'm from the embassy in Saigon. I got your report yesterday."

Bishop jumped up. "I knew some one at MACV would believe it," he said excitedly.

"Well, you were wrong." Lord glanced about the bunker with a bored look. " 'Hysterical' was how they described your report, Captain."

"The NVA is going to overrun this place," Bishop said hotly. He pointed to the ridge across the plain. "Ten thousand gooks are up there waiting to attack. You know what I was writing?" He held up a piece of paper. "A goodbye letter to my parents because *nobody* is going to survive this massacre."

Lord yawned. "That's why I'm here—*I* believe you."

Bishop eyed him curiously. "You do?"

Lord gestured to Bishop's rifle and backpack. "Get your gear, you're leaving." Then he pointed at Bishop himself. "Do you have any clothes, or are you going with me to Saigon naked?"

Bishop stared at him intently. "Who are you?"

"I am the man who is saving your ass, Captain. Someday I'll expect you to return the favor. I'm with the CIA. I don't like to see good men get killed. Now get your shit and let's get out of here. We haven't much time."

"I can't leave here. I have my orders."

Lord shook his head in disdain. "Marines are so tiresomely predictable." He pulled a sheet of paper from his pocket and handed it to Bishop. "You've been reassigned to the embassy in Saigon."

Bishop considered him a moment. "Who the fuck are you?"

Lord moved so close that their bodies touched. *"Never* talk to me this way, Mr. Bishop. Ever." He held out his palm.

Bishop dropped his gaze to Lord's hand. Lord held the palm open. "You're alive, Luke." He clutched it into a fist. "You're dead, Luke."

Bishop looked into Lord's eyes. They were so intense and commanding that Bishop moved back, understanding that it was in the power of this man to kill or save him.

Luke bowed in submission. "Why me?"

"Because I can use you; you are what I have been looking for—a brave, principled man; they are hard to find. Get your gear, Captain."

As they crossed the hill toward the helicopter, Bishop bringing only his rifle and backpack, Lord asked offhandedly, "Do you play baseball, Captain?"

"Yes, sir," Bishop snapped out, overwhelmed and intimidated.

Lord stopped and pressed a finger into Bishop's chest. *"Don't* be afraid of me. I didn't come up here to get a yes-man."

Bishop knocked his hand away. "I played *football;* baseball is for pussies."

Lord smiled. "Very good, Mr. Bishop. Did you master *that* sphere?"

Bishop cocked his head at the quaint phrasing, but he nodded. "I was *great."*

Lord put his arm around Bishop's shoulder and steered him toward the helicopter. "Then this is your first order, Mr. Bishop. Get me a baseball bat, *and* a football. I'm sure you can find them among the Marines at the embassy."

Bishop looked at him curiously. "That's it—a baseball bat and a football?"

Lord smiled. "There will be other things later. You're in the major leagues now, Captain. I expect you to play like a pro—no fuckups at all."

When the chopper took off a few minutes later, Bishop looked down at Gio Linh and pointed to General Lam's helicopter. "When the first round is fired, Lam will sky out."

Lord turned to his pilot. "Will he, Mr. Corcoran?"

The pilot held up a pair of wire cutters. "I think the only way they'll get that chopper off the hill is if they carry it."

Bishop turned to Lord, who nodded complacently. "I told you, this is the big leagues. General Lam just struck out."

CHAPTER 6

Ron Mead drove straight through to St. Louis and slept the night in his car. He cleaned up at a truck stop and after breakfast got directions to the Veterans Hospital.

The day was rainy and miserable, his windshield wipers so badly worn that he could hardly see, and he got lost several times, once even crossing the Mississippi into East St. Louis, driving through boarded-up ghettos and old stockyards.

Finally in late morning he pulled into the massive medical complex and parked.

The hospital was huge, gray and somber in the rain, and he did not want to go in.

Sitting in the car, the rolled-up windows steaming from his breath, he pulled Frizzell's letter from the glove compartment to read a last time.

Hey Ron!

Remember me? Les Frizzell from Nam? I got your address from the Corps and called your Dad. We had a good talk. He said you were the same ol asshole—guess a father would know, huh? He said you were married and ok. Anyway, I was lying around—I do that alot—wondering about some of the guys from

Bravo One and thought maybe I'd try to get hold of some of them.

I don't do much travelling these days—kinda hard without legs, but thought maybe if you were ever passing through here, maybe you could stop in and see me. I'm in and out of here all the time—they keep shaving off a little more of the stumps cause of some fucking infection they can't do much about. Man, when the gooks get you, they really get you.

Anyway, sure would like to see you. Shit, anybody. But I understand if you don't. I mean, the war's over, man, and let's forget that fucker. Besides, I'm no centerfold. I mean, I'm a mess, man.

Anyway, best of luck. Sure remember some great things.

Take it easy. Semper Fi.

Your buddy,

Les Frizzell

Mead put away the letter, took a deep breath, then got out of the car. Inside the hospital, he made his way down corridors crowded with old men in bathrobes and wheelchairs to the orthopedic ward. At the nurses' station he asked for Frizzell's room.

"How nice," the nurse said. "I'm so glad he has some one to see him; he's such a nice young man."

"Is he all right?" Mead asked.

The nurse smiled. "Considering every thing, he's done remarkably. We're very proud of him; he's our favorite. I'm happy you came. He doesn't get many visitors."

"Is he going to be all right?"

The nurse looked at him strangely, then merely smiled and told him the room number.

He walked down the ward nervously and stopped a moment before the open door, afraid of what he was going to find, knowing it was going to be another heavy weight to carry for the rest of his life.

Les Frizzell was the friendliest and most simple man he'd

known in Vietnam. Six feet, eighteen, a high school dropout, he had an infectious grin and love of jokes.

Mead braced himself, then walked into the room.

There were four beds, but only one was occupied. The figure was turned to the window, but rolled over on hearing footsteps.

Mead recognized him instantly; the face had not changed, only the hair was longer.

"Fucking hippie," Mead said.

Frizzell's face lit. He grabbed the bar over his head and pulled himself up. "Corporal Mead! Hey, man, how ya doing? God damn, I don't believe it." He pounded the bed happily. "Jesus, you came to see me."

Mead walked to the bed and was about to put out his hand when Frizzell opened his arms with tears in his eyes, and Mead reached out and hugged him.

"Man, you look great," Frizzell said. "Just great."

"So do you."

Frizzell laughed. "Yeah, what there is of me." He depressed the covering sheet at the bottom of his waist—there was nothing there.

Mead looked up to Frizzell's face.

"It's okay. I'm used to it." Frizzell shrugged. "It's better than being dead, like Snags and Landis, or Miller or Donnadio, and . . . lots of them. I'd show you, but it's kinda nasty."

He gazed into Mead's eyes expectantly. "Do you want to see?" he asked at last.

Knowing that it was important, Mead nodded slowly.

"I kinda wanted to share it," Frizzell said, pulling away the cover. There were no legs, no penis, just the hollowed-out sockets of his hip joints and two tubes running out of his body cavity carrying waste into plastic bags. The abdomen and chest were crisscrossed with scars.

Mead raised his eyes to Frizzell's.

"I'm almost three feet long and weigh sixty-eight pounds. But I still got a good face, huh?"

"Yeah." Mead swallowed. "You got a nice face, Les."

Frizzell brushed at his eyes. "Sorry. They don't want me to get depressed so they dope me up, but it makes me kinda teary real easy. They pump me up with Demerol 'cause otherwise I get all fucked up. Depression and stress are supposed to be bad for my system, and I ain't got much system left. I'm out of large *and* small intestines—I'm down to tiny intestine."

"Then what?"

Frizzell laughed. "Then I'm gonna die. I'm a KIA, man; it's just taking a while—like the war: we lost, but it wasn't quick."

Mead could not find his voice.

"There's nothing they can do," Frizzell said quietly. "Oh, they don't tell me that, but when you've been around hospitals and doctors as long as I have, you *know*. You can smell death—and man, I stink."

Mead brought a chair to the bedside and sat; then he got up quickly. "Can I get you something?"

Frizzell shook his head. "They got Red Cross women and lots of volunteers for that. They come in all the time. It's not lonely—people are always running around, church groups and do-gooders, but it's not like having some one you know come see you."

Mead tried to steady his voice. "I . . . I didn't know."

"I told your old man on the phone."

"He said you were bad, but he didn't tell me you were going to die."

"I'm used to it now. And if I get any smaller, I'll be ready to go. I'm in good shape now, but when I get infected, it's really gross—I'm delirious and screaming, and they dope me senseless. That's no way to live."

"What happened, Les?"

"A mine. I had forty-seven days left. I thought I was gonna make it. Coney and Sutherland and me had this pact. You remember them?"

"Sure. I liked Coney—funnier than hell, but Scott was a prick."

"That's Sutherland all right, mean motherfucker."

"He make it?"

"Yeah, both him and Coney. I guess the pact worked; I mean, we all got out of Nam—just not in one piece. Anyway, I was squad leader, and we were on patrol. A new guy was with us; he tripped a mine. The blast just took my legs off."

"Were you conscious?"

"Yeah, but I kept wishing I wasn't. I could see one of my legs. It was about ten feet away, just lying on the ground. I tried to crawl to it. I mean, it was *my* leg—I wanted it back. Then I started screaming for it."

Frizzell shook his head. "Coney got it for me. Then he sat beside me, holding it in his lap while he talked to me. Then the corpsman jabbed me with morphine, and that was it for a long time. I was in intensive care in Japan for three months. They thought I was gonna die. I think they were getting bored with me hanging on. My fever wouldn't go down, but I wouldn't die either."

Mead watched him silently.

"By the time I got to the States, I was down to stumps six inches long, then they took that away inch by inch."

Frizzell said almost casually, "I lost my cock right away, in Japan while I still didn't know what was going on. They said they'd make me a new one. Plastic surgery. But things kept getting worse, so now I got this rubber tube."

He smiled. "It's long, but it won't get hard."

A wistful look crossed his face. "I remember joking with Coney once about being circumcised. I wasn't, and he was telling it was better for women if you were."

He shrugged. "Turned out it didn't make much difference after all."

Mead bowed his head.

"Anyway, how about you? You look great. You're even bigger than I remember. Course, everybody is nowadays. Every thing all right?"

"I'd sure feel like an asshole complaining to you. But, yeah, things are fine. I was thinking maybe of going to college."

"Yeah? That's what I always wanted to do, if I ever finished high school." Frizzell shrugged. "For me now though it'd be like having a plastic-surgery dick—what would be the use?"

The nurse came in with a syringe. "It's time," she said. "Actually it's past time. You must be having a good visit."

"It's my pain shot," Frizzell said to Mead. "I'm a dope addict."

"You are not," the nurse said.

"I'm down to a shot less than every four hours, and I

start to shake and slobber after five, so what does that make me?"

The nurse took his arm, pinched it gently, and stuck in the needle, then she left.

"I'll start to float away in about fifteen minutes," Frizzell said.

"You really need the shots?"

"Oh, *yeah.* It's all I look forward to. I last about thirty minutes, then I nod off. Just blow me a kiss when you leave. But if I forget to tell you, thanks for coming, Ron. It meant a lot. I get kinda lonely sometimes."

"I'd have come sooner if I'd known."

"Then you might not have come back, and I wouldn't have you here now. Most people never come back. I mean, it's kinda depressing, huh? People come all the time, fucking veterans groups, and they tell me how great I was to go to Vietnam, how we were fighting for freedom and all that shit, and they tell me how the POWs will be coming back any day. I mean, like I give a shit—fuck the POWs, I want my legs back."

Frizzell closed his eyes and said bitterly, "I want my legs, man. I want a girl. I want a life." His fist slammed the blanket. "Shit!"

Mead steeled his eyes shut.

In a moment Frizzell recovered. "I'm sorry. I don't normally do that. I try to keep it all in. I guess seeing you, and . . ."

"I understand," Mead said softly.

"Yeah, I see you do. Others just see some gross, pathetic freak."

Mead took his hand. "Man, we're all freaks, all of us who came back."

"You too?"

"Oh, yeah. I get dreams that . . . are real. I wake up seeing the dead and the blood. Sometimes I'll be walking down the street, and suddenly I want to cry. I don't know why. It's all so fucking sad. And I can't tell it to anybody; you can't explain it. You're perfectly all right, then suddenly there's a smell or a sound or just a leaf falling, and you want to cry like a baby. Whadda ya suppose it is, Les?"

"It's death; we saw it too soon. It's supposed to come

later, after you've already fucked up your lives, missed your chance, fallen out of love, and had rotten kids. After your job has turned to shit, and you're tired and sick. Then you're ready to see death, but not when you're starting out. We saw the end first. It's like a book or a movie. If you see the ending first, you lose interest in the story—there's no suspense."

Frizzell shook his head, trying to fight the morphine muffling his thoughts.

"Seeing those dead gooks did it for me. Remember on the DMZ after Donnadio and Perez got zapped, and we knew we'd killed at least twenty of them, but when we went out to get the bodies, there was not one dead gook?"

Mead nodded at the memory. "Can you imagine we were like that once, fucking ghouls, looking for corpses?"

"Then weeks later up in the DMZ, coming across their burial ground. Digging them up did it for me. It was dark, rainy, and we were digging up bodies, and there was nothing left of them—just soup from the wet ground. I remember standing over them, guys no older than us, just soup. That day was like looking into the grave, seeing yourself."

Frizzell's eyes closed. Mead thought he was asleep until Frizzell said softly, "We found out about life and death too early. You oughta be spared, like you don't tell little kids about Santa Claus and the tooth fairy—you let them believe for a while. I could have gone on believing a lot longer that I was gonna have a life, a wife and kids, a good job. Maybe it wasn't going to happen, but it'd been nice to have dreams about it."

Frizzell gestured about the room. "Now this is my life. It's like being buried above ground."

Mead bowed his head.

Frizzell started to fade. "It's all right. We're all gonna end like soup, you and I know that better than anybody—we were there; we saw. I'm just closer than most."

He shook his head. "You know what bothers me? It's crazy—I'll never get in the paper, even when I die. There won't even be a story in the obituaries. I read those now, isn't that dumb? I'm twenty-two, and I read the obits, and I know I won't even make the paper someday. Ever wonder who decides those things, who gets the big write-up and their picture in the paper?"

"Assholes do. And the bigger the asshole, the bigger the write-up."

Frizzell was quiet for a long time, breathing softly, and Mead was sure he was asleep, but just as he got up to go, Frizzell opened his eyes.

"Do me a favor, Ron?"

"You got it."

"Live for me."

Mead brought up his hands as if to ward off a blow. "That's not fair, Les."

"You got to. I can't live for myself. I don't have a life. Neither does Donnadio or Perez, or Landis or Dutton. None of the dead have lives. But what wouldn't they give for one? Think of the people who *have* lives. What do they do with them? It isn't right those people waste their lives—they don't laugh or dance or run or enjoy anything. Why should they have a life? *I* want one. All those guys in Nam want one too."

He sank back into his pillow. "That's why you got to live for me. Don't screw it up, man. I want you to do all the things I can't. I want you to eat for me and laugh for me and fuck for me."

"Les, I can't carry that; that's too heavy."

"You gotta," Frizzell said simply. " 'Cause I can't. But don't worry, I won't be watching or anything. It won't be like I'll be looking over your shoulder. And if you screw up, I'd understand. I mean, it's not like *I* wouldn't have fucked up. Okay?"

Mead nodded at last. "Okay."

Frizzell settled into the pillow with a happy look. "I'm gonna check out."

He sank away. "Take it easy." Then, faintly, "Semper fi."

"Semper fi," Mead whispered back.

He waited a long time after Frizzell fell asleep, watching his face shift like a sea, easing and tightening, then he kissed him on the forehead.

Then he left.

* * *

When Ron Mead walked out of the hospital, he didn't know where to go. The gray day and threatening rain added to his melancholy, and he stood a long time on the steps.

He didn't want to be a garbageman any longer. If he was going to live a life for Les Frizzell, he couldn't go back to that. But he couldn't go to college either. Go to college and be what? An accountant? Sell insurance? Mortgage a rancher, learn to play golf, wear polyester clothes?

He didn't want any of that, and Frizzell wouldn't want that for his life either.

It was midmorning; the rain had stopped, but it was overcast and cold. Gazing over the parking lot, debating whether to go back to his car—not knowing where to go—he saw a flag flying over rows of crosses in the distance.

Drawn, he walked toward the cemetery. It was a half mile, and there were no visitors on this miserable day, so he walked down the neat rows of white crosses alone, stopping now and then to read a name, determine what war he had fought in, and how old he was when he died.

It was an orderly place, a barracks for the dead, and he felt peaceful here—a place where he seemed to belong, as though he were among his own.

He wandered for hours and sat on marble benches, gazing at workmen digging new graves. In late afternoon, he walked to one and stared into the hole, thinking of the day years ago in Vietnam when he and Frizzell had peered down on the enemy dead.

He thought of those who died, and of Frizzell soon to lie in a grave like this.

As he would too someday. The thought didn't frighten him. When that time came, he would be ready; what frightened him was the time before then.

What was he going to do between now and the grave? He gazed into the hole searching for an answer, but there wasn't one.

Rain began to fall, lightly at first, then heavier, and water started to fill the grave.

He turned away and left the cemetery.

He was too tired and depressed to drive home and wasn't ready to face Sung, so he searched for a cheap motel and found one across the river near the railroad tracks.

The room was shabby and not clean. He dropped on the bed without taking off his clothes and fell asleep almost immediately.

He slept fitfully as sapper thoughts and images penetrated the barriers of consciousness, and when he woke at three A.M., he could not get back to sleep.

He turned on the television. A war movie was on, a World War II film about the Pacific. He flipped it off immediately to sit in the dark.

He looked at the dark screen, stared intently at it trying to see a future for himself, but the screen remained blank, and he couldn't even see his own reflection; it was as unrevealing as the grave.

He turned on the television again; the movie was still on. He saw a jungle, and the screen filled with a soldier's face. Mead sat forward, gripping the armchair.

He stared at the frightened, sweat-beaded face of the soldier. It was night; the jungle was alive with sounds, and the soldier's eyes looked about furtively, then the soldier started to move down the trail. He looked so young, Mead thought, and was so scared, and he knew, just knew what was going to happen.

The soldier was going to die. But he had such an innocent, vulnerable look, a boy like Frizzell, like himself long ago, a boy who was never going to grow up, who was never going to get out of that jungle.

He could hear the jungle, the brush rustling, and he could smell it.

There was terror in the boy's eyes; they grew wider, filling the screen.

Mead jerked forward and shut off the television.

But the image did not go away; the soldier continued down the trail, and it was himself, Mead saw.

It was that night with the enemy's rifle bead aimed at his heart.

Sweat poured from his body; he tensed, waiting for the impact.

He could hear the enemy breathing and feel the finger squeezing the trigger.

Then he jumped up, whirling from the screen, holding up

his hands to shield himself. He stood in the dark room, drenched and shaking.

He was never going to get away from Vietnam; he couldn't. He was doomed to carry the dead with him the rest of his life. He would never purge Vietnam.

He couldn't run away from Vietnam any more than he could run from the men who had attacked Sung.

Then he went slack, and staring now at the dark screen, he finally saw his reflection, and in it, his future.

He took a deep breath, then went to the night table for his car keys. He knew what he had to do. It's what his father had told him. It's what Frizzell would want him to do.

He left the room and got in his car and drove through the night.

When he arrived at the trailer in early morning, the Buick was parked in front.

Sung turned from the kitchen sink when he went in. "Did you have breakfast?" she asked as if he were just coming in from work.

"No," he said with a smile. "I don't think I ate since I left."

"Would you like breakfast?"

"Yes," he said, taking her in his arms.

Then he looked into her eyes. "Is it okay if I don't go to college, Sung? Would you still stay with me?"

She lowered her head in mirth. "Yes, Ron, I will stay with you—I love you."

"Then I want you to pack. We're getting out of here. I guess I better go back to work. Think I can get my old job back?"

She looked at him curiously. "What is that?"

"The only thing I was ever good at, being a Marine."

Then he hugged her tightly. "I gotta keep moving, Sung. I'll die if I don't."

She smiled. "You always looked so handsome in your uniform."

"Yeah, and I'll get to wear all my medals."

He bent and kissed her hair. "We gotta make it, Sung. We gotta prove that. Otherwise nothing out of that war means anything. You and I are gonna make it."

CHAPTER 7

Marshall did not open his eyes when the flight attendant on the presidential aircraft told him they were approaching touchdown in Saigon. When he left in 1968, he had flown over a napalmed wasteland that looked like a colossus's junkyard, some cruel Homeric joke, and he did not want to see the devastation four more years of war had wrought.

Once it had been a paradise of color and life that his own country had savaged and mutilated, brilliant jades and lapis that had been shattered not by a colossus but by foolish dwarfs. The destruction was neither a joke nor Homeric, but merely bad lines of ungifted poets writing Policy. And he was one of them, he knew.

When the plane taxied to a halt, he exited to a blast of humid heat that took his breath away and he was blinded by sunlight reflecting off the metal tarmac and silver Quonset huts of Ton Son Nhut. He gripped the handrail for support, then drew a deep breath and tried to focus on the surrealistic scene below him.

Anyone who had invested the slightest research into the President's envoy would have known Marshall despised ceremony, but on the tarmac below was an extravaganza of honor guards, dignitaries, and pomp. He was so angry he almost went back into the plane, but instead he swallowed his anger, and as he descended the steps to speak some inconsequential lines to the assemblage, an army colonel, a tall, formidable man of commanding presence and severely cropped hair, saluted him and said, "Your car is waiting, sir," and he led a slightly dazed Marshall from the U.S. ambassador to Vietnam, Ellsworth Bunker, startled generals, and ministers to a black sedan and directed the driver to leave, an advance of police jeeps clearing the way.

"Am I being kidnapped?" Marshall asked, turning to see the dignitaries staring at one another in surprise and confusion, and the elderly Bunker storming off to his own car.

"Do you want me to take you back?" the colonel asked.

"No," Marshall said, settling back in the seat. "I'd rather be kidnapped."

The man handed him several folders. "Nothing in them is important, but you'll need the background to understand the crap you're going to hear in the next few days."

Marshall accepted the folders and stared at the man.

"Lt. Col. Paul Jaeger; I've been assigned as your aide, but if you don't like me, or anything about me, they'll get you some one else."

Marshall was somewhat taken aback. "Who assigned you to me?"

"I was in the Pentagon working liaison with Congress when I was asked if I'd like to work for you. They told me you were a former Marine who knew crap when he heard it and didn't want to hear any; they said you were tough and fair. I jumped at the chance."

He handed Marshall another folder. "That's my personnel file; no one else is allowed to see it."

Marshall tried to slow this down and gain control. "Do you know why I'm here?"

"Supposedly to get the South Vietnamese to sign the peace treaty."

"Supposedly?"

Marshall studied Jaeger a minute, then made his decision: this was exactly the man he wanted—tough, direct, savvy, and unafraid; he had not expected anyone like this. "All right, you're hired, but you work for me, *no* one else. I represent the President—I report only to him; you report only to me. Is this going to be a problem?"

Jaeger shook his head. "No, sir."

"I mean that, Colonel—you report to me alone—unless you have a private line to Richard Nixon."

Jaeger smiled. "I can't even get a call through to my wife in Minneapolis."

Marshall nodded. "Fine. Now drop me off at my residence. I need sleep, but have some one pick me up at eight in the morning, then show me how good you are."

Sirens screamed a path through the crowded streets so quickly that Marshall saw only a blur. Though an entire floor of the most modern hotel had been readied for him, he had demanded to stay where he had before, at the villa of the former French legation on a wide, tree-lined boulevard in a residential area not far from the embassy. The old colonial-style building of terraces and columns, expansive gardens, and an inner courtyard with a marble fountain had been refurbished for visiting dignitaries, but the luxurious serenity had been marred by an electronically wired concertina fence so that the estate had become a heavily guarded compound with a Marine sentry booth at the entrance.

A deferential staff greeted him, but he withdrew immediately to his room, where he dropped onto the canopied bed underneath a clacking overhead fan. He got off his jacket and shoes, then fell back on the mattress and slept soundly until he was awakened at seven by a young Marine knocking at the door.

"Corporal Wesley Bonnard, sir. Colonel Jaeger sent me to get you. I'm your driver, sir."

Marshall, disheveled in his clothes from the day before, yawned at the rigid youth before him, muscular and clean-cut, awed and slightly afraid, but displaying the bright eagerness that had been the hallmark of Ron Mead, his bodyguard years ago.

"Are you my bodyguard too, Corporal?"

Bonnard frowned. "I . . . nobody said anything about that, sir." Then he snapped even more rigid. "Yes, sir, I'll be your bodyguard too."

"Am I likely to need one, Corporal?"

Bonnard frowned again. "I . . . I guess that depends on what you plan to do, sir."

Marshall reached out and shook the Marine into a looser stance. "Relax. I have no plans for anything dangerous; driving through Saigon is going to be the most frightening thing you'll be called upon to do. Give me thirty minutes to shower and change, and another thirty minutes for breakfast. I'll meet you outside."

An hour later at the huge squat embassy in the center of town, Jaeger met Marshall's car and ushered him through security and the lobby to a private elevator that brought him to his suite of offices on the top floor overlooking the embassy compound and the city that stretched to the horizon. After meeting the clerical staff, Jaeger introduced Marshall to his other aide.

Captain Kurt Seidel was a powerfully built young man with whitewall haircut, strong, thick features, paratrooper wings, and menacing demeanor.

"I don't think I'll need Corporal Bonnard as a bodyguard after all," Marshall said pleasantly, shaking hands with the slight fear that Seidel would crush his fingers.

"No, sir, you won't," Seidel said without humor.

"West Point?" Marshall asked.

"The Citadel, sir," Seidel snapped out.

Marshall turned to Jaeger. "Why do I need two aides?"

Jaeger smiled. "He's the brains; I'm the brawn."

Marshall nodded, liking his aide more and more, but when he stepped into his inner office, he pointed to the ornate furnishings of chintz and brocade. "Get rid of this foo-foo shit. Last time it was decorated for Conan the Barbarian, this time it's for Liberace. Isn't there anything in between, something functional—U.S. Government dull?"

"We'll get right on it," Jaeger said, leading him out of the office to his own. "In the meantime you can work in here—you'll need an hour to go over the papers I gave you yesterday before we go to the MACV briefing."

"Knowing that you're on a very tight schedule, Colonel, I read them at breakfast."

Jaeger nodded approvingly. "Good. Then I'll call MACV and tell them we'll be earlier than expected so we can get that bullshit out of the way."

"If I'm going to hear 'bullshit,' why go?"

"You're in a play, Mr. Ambassador, a bad one; consider this a rehearsal where you meet the rest of the cast and hear the lines."

Marshall nodded, then handed him back his personnel file. "I read that this morning too. You've had a remarkable career, medals and battlefield commands, and you're on the promotion list—thirty-six for a full colonel is quite an achievement."

"I bought all the rank insignia from second lieutenant to four-star general in the PX at West Point when I graduated," Jaeger said without expression. "I'm halfway there."

Marshall sat on Jaeger's desk; he had never met anyone with the brusque confidence of this colonel. "I get the feeling you're somebody's golden boy. Who's behind your career?"

"Do I look the type who needs a patron?"

"They come into the lives of all lucky people, Colonel; it's hardly an indictment. I was fortunate to first work for JFK. Captain Seidel has you; who's *your* benefactor?"

"I worked for General Westmoreland here years ago; he brought me to Washington when he was appointed chief of staff. I guess I owe the most to him."

Marshall passed over that and stood. No protégé of Westmoreland's would get a congressional liaison job or be sent on this mission; he would have been buried in the Pentagon as soon as the former Vietnam commander retired. Jaeger was hiding something; he had made his first mistake.

Marshall hopped off the desk. "We'll keep to the schedule. I need to pay my respects to Ambassador Bunker—if he'll see me after leaving him on the tarmac yesterday."

Marshall's sudden and unannounced arrival in Bunker's office caused a sensation. His aides didn't know how to handle the situation, leaving the President's envoy standing alone as they rushed into Bunker's private office to announce his presence.

In a moment the seventy-eight-year-old diplomat came out, peering over his wire-rim glasses. "Why, it *is* you, Brad. I wasn't sure you'd really arrived. I saw this blur rush past me yesterday, and I was *told* I was there to meet you, but I thought—well, at my age, with failing eyesight and advancing senility—maybe I had made a mistake."

Marshall laughed and shook hands with his old friend. They had known each other since the midsixties when they had both served as envoys for Lyndon Johnson. Bunker was a taciturn New Englander of sharp wit and good humor, a career diplomat Marshall liked and esteemed.

Bunker led him into his office, and Marshall realized where his own decor had originated. Bunker's office was softly sumptuous, but fitting for an elderly man of refined taste. The old man directed him to a sofa and sat beside him, opening his hands expansively. "So here you are again. Last time for Lyndon, this time for Nixon."

"Do you suppose we'll burn in hell for this?"

"Probably," Bunker mused. "But think of the fascinating company. Can I get you something?"

Marshall shook his head. "I only dropped in to pay a courtesy call and apologize for yesterday. I was hustled out by my aide—Christ, he looks like an SS commando, and *his* aide looks like camp director at Auschwitz."

"Mmmmm," Bunker murmured.

Marshall nodded. "Yes, I've thought of that too—the obvious White House connection, all those Prussians, but they seem remarkably competent, and my mission is hardly a subtle one."

"Exactly what *is* your mission?"

"To convince the South to sign the peace treaty."

"Mmmmmmm."

"You don't buy that one either?"

Bunker smiled. "I know you too well, Brad. I think you have an ulterior purpose. But don't worry, I won't say a thing."

"And I won't cause you any complications, Ellsworth. But I may ask your help on several things—one very personal."

Bunker's eyes fixed him shrewdly. "Your son?"

"You know about it?" Marshall asked in surprise.

Bunker nodded. "The White House informed me." He held up his hand. "They don't put much stock in it, Brad, but they've asked me to do every thing to assist you. We all understand, and we sympathize, yet I don't want you to get your hopes up. I've already started inquiries. I'll let you know as soon as I learn something."

Marshall stood. "Thank you," he said gratefully. "I don't want this to interfere with my mission, but you understand how . . ."

"Of course." Bunker ushered him to the door. "Should I say good-bye now, or risk another trip to the airport when you leave so that you can run by me again and perhaps knock me down this time?"

"I'll come see you. You can snub me instead."

When Marshall returned to his office, he found the furniture already replaced with standard government-issue tables, desk, and chairs.

"My God, you *are* competent. And fast," Marshall said.

"Captain Seidel did it all himself in one trip," Jaeger said.

"I wouldn't be surprised. Now, let's go to Act I rehearsal, Colonel."

The raising of the curtain at MACV twenty minutes later opened a first-act fiasco even Marshall wasn't prepared for.

Despite a drastic reduction of troops, MACV headquarters was even more martial—there were crisper uniforms, brighter brass, more polish, more medals and decorations, and even more swagger—than in 1968. He felt as if he had walked into an Adirondacks military camp run by crazed commandos for the recalcitrant youths of wit-ended parents.

And the rehearsal wasn't for a new drama, but for an old warhorse of a play once the vehicle of leading stars, now restaged for after-dinner theater with over-the-hill actors compensating for lack of professionalism with exaggerated gestures and outlandish costumes.

The drama was dead, stilted and stylized—a dinosaur production staged by midgets unable to get their lines straight. One minute Marshall was briefed on how more men and matériel would end the war, and the next, as if the actors were snapping their fingers at forgotten lines, he was told that the South was winning the war on its own.

It was an altogether schizoid performance, interrupted finally by Colonel Jaeger, who told a two-star general that Ambassador Marshall had no more time to waste.

Back in his office, looking out over miles of crumbling apartment buildings, shops, and bars and whorehouses crumpled together as if a huge fist had closed on them, Marshall had the discouraging feeling that he too was just part of the tired cast in a turkey revival, speaking lines from a bad script. He could improvise gestures and snatches of dialogue, but he could not rewrite *Vietnam: The War,* nor change its ending—that had been written by Richard Nixon and Henry Kissinger, dramatists not noted for enduring works.

But *could* there be an ending besides the Porky Pig "That's all, folks" in the script now? he wondered. South Vietnam victorious? A stalemate like in Korea? It didn't seem likely. America was weary of war. Not just inured to young men and civilians slaughtered on the six-o'clock news, Americans were bored. The war was down in the ratings, so it was going to be canceled.

The play had become tedious; the audience had left, and now even the actors were walking offstage. There would be no extension of the run; the play was closing—that was the message of the second act he was supposed to deliver to Pres. Nguyen Van Thieu and Vice Pres. Nguyen Cao Ky shortly, the second meeting of the day that Jaeger had scheduled for him.

"You were right about MACV, so what are Thieu and Ky going to tell me?" Marshall asked Jaeger when he brought in yet another background report.

"That we're betraying them, the North can't be trusted, we're dooming them to a communist takeover, and that they won't sign the peace treaty."

"Why didn't Washington appoint you envoy? I seem irrelevant to this exercise."

Jaeger smiled with perfect teeth and only slight irony. "I'm a military officer, a cameo player—I just follow orders. You're a diplomat, the star—you get to improvise."

Marshall nodded. "You *are* good, Colonel. Much too good for the Pentagon."

Indeed, Marshall knew, Jaeger *was* too good, and walking out on a two-star general who might someday be his superior indicated a power base beyond the military. His aide obviously had friends in very high places; higher than his own perhaps.

"What should I improvise to Thieu and Ky, or should I just follow orders too?"

Jaeger shook his head. "I have no answer, sir. I spent two years in this country leading troops in battle. I saw many men die; I hate to think it was for nothing. I hate quitters; if my son ran from a fight, I'd kick his ass harder than the guy chasing him—or woman, as seems more likely in these feminist days."

"Would you let your son fight in this war?"

Jaeger's voice softened for the first time. "I know your son died here, sir. My boy is nine; he's happy and safe. I'm not qualified to discuss this with you."

Marshall nodded silently. Should he tell Jaeger that Ryan might be alive? Could he help him learn about Ryan? Or did he already know?

He debated a moment, then glanced at his watch; later, he decided.

"What about the secret talks between Hanoi and Saigon? Since they're being held here, surely we have an idea of what's going on."

"You think the CIA might be eavesdropping?" Jaeger asked with a smile.

"I couldn't imagine such a thing, but perhaps some one has *legitimately* learned what's going on."

"You'll have a report in the morning; legitimately acquired, of course."

Marshall pushed himself from his desk. "I'm going to have you and Captain Seidel sit out this meeting with Thieu and Ky; you might frighten them."

When Marshall's car pulled into the Presidential Palace compound twenty minutes before his scheduled appointment, the South Vietnamese were thrown into confusion. They had prepared an honor guard, but it was not ready, and when he stepped out of the car and bounded up the palace stairs, he caused an uproar.

Going up the staircase, he encountered Vice President Ky. The erratic and unpredictable former Air Force general, trim and athletic, had traded his flamboyant jumpsuits and scarves for well-tailored pinstripes. Ky shook hands, then put his arm around Marshall familiarly. "You're early. I thought we were going to have some dreary ceremony with rifle salute. Didn't you trust us, or were you afraid we'd miss?"

"What I'm afraid of is that you won't miss on my way out."

Ky laughed. "The news you're bringing is that bad? But you look so good, just as before." He led him down the corridor. "It was a great surprise to learn you were coming. We never expected *you* to be working for President Nixon; are you here to disarm us?"

Marshall smiled. "I am here to *serve* you."

"That would be a welcome change for your country," Ky said, walking into Thieu's office without knocking.

The room was large and ornate, filled with rosewood and carved-teak pieces; heavy damask drapes shut out the searing sunlight, creating a somber setting, and an Aubusson rug muffled sound. At the far end of the room stood the South Vietnamese president.

Thieu, short and stocky, in his late forties, a former army general, shook hands with Marshall and ignored Ky, for the two men, rivals for many years, were not friends.

As soon as the official photographs were taken, Thieu said without preliminaries, "You are abandoning us."

"We are not going to sign our own death warrant, even for you," Ky added flatly.

Marshall opened his hands encouragingly. "I am here to listen."

"Do you think the North Vietnamese will honor the peace treaty?" Ky asked.

"I believe we can work out guarantees," Marshall said.

"The only guarantee would be your country's willingness to support us when the North violates the treaty and attacks us."

"President Nixon has given you that guarantee," Marshall said.

Thieu stared at him stonily. "Do you expect me to trust Nixon's word that the United States will stand by South Vietnam after the treaty is signed? Be honest."

Marshall met his gaze blandly and smoothed the trouser leg of his white linen suit, feeling like a physician confronting a patient with a fatal diagnosis.

What would the kindly physician do? the moral man? he wondered.

The moral man wouldn't *be* here, he realized. Machiavelli would, and like Nixon and Kissinger, would lie without qualm or conscience; as physicians, they'd administer a euthanasic dose without hesitation.

But he couldn't, and he let out his breath slowly. "President Nixon is going to make peace with North Vietnam—you know that as well as I do. Kissinger is negotiating a treaty in Paris now, and Hanoi's negotiators are here meeting with your representatives. There *will* be a treaty. President Johnson was forced out of office because he could not end the war. Now time is running out for Nixon."

Thieu opened his mouth to speak, the contempt on his lips so evident that Marshall raised his hand to silence him. "Americans are impatient. We use the minute hand of a watch to gauge time while others use the calendar. We are accustomed to rapid change—get excited for some cause, expect it settled within a few newscasts, then people want something different. We want every thing resolved within the course of a thirty-minute television program, and even the most popular show can count on only a few years' run. This war has lost all popularity; the majority has shifted against it. President Nixon, *any* president, is bound to accede to the majority's will."

Ky reached for a cigarette on Thieu's desk. "Of course; we understand that, but now we are talking practical matters. Can American public opinion be changed?"

Marshall shook his head. "President Johnson did every thing he could; so has President Nixon. I can't come up with anything either."

"But thousands of your young men died in this cause," Thieu said. "The cause is right. *Surely* we can change American public opinion. We must. How?"

Marshall thought a moment. "Find proof that the North will violate the treaty."

"You'll have that proof when they attack, but then it will be too late," Thieu said.

"What kind of proof?" Ky persisted. "A politburo memo admitting the treaty is phony? A copy of their invasion plan?"

Marshall shrugged. "That would probably do it, but I think it's unlikely we'll uncover those, so we should concentrate on treaty safeguards—troop withdrawals, timetables, elections. I will work with you, but you must help me move towards peace because if Washington feels you are stalling, they'll ignore both you and me."

He handed them a thick folder. "I've come with several

new proposals; I'll contact you in a few days to see if we can't find agreement. In the meantime, I hope you are taking the talks with North Vietnam seriously; they could play a significant part in the peace."

"We are deliberating carefully," Thieu said noncommittally.

"Good, because there is little time left. Democracies are fragile—they depend upon elections. Surely you can appreciate President Nixon's anxieties."

Marshall stood, shook hands, and said good-bye.

At the door, Thieu stopped him. "Ambassador Marshall. This might be geopolitics to your country, but it is our *existence.* We will cease to exist if you abandon us."

Marshall nodded. "I understand, Mr. President."

"I trust you, Mr. Marshall," Thieu said. "I know about your son. I am very sorry. He gave his life for our country. Help us like he did."

Though Marshall felt a body blow had been delivered, he said impassively as he turned away, "I will do every thing I can."

He bounded down the palace stairs, shielding his eyes from the sun.

"Where to, sir?" Corporal Bonnard asked, holding the door open.

He dropped into the backseat and closed his eyes. Ryan, Ryan, he thought.

"Bad shit, sir?"

"Yes, Corporal, it was very bad shit."

The young Marine smiled. "A woman is always best when you got bad shit to deal with. They have a way of helping out."

Marshall rubbed his forehead. Indeed, he mused; they dig you into even deeper shit.

"I know a great cathouse."

Marshall laughed despite his pain; the President's envoy could hardly go to a whorehouse. What he really wanted to do was see Teresa Hawthorne. They had shared a perfect moment long ago in the middle of the war when he seemed so much younger and there had been hope, but perhaps it was best to keep the moment in memory. If he sought to recover and relive it, he might shatter the jewel.

Four years had passed. He had written her twice after his return to America, but there had been no answer. Perhaps she never received his letters, or perhaps she wanted to safeguard the jewel in the vault of memory too. He had changed; had she? Perhaps she had become jaded. Yet he knew she hadn't.

I *will* go see her, he decided. But he did not want anyone to know.

"Better take me back to the villa, Corporal. What works for a young Marine might not be the best thing for a middle-aged diplomat."

Bonnard grinned. "I don't know, sir; if politicians and diplomats spent more time in whorehouses, the world might be a better place."

Catherine would agree with that, Marshall thought; she might even approve—better Nixon and Kissinger in a cathouse on Tu Do Street than the White House for sure.

"Take me home," Marshall said.

When the sedan drove through the security gate at his villa and stopped in front, Marshall waited until Bonnard drove off, then walked back through the sentry booth, startling the Marine on duty, who ran out to block his exit.

"Sir, you're not supposed to leave except with Corporal Bonnard."

"Corporal Bonnard wanted me to go to a whorehouse. I thought I'd go for a walk instead. Isn't that all right?"

"Well, sir," the Marine said in confusion, "I . . . I have orders, I mean you're . . ."

"Am I a prisoner?"

"No, sir, of course not, but . . ."

But Marshall was on the busy boulevard in front of his residence, flagging a taxi, and he was gone before the guard could sound the alert.

"Cholon," he told the driver as the decrepit car rattled down the choked boulevard, plowing its way through pedicabs, bicycles, carts, pedestrians, its horn blaring at them all.

He didn't have the address of the clinic or any idea where it was in the labyrinth of Cholon, the ancient Chinese district, a teeming underworld even Dante could not have imagined. In this mazelike district of bars and whorehouses, dope dens, intrigue, murder, and sin, every thing was for sale with no fixed prices. Multilayered, with rings upon rings of circles within circles, the ninth one barely scraping the surface—here Judas Iscariot would have been only a minor figure scratching out a living, and Dante would have been shocked to see Beatrice violated and sold in this hell.

"The church where the Diems were killed," Marshall said to the driver.

"Saint Xavier," the driver said in satisfaction, probably at the memory of the assassinations, Marshall thought.

"There's a clinic near there run by an American woman. Do you know it?"

The man shook his head.

A whorehouse he would have known, Marshall felt sure, but those who went to Teresa's clinic did not arrive in a cab. Marshall handed the man a large piaster note. "Find the clinic—prostitutes go there to deliver their babies."

The cab threaded the streets, the driver shouting questions out his open windows as people pressed their faces into the cab and banged on the doors.

Within minutes the cab pulled to a curb and Marshall jumped out, pushing his way past begging women and children who held out their hands and clawed at his clothes.

The alley was as before, trash-littered and strewn with human debris, amputees and cripples with barely the energy to tug at his trousers.

He opened the heavy door and was immediately overwhelmed by a bedlam scene out of Hieronymus Bosch: cots were jammed side by side, women sat or sprawled on each, holding shrieking and deformed infants.

He froze, but in the midst of the confusion she sensed him; turning toward the door, cocking her head, she straightened from bending over a bed and he saw her.

He raised a hand and watched her move toward him, patting and comforting those she passed. Then she was before him. "Well," she said.

He grabbed her in relief and held tightly. "My God," he choked, "I'd forgotten."

"I thought I'd never see you again," she said in amazement.

He looked beyond her to take in the horror. Everywhere

was disease and despair, deformity and emaciation, suffering and pain. "It's worse," he said in disbelief.

"Yes," she answered, turning to follow his gaze. "Much."

He *had* forgotten. Before it had been bright, an attempt at lightness, some cleanliness, but now it was a clogged sewer, reeking and filthy. "My God," he whispered.

She brushed at hair wisping about her face and led him away, saying matter-of-factly, as if he had walked out of the clinic a week ago, "We've been quite busy since we last saw you, and we've made many changes; I'll show you, then you can take me to dinner."

She pulled him through the ward, stopping now and then to comfort a woman or hold a baby, thrusting a diseased or deformed infant into his hands, clinically pointing out all the problems—retardation, unformed limbs from malnutrition, prematurity, drug addiction, venereal disease, child after afflicted child. She led him past women who stared blankly at the wall, slack mouthed, eyes mad, past little girls with swollen bellies, and others with no breasts trying to feed infants.

All he could do was stare in disbelief. How could one place house so much suffering? he wondered. Here was hell in the midst of a war his own country had wrought, and no one knew of it, and he himself had forgotten.

When she started up to the second-floor ward, he held the railing. "No more," he said, dropping on a stair, feeling sick to his stomach from the noise and stench.

She looked at him curiously. "Had you truly forgotten? Did you think it all went away when you left? Did you think only *Americans* were suffering and dying?" She gestured about her. "This is just a tiny island in a sea of suffering; only one little clinic in Saigon—I don't even have an idea how many are in the streets worse off than those here, or how many babies are thrown into refuse heaps."

She dropped beside him. "How could you have forgotten? You of all people."

He closed his eyes. "I tried not to remember. After my son died here, I tried not to think of Vietnam."

"Oh, dear," she said, bringing her hands to her mouth. "I had no idea. I'm sorry. Forgive me." She jumped up. "Come, let's go to dinner."

He remained seated. "No. I *had* forgotten; I'd thought

only of my own loss. I read reports and saw the papers; I watched the news and went to meetings. I talked and I lobbied. But I had forgotten how awful this was."

"Enough!" she said, pulling him up. "You don't have to tell me how bad this is, and I don't want to watch you take center stage in this tragedy. I want you to take me to dinner—I haven't eaten out since the sixties when you took me last time, four years ago—*my* how time flies."

She brushed at her tattered dress and said briskly, "Four years. And here you are again out of the blue. I can't believe it. Come, I'm starving. Where should we go?"

Marshall smiled. He *had* assumed center stage with his grief, and she had rightly nailed him, for who was he to feel remorse or self-pity in the midst of others' pain and suffering? He looked out over the clinic and said with an attempt at levity, "Corporal Bonnard said I should have gone to a whorehouse; maybe he was right."

She did not laugh. "Don't; where do you think all these babies come from? I'll have Father Dourmant talk with you and your corporal."

"Father Dourmant is still here?" he asked incredulously. "He must be eighty."

"He's thriving. He's a Jesuit—the worse things become, the better he feels. Right now he's . . . Never mind."

He took her hands and kissed them; she hadn't changed at all, he saw, and realized with a mix of pain and happiness that he still loved her. "You look lovely, Teresa."

"I don't," she said, pulling her hands away. "I look tired and old."

He shook his head. "*I* look tired and old."

"Then we'll find the brightest, noisiest, most garish restaurant and forget how old and tired and dreary we are," and she took his hand and led him through the clinic.

Outside, it was early evening, just before the carnival of night began. Shops were still open, vendors and peddlers shouted down the traffic, and unkempt, tired girls straggled into the bars to begin their shift, hoping that tonight they might get lucky and be chosen by a soldier to take them home or at least buy them a drink.

Teresa strode down the sidewalk, plowing through the masses while Marshall struggled in her wake, but the crowd was too thick, jostling and buffeting him as she looked into several restaurants before finding one that satisfied her.

"Isn't it bright?" she asked happily when he finally reached her side.

"Blinding."

"Well, to me it's a welcome relief. If you want dark and quiet, you'll have to go to a bar or a brothel as your corporal suggests. I hope he's using contraceptives."

"I'll be sure to ask him."

She shouted an order to a waiter as she sat at a crowded round table where the other diners ignored them. Two bottles of beer were slammed before them as Marshall dropped into his seat, his shirt clamped to his body in sweat. He was so hot and thirsty he drank half of it before he pulled the bottle from his mouth and held it up to her in silent toast.

She raised hers, and then they just stared at one another.

"I wrote you," he said softly. "Did you get my letters?"

"Yes, but what was there to write back—a child died? More women came?"

She *did* look tired and older, he realized, thinner and more worn, but an ethereal beauty about her defied time and flesh, an almost translucent softness that made her otherwordly, beyond him, as unpossessable as music.

There had been that one night, one interlude in war and their lives when he had transcended self and they had lain together, and now looking at her, he saw in her light smile that she was remembering that night too.

He looked tireder and older too, she was thinking, but in his features she saw the same strength and decency that had been there before. She had never felt such comfort and protection as she had that night.

It was the briefest moment when she had been able to forget the war, all the suffering and pain, and it made no difference that it would not last, that he would never leave his wife, or that she would return to the clinic in the morning. That the moment was impermanent did not matter—for what beauty lasted? How long a rose? How long love? That it lasted a night was more than she had dared hope, for it gave her a vision of a world of happiness and children, comfort and home, so warm and fulfilling that it would sustain her forever. She would never achieve its reality, but just the knowledge that such love and wonder existed was enough. The memory was a touchstone in her heart to another life, and in the most awful moments, in her most terrible trials, when she was overcome by sorrow and pain, she had that moment in memory. She would never be so happy again; her heart would never soar as it had that night, but she had tapped into a richness and depth of feeling that was enough to last her life.

She wanted to thank him for it now, but she knew he would never understand—no man could feel so deeply, no man's heart could hold such love and wonder.

Instead she merely leaned across the table and touched his hand.

Yet he *did* have some sense of that feeling, and it made him bow his head, in gratitude, but in the knowledge of what he had lost too.

"Are you all right?" she asked in concern. "You don't look well."

He drained the bottle. "I haven't been well since my son was killed. And your tour of the clinic just reinforced the hopelessness. I came four years ago to stop the war. Now it is ending, but things will only get even worse. That's why you and Father Dourmant must leave, Teresa. The communists will take over; you've got to get out."

Oh, dear, he was being practical, she thought, and she withdrew her hand. "Will they take care of the women and children?"

"No! They're not interested in prostitutes and their GI babies."

She sipped her beer. "Then I guess I'll stay—*some one* has to care for them."

When their food arrived, he pointed a chopstick at her. "I could have you arrested, dragged out on espionage charges."

"And Father Dourmant? Will you have him arrested too?"

"I'm sure he'll have better sense."

"I doubt it. He's . . ."

"That's the second time you've broken off a sentence about him. You'd never make a diplomat, Teresa."

"I certainly hope not. I want to *help* people. But enough of this, it's too depressing; I might as well have stayed in the clinic. You know I'm not going to leave, walk away from Vietnam or these people who are suffering, so tell me about your life. All the exciting things and people. And tell me about Corporal Mead, your bodyguard, that wonderful boy who married that sweet girl."

"I don't know what happened to him."

"What is the fate of warriors after the war?"

"They grow old and tired like the rest of us."

"My goodness, you're *not* happy, are you?"

He put down the chopsticks. "What did my son die for? What did any of them die for? What was the point of it all?"

"There is no point to war," Teresa said softly. "Did you think there was?"

He smiled. She hadn't changed at all, he saw. She was even more wonderful.

"Don't patronize me," she said hotly.

"I wasn't; I was thinking how much I love you, and remembering that night."

"Stop that! I am a tired, old woman."

"Nonsense, you are—"

She put her hand on his mouth.

He laughed, taking it away. "All right. But I truly admire you."

"You *should.*"

He took her hand again. "I wanted to do as much good as you. I thought I could make a difference, but I can't even get my government to help your clinic—the government won't recognize those children. I tried last time. My plan was to get you and the children out, but Ambassador Bunker told me it wasn't possible. Now with the war ending, there's no hope at all."

She considered him a long minute. "Maybe there's some one you should talk to." Then she lowered her head. "Oh, that's ridiculous. We're having a lovely dinner. Well, *I* was, you didn't eat anything. And we haven't seen each other in years, and you're an important diplomat, and I'm a . . . what?"

"Saint."

"Yes, and maybe we can meet again and I'll find something to wear and you can take me to an expensive restaurant where we'll have wine and you will not be maudlin."

"You are debating whether to tell me something," he said, nonplussed.

She laughed. "You're right, I could never be a diplomat, but I don't know whether I should say anything. I don't know whether I *can,* at least until I talk with some one."

He smiled. "Father Dourmant. You would make a *dreadful* diplomat. Tell me tomorrow night at dinner in your best dress at the most elegant restaurant I can find. I'll pick you up at six o'clock."

"Bradley," she said softly, "I don't have a good dress."

He kissed her hand. "I don't think there are any elegant restaurants."

She reddened at the touch but did not pull away.

He placed money on the table and stood. "I'll pick you up around six."

Outside, he put his arm around her and led her back to the clinic down streets still so filled with people and commerce in the hour the shops closed that neither noticed the tall, thin American following them.

Wilson Abbot Lord had been in the embassy when the call came that the President's envoy had disappeared. He knew where Marshall was going, and while security frantically sought him throughout the city and Colonel Jaeger went wild, Lord drove directly to Cholon where Marshall had spent time four years ago.

He saw them leave the clinic, and as he watched them dine, he remembered the French priest at Saint Francis Xavier's and made the connection to Huong's remark about Job. Where else would he get such an idea except from a priest?

Looking over the bright beckoning neon of the bars and whorehouses, Lord saw the dark steeple of the church. Of course, and Dr. Trung had been raised a Catholic. He was hiding in there; he knew it.

The North Vietnamese defector was no gecko; he wasn't going to get away. And Bradley Marshall wasn't going to get him either—Marshall would wreck every thing.

A cripple huddling against the wall reached out and tugged on Lord's trousers.

Looking down, he nodded without condescension or annoyance, spoke a pleasant greeting, then reached into his pocket and handed him a large piaster note.

As soon as he did, he was besieged by beggars thrusting out their hands, and a legless man crawled toward him.

His eyes fixed on the steeple of Saint Francis Xavier. Where was God for these people? he wondered. Where was his own country? And what was Marshall doing for them? Nothing. Marshall had walked past them, seeing and feeling nothing.

Lord spoke to them softly in Vietnamese, gave them every thing in his wallet, then he crossed the street and walked toward the church.

The Diems had sought sanctuary there. It was fittingly ironic that a North Vietnamese defector would attempt the same.

But, he thought, the CIA didn't honor sanctuary any more than God did.

CHAPTER 8

Though not yet eight in the morning, Cholon throbbed with activity. The whores and dope dealers were gone, their shift over, replaced by merchants and vendors setting up their displays for the day's black market—a vast bazaar of goods nowhere else to be found and laid out like a banquet set in an asylum, with leather goods beside bicycle parts, exotic fruit next to plastic toys, every thing offered except art, or what passed for it, and that was to be found in the shops downtown or in front of the hotels where the foreigners stayed, the only ones who could afford *that* luxury.

Trucks rattled by with beer and ice for the bars, shopkeepers swept out their stores and the sidewalks, and beggars and children sorted through trash as Teresa left the clinic after she finished serving breakfast, fairly running through the back streets and alleys to the church. She pushed through the wrought-iron gate that led to the rectory and darted up the stairs. There was no answer to her knocking, but when she tried the door, it opened. She walked into the dark vestibule, then looked into the kitchen. Father Dourmant was an early riser, yet there was no sign of life.

She closed her eyes and clasped her hands in an involuntary gesture of prayer. He was an old man; she kept forgetting how old until times such as this. The day would soon come when he would not rise, she knew. She went down the dingy hall to his room and held her breath before tapping lightly on the door.

There was furtive rustling, then an angry voice. "Who is it?"

"Teresa, Father. Are you all right?"

He cracked the door; he wore a frayed bathrobe, and disheveled white hair poked from the stocking cap on his head. "What are you doing here?" he demanded.

"I came to talk to you," she said in relief. "Actually I went to church for morning mass but apparently it was too early. God and his priests seem to keep banker's hours."

"I'll be right out," he said, slamming the door in her face.

The kettle was boiling and she had set two places at the table when he shuffled in, dropping tiredly into a chair. "A damn dog barked all night; I didn't get any sleep. I hope somebody ate it."

"Good thing it barked; you left your door open last night."

He looked up in alarm. "I'm losing my mind. I go to all that trouble to hide the wretched man, then I leave the door open."

"He's here?"

"In my room. Between him snoring and that damn dog, I didn't sleep at all."

She poured coffee, her eyes betraying a gleam, and she could not contain herself any longer. "You'll never guess what happened. It's a miracle."

He gingerly sipped the hot coffee. "I am seventy-six years old and have never seen a miracle. I suppose the final indignity of my priesthood is that a defrocked nun will witness one next door."

She leaned forward and said excitedly, "Bradley Marshall is here."

"That's the miracle?"

"Isn't it wonderful? I was working in the clinic, and then I looked up and he was there." She brought up her hands to suppress a giggle. "He asked me to dinner tonight."

Father Dourmant blew loudly on the steaming coffee.

"Anyway"—Teresa coughed—"I am sure he will help your man."

Father Dourmant rapped the cup against the table, spilling

coffee. "But will he get us any *money?* The Chinaman will sell the man's information. What can Marshall do except take you to dinner?"

"I thought the idea was to save the man, not exploit him," she said testily.

"It's *both.*"

"Oh, Father, money won't make any difference; it won't change the lives of those children—it won't give them love. I think Bradley should talk to the man tonight."

"Money *does* make a difference," Father Dourmant said angrily. "We need it for food and medicine, Teresa, and since God isn't minting any, we have to get it any way we can. I think the Chinese man is the way. I'm sick of seeing so much suffering. I don't have much time left; the least, maybe last, thing I can do is help those poor women and children—not their souls, their bodies—and that means *money.*"

"It can't *hurt* for Bradley to talk to Dr. Trung."

"I don't know," he said dubiously. "Let me see if that damn Chinaman has come up with anything." He mused a moment. "Besides, if I let him know someone else is interested, we might get even more money. I'd rather deal with him anyway; the Chinese have been around longer than the Americans; they have a better understanding of things."

Teresa laughed. "Did they teach you this in the seminary?"

"No! The seminary didn't teach me anything useful; I learned every thing in this damnable hellhole."

Teresa smiled. "You should hear yourself, Father," she said, getting up to leave.

"You should hear *yourself* talk—Bradley Marshall and dinner, indeed," he snorted.

She waved to him sweetly.

"Lock the door behind you," Father Dourmant shouted.

Wilson Lord was at his desk after a sleepless night—a barking dog caused too much disturbance for him to get into the church or the rectory at Saint Xavier, so now he was back to the Chinese man, Huong, as his best lead for getting the defector.

He was tired and annoyed and further aggravated by what

he had just learned about Marshall's aide. Lt. Col. Paul Jaeger was indeed a wunderkind, but Lord had had to go far out of channels to learn about him because Jaeger's personnel file was unavailable even to Langley.

He had been forced to call his mentor in Washington, a man who had served every president since Franklin Roosevelt, an insider to every secret and source, perhaps the wisest of the Wise Old Men, and the only man who knew Lord's sacrifices in Korea, and that thousands of lives would have been lost had he been broken. Though he had been Lord's secret patron for two decades, even he was reluctant to discuss this.

"You *did* get the message, Wilson," the man asked in his cultured, always ironic voice. "This is not something you should pursue."

"I got the message," Lord had answered.

"You're calling in a very big chit, Wilson. Your credit is good, and you know my regard for you, so I must ask before I grant the request—are you *sure* you want to cash in this IOU?"

"I do," Lord said without hesitation.

The man sighed. "Mark my word, Wilson, this is not information you need or want. I know you too well; this will get you in trouble. Colonel Jaeger is a protégé of someone highly placed in the White House—even I'm not sure who. Nor do I *want* to know. Knowing things can be bothersome—one can't reasonably deny anything then. Let's just say Jaeger works for someone in the basement of the White House, some rogue warrior. But he might not be a rogue at all, instead acting on authority, though you would never be able to trace it back to the source—the deniability is complete. It's rather like Peer Gynt's onion—if you strip away all the layers, you'll find nothing at the core. Nevertheless, the onion smells and definitely can cause tears of discomfort. Strip away all the layers at the White House—who's at the core? The Prussians, Haldeman and Ehrlichman? Chuck Colson? Alexander Haig? Or does it go higher? Are you getting my gist, Wilson?"

"Yes."

"What about yourself, Wilson—are you a rogue, or acting on orders? Do I want to know? Would you tell me?" The man chuckled. "Wisteria is a gorgeous plant, but insidious; its trailers lead everywhere, choking and killing every thing; it's indestructible. You're dealing with wisteria, Wilson—stay out of its path."

His mentor was right, he knew. He was over his head here, but now more than ever he was determined to get the defector out of Saigon before the man was tracked down and killed by the North Vietnamese, MACV, or his own colleagues—some other rogue operating for someone else, with or without authority.

Three forceful knocks interrupted his concentration. Lord looked at his watch; it was exactly eight A.M. "Come in, Captain," Lord said, knowing only the Marine officer would be bold enough to knock so loudly.

Bishop had slept twenty hours, showered three times, washed and starched his uniform, polished his boots, and gotten a haircut, but though he felt restored and confident, he was nervous because he didn't know what Lord wanted of him.

Unsure how to report to a civilian superior, especially with a baseball bat gripped in his left hand and a football clutched in his right, Bishop entered with what he thought was offhanded casualness, but still with martial stiffness. He held out the bat and ball to Lord.

Lord suppressed a smile, took them, and motioned to a metal folding chair. "You have a choice, Mr. Bishop," he said diffidently. "You can work for me or get assigned to the Marine guard detachment here."

Bishop sat rigidly in the chair. "Embassy duty means rifle and short-arm inspections. I'll pass on that."

"What do you imagine you'd be doing for me, Captain?"

Bishop locked his gaze on Lord. "Something worthwhile. Something that would make a difference. I owe you my life, Mr. Lord; if you hadn't gotten me out of Gio Linh, I would have been killed. Now let me start paying you back. I want to win this war."

Two nights ago, in a surprise offensive that caught the U.S. off guard and overwhelmed South Vietnamese positions along the DMZ, Gio Linh had been overrun and the corps commander, General Lam, killed in the fighting. His last communication was that he was flying out in his chopper, but for unknown reasons he didn't make it.

"You don't owe me, Mr. Bishop. I want you to do things out of conviction, because you *believe*. I don't want a vassal or a robot."

"I'm not a robot, Mr. Lord—I do *only* what I believe."

"What would you do to win this war?"

"Anything."

Lord eyed him appraisingly. Here was a man he could use, dedicated and passionate, neither cripplingly stupid nor dangerously intelligent. What a weapon, Lord thought—a cold professional who would do Lord's bidding because he *believed* in it.

Yes, Lord thought, he had found a match for Jaeger, though a man like Bishop could be dangerous in the wrong cause, acting on his own while his handlers napped. Now he'd be putty to mold, but later, as a colonel, an aide in the White House, he could be dangerous—contemptuous of civilians, knowing what is best for the country, looking so good in his uniform with medals and decorations—oh, he could be evil, Lord thought; he would take care not to doze. "Anything?" he asked.

"Anything," Bishop answered. "There is no morality in war."

Lord pressed closer, eyes hypnotic. "Any weapon? Any means?"

"It would be immoral not to use them. How could I tell a Marine he had to die because it wasn't moral to use the weapons that might save him? Or tell a people they had to lose their freedom because it isn't right to use certain weapons to defend them?"

"No limits, Mr. Bishop?"

"Once you join the rodeo, you can't bitch about the bumpy ride."

Lord nodded approvingly. "I think we understand one another, Lucas." Then he sat back, all business. "You'll need special clearances—that will take several days; in the meantime, relax—get laid, read a good book, write your mother. Come back Thursday."

Bishop stood. "You don't know how much this means to me. I'd do anything to win this war. I owe you my life."

"Let's not get sentimental, Captain. However, there is *one* thing you can do. Familiarize yourself with Cholon, especially around Saint Xavier Church."

Bishop smiled. "Maybe instead of getting laid, I'll go to church."

"Perhaps you can manage both," Lord said dryly. "Pope Alexander VI did; two of his eleven children were Cesare and Lucrezia Borgia."

Bishop grinned. "I see that working for you is going to be educational, sir."

Bishop bounded down the back stairs of the embassy so keyed up that he had to restrain himself from whooping: at last, something to do that mattered. All he had ever wanted was to serve his country. He was the ultimate team player who would throw himself into the fray against any odds. He had been a loyal halfback for Oklahoma, a good fraternity man, and a dedicated Marine, but the Marines had given him only menial tasks—now he was working for Wilson Lord and the CIA.

To Bishop, the CIA was a hallowed world of masculinity where the secret codes and handshakes meant something, a fraternity serving a great cause. Wilson Lord, a true warrior for democracy, had invited him into the order, and Bishop was overwhelmed with pride and gratitude.

He returned the salute of the Marine guard as he walked through the security door.

Outside, the slap of the city's polluted heat stopped him on the portico. He stood adjusting to the wet blanket Saigon threw on him and considered what to do until Thursday. It was only nine A.M. He would get gloriously drunk and fuck himself senseless, he decided with no deliberation.

As he stood on the steps, a black limousine drove into the compound and headed toward the embassy. An honor guard rushed out presenting arms.

Bishop bent to see who was in the limousine, but a man he did not recognize stepped from the car. He was tall, in his forties, striking and dignified in a white linen suit, yet there was something familiar about him.

The man started up the stairs and noticed Bishop, the only person not saluting.

At the top of the stairs Marshall turned and looked directly at him. Then there was a bullet-headed army captain beside him. "Salute, asshole," the fireplug said.

Then a colonel was before him. "You *better* salute, Captain, or I'll rip those bars off your uniform before you can get an intelligent look on that stupid face of yours."

Bishop brought up his hand in an immediate salute, but Marshall had already disappeared into the embassy.

Jaeger pressed his face into Bishop's. "I *never* want to see you again. Get the fuck out of here," and he mounted the steps after Marshall, followed by the army captain.

Bishop stood stunned. Then the sergeant in charge of the honor guard went up to him. "I thought he was going to arrest you, sir. That was Colonel Jaeger, Ambassador Marshall's aide. Be *real* careful around him—the colonel, I mean; the Ambassador's okay."

"That was Ambassador Marshall? I thought I knew him."

Bradley Marshall, that was his name, Bishop remembered. He had seen him four years ago when Marshall was touring forward outposts just before the Tet Offensive. Bishop commanded the most exposed position at Khe Sanh, and Marshall had surprised everybody by spending the night on the hill. They had talked several times and Marshall had played cards with his men and, in the morning, had flown to Hue just as the North Vietnamese attacked.

He had seemed a decent man, Bishop remembered, but if he had people like that colonel and captain working for him, he was definitely a man to avoid.

And he would avoid them, especially now that he was working for Wilson Lord.

He dropped Marshall and the colonel from his thoughts and, springing down the steps two at a time, returned to the happy prospect of drink and women.

Marshall was in the elevator going up to his office when he remembered who the Marine officer was and the night he had spent at Khe Sanh. The young lieutenant had reminded him of himself years ago in another war; it had been an altogether depressing night, sitting among young men before the battle.

At least this one had lived, Marshall reflected. He seemed a decent young man.

But then gloom settled over him as the elevator door closed; some things never change, and some men never learn—here he was back in war again. How could it end, he wondered—this war or any—when men ran from safety and family back to the battlefield? But that had been the story of his own life too—World War II, and then Korea, and he knew the reason: he had loved war just as much as that Marine lieutenant. Maybe Ryan had grown to love it too.

Christ, he thought in depression, entering his office, but even before he reached his desk, Jaeger brought in the morning's intelligence summaries.

Marshall accepted them with desultory interest, his mind now on Ryan. He had heard nothing from Bunker and knew how long diplomatic overtures took, so he had decided to confide in Jaeger about his son. If anyone could determine whether Ryan was a POW, it would be Jaeger. "Give me thirty minutes to glance over these, then I want to talk to you about a personal matter."

Jaeger smiled. "Not women I hope. You'd probably be better off talking with Corporal Bonnard."

"I've already discussed women with Corporal Bonnard—his belief is that all problems can be solved in a whorehouse."

Jaeger nodded as he left the room. "He may be right, as long as one has access to penicillin afterwards."

Marshall was almost finished with the intelligence summary when Jaeger interrupted to tell him that he had a call from Vice President Ky.

"What about Trung?" Ky asked without preliminaries when he picked up the phone. "Isn't this just what we want? Could this be it?"

Marshall had no idea what he was talking about. "I don't understand."

"Pran Ba Trung, Hanoi's negotiator," Ky said in exasperation. "He's gone. They say he's sick, but we think he's defected. You know *nothing* about this?" Ky asked incredulously. "This is the most important thing that's happened in years."

"I haven't finished my briefings this morning. I'm sure

something is in them. Let me get back to you as soon as I have something."

Marshall flipped quickly through the last of his intelligence summaries, but there was nothing in them about Trung. He sat back perplexed.

Just then Jaeger entered with another folder. "This is the summary on the secret talks—every thing legitimately acquired of course."

Marshall stared impassively at the coincidence—was his phone tapped? Undoubtedly it was, but this report would have been worked up before Ky called. Perhaps Jaeger had hoped Marshall would have forgotten about it or never learned of Trung's disappearance. Or was he just being paranoid? He wanted to trust Jaeger, *needed* him to find about about Ryan, but now he was torn.

"Anything of particular interest, Colonel?" he asked casually.

"The talks are going nowhere; they can't even agree on what to order for lunch. We're talking *nowhere.*"

He handed the file to Marshall and was about to leave when he stopped. "The only interesting thing is some speculation about Hanoi's chief negotiator, Dr. Pran Ba Trung. He missed yesterday's sessions. Hanoi claims he's ill; the South Vietnamese think he's defected. That's quite a development except he hasn't thrown himself in their hands or shown up here for asylum."

Marshall nodded. "I can imagine how excited the South would be at a defection."

"Orgasmic."

"But we're not putting much stock in it?"

"MACV gives it a zero on the Peter Meter and the CIA even less."

"So where is this Trung if he's not at the negotiations?"

Jaeger shrugged. "All anyone knows is in the file."

Christ, what a turd in the soup a defector would be, Marshall thought as Jaeger withdrew—no wonder MACV and the CIA dismiss the possibility—he would throw the peace negotiations into chaos. The man could waltz through the embassy doors wearing a tiara and a jockstrap and everyone would pretend not to notice.

He put down the folder and leaned back in his chair. A

defector would alter the situation drastically. But isn't that what he wanted?

Marshall flipped through the file to see who in the CIA had dismissed the possibility of defection—the station chief himself, emphatically.

Yet what would Wilson Abbot Lord think about the defector? he wondered.

He hadn't forgotten Lord, but Lord couldn't be concerned about his mission. He wasn't *doing* anything, and the South was resisting the treaty well enough on its own.

But what would Lord think about a defector? He'd be as excited and eager as the South Vietnamese, Marshall realized, seeing his value in torpedoing the peace talks.

What a bizarre development, Marshall thought—yet the rumor was probably only that, and even if a defector did exist, he was hardly going to walk into his office. He would never get through the door—the NVA, the Vietcong, MACV, the CIA, or, if no one else, Jaeger would see to that.

No, he realized, even if a defector existed, they would never meet. Unless, and he laughed to himself, Teresa Hawthorne invited him to dinner tonight.

Then he thought wildly, was *that* what she was hinting at yesterday? It couldn't be.

Jaeger interrupted again. "Your daughter is on the line. She says it's urgent."

Marshall grabbed the phone. "Sarah! What's wrong?"

"Dad? I can hardly hear you. This is a terrible connection."

"What's the matter? Are you all right? Your mother? Chris? What's wrong?"

Chris came on the line. "Relax, Dad, we're okay, but something's come up."

"What?" Marshall cried in panic.

"I got a manila envelope with pictures of Ryan in the mail yesterday," Sarah said on the extension. "I didn't know what to do, so I flew out to show them to Chris."

"They *look* like Ryan, Dad. What's going on?" Chris asked.

Marshall didn't speak for so long that Chris said, "Dad? You still there?"

Marshall drew a deep breath and finally asked, "Have you told your mother?"

"No. We thought we'd talk with you first. How come they were sent to Sarah? What kind of asshole would do anything like that? Is he alive, Dad? Is Ryan a prisoner?"

"I don't know. I've seen those pictures."

"What? And you didn't tell us about them?" Sarah shouted. "If my brother's alive, I want to know. How could you not tell us?"

"Those pictures can't be authenticated. They might be real, but they could be faked. I didn't tell anyone because I didn't want you to get your hopes up."

Chris's voice turned cold. "Had you seen those photos when we talked?"

Marshall did not answer.

"You already knew. And you didn't tell me. While I was spilling my guts to you, you were thinking about Ryan. That's what your mission is about, isn't it?—to chase after Ryan. You can't let him go. And you didn't even have the decency to tell me about him."

"That's not how it was, Chris."

"I understand," Chris said evenly. "Look, if Ryan's alive, get him back. That's all that's important. Then you and I can move on. Now Sarah wants to tell you something."

"I'm coming over."

"What!"

"I have my ticket. I'm on a flight leaving from San Francisco tonight. I'll arrive in Saigon tomorrow morning at nine-thirty."

"Are you crazy! You can't! This is a war zone. Chris! Talk sense to your sister."

"I think she should go," Chris said. "I think she needs to be there."

"She does *not* need to be here."

"Dad, if there's a chance Ryan is alive, I have to help get him back."

"Sarah, you'd just complicate things. I couldn't do my job here if I had to worry about your safety too."

"Chris and I have talked about this a long time. There was a reason those photos were sent to me; it's a message from someone. Can't you see, I *have* to go."

"Sarah! Listen to me. You *can't* come. I'm doing every thing I can to end this war. I'm doing every thing to find out about Ryan. For the love of God, *don't* come. It's much more complicated than you think."

"No, Dad, it's very simple: someone sent me photographs of my brother. We thought he was dead, but he's alive. I have to go get him."

"Sarah, I'm serious. I'm your father and I'm telling you not to come. I'm *ordering* you not to come."

"You can't do that, Dad; I'd never forgive you. Can't you see—I *have* to go. If Ryan's alive, I have to try to save him. Chris wants to come too, but we decided that you and he have too many problems—he *would* get in the way, but I won't. I'll see you at nine-thirty tomorrow morning," she said, hanging up.

Marshall was holding the dead phone when Jaeger entered the room.

"Is something wrong, sir?"

Marshall just stared at him.

"Did you want to talk about the personal matter now?"

Marshall looked at him incredulously, then he shook his head and Jaeger withdrew.

My God, Marshall thought wildly. How could he have been so naive? He had completely underestimated those behind this. The pictures had been sent to Sarah to lure her over; someone had anticipated his every move. Catherine was right: he *had* been a fool, and now here was his daughter, like Iphigenia, about to be sacrificed. That was the threat held over him now—Sarah. If he stalled on the treaty or failed to convince Thieu and Ky to sign it, Ryan would never come back and Sarah would be killed.

And of course Jaeger was in on it. And Seidel too; he wouldn't hesitate to kill Sarah.

She couldn't come; Marshall had to stop her. But how? He couldn't even have her passport pulled—whoever wanted her to come would see to that. There was no one he could go to because he didn't know who was behind this, or how high his influence reached. Someone was orchestrating this, someone with access to the White House and all information, with tentacles that reached into the State Department and even the CIA. He would be stymied at every turn because every turn would either be anticipated or immediately discovered. He could not outwit his enemy because he didn't even know who his enemy was, or whom he worked for.

Father Dourmant stabbed the bell on Huong's door. The same guard opened the door and glared at him with the same hostile look. As he waited to be announced, Father Dourmant wondered if he was in time for breakfast, or if he had missed it by oversleeping. Once again he cursed the dog.

But the table was set and he beamed, sitting down, reaching for a roll even before Huong finished bowing in greeting.

"I've started inquiries," Huong said, motioning a servant to pour coffee.

"Good," Father Dourmant said, breaking the roll. "How much money do you think we'll get?"

Huong smiled. "First we must establish the value of the merchandise, then secure a buyer."

Father Dourmant dropped the roll. "But you have a buyer?" he asked anxiously.

"Someone has expressed interest. I expect an answer shortly."

In relief, Father Dourmant chose an apple from the fruit basket, compared it with another, then pocketed both in his cassock. "I'm not getting *any* sleep over this matter."

Huong motioned to his daughter standing shyly in the doorway. "Come," he urged. She was small even for five, with large, inquisitive eyes and an intelligent face.

Father Dourmant turned and held out the basket of fruit. "Take an apple before I eat them all—old men are terribly greedy, or help me choose one for a nice lady who helps poor children. I can't see very well; I might choose one with a worm in it."

The little girl laughed and approached without fear. "Daddy doesn't have worms in his apples. Take the whole basket like you did last time. Give them all to the nice lady and the children."

"That's a good idea," Huong said.

"Would they like my dress?" she asked. "They can have my shoes too." She started to unstrap them when Father Dourmant put his hand on her arm.

"That is very kind of you, my dear, but no." He raised his hand and blessed her, then turned to Huong. "Miss Hawthorne had a chance encounter with someone who might be interested." He looked to the little girl. "But I would rather deal with you."

The Chinese man nodded gravely. "I will do what I can."

Father Dourmant pocketed several rolls in his cassock. "Maybe God pays attention, after all."

"Did you doubt it?" Huong asked.

"Oh, yes. Frequently," the priest said, sipping coffee luxuriously.

Wilson Lord arrived at noon for his appointment with Huong. The guard showed him into the courtyard, and Huong greeted him on the veranda. "Would you like to see my garden before we dine? Do flowers interest you, Mr. Lord?"

"Every thing interests me," Lord said politely. "Just the other day I made a great discovery from a gecko."

Huong led him down the steps onto a gravel path that wound through a garden of exotic flowers: peonies, orchids, roses, and bougainvillea created a riotous blaze almost too much for the eye to manage. They walked past blossoming apple and cherry trees, then strolled along a pond on which huge white lotuses floated. When they returned to the veranda, the table was set.

"I've chosen a California chardonnay," Huong said. "It is as good as any French burgundy at a fraction of the cost, with none of the pretension."

Lord drew the wine over his tongue. "The French make lovely novelties—dresses, perfumes, wines, objects for the table and palate, but only a frivolous people take such things seriously. What is fashion, after all, except mad queers telling silly rich women what to wear."

Lord gestured toward the garden. "Gardens are another matter. They are man's attempt to impose order on the natural world—enhance beauty, marshal color and form, then lay it out to give beauty meaning. Gardens are art. The Japanese distill art in a single brushstroke, or in a raked-gravel garden with a solitary rock. You have done it by unleashing color and form, giving beauty freedom."

Lord sipped wine. "Gardens reveal much about the gardener; the French are not noted for their gardens, but I like yours very much."

Huong nodded appreciatively. "You *do* learn interesting things from surprising subjects. I would like to see your garden, Mr. Lord."

"Alas, I have neither time nor thumb for that; I usually buy cut flowers. Some might find that revealing."

Huong laughed.

They chatted politely over a light lunch of chicken and fresh vegetables, then Lord set down his knife and fork. "You know where Dr. Trung is. I would like to talk with him. Your help would be compensated, of course."

Huong waved a dismissive hand. "My compensation would be a worthy cause advanced. The party I am representing has meager needs and no great expectations. I think a million dollars would suffice."

Lord shrugged as if the sum were inconsequential.

"I must inform you of a complication, however. Another interested party."

Marshall, Lord thought; the bastard has made the connection, but he said blandly, betraying no urgency, "There are always complications—it is in the nature of the business."

But it *was* urgent—the battle plan would reveal the North's treachery. He had to get it. If he didn't, the South would fall and his wife and child would never be free.

Yet he had no money and nothing to barter with. Now he needed Bishop more than ever; he had to get into the church—nothing and nobody could get in his way.

He lifted his wineglass. "The complication will be eliminated." He toasted Huong. "To a free Vietnam."

CHAPTER 9

When Marshall's car drove through the gate at his villa, the guard saluted warily. After Marshall's disappearance yesterday, every Marine had been threatened with court-martial if he escaped again, so now a jeep with three Marines was parked outside the gate.

Too distraught at the prospect of Sarah's arrival to work, Marshall had summoned Bonnard to drive him home. He needed to talk to someone, but the only person he could go to was Teresa Hawthorne. Yet now more than ever he needed to keep his movements secret.

Seeing the jeep and heightened security, Marshall directed Bonnard to drive him back to the embassy for papers he had forgotten.

"I can get them for you, sir," Bonnard said.

"They're in my safe; I've got to get them myself."

As the gate guard waved the sedan back through, the jeep started up, but Bonnard called that they were just returning to the embassy.

Halfway back, blocked in traffic on Nguyen Hue Street, Marshall opened the passenger door, jumped out, and crossed the street to hail a cab going in the opposite direction.

Bonnard leapt from the car in disbelief as horns blared furiously.

Settled in the cab bouncing toward Cholon, Marshall

knew that tomorrow they would probably handcuff a Marine to him.

Teresa, harried in the midst of the confusion and squalor of the clinic, turned in distraction when Marshall appeared at her side. "You're early," she said, bent over a crib. "I haven't changed into my evening gown yet."

"I needed to see you. Can we talk somewhere?"

She frowned. "I have many things to do," she apologized. "I have to oversee the kitchen."

Deflated, sensing the immense sorrow about him and his minor place in it, he nodded, but she saw how disturbed he was and led him to the staff room.

He gazed about the cubbyhole room with curtained-off cubicles that offered no relief from the cries and screams of the ward. "How can you sleep? *When* do you sleep?"

"Oh, one grows accustomed to being tired. Every time I lie down or get depressed, I think of those out there—it's difficult to feel sorry for yourself when others are so much worse off, and it's hard to stay tired with so much to do. So now, what can I do for you?"

"Now you're patronizing me."

She shook her head. "Only those with terrible problems come here, Mr. Marshall. Tell me yours."

So he told her about Sarah's arrival and the possibility that Ryan could be alive.

"What should I do?" he asked when he finished. "She could be killed; they *would* kill her."

"Why not bring her here? It's a terrible place, woefully depressing, but she'd be safe; no one would guess she was here. I could hide her easily among the women."

"Here?"

She gestured across the room. "Two beds are empty. No one stays long."

"You do," he said mildly.

"Yes, but I'm a saint."

"Well, my daughter isn't."

"She sounds like a remarkable girl, coming to save her brother, putting him before her own safety."

Marshall's jaw clenched. "I should stop her. Maybe it's not too late to prevent her from coming."

Teresa shook her head. "I wouldn't do that, Brad. She'd never forgive you or *herself* if she didn't come. The best you can do is keep her out of danger, and that might be by having her stay here."

Marshall considered several minutes, then nodded. "I guess I don't have a choice." He took her hand. "Thank you. I knew you'd come up with something."

She smiled. "Now you can help me."

"Anything."

"Come with me to the rectory. Father Dourmant has something to discuss. He's making dinner, though I'm afraid he's not much of a cook."

"Teresa, I have an awful feeling that I know what this is about."

"How could you possibly know what it's about?"

"It's called 'worst-case scenario.' "

She pointed toward the ward. *"That's* called worst-case scenario, Brad."

She took his hand and led him through the clinic, out the alley, down crowded streets to the unhinged gate that led to the rectory.

The old priest, shuffling from the kitchen, met them in the hallway. "I thought I locked the door."

"You remember Bradley Marshall, don't you, Father?" Teresa asked.

"Of course," he said absently, staring at the door. "Did I really leave it open again?" He contemplated the door, then shouted, "No! It was that damn woman—I told her to lock it after she cleaned, and she didn't. You see, I'm not losing my mind."

Much relieved, and forgetting to lock the door, he shuffled back to the kitchen.

Teresa and Marshall followed down the dark, narrow corridor to the cluttered room lit by a single bulb. "You're looking wonderful, Father," Marshall said. "Apparently charity has its rewards."

"It's not charity that's doing it," Teresa said, watching the old priest bustle about, tossing utensils on the table, searching for clean plates and napkins, kicking a chair out of his way. "It's intrigue," she whispered.

"True," Father Dourmant said, opening the oven, then

slamming it shut as smoke billowed out. "I'm coming to the true calling of a Jesuit late in life. If I'd started earlier, I'd probably be in Rome now, instead of this hellhole."

Teresa glanced nervously at the stove. "Can I help?"

He handed her a hotpad. "Yes, unless you want to starve tonight."

Teresa pulled what might have been a roast from the oven. "I think everything is ready, or at least that it shouldn't cook any more." She put the meat on the table. "I haven't told Brad anything, Father. But he told me his daughter is coming tomorrow. It's about his son, who may be alive after all."

Father Dourmant dropped into a chair. He twisted strands of wisping white hair and contemplated Marshall. "Why are you here?"

"To end the war."

Father Dourmant shook his head. "It will never end. The Vietnamese are like ants—they love war. When this phase ends, they'll turn on themselves."

Teresa set the smoking meat on a platter. Father Dourmant glared at it balefully. "It looks like a burnt dog."

"I'm sure it will be very good," Teresa said.

Father Dourmant poked it with a finger, then looked to Marshall, who took a deep breath and told him about Ryan and the pictures.

When he finished, the old priest poked the roast again. "That's as clever as anything the old Borgia popes could have come up with."

Teresa sliced the meat and handed the priest a plate. "See, it's not so burned, and the vegetables are perfectly fine."

Mumbling an incoherent blessing, Father Dourmant cut a piece and chewed tentatively. "Awful. Maybe it is that damn dog from last night. I wouldn't put it past them to sell me something like that."

"Tell him about the man who came here for sanctuary," she said.

Father Dourmant pushed his plate away. "This may have to do with him."

"If this man is Pran Ba Trung, it might indeed," Marshall said.

"You know about him?" Father Dourmant asked.

"Everybody knows about him; everyone is looking for him."

"He says he'll be killed if he's discovered."

"That's probably true. So he came here for sanctuary, and you want to help him."

"For a price," Teresa said sweetly.

Father Dourmant ignored her. "He says he has important information."

"Father Dourmant thinks you can arrange some kind of payment."

"Shut up," the priest said.

"Father Dourmant wants the money to help with the clinic," Teresa said. "We need it desperately, but what matters is helping that poor man. You must help him, Brad."

Marshall chewed a piece of meat, then swallowed, suppressing a shudder. "It's not a simple matter. Negotiations are at a critical stage. He could cause incredible complications."

The priest nodded. "Especially for you. Helping him might hurt your son."

"If he's alive."

"Could you take the risk? What would your daughter say about that? How clever to have had the photographs sent to her—a very diabolical mind is behind all this; he missed his calling; he should have been a Jesuit."

"What should I do?" Marshall asked.

"You should talk to the man," Teresa said in exasperation. "Perhaps he knows something about your son."

"He wouldn't tell me even if he did know. We want our POWs back—his defection would delay that."

"Talk with him anyway. You know you have to; the man needs help—he's desperate."

Marshall put down his knife and fork; she was right of course—it wasn't even a matter for debate. "Is there a quiet place where we could talk?"

"The church," Father Dourmant said. "Use the side door; I'm sure I forgot to lock it. I'll bring Dr. Trung over in a few minutes."

Shuffling from the kitchen, the old priest stopped in the

doorway and turned. "Money! We forgot to talk about that."

"I will get you money, I promise," Marshall said.

"How much?" the priest persisted.

"How much would you like?"

The question took Father Dourmant aback. He had never entertained a sum in his mind. The only money that passed through his hands were the crumpled, soiled notes in the poor box and his own meager allowance. He had no concept of money; his last dealings with currency were in France over fifty years ago.

"Ten thousand dollars," he said out of the blue, then pointed his finger. "Not a penny less."

"Done," Marshall said. "Thank you for dinner, Father."

When the priest was gone, Teresa smiled. "He's right, of course."

"About what?"

She pointed to the roast. "It's a dog."

The interior of the church was cool, and the stained-glass windows, filthy from pollution and unwashed for years, muted the fading evening light. Marshall stood before the altar, then sat in the first pew soothed by somber silence and lengthening shadows.

The church was calming, and he bathed in its serenity, perhaps the last pocket of it in Saigon, until the side door opened and Father Dourmant entered with a short, middle-aged man, nervous and frightened.

The priest pointed toward Marshall, then turned and left.

Marshall stood and shook hands, gesturing to the seat beside him. "How can I help you?"

"Save my life." Then Trung sighed. "But I know you can't; you don't even want to talk to me. You represent a government that wishes to make peace at any cost. I represented one wishing to make the same peace for the same price. I am a complication."

"Why did you flee if you knew this?"

"You should understand, Mr. Marshall. I know your background. You are a principled man; therefore, you should understand mine. I cannot lie for my government any longer."

"Are they asking you to lie?"

"That is why I was sent to Saigon."

"My experience among diplomats is that lying is in the nature of the calling. Why this sudden sensitivity to truth?"

Trung considered the question, then said more to himself than to Marshall, "I lied easily when I was young, rationalizing it for a purpose. I'm not sure why—you would think a young man would be more idealistic."

Trung shrugged. "Maybe willingness to lie for ideals *was* idealism. But then I had to tell bigger lies, covering up others: lies about production and the economy, purges and disappearances. Lie after lie, year after year, until I couldn't do it any longer."

Suddenly Trung's anger broke through the silence in the church and his face was a mix of fury and grief.

"But the biggest lie was about my son. He died for the Party, killed in a mindless assault, and there was *nothing* I could do because my government is incapable of error. Thousands died with my son in the Tet Offensive of 1968, but the party decreed a great victory. No one could dispute this, even myself, a politburo member."

He bowed his head. "I cowardly swallowed my son's death. But his death wasn't the first I desecrated—many others were executed in the name of communism."

He held out his hands. "There is much blood on these." He folded them in his lap. "I won't lie anymore. I must atone for my son."

He reached into his jacket for an envelope. "Here is General Giap's plan for an invasion after the peace treaty is signed. There are notations in his own handwriting."

Marshall looked at the envelope in amazement. "How do you have this, and why are you offering it to me?"

"I was in the politburo. I copied it to gain the currency to defect. I am trying to buy my life."

"You are a traitor," Marshall challenged.

"To what?" Trung demanded scornfully. "A German who killed Hitler—would he have been traitor or hero? Should we debate the ethics of serving an immoral cause? Do you want to justify serving Richard Nixon?"

Trung held the envelope before Marshall, but when he didn't take it, Trung wedged it in a crevice under the pew.

"I came here to reassure the South that we would honor the treaty. We won't. That envelope proves it. Help me get out of here with it."

Marshall stared at him for a long minute. The church had grown dark; only the brass candlesticks and crucifix were visible, reflecting burnished light from the outside traffic and streetlamps. "That envelope could destroy the Paris peace talks and prolong the war. The POWs would not be returned."

Trung nodded. "But South Vietnam would be saved."

Marshall took a deep breath. Here it was as he had known it would come—the choice between duty and love, Vietnam and his son. But now there was even more at stake—Sarah. He sat silent for many minutes, then said, "I need to think about this."

Trung pointed toward the envelope under the pew. "You are my only hope. You are perhaps the last hope for South Vietnam." He stood, bowed, then left.

Marshall sat alone in the church for another twenty minutes, torn by indecision. Could it be true about Ryan? he wondered.

He looked to the altar. Was his son alive, or was this just a trick?

Yet surely no one could be so callous and cruel—resurrect a man only to murder him again.

He wanted so desperately to believe, but to do so, to raise Ryan from the dead, he would have to sacrifice Trung and South Vietnam's last chance for survival. Marshall fixed his gaze on the crucifix above the altar.

His gaze hardened. Did he dare *not* believe? Was the risk worth the wager?

Finally he lowered his eyes from the cross. He had no choice. He would do anything to get Ryan back—honor and principle weighed nothing against his love for his son, and even if it was not Ryan held hostage, only the illusion of him, he would not deny the illusion as a conjurer's trick. He could not save Trung at the expense of his son, nor would he spare Vietnam to save Ryan.

Maynard had been right, this was all about POWs, and he was caught in the game. He would sacrifice Vietnam for

Ryan. But who could fault him? What kind of a man would not save his son?

It wasn't even necessary to have tricked Sarah to come over—his love for his son was enough to twist him to the will of whoever was behind this.

He glanced to where the envelope was hidden, then he stood and left through the side door.

Outside on the dirt path leading from the church to the rectory, he took a last look at the church, a disheveled remnant of colonial rule, flotsam of a past civilization, soon to be forgotten.

Turning, he heard the sounds of the city, traffic and horns, shouts, music, laughter, mingling in the fetid air glowing in a yellow haze from the lights of the bars.

The night was warm and carnal; beyond the church and rectory, a tiny refuge in the squalor of Cholon, whirled a tempest of whores, hustlers, and dope peddlers, tight-skirted women and leering pitchmen, a carnival midway of neon and music where soldiers and Marines gawked at the freaks and bartered for flesh.

He listened to the cacophony, staring up the trash-littered path that led from the church to the world, then he stepped back quickly—someone was watching him: a tall man, young and powerful, too large to be Vietnamese.

It was the second time today that Marshall had seen the man. He left the shadows and walked toward him. "How did you find me, Captain?"

Bishop came to attention. "Good evening, sir. Find you? Are you lost?"

Marshall stared at him curiously. "Weren't you looking for me?"

Bishop shook his head. "No, sir. I was just walking by."

"Captain, are you asking me to believe this is coincidence—a Marine surrounded by two thousand whorehouses is walking into a closed, deserted church as a fugitive ambassador is walking out?"

Bishop grinned. "Are there really that many cathouses here? I better get busy."

"Captain, what are you doing here?"

"Walking around, sir."

"Bullshit."

Bishop laughed. "On my honor as an officer, I was not looking for you, sir."

Marshall shook his head. "This war is completely out of control—ambassadors running loose in a combat zone, and Marines walking past whorehouses to go to church." Then he extended his hand. "Bradley Marshall. I remember you from Khe Sanh."

"Luke Bishop, sir. That night was the biggest surprise I ever had."

Marshall considered him. This man wasn't casually here; he had been sent. But by whom, and why? Did he know about Trung?

"How about a beer, Captain?" Marshall coaxed. "Think we can find a bar? Or are you in a rush to get to church?"

They headed for the main street and looked into several bars before finding a quiet one with booths. A girl shimmied up to Bishop and groped his crotch, but he pushed her away. She flounced off disdainfully while an older woman brought them beers.

Another bar girl appeared from behind a beaded curtain and started toward them, but the first girl called her over. They whispered together, glanced derisively at the two men, then were hushed by the older woman, who didn't care about the sexual preferences of paying customers.

"You're going to have to come back here on your own to save our honor, Luke," Marshall said, easing back into the booth.

Bishop held up his hands. "I'm a churchgoing Marine, sir—you'll have to do it."

"I'm a churchgoing ambassador," Marshall answered, smiling at the young man who had reminded him so much of himself long ago. "What are you doing back in Vietnam? Didn't you get enough action the first time? Tell me the story; I'd love to hear it."

Disarmed by Marshall's interest and another beer, Bishop told him of his troubles after Vietnam and his experiences at Gio Linh.

"You were fortunate to get out alive; you should be grateful to Wilson Lord," Marshall said, nursing his second beer, watching Bishop begin to glaze over now with his fifth. "But maybe if you had stayed at Gio Linh, it wouldn't have been overrun."

"That's true. The South Vietnamese aren't bad soldiers; they just need help. That's why we can't cut them loose just when they're starting to make it."

Marshall sipped at his beer, motioning a girl to bring Bishop another. He had learned what he wanted—Bishop was working for Lord, but to do what? "So tell me, Captain, why were you at the church? Wilson Lord saved your life, but I doubt he's concerned about your soul—if you weren't looking for me, what were you doing?"

Since Lord hadn't given him a cover story, hadn't told him anything, Bishop merely shrugged. "He gave me a couple days off until my security clearances come through. Actually he told me to get drunk and laid."

"He *is* a good friend."

"He suggested I familiarize myself with Cholon, especially around the church. That's what I was doing, but I don't know why."

Marshall set his empty bottle on the table. So Lord *did* know about Trung. But he hadn't gotten to Bishop yet; the young officer hadn't been turned.

Then, staring at the slightly drunk Marine, a powerful-looking young man who seemed genuinely decent, Marshall saw that he could use him. He needed time more than anything, another day to safeguard Sarah, decide about Trung, and see about Ryan. He needed twenty-four hours to outwit Jaeger and come up with a plan to get Trung out of the country without jeopardizing Ryan, but Trung might not last that long. Surely NVA and CIA teams were fanning out through the city to find him, and Father Dourmant could hardly hold them off, but Bishop might—he could be Trung's only hope.

Too much was happening too quickly; he wanted time to explore all possibilities before making a decision, yet it seemed that if he could hide Sarah and have Bishop protect Trung, he might even be able to save Trung and negotiate Ryan's release. At least it would give him a powerful bargaining position. But it all rested on safeguarding Sarah and protecting Trung.

Marshall leaned across the table. "I'm going to give you an order, Captain."

Bishop grinned, saluting stupidly. "Yes, sir."

Marshall took away Bishop's beer. "I'm serious, Captain. I represent the President, your commander in chief, and I'm giving you an order."

Realizing that Marshall wasn't joking, Bishop shook his head to focus and said crisply, "Yes, sir."

"Meet me in the VIP lounge at Ton Son Nhut tomorrow morning at nine-thirty."

"That's it?"

Marshall stood. "That's it." He stepped from the booth. "But I have a suggestion for tonight." He nodded toward the girls at the bar. "Get drunk and laid."

Bishop grinned.

Marshall headed for the door. "I'll see you tomorrow. Nine-thirty."

But Bishop was already at the bar, dropping into a seat between the two girls.

CHAPTER 10

A bleary-eyed Bonnard arrived at the villa at seven A.M., two hours before his scheduled time, and was met by Marshall waiting on the steps. He had called the embassy dispatcher as soon as he woke and directed his sedan be sent over immediately.

"Rough night, Corporal?"

"I was just getting in when I got the call to pick you up, sir."

"I hoped you used contraceptives," Marshall said, dropping into the backseat.

Bonnard turned. "Sir?"

"Rubbers. Use rubbers, Corporal."

Bonnard searched his face. "Is that an order, sir?"

"Yes. You armed?"

Now Bonnard looked at him with real concern. "Yes, sir, M16 and a .45 pistol."

"Good. Take me to the embassy."

He had hoped to arrive before his staff, but Jaeger was already there. Marshall did not mention Sarah's arrival, though he was sure Jaeger already knew of it, and had withdrawn to his office to read the updates on the secret talks to gauge the authenticity of Trung's defection when, unknown to him, Wilson Lord entered his suite of offices.

"I need to see Ambassador Marshall," he said, presenting the secretary with his identification card.

"Do you have an appointment?" she asked politely, consulting her log.

"No, but he'll want to see me; please give him my name."

"The ambassador has *no* time to see you," Colonel Jaeger said from the doorway of his own office.

Lord turned to him with desultory interest, masking his desperation to see Marshall. He *had* to convince Marshall to work with him to get Trung out of the country. "Let's leave that for him to decide, Colonel."

"*I* decide these things, Mr. Lord."

Then Captain Seidel stepped from his office and approached Lord threateningly.

"Leave, Mr. Lord," Jaeger said.

"Beat it, asshole," Seidel said.

Lord smiled, leaning into Seidel's face. "You're not even the batboy in this game, stupid, so butt out before you get hurt." Then he turned to Jaeger. "And continuing this analogy, Colonel, you're just a weak pinch hitter on a losing team of true psychotics, strictly bush league, playing *way* over your heads. If I were you, I'd be looking beyond this one *brief* season, Colonel—the lineup could change drastically."

"Any chance you might be out of the game yourself, Mr. Lord?" Jaeger asked.

"None," he said flatly. "Psychotics might have one spectacular season, but their careers are brief—they make stupid mistakes; I'm immortal. Those behind you won't have another season, but I'll be on the mound for many more years. Now, like a good lackey, a designated runner for real players, go tell Ambassador Marshall I'm here."

Jaeger smiled and went into Marshall's office.

"Wilson Lord wants to see you. He says you'll want to see him."

Marshall sat back. "He's wrong. But send him in."

Lord closed the door behind him, and the two studied one another warily; they had not met since Lord's assassination attempt four years ago.

"May I sit?" Lord asked.

"Are you going to be here that long?"

"That depends on you."

"In that case, there's no reason for you to be here at all."

Lord smiled as he crossed the room to sit in front of Marshall's desk. "Undoubtedly the room is wired and Jaeger listening in. Surely you've figured him out—he works for one of the White House Basement Boys."

"Basement Boys?"

"We're talking Fellini here, Brad, *Satyricon.* The White House basement is filled with freaks speaking in tongues, and you never know which one has authority, or who he reports to. But they've managed to place Jaeger as your assistant, and dressed the village idiot in an army uniform to be his assistant."

"How do you know this?"

Lord put his hand to his head in mock thought. "Oh, let's try to guess—did I read it in Ann Landers, or could it be my sources at Langley? Wake up, Brad—smell the coffee, as Ann says. Now let's get to the point. Trung's defection is authentic, and a man as clever as he did not leave with just his toothbrush—he must have brought secret documents with him, like Giap's plan for an invasion."

Lord did not indicate his information was from Huong, and Marshall did not register surprise, but he wondered how the bastard knew.

"Trung offers the only hope of saving Vietnam," Lord continued. "As disturbing as the thought is, you might be the only one who can get him out of the country. I know you've met with him; your excursions to Cholon haven't been sight-seeing expeditions."

"Oh, your resources are greater than mine, Wilson—spies and informants, an entire airline, Air America; smuggling one individual out shouldn't be too difficult."

"If all that was at my disposal, it wouldn't be," Lord said dryly. "But I can't book passage for Dr. Trung on Air America."

"No, not if you want him to arrive in one piece anywhere. I've heard the CIA line—unsurprisingly, it coincides with the White House's."

"Yes—abandon ship," Lord said contemptuously. "The lifeboats are in the water, and there's no room for Dr. Trung. Or 'gook' women and children. Someday helicopters will lift off this building carrying the last Americans kicking at those we're abandoning."

Marshall shook his head. "Melodrama, Wilson."

"It *will* happen unless I get Trung out."

"So you've come to me, thinking I might be interested in helping Dr. Trung into a lifeboat, save the sinking ship, oppose the policy of our government, and work against the President, at whose discretion we both serve?"

Lord crossed his legs leisurely, betraying none of the anxiety rising in him. "I'll give you credit for that. I even expect you to be around longer than those loonies in the basement of the White House—a frightening thought if there ever was one."

Marshall nodded toward a sheaf of papers on his desk. "Neither the CIA nor MACV believes Trung defected—they call it wishful thinking."

Lord shrugged. "A gift horse isn't *necessarily* hiding Greeks."

"Do you play chess well enough to distinguish a poisoned pawn from a blunder?"

"Well enough to know that good players poison their pawns and poor players just make mistakes."

"What kind of player is Hanoi?"

Lord opened his hands. "Very erratic; one has to rely on one's own skills."

"And your skills?"

Lord smiled. "I've played accomplished opponents; you and I are about even."

"You tried to kill me, and I had you relieved—that makes us even?"

Lord shrugged. "I know nothing about an attempt to kill you; I made a special trip one day to warn you about danger—I tried to save you. It was your retarded Marine bodyguard, Corporal Mead, and your own stupidity that almost got you killed. But here you are back again—older and wiser, I hope, maybe even on the same side with me. I'm sure it's just passing coincidence, nothing to make us reconsider our feelings about one another, but we might have similar views and goals on Dr. Trung."

"You expect me to trust you?" Marshall shook his head in scorn. "You are a liar and a murderer. You're like the boy calling wolf—I would *never* trust you."

Lord leaned forward. "You'd better—the wolf's out there

this time, and unless you trust me, you'll destroy the last chance for this country. Dr. Trung is legitimate."

Marshall stared at him for a long moment. He despised Lord and everything he stood for, but he sensed he could be right in this case: they might have a similar interest in Trung—they might be the only two who wanted to save him to help South Vietnam.

But could he trust him?

His eyes bored into Lord's, searching for a clue, but his mask was impenetrable.

Then he remembered their last meeting four years ago. Lord had set him up to be murdered, had arranged a phony meeting with a North Vietnamese general to end the war, had it planned so meticulously that the murder would have been blamed on the North, torpedoing any future peace talks, and even when Marshall forced Lord to go along, Lord had played his part perfectly. He was willing to die, Marshall understood later; he *would* have died for the cause he believed in. Lord never wavered. It had been a remarkable performance, a true Nathan Hale act, and he, Marshall, had fallen for it. He had been tricked completely and owed his survival to Ron Mead.

Marshall shook his head. No, he could not trust Wilson Lord; this time he had no one to save him if he made a mistake. "*Nothing* you say will make me trust you."

"You are such a hypocrite," Lord said scornfully, starting another tack, beginning to fear he would not succeed. "You pontificate and act so principled, but you're as corrupt and self-serving as everyone, only without the courage to admit it." He reached into his jacket and tossed an envelope on Marshall's desk. "*This* is why you won't help Trung."

Marshall opened it and saw the same photographs he had seen at Langley, the ones sent to Sarah. "Where did you get these?"

"*Everyone* has them," Lord sneered. "Do you want others—different poses? Close-ups? Tell me what you want and I'll get them for you. So can your aide, or anyone in Washington." He sat back in disgust. "You're going to sell out Trung and Vietnam for faked photos, *not* because you don't trust me. Christ, I expected more even from you. Can't you see what's happening? You're being blackmailed, and now they have your daughter on her way here. They have your number, Excellency."

"You know about Sarah?"

"Everybody knows everything. They've set you up beautifully. You're their patsy, and those photos and your daughter are their trump cards. You're playing a worthless hand at a rigged table where your own aide is the house shill."

Lord shook his head with a mix of sympathy and disdain. "Your son is dead. I understand your desire, your *desperation,* to believe otherwise. There's nothing I wouldn't do to save my son—but yours is dead; those photographs are a trick. You can't save your son, but you *might* be able to save this country."

Pushing the photos away and suppressing the fury raging through him, Marshall asked evenly, "How?"

"Give Trung to me. Let me get him out—you can't. You're trapped; they're watching your every move, just waiting for your daughter to arrive. If you don't give me Trung, he'll be killed. As soon as your daughter arrives, they'll take her hostage and force you to give him up. They'll kill him because they're not going to let anything stand in the way of the treaty."

Marshall shook his head. "I hardly think Richard Nixon and Henry Kissinger have put out a contract on Dr. Trung."

Lord stared at him incredulously, now desperate because he realized Marshall was not going to help. "Are you really that naive? Of course *they* won't put out a contract, they'll merely mention this 'complication.' The Basement Boys will take it from there, acting entirely on their own. They'll contact Jaeger, or someone working with them at Langley or State or at the Pentagon. The word will filter out from there—everything completely sub-rosa, with *no one* taking responsibility, no one you can trace anything back to, but probably *I'll* get the contract to terminate him, yet *you* will have killed him."

Again Marshall vacillated. But then he remembered sitting across from Lord on the helicopter an instant from death, Lord's face utterly expressionless. Then he glanced to the photographs of Ryan. If he worked with Lord, he would doom any chance of getting Ryan back.

Marshall shook his head. "You are asking the impossible—for me to trust you; instead, why don't you trust me? Let me handle this matter."

"You *can't!* I just told you—you're being blackmailed. They'll kill your daughter."

Marshall stood to dismiss him. "What chance do you have against *your* handlers at Langley, those unnamed, untraceable people? None. Let me handle this—stay out."

Lord held out his hands in a final plea. "Then let's work together; we've got to save Trung."

Marshall checked his watch. "I have an appointment."

"Stop!" Lord cried. "How about if we take him to a correspondent? What if we bring Trung to a journalist, set him up with a network interviewer? He could hold up the invasion plan. All we need is publicity."

Marshall shook his head disdainfully. "I am the President's envoy. You expect me to turn this into a media circus to embarrass the administration I work for? And what are Trung's chances of surviving once he's brought to a journalist? Which one of them do *you* trust, Mr. Lord? They're all bought and paid for—the military and the CIA control this environment. No journalist here would touch this story: he'd be gone faster than Trung. How long did Lee Harvey Oswald last in custody? And you call *me* naive."

Lord stood, shaking with anger. "You self-righteous, hypocritical bastard. You're just rationalizing. You're going to kill that man and destroy this country."

Marshall nodded in dismissal. "Good day, Mr. Lord."

Lord started to say something else, then swallowed his rage and went to the door. "You won't get away with this," he promised.

When he passed through the outer office, both Jaeger and Seidel were waiting.

"How'd the game go?" Jaeger asked.

"Strike out, asshole?" Seidel sneered.

"It's an early inning, gentlemen," Lord said pleasantly, suppressing his fury.

In his office, Marshall grabbed his jacket. It was nine, with barely enough time to meet Sarah's plane. He left through the back of his office and took the elevator to the lobby.

Outside in the sedan, Bonnard was asleep at the wheel, but jerked awake when Marshall rapped the window.

"Ton Son Nhut," he said grimly.

When the sedan pulled up to the air-base terminal, Marshall jumped out and ran inside as Bonnard sprinted behind him with his rifle. Outside the VIP lounge, Bishop came to attention, and though he was shaved and his uniform immaculate, Marshall saw the same recovery daze in his eyes that had been in Bonnard's.

"Did *you* use rubbers, Captain?" Then he pushed through the lounge and went out the VIP door to the flight line. "Follow me," he said to them.

Outside on the tarmac, a huge Pan American jet shimmering in the blinding sunlight taxied toward them.

"I'm only going through this once, so pay attention. My daughter is on this flight. Captain, I want you to take her to the priest at the church where we met last night; he'll bring her somewhere else. Make sure she stays there. I don't care what you have to do to restrain her—knock her unconscious if necessary—but don't let her out of your sight."

"Is she likely to cause me a problem?" Bishop asked.

"Very likely."

"I'll go with her," Bonnard volunteered.

"You will drive us out of here, get us in the biggest traffic jam you can find, then the captain and my daughter are going to jump out, disappear, and go to the church. Then you will bring me to the embassy."

A ramp was rolled toward the plane and the door opened. Not to Marshall's surprise, the first person out was Sarah, holding up her hand to block the scorching sun.

She was taller than he remembered, older-looking than twenty, striking and assured. Her hair was long, fashionably frizzy, and she was wearing jeans, sandals, and a psychedelically colored blouse.

"Sarah!" Marshall called as she started down the stairs.

They hugged for a moment, then she stepped back. "Thanks for meeting me. Or am I under arrest?" she asked, nodding toward Bishop and Bonnard standing with his rifle.

"Sarah, this is Captain Bishop, he'll be with you while you're here."

Bishop held out his hand. "Luke," he said with a friendly smile.

She looked at his uniform disapprovingly. "Nice to meet you, Captain," she said without enthusiasm.

"And my driver, Corporal Bonnard."

Bonnard nodded shyly and tried to hide his rifle behind him.

She turned to her father. "Tell me about Ryan."

He took her arm. "I'll explain on the way out."

Bonnard rushed to hold the car door open for Sarah, and daughter and father got in back while Bishop rode up front.

"Listen carefully," Marshall said as Bonnard drove away. "You were tricked into coming here. Those pictures were sent to you to lure you over. You're in great danger. I've got to hide you because if the people behind this find you, they'll use you to blackmail me. And they wouldn't hesitate to kill you. You can't stay with me—they could get at you too easily. I don't trust them because too much is at stake."

"Isn't this a little theatrical, Dad?"

"This is not a game, Sarah. Many lives are at risk, and the peace treaty depends on what happens in the next few days. You're going to have to do exactly what I say, and Captain Bishop will see to it. I told him to knock you unconscious if you cause him the slightest difficulty."

"He looks like he'd enjoy it," Sarah said dryly.

"After he hears your antiwar views and feminist rhetoric, I'm sure he would, so be careful. Please spare him the histrionics, he's just doing his job."

"Dad, I'm over here because of Ryan. That's the *only* reason I'm here."

"I know. I understand why you're here, but I doubt those pictures are real, Sarah. It's too much of a coincidence."

"You don't know for sure. They might be Ryan."

"Yes, they *might,* that's why I'm going through all this. I *want* him to be alive; I want to save him more than anything, but I can't let anything happen to you. That's why you've got to hide. Captain Bishop will take you to a clinic run by an American, Teresa Hawthorne, one of the most depressing places on the planet, but you'll be safe there."

She wasn't listening. "Do you think Ryan's alive, Dad?"

Marshall drew a deep breath. "No, Sarah, especially after

I talked with someone this morning. He had the pictures too—he says everyone has them. I'm afraid we just want him to be alive."

She turned to stare out the window. "That's what Chris thinks too."

"But he still thought you should come?"

She nodded. "He thinks I have to find out for myself. You know what he said? 'Discovery isn't learning something new, just finding what's always been there.' I guess he ought to know, Dad; he's been through a lot. He told me about his talk with you."

Marshall looked to the two Marines in the front seat. "Let's not go into that now."

He tapped Bonnard's shoulder. "Find some traffic, Corporal."

"There's heavy construction just down the road, sir."

Marshall turned to Sarah. "Captain Bishop will take care of you; just do what he says, and *don't* cause him any grief. Your life depends on it."

The sedan slowed. "It's coming up," Bonnard said. "Get ready."

Finally the car stopped, completely wedged in.

Only one lane was in use, and though a policeman directed traffic, his efforts were futile as bikes and cycles and pedicabs clogged an intersection and two trucks faced off.

Bishop turned to Sarah. "You ready?"

"Are you sure this is necessary, Dad?"

He reached over, hugged her tightly, then pushed. "Yes. Go."

Bishop opened his door, pulled open Sarah's, grabbed her arm, and together they ran across the road and disappeared down a side street.

Marshall watched long after they were gone.

"The captain seems okay, sir," Bonnard offered encouragingly, then amended, "For an officer, I mean." He listened in satisfaction to blaring horns and screaming motorists, then he turned. "Tell me when you've had enough and I'll get us out of here."

"How?" Marshall asked, staring at the jumble of vehicles.

"Hang on," Bonnard said, putting the car in reverse and backing up. The heavy American sedan crumpled the front end of the car in back, then Bonnard put the car in forward and crumpled the back end of a Vietnamese truck in front, then he swung the car into the other lane, and smashing into two more cars, made a U-turn and accelerated, leaving a wake of destruction.

"Oh my God," Marshall cried. "Don't *ever* do anything like that again."

Bonnard was stung. "They'd have done it to us if they had a car like this."

Bishop led Sarah through tenements and back alleys, into the front of one shop and out its back door, down side streets until she wrestled from his grasp and dropped onto a crate of garbage.

"I didn't come from boot camp, Captain," she said between breaths. "*Nobody* could have followed us. Let me catch my breath."

Bishop jerked her up. "If you can talk this much, you have plenty of breath left."

He forced her on; two blocks later they came to a busy intersection where he hailed a cab. "Cholon," he told the driver as they got in, cramped together in the backseat.

When the cab sped off, Sarah dropped against the seat and closed her eyes.

"Maybe boot camp wouldn't be a bad idea. You're not in very good shape," Bishop observed disapprovingly.

She opened her eyes balefully, started to speak, then closed them and rested back.

Marshall had Bonnard drop him a block from the embassy. "Hide the goddamn car. If anybody sees this wreck, they'll think I've been drag racing. Go get another rifle for Captain Bishop and meet me here at one."

Marshall walked past startled guards and crossed the compound into the embassy.

Though Jaeger didn't question his absence and tried to appear nonchalant at his return, he wasn't able to bring it off.

"Have some lunch sent up. I want to go over the files again before I see Thieu and Ky this afternoon."

"I didn't know you were seeing them," Jaeger said in surprise.

"That's why Ky called yesterday. They want to discuss Trung," Marshall lied, going into his office, closing the door.

When the cab dropped Sarah and Bishop at the church, Bishop led her around back to the sacristy. Knocking on the door without answer, he pushed it open to confront a startled Father Dourmant, who glared at him so sternly that he stepped back.

"Sir, Ambassador Marshall told me to bring his daughter here."

"Stupid girl," the old priest said, he thought to himself, but quite audibly, then he grabbed Sarah's hand. "Come with me."

When Bishop sought to follow, Father Dourmant turned on him. *"You* stay here; those poor women don't need to see another soldier."

"I'm sorry, sir, but my orders are to stay with Miss Marshall."

Father Dourmant glowered at him. "Yes," he said at last. "You *should* go, you should see what you soldiers have done."

Then the old man turned and led them to the clinic, so accustomed to weaving through crowds that Sarah and Bishop had to struggle to keep up. He pushed past the beggars, cripples, and amputees in the alley, but Bishop and Sarah, trying to ease around those clawing at them, holding out their hands, stopped in their midst, until Father Dourmant grabbed their hands like children and yanked them into the bedlam within.

"Stay here," he said, leaving them to find Teresa.

Bishop and Sarah reeled against the door, recoiling from the screams and wails, staring in openmouthed disbelief at the suffering before them.

"Miss Marshall," Teresa said three times before Sarah finally turned to her. "I'm Teresa Hawthorne. You'll be safe here."

Sarah couldn't speak for a full minute, then she whispered in shock, "What is this place?"

"It's a clinic," Teresa said; then she shook her head. "Actually that's too grandiose. We don't have a doctor, and I'm not really a nurse. We just do the best we can to help."

"Who are these women?" Sarah murmured. "And these babies?"

"Most of the women are prostitutes, though I don't like that word. The only way they could survive was in a brothel, and they became sick or pregnant. They come here because they have nowhere else to go."

Then Teresa turned to Bishop and held out her hand. "Will you be staying with us too? I suppose you're here to protect Miss Marshall, though no one here will harm her."

"Captain Luke Bishop," he said absently, shaking her hand, staring over her head to the pandemonium beyond.

"Soldiers did this," Father Dourmant accused. "American soldiers."

"Father," Teresa admonished. "It's hardly this young man's doing. Come," she said pleasantly, "I know this is terrible at first, but don't be upset. The women and children are well cared for. It's mostly the noise that's so disconcerting; you'll get used to it, and you must always tell yourself, it is *they* who are in pain, not yourself, so you never have cause to feel sorry for yourself, or even *think* about yourself."

She smiled. "Forgive me. I'm getting to be as pontificating as *any* old priest," she said, leading them through the ward to the staff room.

"This will be your bed." She pointed to Sarah. "And that one yours, Captain. Not very luxurious accommodations, I'm afraid."

The two just stood staring at her.

"Did you have a nice flight?" she asked Sarah. "And is the war going well for you, Captain?"

At that Sarah laughed, but the laugh turned to a choked cry. "I'm sorry," she said, catching herself immediately. "My God, that's the most awful thing I've ever seen."

Then she held out her hand firmly. "My name is Sarah Marshall. Thank you for letting me come here. What can I do to help?"

"I think you're just supposed to stay here," Teresa said.

Sarah shook her head. "No. I'm supposed to *do* something."

Teresa looked at her, an earnest young woman who reminded her of herself many years ago.

"Please," Sarah said. "Let me help. I'll do anything."

"Why don't you rest first? You've had a long trip."

"I'm not tired. I couldn't possibly rest."

"Well, I don't know what your father would say. We only talked about you staying here."

Sarah put her hand on Teresa's arm. "You *have* to let me help. I won't stay otherwise." She turned to Bishop, eyes blazing. "I don't care if you do hit me."

Teresa said in slight admonishment, "There's no blame here. We don't allow it; there's no time. And of course you can help. You can work with me on the ward."

Then Teresa turned to Bishop.

He looked self-conscious, as if this *was* his fault. "Is there anything I can do?" he asked.

Teresa smiled. "Oh, I am sure we can find something for a strong man. All we have here are frail women."

Bishop stared at the two women, then he shook his head. "No, I don't think so," he said.

CHAPTER 11

Ron Mead sat hunched before the telephone in the cramped trailer in Sneads Ferry, North Carolina. Like an uncertain bear with a strange toy, three times his hand went out for it and each time withdrew. In the kitchen Sung cast him sidelong glances, waiting for him to shore up his courage, knowing he would, silently amused at the torture he always put himself through before even the most simple task.

Not that *this* was simple, she knew. Asking for help was a major undertaking for Ron, and she had watched his tension build over the last weeks, listened to his debates and doubts, and finally urged him to end his agony by doing what he knew he was going to do anyway—call Bradley Marshall.

"But what if . . . I mean, suppose . . . ," he agonized.

At last, after an entire week of fretting, he got Marshall's home phone number. Another week was spent rehearsing his speech. Tonight he was going to make the call, but his distress was so acute he had not been able to eat dinner, and when Sung took away the plates, he cast about frantically for something to do, but finally he settled before the phone with trepidation and resignation. Yet still he couldn't pick it up.

After the third reach, he turned toward the kitchen and caught Sung glancing away. "You think I'm a fuckhead, don't you?"

She rinsed a dish. "I don't even know what that means."

"Stupid."

She dried the dish and put it away emphatically.

"All right! I'm going to do it this time. I really am," and he grabbed the phone.

He knew he was going to place the call; he knew he *had* to. He couldn't live like this anymore, and he couldn't subject Sung to life like this either.

He had rejoined the Marines two months ago. Exempted from boot camp because of his past service, he was sent to Camp Lejeune for advanced infantry training. Handling the course with ease, he was promoted to private first class and assigned to the Marine Expeditionary Force. But this meant he would spend at least six months a year afloat, part of the ready-reaction force prepared for any crisis, leaving Sung alone in a raucous redneck town of thirty thousand Marines.

"I will be fine," she said. "You always worry about me, but you shouldn't."

Yet of course he worried and couldn't leave her in a trailer park on a mosquito bog in a place worse even than Arkansas, so he had applied to Embassy School in Washington, D.C., but had been turned down even though he had served at the U.S. embassy in Saigon four years ago as bodyguard to President Johnson's envoy Bradley Marshall.

"You have a good chance of making it next time," his commanding officer told him. "You haven't been in long enough—try again in a couple years."

But Mead couldn't wait two years.

"I'm sorry, Mead, there's nothing I can do. You have a great record, medals and decorations, and they should have taken you, but you've only been back two months. I suggest you get hold of that ambassador and see if he can't put in a good word for you."

"Would that do it?"

The major laughed. "An ambassador calling the embassy school? They'd send a limo here for you. Ambassadors are the personal reps of the President. They are his friends; they give him *money*. People in Washington walk around with puckered lips. Get that ambassador to call for you, and they'd even kiss your unwashed PFC ass."

But still he had debated it for two weeks.

"Do you think he'll remember me?" he asked Sung.

"I'm sure he will. I think he owes you his life."

"I guess we're about even. We couldn't have gotten married without his help. Then what would my life have been?"

She had smiled, dropping into his lap. "You say very romantic things sometimes, Ron, but I don't even think you know it."

"Like what?"

She smiled, jumping up.

"Wait a minute," he said, grabbing her waist. "Let's go back to the romantic part. Was it enough to get me laid?"

"Call him and you might," she said, slipping away.

"You're always blackmailing me with sex, Sung. That isn't right."

"It's the only thing you understand."

So that night he called the Washington operator and got the home phone for Bradley Marshall, but after he had it, he was paralyzed with anxiety and Sung knew it would be a long while before he gathered his courage to call the house—at least a week of thrashing, stammering, and nail biting.

But now the night had come; he was in the last throes of distress. Dialing the numbers, he braced himself, and Sung gripped the sink to give him support.

At first he thought he had the wrong number; it sounded like someone answering in Chinese. Then after he asked for Ambassador Marshall, there was more Chinese, then a long pause.

"Hello?" finally came a cultured woman's voice.

"Ah . . . is this Ambassador Marshall's house?"

"Yes," Catherine said. "I'm afraid our help doesn't speak much English."

"I'm calling because, well . . . is Ambassador Marshall there?"

"I'm sorry, he's not here right now." Then, sensing something unusual in the voice, for this was not a typical call, she asked, "Can I help you? I'm Catherine Marshall."

"Oh." He gripped the phone tighter, and Sung, watching him, held on to the sink, then he said, "Ah, well ma'am, I . . . Do you know when he'll be back?"

"Not for a while, I'm afraid. Who is this?"

"PFC Mead, ma'am."

"Who?"

"Private First Class Ron Mead, ma'am. I was Ambassador Marshall's bodyguard in Vietnam once."

"Of course," Catherine cried. "My goodness, he's talked a lot about you. Where are you? Can you come by the house? What can I do for you?"

"He remembers me?" Mead asked in surprise.

"Brad? Of course. I think he'd leave me for you. My God, you saved his life fifty-six times, didn't you? He told me about the helicopter crash, and the rice-paddy fight, and Hue. The way he tells it, you almost won that war single-handedly. He said you were strong and handsome and brave." She paused. "Maybe *I* should run off with you."

Mead laughed. "He told me about you too, ma'am. He said you were really neat."

"Neat?" Catherine repeated. She was charmed, but then she said with concern, "Is something wrong? Are you all right?"

"Yes, ma'am, I just . . . needed to ask him something."

"Well, let me give you his number. He's in Vietnam."

"He is?"

"Yes, and I certainly wish you were there with him. And why are you a PFC? He always called you Corporal Mead. Isn't a corporal higher? What happened to you?"

"It's kind of a long story, ma'am. That's why I need to talk to Ambassador Marshall."

"Then call him right away. As soon as you hang up. You promise me?"

"Yes, ma'am."

"I'll give you his private number in Saigon. Make sure they let you talk with him. Tell them *I* told you to call. Tell them you are calling for me."

"Yes, ma'am."

"Then call me back. Never mind, give me your number, I'll call *you* back."

He gave it to her, and after admonishing him again to call Marshall, she hung up.

Mead turned to Sung in amazement. "He remembers me. I mean, that was his wife. He told her about me. She told me to call him."

This time he was so nervous he misdialed four times, then finally gave the number to the overseas operator.

"This may take a while," she said. "I'll call you back when I get a connection."

But the call came through quickly; he had had time only to pace the trailer six times, and none to remember the speech he had forgotten during his talk with Catherine.

"Ambassador Marshall's office," a woman's crisp voice said.

Summoning all his courage, Mead blurted, "This is PFC Ron Mead. Mrs. Marshall told me to call the ambassador for her."

Marshall's secretary had been told to route all calls through Colonel Jaeger, but she didn't think he meant those from the ambassador's wife, and fearing that something might be wrong, she said, "Just a moment, please," and buzzed Marshall on his intercom.

"You have a call from a . . . Private Mead. He says he's calling for your wife."

It was nearly noon in Saigon. Marshall had returned to his office after picking up Sarah at Ton Son Nhut and was studying the reports on the secret meetings between North and South Vietnam, trying to determine the authenticity of Trung's defection.

"Private Mead? My wife?" Then he reached for the phone. "I'll take the call."

"Ambassador Marshall?"

My God, Marshall thought. It *was* Mead, and a broad smile broke over his face. "Corporal Mead! How are you?"

"Oh, fine, sir. I mean, great. I . . . well, actually it's not Corporal Mead, it's PFC Mead now, sir."

Marshall laughed. "Well PFC Mead, it's still wonderful to hear from you. Why are you calling?"

"Well, sir, I called your house, and I talked to your wife. She was really great. I mean, she gave me your number and—"

"Corporal . . . Private Mead, this call must be costing you a fortune. Give me your number and I'll call you right back."

"You will, sir? I mean, I know you're busy, and I don't want to—"

"Give me your number!"

As soon as he did, Marshall hung up and told his secretary to place the call.

Mead pounced on the phone at the first ring.

"Now, what can I do for you?" Marshall asked.

"Well, sir, I really hate to bother you. I mean, it's not really important or anything, but . . ."

Marshall laughed silently. Ron Mead had not changed a bit, he could tell, and as he listened to him stammer through his sentences, he recalled with warmth their times together four years ago.

There had been so many remarkable events, and as he remembered them, he forgot his troubles, forgot Trung and his mission, and even Sarah and Ryan for a moment.

"Remember when the chopper crashed?" he interrupted. "And you dragged me out, and the NVA came?"

"Yes, sir, I remember."

Marshall laughed. "And when you almost killed Wilson Lord? He's here too, you know."

"That cocksucker. Begging your pardon, sir, but I *should* have killed him."

"Yes, that was my mistake. And that night at the emperor's tomb in Hue during Tet? I think that was the most remarkable night in my life. And Teresa Hawthorne," Marshall cried happily. "She's here too. She asked about you."

"She did?"

"And about your wife." Marshall laughed again, remembering his reaction when he was told that his fierce bodyguard had fallen in love with a girl he had met in a brothel. "How *is* your wife?"

"Great, sir. She's right here."

"And where are you?"

"Camp Lejeune, sir. I got out of the Corps. That's why I'm a PFC. I didn't do anything wrong, I mean, I wasn't court-martialed or anything. I just got out, and that's what they made me when I came back in. And that's why I was calling you, sir."

"Tell me about it."

"Well, sir, I need a recommendation. I tried to get into embassy school, but they turned me down. I thought . . . I mean, I wondered if . . . Well, sir, could you . . . maybe tell them I . . . I'm not a fuckup?"

Marshall laughed. "I can take care of your problem, Private Mead."

"You can, sir?"

"I'll give Washington a call as soon as I hang up. You'll be hearing from them very shortly."

"Oh, Jesus, sir. That's great. You don't know what this means to me. And I really hated to ask."

"I know. You never even asked me to help you marry your wife. Miss Hawthorne had to do that."

"Well, sir, I really appreciate it. I don't know how to thank you."

"Don't." Then, listening to the voice from long ago, the most earnest, dedicated man he had ever encountered, one who had on more occasions than he could remember put his life on the line for duty, Marshall said softly, "Remember that night at the emperor's tomb when I told you about my son who was coming to Vietnam?"

"Yes, sir, he was joining the Green Berets. You were really pissed and joked about him getting killed because he couldn't throw a grenade. You hoped your wife would lock him in the cellar."

"Well, he *was* killed."

There was a pause and a sharp intake of breath. "Oh, sir, I'm sorry. Oh, shit, I . . ."

"It's all right. But I want to ask you something."

"Yes, sir."

"I've learned that he might not be dead; he may be a POW."

"That's *great,* sir."

"Yes, if it's true. But it might not be; there's a complication and I don't know what to do. I'm torn. I want to ask you what to do."

"Me, sir? *I* don't know anything."

Marshall shook his head in wonder. What kind of godsend or omen was this? If there was anyone he would trust to do right, it was Ron Mead. Ron Mead would tell him what to do about Ryan and the defector.

"If it came to your life or your duty, you would do your duty, wouldn't you?"

"Yes, sir, I think I would."

"Oh, I know you would—you *did,* many times. But what if it was between your wife and your duty."

"My *wife* and my duty?"

"Yes."

There was a long pause. Mead turned from the phone to stare at Sung, who had long finished with the dishes and, unable to make a pretense of disinterest, had sat down across from him in the dimly lit trailer.

She was everything in his life; his life was *nothing* without her, and looking at her, he was overcome with a love wholly beyond his ability to articulate. There were no words for what he felt. "I . . ." He stared, then stopped.

He couldn't speak, but suddenly he was thinking of Les Frizzell, who had asked him to live for him, and into his mind flooded all the lives he could not live, all the dead who could no longer dream or love—Perez and Donnadio, Landis and Page and Peterson, Snags and Davidson, and again there were no words to capture what he felt.

"Tell me, Ron," Marshall whispered.

Then Mead took a deep breath and turned from Sung. "Sir, she's my wife *because* she knows I'd do my duty. She wouldn't love me otherwise. I couldn't love myself if I didn't do my duty."

Marshall nodded to himself. What other answer had he expected? "Do you always know what your duty is, Private Mead?"

"No, sir. But I think *you* do. And I think your son would understand."

Marshall let out his breath; there it was—so easy and right even a Marine private knew it.

Oh, Ryan, he thought with a stab in his heart. Ryan, Ryan—I have to give you up. He closed his eyes against the pain and couldn't speak. Finally, when he did, his voice was choked. "Thank you."

Then there was another pause as neither wanted to break the connection.

"I'll look you up when I get back," Marshall said. "Perhaps we'll work together again someday."

"I hope so. . . . Good luck, sir."

Marshall hung up, bending forward, rocking with hurt.

Mead stared at the phone for a long time, then he jumped

up and ran to Sung excitedly, lifting her out of her chair, holding her tightly. "He's gonna help. Everything's going to be okay. I can't believe it."

He tossed her in the air. "He's so great. God, I hope I can do something for him someday."

Then he said solemnly to Sung, "But I sure hope I never have to make a decision like his."

She smiled and patted his head fondly, for he had been right about her too.

"I hope you don't either," she said.

CHAPTER 12

Luke Bishop had never felt so miserable and helpless. For five hours he had cleaned toilets on his hands and knees, mopped slime and filth, carried out garbage, yet every time he went onto the ward, the women recoiled from him in terror and clutched their babies tightly.

When he struggled out with huge pots of soup, they wouldn't eat, and when he tried to help Teresa and Sarah, women whimpered and turned away.

He had not known this side of war, or what happened in the brothels after he left them—he thought only pleasure resided there; he did not know of the women and children.

Before today, war had been a glorious quest, manly and noble; he had not known this baser side, so now he was torn by new emotions, all of which made him feel small and inconsequential, and for the first time he saw why Anne Tavernise had stopped seeing him, and how a woman like Sarah Marshall would never want anything to do with him.

He had watched Sarah comfort women and tend children. Out of the corners of his eyes he saw her stroke their faces and massage their limbs. She was stoic and composed, just like Teresa, and each time their eyes met, he lowered his, for what he had been most proud of—being a centurion—now made him feel guilty and debased.

At last he fled to the kitchen, drenched in sweat, overcome with remorse and sorrow.

He was turned against a wall when Teresa came in to check on him.

"You burned your hand," she cried, taking it in hers.

"I just spilt some soup," he said, pulling away. "It doesn't hurt."

She released his hand to stare at him, but he couldn't meet her gaze.

"Don't be upset," she said. "It's very good of you to help, but these women have suffered so much. They can't possibly react to you any other way."

"I understand. I . . . I just didn't know about this."

She nodded. "War is very terrible, Captain. I think you have suffered too."

He shook his head sorrowfully. "No. Nothing like this."

"There are so many kinds of suffering, and so many victims. That's why it's hard to level blame. Those truly responsible never see their victims."

"Do *they* ever pay?" Bishop asked bitterly.

She smiled. "You'd have to ask Father Dourmant that. I'm sure he's counting on it though."

Just then Sarah burst into the kitchen. "Teresa! A girl's in labor. I don't know what to do. Come quick!"

Teresa rushed out after her, but in a moment Sarah returned to the kitchen. "You've got to help," she called to Bishop. "The girl's hysterical. We can't hold her down. Teresa said to come. Hurry!"

Bishop backed against the wall. "I, I can't," he stammered.

"You *have* to. We're not strong enough to hold her. Hurry. There's no time, the baby's coming."

She grabbed him roughly and pulled him out of the kitchen.

Immediately he was overwhelmed by noise and confusion and he tried to pull away, but Sarah wouldn't let go and brought him to the middle of the ward where a girl lay writhing on the bed.

All around, other women had begun a chorus of screams. Bishop brought his hands to his ears and closed his eyes.

"Hold her down," Teresa said at his side. "We can't move her—she's already started to push the baby out. Captain!

You've got to help. The baby will die unless we get it out now."

But Bishop couldn't move. Finally Teresa slapped his face, a hard, sharp slap that rocked him. "Hold her down!"

Bishop looked at Teresa, then bent over and grabbed the girl's flailing arms. She screamed into his face, but he gritted his teeth and pressed down. She was only a child, he saw, no more than fourteen, and he pinned her to the cot easily.

"Good. Now press on her stomach with her contractions," Teresa called to Sarah.

The girl screamed louder, contracting in spasms.

Teresa was between the girl's legs; blood was everywhere and she couldn't grasp the small head beginning to emerge.

"I can't get the baby!" she cried. "Captain, help me! I'll hold her while you pull. Hurry, or the baby will suffocate. Twist its head and pull. Hurry!"

Luke wedged the girl's legs farther apart with his body and reached down. The head was motionless, the eyes closed, and his hands slick with blood. He could not get a grip.

He ripped off his T-shirt, wrapped it around the baby's head, and pulled. As the body moved forward, the girl thrashed wildly and, in a final scream, pushed so violently that the torso slipped out. Bishop grabbed the tiny figure and held it up by its feet.

It hung motionless.

"Slap it!" Teresa cried.

He hit the baby's buttocks, but it still did not respond. He reached into its mouth, found the tongue at the back of the throat, and pulled. Then he brought his mouth to the baby's and blew in air.

The infant jumped in his hand, spat out blood, then screamed.

Bishop held it as it yelled. Teresa took the child and placed it on the bed. Bishop backed away, tasting blood in his mouth. He wiped his face with his arm, then ran into the kitchen and threw up in the sink.

He was bent over it when Sarah came. She put her hand on his shoulder, but he turned aside so she couldn't see he'd been crying. "Is the baby all right?" he asked.

When she didn't answer, he turned. "What's wrong?"

He started out of the kitchen, but she grabbed his arm and held him back. "You don't want to see," she said softly.

"What happened? Did I hurt it? Oh, Jesus!" he cried.

She shook her head. "It's terribly deformed. It can't live. You did everything you could. It's not your fault."

He brought his hands up and covered his face. "Oh, God," he cried.

She put her arms around him. He dropped his head on her shoulder.

"I think I made a mistake about you, Captain," she said softly.

Then Teresa came into the kitchen and went to the sink to wash her hands.

"Well," she said brightly. "How about some coffee before we start dinner for the women? There's plenty of soup left, and, you know, we even have some fruit. Father Dourmant brought an entire basket today. That will be a wonderful treat for the women. Some of them haven't ever eaten an orange."

When Bishop raised his head, Teresa said gently, "All we can do is try, Captain. It's never enough, so we have to do it over and over, again and again. And try not to be discouraged."

Shortly after his talk with Mead and a follow-up call to Washington, assuring him that Mead's orders for embassy school would be cut that day, Marshall told Jaeger he was going to the Presidential Palace. He left the embassy, walked to his battered sedan parked down the street, and told Bonnard to drive downtown. "Park near the Continental Hotel and bring the rifle."

Ten minutes later they were in a cab on their way to Cholon.

"Pay attention to how we're going," Marshall said. "Tonight you're going to drive me to the same place, get Captain Bishop and the man he's protecting, then bring us back to my villa. You can't make any mistakes."

When the cab stopped before the church, Marshall brought Bonnard to the rectory. Father Dourmant would not let him in with his rifle until Marshall mollified him by saying that he was coming back later for Trung, then he went to the clinic.

He found the three in the kitchen sitting at the table drinking coffee. Bishop was shirtless, his face and chest still bloody.

Marshall looked to Sarah. "What happened?"

She merely shook her head.

Teresa stood to get him a cup. "Your daughter and Captain Bishop have been working very hard." She brought the pot from the stove. "I'm sorry I can't offer you any cream or sugar, and the coffee isn't very good either, I'm afraid."

Marshall appraised Sarah and Bishop sitting side by side. "Apparently he didn't have to knock her unconscious to keep her here."

"Quite the contrary," Teresa answered.

"Well, I'm sorry to take away your help, Teresa, but I need Captain Bishop."

"We need to talk first," Sarah said. "Tell me about Ryan."

Marshall put his arms around her. "I think he's dead, Sarah. I think he was killed on that ambush in 1968."

"But what about the pictures?"

Marshall hugged her tighter. "Those pictures are faked, Sarah. This is the hardest thing I've done in my life, to deny Ryan, but I have another duty."

"More important than Ryan? Your own son?"

"Yes. A young man I knew long ago reminded me of it." Marshall gestured toward the ward. "Our loss and suffering aren't the only things to consider, Sarah. To help Ryan, I'd have to turn against those poor people out there, and this entire country. Ryan wouldn't want me to do that. The White House wants this treaty signed; I was tricked into coming with those photographs. So were you."

"Who would do something like that? Even Nixon wouldn't."

Marshall shook his head. "No, Nixon would not do that—he's not that clever. I'd shoot myself if I thought Richard Nixon or Henry Kissinger could fool me. But they're not behind this—they don't have to be. Those who work for them are; they're behind this, without authority or authorization, believing the ends justify the means, and nothing will come back to them, unless they're caught—but then *they'd* have to take the blame because they were acting on their own. They're extemporizing, believing they're doing what's desired, though no one has told them this explicitly."

"Is *that* how government works?" Sarah asked incredulously.

He nodded. "Yes, my dear. *I'm* extemporizing. We all do it—it comes with power and position, and it's easily abused. You have no idea what people will do to please those in power. There is no lie some wouldn't tell, no dirty trick they wouldn't pull. There is *nothing* some wouldn't do. They even have a man here, my own aide, working for them. He's masterminded this and wouldn't hesitate to have you held hostage until I convince the South to sign the peace treaty."

Bishop said tentatively to Sarah, "Your dad's right, Sarah, but there's something else you ought to consider. Your brother came to Vietnam because he couldn't live with himself if someone died in his place. Everybody else was dodging the draft by going to graduate school or running to Canada or weaseling out by joining the National Guard. What your brother did was noble. Even if he's alive, how do you think he'd feel about you selling out a whole country to get him back?"

"But what if he *is* a prisoner? What if *you* were one? Wouldn't you want to be rescued?"

"I'd rather die than cause that kind of betrayal," Bishop said. "What kind of coward do you think your brother was? Don't cheapen him like that."

Sarah shook her head angrily. "That's so stupid! Men are so stupid. You made this horrible war, you kill each other, you caused all that misery and suffering out there on the ward, and now you're trying to make it all sound noble and worthwhile, like some epic poem. I want my brother back!" She began to cry.

Teresa sat beside her. She stroked her head softly, then looked to Marshall and Bishop sadly. "Take your captain, Mr. Marshall. I know you have a duty to perform. We women will stay here."

"Is there a chance your son is alive?" Bishop asked as he followed Marshall to the rectory.

"I think it was just a cruel hoax to get me to do what they wanted."

Bishop shook his head. "I can't believe anyone sent pictures to your daughter." He was silent a moment, then said, "You know, at first I thought she was . . ."

"Spoiled? Obnoxious?"

"I've never met anyone like her. Maybe once I did, at LA airport, but she spat on me. I was expecting Sarah to do the same, but . . . Has she got a boyfriend? Could you fix me up with her?"

Marshall smiled. "Do what I tell you tonight, get us all out of here, and I will."

"It's a done deal. What do you want me to call you after we get married? Ambassador Dad, or just Dad?"

Marshall stopped at the gate. "You really like her?"

"She's terrific. She came over here to save her brother, and you should have seen her with those women and children."

Marshall pointed to the rectory. "Save the man in there and we'll discuss a dowry—a heavy dowry."

"Save *one* man? That's it?"

"His name is Pran Ba Trung; he may or may not have defected from Hanoi with important information. He could be legitimate or a setup—I don't know. But he is in great danger. I want to get Trung out of the country with his information. I have a plan, but I need several more hours to work on it, so my order to you is: protect him until nightfall when I come back for him."

"That's it?" Bishop grinned. "I might as well go get Sarah right now."

"You don't understand, Luke. Many people, including some in our own government, are trying to kill him. This could be very dangerous."

"You're just trying to turn me on."

"Luke, I'm serious. The chances of this working are almost zero. Everybody is trying to prevent me from getting Trung out. I am the only one who can help Trung, and you are the only one who can help me. This might come down to just you and your rifle."

Bishop cupped his groin. "Now you're really turning me

on. You mean this is an Alamo kind of situation? You're talking a Marine's wet dream."

Marshall put his hand on Bishop's shoulder. "Luke, this is not a game: we are not playing cowboys and Indians, Marines and bad guys. *Everyone* is trying to kill Dr. Trung. The only reason he's alive is because no one knows where he is, but they could find him any minute—if they do, both of you are dead."

Bishop nodded confidently. "I'll take care of him. But what about Sarah? Maybe she should be with me too?"

Marshall shook his head. "She's safer in the clinic. The women could hide her; no one would find her there. It's you and Dr. Trung I'm worried about."

When they entered the rectory, Bonnard jumped up in relief. He had spent an uncomfortable hour under the watchful glare of Father Dourmant, and when he saw Bishop, he thrust the rifle and clips of ammunition into his hands.

"Is he going to sleep in my room too?" Father Dourmant grumped, visualizing a barracks of snores.

"The church would be safer," Marshall said.

"I can't have a rifle in the church," Father Dourmant said.

"Do you really think God would mind?" Marshall asked.

The old priest considered, then shook his head. "Probably not. Actually there's one on the wall in Saint Mark's in Venice." He shrugged in acquiescence. "You can use the balcony. No one ever goes up there."

Fifteen minutes later, they all gathered in the church balcony.

"I'll be back after dark," Marshall told Trung. "I'm doing everything I can to save you. I can't bring you to the embassy or grant you asylum because the secretary of state would not approve it—you'd be turned over to others, and you know your fate then."

Marshall nodded toward Bishop. "The captain is going to protect you until I return. I need to finalize a few things, then I'll bring you to my villa. You'll be under my protection and leave the country when my daughter and I do."

"Why don't we just go now?" Bishop said. "Bonnard could get the car; we could make a run for it."

"You're forgetting Sarah. They're watching my villa; they'd never let her in. They'd stop the car. Jaeger knows something's up. They'd grab both Trung and Sarah. You don't understand the stakes, Luke. Believe me, I've thought this through carefully. Besides, I need time to arrange a surprise for Jaeger. Wilson Lord gave me the idea. I'm going to call a press conference for nine o'clock. When I show up with Dr. Trung, it will be before the cameras. Later I can bring Sarah to the embassy; no one can harm a U.S. citizen there."

Marshall looked at his watch. "It's nearly five. I'll be back after dark."

He hesitated on the stairway staring at the two incongruous-looking men huddled together on the balcony, one old, small, and very afraid, and the other young and muscular, not a bit afraid, and he turned and left.

Washington would be apoplectic when it learned he had granted Trung sanctuary in his villa, but that's what the Basement Boys get for trafficking with liberals, he thought. They would be wild, but they could hardly starve out their own envoy or lay siege to his home with a SWAT team. They would have to let him leave with Trung and Sarah. Once in the United States, Trung would be safe; his notoriety would protect him. What happened with the battle plan would be up to others, and what the media made of it.

Marshall felt he had nothing to lose. Catherine would approve, and more importantly, so would Ryan.

Andy Maynard had been right—the POWs were the soft issue and he was being exploited, as others would be in the future, no doubt. The prisoners were merely pawns: having lost their purpose in war, they were now being exploited in peace.

But everything could work out yet.

All Bishop had to do was hold out for a few hours.

When Wilson Lord left Marshall's office, he knew Trung would soon be tracked down, then a country and Lord's wife and son would be lost.

Already teams from all sides searched through the city. A mad scramble of NVA sapper units, South Vietnamese Special Forces, and CIA squads fanned out in a huge dragnet. He had to get to him immediately, but there was no safe house in Saigon where he could be brought. There was only one hope—Huong, yet Lord had no money and nothing to offer the Chinese man.

By the time he reached Huong on the phone, it was midafternoon. They had met clandestinely several times before in obvious places because Lord believed the obvious was always overlooked, the obscure, never. This time they arranged to meet when Huong's car stopped at a busy downtown intersection.

Thirty minutes later Lord got in as Huong's car inched through traffic.

"I need help," Lord said. "I have to get Trung out immediately. My own people are as likely to murder him as the North Vietnamese. They see his defection as a threat to the peace talks. He's a dead man if he's found, and they're closing in on him. I've heard they've narrowed the search to Cholon. They'll be going block to block soon."

Huong turned to look out the window. "Then the priest was right—your country is abandoning us."

Lord was silent.

"What about those who served your cause? What will happen to them when the communists attack? Who will help and protect us when we are hunted down?"

Huong turned accusing eyes on Lord. "What will happen to my wife and child? My mother? Can you understand what this means? I *believed* in the United States. People look to America—you are our ideal, our hopes. If you let us down, what is there to believe? Who is there to trust?"

He reached for Lord's hand, his desperation breaking through as he saw his world disintegrating. "My child is five. Whether she lives in freedom or tyranny depends on *your* country. Only you can save her—without America, she's lost. So are my wife and my mother. I cannot let anything happen to them."

"My wife and child are here too. I am doing everything I can to prevent this treaty. The last hope is Dr. Trung."

Huong shook his head at the looming disaster. "What am I to do?" he cried. "I'm lost. My daughter, my wife, my mother . . ."

"It's not over yet. There's one last chance. That is why you must help me. But there's no time left—sapper units are everywhere."

Huong closed his eyes and bowed his head. He was silent a long moment, then he turned to Lord, for he saw he had no choice, no other hope. "I will trust you," he said at last. "I will trust you because your stake is the same as mine, the lives of those we love."

Lord clutched his hand gratefully. "Perhaps you are like Job after all."

"What can I do?"

"Dr. Trung is at the church in Cholon. He will be killed unless I get him out immediately. I will save him, forcibly if necessary. Meet me on the quay in front of the Majestic Hotel at nine P.M. I will turn him over to you and you will get him to Hong Kong." Lord glanced at his watch. "It's nearly five. Is four hours enough time to arrange this?"

Huong frowned as he contemplated the logistics, but he nodded.

Lord clasped his shoulder. "Then until tonight."

The car stopped at the next intersection; Lord got out and flagged a taxi. He would save Trung; nothing was going to stop him.

CHAPTER 13

Bishop and Trung sat across from one another on the floor in the small cramped balcony of the darkened church. The upper alcove was stuffy and close with the smell of mildew, and night had not cooled down the day's heat and humidity. It had been a long while since any choir had sung from here, and mice had eaten the psalm books and now scampered overhead on the creaking beams. Outside lights from the bars and whorehouses strained through the grime of the once rose-colored stained-glass window, and they could hear the shouts from the streets and the blare of traffic, and now and then a gunshot.

Bishop was braced against the wall at the top of the staircase, his rifle within easy reach. Across from him, Trung sat primly in a dark suit. They had not spoken since Father Dourmant had locked the doors.

Though he had only a vague understanding of his mission, Bishop knew there was nothing he could do if an enemy—and he didn't even know who the enemy was—assaulted the church. He could lay down heavy fire on anyone coming up the staircase, but if all they wanted to do was kill Trung, he would be helpless—they could toss grenades, rake the balcony with machine-gun fire, or set fire to the church. If this was indeed the Alamo, massacre was inevitable.

But he had survived so many life-and-death situations that

he was not afraid; he was thinking of Sarah and what he had witnessed in the clinic.

"I've never known an American soldier before," Trung finally said.

Bishop drew his knees to his chest. "We're like everybody else."

"You would die for me, truly?"

"That's not my intent."

Trung sighed. "Belief is such a strange thing. Before, I believed things you would have killed me for. Now you will protect me from those who would kill me for believing what you do. It is all quite curious, don't you think, Captain?"

Bishop smiled. "Considering the way you politicians talk, I'm surprised more people aren't killed."

Trung laughed. "It isn't politicians who kill, it's *beliefs.*"

Bishop shook his head. "We do it because politicians or popes tell us to. We believe in *them,* but that's natural—we get that from when we're born, doing what our parents tell us to do, then our teachers. Our whole life is doing what we're told. It'd be okay except some sorry politician or religious nut sends us to do the wrong thing."

"Yet you do it."

Bishop shrugged. "My folks used to send me to bed at nine P.M.; I didn't want to go, but I did. My teachers used to give me homework: I didn't want to do that, but I did. I think it's a matter of trusting, not believing."

"And now you are trusting Ambassador Marshall."

Bishop grinned. "Is this some kind of psychological warfare? I never met a communist before."

"We're like everyone else," Trung said ironically.

Bishop shook his head. "I just want to do what's right, but that's not always easy to know; lots of men die for the *wrong* thing. Trusting is like that—you can't always be sure. I guess that's the main thing I learned in this war—not to trust anybody."

"I don't trust anyone either."

"Not even Ambassador Marshall?"

Trung shrugged. "With whom would you trust *your* life, Captain?"

"The only guy I'd trust would be the Marine next to me."

Trung opened his hands and said kindly, "Then I could not be in a safer place, or with a more trustworthy man."

Sudden rifle fire, screams, men running, and overturning garbage cans sent Bishop and Trung to the floor. Lights flashed across buildings and bright flares lit the sky in a harsh glare. They heard shouts and strident orders. The city grew ominously quiet; even the traffic abated.

"Jesus," Bishop whispered. "They're out there."

Trung cringed, holding on to the floor, but there were no further noises. In a few minutes the flares died out, then traffic resumed, and the noises of the city gradually returned to normal.

The balcony had become sweltering; Bishop wiped sweat from his forehead and reached over to reassure Trung. "It's okay; whoever was out there is gone."

Trung's breath calmed, and at last he sat back up in the corner.

Bishop studied him curiously. "You're the cause of all this. What about you? Who can trust you? Somebody is the sucker—either your government or ours."

"Why do people find it hard to believe that someone might change his mind?"

"Because people don't do that very often. It makes us nervous—then we might have to change our own minds. I should know, it just happened to me today."

Trung contemplated him a moment. "You are a wise young man. Are all American officers so clever?"

Bishop shook his head. "Nope. I'm the smartest."

Trung laughed. "I would like to know you in better times, Captain. Do you have a wife and family?"

"Nope. I just told you, I'm the smartest."

"Your life is your career?"

Bishop took a deep breath. "I haven't been very lucky in love."

"The war," Trung said softly.

"Yeah. I became a professional killer. I've found that the women attracted to men like me . . . well, I don't want to spend the rest of my life with them. I'm having trouble finding a socially acceptable woman who doesn't mind living with a psychopath."

Trung smiled. "You are young, and though your eyes are

round and blue, and your hair blond, I suppose *some* girl might find you attractive. I am sure you will find a lovely girl to share your life, and have lovely children."

"I hope so," Bishop said with more fervor than he supposed.

Trung nodded, trying to be solemn for the young man. "The best women are reformers. They want to make the world better, and that means changing men. Since you tell me there is *so* much in you to reform, you will find one of the best women."

"I wasn't aware communists knew much about women."

"As much as any men—we too are always underestimating them. There are lots of unhappy marriages in Hanoi; in Moscow also, I'm sure."

Bishop laughed, then at the sound of a door opening, he grabbed his rifle and rolled into a prone position at the top of the stairs, aiming toward the stairwell.

In a moment came whispering, the clattering of plates and utensils, then the labored breathing of Father Dourmant climbing the stairs, and Bishop sat up and put down his rifle.

"Don't worry," Teresa Hawthorne whispered. "It's only us."

Bishop suppressed a laugh. "I know."

"We brought food," she said, helping the old priest up the last steps. "We thought you might be hungry."

She laid dishes before them, then asked solicitously, "Are you warm enough? Do you need anything?"

"No, ma'am," Bishop said, then trying not to sound censorious, added, "Maybe it isn't a good idea to bring food in here. Somebody could be watching."

"Oh, dear," she said. "Yes, you're probably right, but I think the people who were looking for you are gone."

"What people?"

"Soldiers, many of them," Teresa said. "They came into the clinic."

"Sarah!" Bishop cried.

"She's all right," Teresa reassured. "The soldiers didn't stay. The women started screaming and the babies were yelling; it was more than the men could stand. Sarah was on the second floor. The soldiers never went there."

"They came to the rectory too," Father Dourmant said. "But they didn't stay because I had Vinh with me."

"Who's Vinh?" Bishop asked.

"A leper; I frequently use him in tight situations. I've taught him to grimace and moan in the most appalling manner; he's quite effective. His slobbering is the pièce de résistance. I told them he lived in the church with other lepers. I offered to bring them over, but they didn't want to come. I think they were very angry, so they starting shooting in the air and chased some youths down an alley."

Bishop smiled. "I don't think Dr. Trung needs me with you two to help him."

Trung accepted a plate gratefully. "We are getting along very well. We've managed to pass the time talking about philosophy and women."

Father Dourmant looked at him sharply. "This is a church."

Trung held up his hand. "Only chaste talk, I assure you."

"Not women—philosophy," the priest said. "That's an affront to God."

Bishop smiled. "Actually, it was politics."

"Even worse," the priest grumped.

"We'll just pray from now on," Bishop said solemnly.

"Good. This will help." Father Dourmant reached into his cassock and handed him a rosary. "Do you know what it is?"

Bishop held it curiously. "No, sir."

The priest shook his head in disgust. "A communist Catholic, and an American heathen." He glanced angrily toward the altar, then he turned to Teresa. "We'd better go."

She stood. "Are you sure you don't need anything? Blankets? A pillow?"

"No, ma'am, thank you. We'll be fine."

She gazed at Bishop a minute, then reached out to stroke his head; he seemed so young, incongruously fierce with rifle and uniform, and so vulnerable. How much better it would be if he could help with the soup in the kitchen, she thought, and save a child now and then. Then she smiled and nodded toward the rosary in his hands. "They're worry beads for those who are worried about their souls. Do you need them?"

Bishop smiled back. "Yes, ma'am, I think I do."

"You certainly do," said Father Dourmant, glancing toward the rifle; then he turned to Trung. "You too. You can share them."

Teresa started down the stairs after the priest, then stopped and looked intently at Bishop. "Good night," she said, and again she was thinking of when she was young, and wondered why it was she had never found love.

When they were gone, neither man said anything for a few minutes, then Trung reached over and took the rosary from Bishop. "I think I need these more than you do."

They were eating silently when Bishop heard the downstairs door open again.

He stopped chewing and listened, thinking Teresa or the priest had returned, but this movement was different, professionally stealthful. He motioned Trung quiet, then reached for his rifle and rolled into position at the top of the stairs, aiming into the stairwell.

A dark figure entered his rifle sights. Bishop aimed at the center of his chest.

Suddenly, as though sensing danger, the figure stopped.

"Dr. Trung? I am here to help you. I am not armed."

Bishop breathed in relief and laid aside his rifle. "Mr. Lord?"

"Captain Bishop?" Lord mounted the stairs to the landing, saw the rifle on the floor, and Trung crouched against the wall. "What are you doing here, Luke?"

"I came yesterday like you suggested. Ambassador Marshall was here; he told me to guard Dr. Trung until he came back."

"Do you know who Dr. Trung is, Captain?"

"The ambassador told me."

"He is in great danger. We've got to get him out of here. Cholon is crawling with units searching for him. The NVA and Vietcong know he's in the area; they're sweeping door to door right now. It's only a matter of time before they break into the church. I had to slip by two teams to get in here."

At first shocked by Bishop's presence, Lord felt immense relief; now he had someone to help him, but to his surprise, Bishop balked. "I can't do that, sir."

"You don't understand. Dr. Trung is going to be killed unless I get him out immediately. Sapper teams will be here any minute—they're going to kill him. Don't you understand, he's the last threat to the NVA for winning this war."

Bishop shook his head. "I can't let him leave. Ambassador Marshall told me stay here with him until he returned."

Lord started patiently, "Captain, I know you are doing what you think is right—"

"I have no idea what is right. I'm doing what I was *ordered* to do. The ambassador is the personal representative of the President."

Knowing that he was not going to overpower Bishop, Lord checked his anger and started again. "Captain, orders are frequently wrong—of all people, *you* should know that. Following orders, you'd be dead at Gio Linh. If you follow *this* order, Dr. Trung will be killed."

"That's why I'm here, to make sure he isn't."

"You're going to be killed *too,*" Lord exploded. Then he caught himself. "Luke, listen: the U.S. doesn't want Dr. Trung—they think he'll ruin the peace talks. Marshall can't save him; they lured his daughter here, and as soon as they find her, they'll force him to turn Trung over to them, then they'll kill him or turn him over to the Vietcong. That's why *I've* got to get him out of this church."

Lord pressed Bishop. "Think: if the ambassador could save Dr. Trung—if the U.S. *wanted* him saved—Marshall could bring him to the embassy and grant him asylum. Why hasn't he done that? Why are you hiding in this church?"

Bishop looked confused.

"Ask Trung—he knows he has as much to fear from our government as his own."

Bishop turned to him, but there was only uncertainty and terror in Trung's eyes.

"I saved your life, Captain. I'm calling in that chit. I can save Trung; someone is waiting now to get him out of the country."

Bishop wavered; Lord watched his fists clench.

Lord's voice continued soft and reasonable. "Your duty is beyond orders. Luke—help me like I helped you."

Bishop stared at him in agonized debate.

"You are never going to make a more important decision," Lord coaxed gently. "Everything in your life has brought you to this moment."

Bishop closed his eyes, besieged with conflicting thoughts and feelings. Suddenly he saw himself as a small boy in front of a white frame house on an Oklahoma plain, then an older self on a football field, grinning with chip-toothed smile, then older again with shaved head and fiercely proud face, on a cold, drizzly morning standing on a parade ground at Quantico beside others, many soon to die.

He wanted to do what was right. *Semper fidelis.* But faithful to *what?*

Then for a reason he could not understand, he thought of Sarah Marshall. He opened his eyes on Lord and shook his head. "I can't let you take him, sir."

Lord sighed. "Orders are orders, right?"

"That's the oath I took."

Lord nodded in resignation. "All right, Captain, I'll see if I can't get Ambassador Marshall to issue you another order."

Lord turned for the stairway. He started down, but unseen by Bishop, he reached into his jacket for his pistol. He didn't want to do this, but too much was at stake, and in his mind he saw his wife and son, everything he had fought for his entire life, and he whirled and fired at Bishop.

The bullet tore into his skull, slamming him backward against the wall.

As Bishop lay motionless, Lord trained the gun on Trung, cowering in the corner.

"Hurry, unless you want to die too." Then he yanked him up and forced him down the stairs.

Hearing the shot, Teresa and Father Dourmant ran from the rectory and reached the church as a car raced away.

"Oh my God, my God," Teresa said.

Father Dourmant stood at the open door. "I forgot to lock it," he cried. "I am a stupid, stupid old man." He ran inside and, clutching the banister, dragged himself up the stairs one by one as Teresa followed.

At the top Bishop lay sprawled on the floor, blood bubbling from his mouth.

Seeing the terrible wound, Teresa turned for the stairs. "I'll get a doctor."

Father Dourmant knelt beside him and made the sign of the cross on Bishop's forehead. "It's too late."

Below, the sacristy door was thrown open and three Vietnamese soldiers rushed in.

Seeing Teresa in the balcony, they ran up the stairs toward her. They were the same soldiers she had seen in the clinic, and though they wore uniforms of the South, she knew they were a Vietcong sapper team.

"Father!" she cried, trying to block them, but they knocked her down and pointed their rifles at the priest.

Father Dourmant rose ponderously. "Who are you?"

They pushed him aside roughly and looked down on Bishop. "Where is he?" one demanded in Vietnamese. "Tell us or we'll kill her."

The man grabbed Teresa's hair and yanked back, pressing his rifle under her chin. "Where did he go?"

Father Dourmant drew himself up. "I don't know. We don't know anything."

"That was clever about the leper, old man," the leader said. "But you won't fool anyone ever again."

Father Dourmant closed his eyes to pray, but there was no shot; instead, a voice came from downstairs.

"Captain Bishop! Teresa!" Marshall called, standing before the altar, Bonnard beside him with his rifle.

As soon as Bonnard saw the man in the balcony, he threw himself on Marshall, knocking him to the floor, aiming his rifle, but a second Vietnamese pushed Teresa to the stairs, shielding his body with hers, while the third grabbed Bishop.

Marshall rolled from under Bonnard. "Let them go," he said, standing up.

"Brad, they don't understand you. They're Vietcong."

Then he saw Bishop's head, the blood-matted hair and torn-away skull.

"They didn't do it," Teresa cried. "Someone got here first and took Dr. Trung."

They faced off for a full minute, then Marshall said to Teresa, "Tell them I know why they're here. Tell them I know what they want."

As she translated, he went to the front pew. The envelope

was worthless. Washington did not want Trung or his information, and maybe Lord hadn't gotten it, for it must have been Lord who had shot Bishop—no one else could have gotten up those stairs.

He felt under the pew and held up the envelope. "This is what they want. Someone else has Dr. Trung. Tell them to let you go and they can have this."

He nodded toward Bonnard. "He won't let them take me or you. Tell them their hostages are no good to them. Bonnard will kill them before they get to the door."

Teresa spoke to them quickly. Gripping their hostages close, the Vietnamese talked among themselves, then looked to Bonnard, whose rifle was trained on them.

"Tell them to let you go first," Marshall said, walking toward Teresa.

The man holding her considered a moment, then released her as the other two kept their rifles on Father Dourmant and Bishop.

"Now Father Dourmant," Marshall said, holding out the envelope.

The man took it as he released Father Dourmant.

Marshall nodded to the soldier holding Bishop. "Now him."

The man let Bishop drop to the floor, then the three, using Marshall as a shield, moved to the door and ran out.

Marshall knelt beside Bishop. "Help me with him," Marshall called to Bonnard. "We have to get him to the car."

Bonnard put his rifle on the floor, but just as he got his arms around Bishop's shoulders, the church door was flung open and Jaeger rushed in with four armed soldiers.

"You're too late, Colonel," Marshall said. "In fact, you're last—two others got here before you."

"Where's Trung?" he demanded.

"With the man you *really* don't want to have him," Marshall said angrily.

"You mean that old man Wilson Lord has him?" Jaeger asked contemptuously. He laughed. "He's one I *want* to have Trung. That simplifies everything. We know all about Lord. He made the same mistake you did. Captain Seidel is at his home right now; he has his family. We'll have Trung shortly. Thank you for your efforts, Excellency. You did a wonderful job setting this all up for us. You played right into our hands."

"Our?"

Jaeger laughed again. "I was told you were naive, but I never suspected you'd be this easy. It's truly frightening that men such as you control our foreign policy."

"No. What's frightening are men like you and your handlers."

"Give me the papers Trung handed over to you. We know he had documents. I want them, then this sorry affair will be over."

"I wouldn't give you anything. Get out of my way, this man needs help."

"I want the papers. Are you going to make me threaten these people?" Jaeger turned to Teresa and took careful aim with his pistol. "Give them to me."

"Dad!" a voice called behind him. Then, seeing Bishop's blood, Sarah screamed.

As Jaeger whirled, Marshall reached for Bonnard's rifle, swung the butt around, and charged, driving it into Jaeger's chest with such force that he heard the breastbone crack. As Jaeger slumped, Marshall smashed the butt into his face.

Jaeger fell to the floor and didn't move. Marshall looked at the soldiers. "Get that bastard out of here." Then he ran to Bishop. "Help me with him," he yelled to Bonnard. "We've got to get him to a hospital. How long will it take?"

"Fifteen minutes if I cut through town."

Marshall struggled to lift Bishop. "Don't stop for anything."

"Don't go, Papa, read me a story," the little girl said in her bed. "You promised."

"Is the story more important than my business?" Chien Lin Huong asked lightly.

"It's night. You don't work at night, Papa."

"Sometimes I do, after you go to bed. Tonight I have to work *before* you go to bed. I have to meet someone."

She considered. "Maybe you have time for a *tiny* story."

Huong looked at his watch. It was eight-thirty; all the arrangements had been made to get Trung out of the country. He would be taken directly to the dock, put on one of

Huong's cargo ships as a crewman—the papers had already been readied—and in a few days he would be in Hong Kong. But Huong had to leave now or he would be late for his rendezvous with Lord. "How about if I sing you a song instead?"

"Papa, you have a terrible voice."

"You'll be sorry when I never sing to you again."

"No, I won't."

He laughed and hugged her. "You make me very happy, Ai-ling; I love you so much. Instead of the story or a song, how would you like to come with me to the car?"

Her eyes lit in wonder. "Outside?" Beyond the gate was a fabled place where she was rarely allowed.

He hesitated. He meant to the garage, for he always kept her within his guarded walls. "I don't want you to go outside, Ai-ling. It's dangerous."

"Oh, just to wave good-bye, just for a moment. Then I'll go to bed."

As he wavered, she pressed, "I'll never get to go. Mother *never* lets me outside. Please, Papa, just to the street to see your car leave. A guard will be there."

"I don't know," he said unsurely.

"Just for a minute. It's such a nice night. Oh, Papa, please."

"All right," he relented.

She clapped her hands happily, but when he made no motion to leave, she tugged on him. "Well, aren't you going?"

"First you didn't want me to go, now you want me to hurry." He stood, set her down, then walked out with her holding on to his finger.

"Watch her carefully," he said to the guard on the porch as he went to the garage. "Let her stand on the sidewalk as my car leaves, then bring her right back to the house."

The limousine was brought from the garage. Before getting in, Huong kissed his daughter, then motioned her aside solicitously and admonished the guard again.

Another guard opened the gate as the little girl and her guard walked to the curb.

Inside the limousine, Huong waved as the car started down the driveway. Encapsulated in the luxurious machine, he did not hear the squealing tires of a car turning a corner at the head of the street.

The guard looked up at the sudden sound, but the child was not paying attention. She was watching a puppy cross the street toward her, wagging its tail.

Before the guard could grab her, she darted toward it.

The puppy crouched at her approach. Smiling happily, she reached for it.

Marshall cradled Bishop's bleeding head in his lap. "Hurry," he said fiercely to Bonnard as the car rounded a corner.

Accelerating, Bonnard raced down the residential street.

Suddenly a dog wandered into his path. Unable to stop or swerve without hitting parked cars, Bonnard closed his eyes, not wanting to see.

He did not see the little girl dart into the street, or the vehicle slam into her with incredible velocity, hurling her under the wheels of another car backing from a driveway. All he saw in his rearview mirror was the animal splattered on the pavement.

"What was that?" Marshall called.

"A dog. A fucking dog was in the street," Bonnard said, gripping the wheel.

"Stop! Stop the car."

Bonnard threw on the brakes. Marshall turned to look out the back window and saw a man running toward the car, a well-dressed man his own age, running blindly, hands outstretched, mouth open, screaming in anguish.

"No! No! No!" Huong cried. He threw out his arms screaming, *"Ai-ling, Ai-ling,"* so loudly he felt his lungs bursting.

When he reached the stopped car, he began to beat on it, pounding his fists against the window, trying to break it to get at the man in the backseat, clawing at the door, howling with pain and grief.

Marshall stared into the wild eyes, then he looked back and saw the dog in the road.

He turned to the man beating on the window, then he looked down at Bishop.

He saw Bishop's blood, saw matted hair and exposed

brain, and his own eyes filled with fear and terror. "Are you sure that's what you hit? Just a dog?"

Bonnard slammed his fist against the steering wheel. "Just a fucking dog."

Marshall clutched Bishop in his arms. He glanced back to the animal, turned for a last look at Huong, then his mouth set. "Go on," he ordered Bonnard.

The car squealed forward.

Huong sank to his knees, clutching his heart as if it were about to implode in grief.

Finally, long after the car disappeared, he stood.

When he turned, his guards stepped back from the fury in his eyes, but he didn't see them. All that was seared into his mind was the face of the man in the car.

CHAPTER 14

Wilson Lord sat in mounting agitation in his car parked along the quay of the Saigon River across from the Majestic Hotel. It was nine-fifteen. Something had happened to Huong, he knew.

Huddled across from him, Pran Ba Trung shook uncontrollably.

Vendors and black marketeers converged on the car, banging on the doors and tapping at windows. A prostitute lifted her skirt and pressed against the glass.

"We've got to walk," Lord said, reaching to unlock Trung's door.

Playing for time, he steered Trung to Tu Do Street, the midway of bars and brothels, then he walked him back, past beggars, soldiers, whores, and money changers, but there was still no sign of Huong.

Trung slumped under the strain. "It's hopeless; I'm lost."

"No," Lord said defiantly.

Hooking his arm through Trung's, he led him to the dock that overlooked the river. "Wait here," he said. "I'll be back in a few minutes."

Inside the Majestic, an ornate relic of French-colonial days, he went to Reception. "I need to make a call," he told the clerk.

The man pointed across the lobby to a long line.

"It's urgent."

The man shrugged.

"All right, I'll call from my room." He pointed to keys behind the desk. "Five fourteen."

The man handed him the key and Lord went to the elevator. He knocked on the door, then opened it. At the window he pulled the curtain aside and saw Trung standing on the quay, then he picked up the telephone on the nightstand and gave the operator Huong's number.

A sobbing woman answered.

"Is Mr. Huong there? I must speak with him."

The sobbing continued.

"I must talk to Mr. Huong."

The only sound on the other end was the crying woman. Huong was at the hospital, she finally said. Lord put down the receiver. He went to the window, saw Trung glancing about fearfully, then he gave the operator his home number.

It was answered on the first ring.

"Dad?"

"Lance! Are you all right? Where's your mom? Put her on."

"Dad," the boy said plaintively. "Come home."

"What's wrong? Lance, what's wrong?"

There was silence on the other end.

"Lance," he begged. "Say something."

"This is the batboy, asshole," Captain Seidel said. "In fact, I found a bat here at your house. You want your kid to say something? How would you like to hear him scream when I break his hand with it?"

Lord closed his eyes.

"You fucked up bad, and now you're going to pay. I want Trung. You have him, but I have your kid. Here he is—say something, little boy."

"Dad!" Lance cried. Then he screamed in pain.

"Next time you're really going to hear him scream, so cut this shit right now. I don't want to hurt him, but you *know* I will, and then we'll start on your wife. I'd enjoy that a lot more."

"You bastard," Lord seethed.

"Watch it! Be nice to the batboy or you'll be sorry. Where's Trung?"

"Dad! Dad!" he heard his son call.

"All right!" Lord yelled. "He's on the quay in front of the Majestic."

"He better be," Seidel said, hanging up.

Lord dropped the phone. Lance. Anh. Seidel would not hesitate to kill them, he knew. But if Seidel touched them, Lord would pursue him to the end of the world; he would make him plead for death long, long before he killed him. He went to the window and rested his head against the glass.

He had just murdered Trung, he knew, and the last hope to save South Vietnam.

Ten minutes later, two cars pulled up at different ends of the quay. Four men got out of each car and converged on Trung.

One struck him from behind and he collapsed, then, as though helping a drunk, they carried him to a car, threw him in the backseat, and drove off.

When the car disappeared, Lord grabbed the phone.

Anh answered.

"Are you all right? Is Lance all right?"

"We are fine. The men are gone."

"I'll be right there," he said, hanging up.

He dropped into a chair and covered his face with his hands, overcome by relief. Then he rose, gorged with fury. Bradley Marshall was responsible for this; Marshall had murdered Trung. If Marshall had listened to him, they could have saved Trung. Now everything was lost.

He shook with rage. That bastard! That lying, hypocritical, self-righteous son of a bitch—he would pay for this, Lord promised. If it was the last thing he did, he would make Marshall pay.

As he left the room, an overweight, middle-aged man confronted him, a defense contractor here on a billion-dollar deal, Lord surmised—the mortician making a house call.

Lord held out the room key to him. "A mistake. They gave me the wrong key."

"Stupid gooks," the man said.

"Yes," Lord said, walking toward the elevator. "Wrong room. Wrong country. Wrong war."

CHAPTER 15

Two days later, on his last morning in Vietnam, leaving his villa for breakfast with the U.S. ambassador, Ellsworth Bunker, Marshall was met by a new driver, and three escort jeeps mounted with machine guns.

"Where's Corporal Bonnard?" he asked the civilian driver.

"I have no idea, sir. My orders are to drive you to Ambassador Bunker's residence, then pick up your daughter, then bring you to catch your flight at the air base."

Marshall pointed toward the three jeeps. "What's that all about?"

The driver shrugged. "Orders, sir."

When Marshall arrived at Bunker's downtown residence, the seventy-eight-year-old ambassador greeted him on the portico. "I'm glad you arrived safely."

Marshall gestured toward the jeeps and soldiers. "Is there an alert? Or are you just eager to see me out of here safely?"

The old man murmured noncommittally, then took his arm and led him inside. The table was set and the two sat in the dining room. Servants set plates before them and poured coffee; an overhead fan clacked soothingly. Bunker sipped orange juice and waited for the servants to withdraw.

"Your resignation last night took the White House by surprise," Bunker said. "They cabled me for information, but I didn't have any—only that your aide is in the hospital along with a critically wounded Marine officer."

Bunker buttered a roll. "Do you want to fill me in? What happened to your aide?"

Marshall sipped coffee. "He tripped over me," he said blandly.

Bunker nodded. "Very clumsy of him. How about the Marine captain with the bullet wound? The doctors don't think he'll live."

"The only witness was Dr. Trung. I doubt he'll be coming forward to testify."

"No, probably not," Bunker mused. "So, this is a closed matter?"

"A complete washout, like my mission."

Bunker shrugged. "We have those now and then—sometimes a washout, sometimes a grand-slam homer, usually just a lot of bench-sitting."

"But I wanted to make things *better*. I wanted to save this country. And my son." Marshall shook his head sorrowfully.

Bunker sighed sympathetically. "Yes, I know, but it wasn't true, just one of the many rumors. My sources say he died four years ago on that ambush; they have no reason to lie to me."

"God, that was cruel, preying on the dead, trading on hostages."

Bunker blotted his mouth with his napkin. "Get used to it. Since our enemies don't have our technological weapons, they use cruder ones. How can one complain about their tactics as we napalm them? It's fair reparations."

"Reparations?"

Bunker nodded. "The bill always comes due, Brad. You don't think we were going to get away from Vietnam without paying, did you? There's no escaping it—nationally or *individually.*"

At the emphasis, Marshall looked up from his bacon and eggs. He sensed suddenly that this breakfast was not just a formality after all, but that he had been set up for something else.

"Yes," the old man said. "I think the troops have a phrase for it—'pay back.' Apparently that's what happened to your driver—very curious business."

"Corporal Bonnard? What happened to him?"

"We're not altogether sure. He was found dead early this morning."

Marshall clattered his cup into his saucer, spilling coffee on the table. "What?"

Bunker said in almost bored tones, "Very curious. It could have been drugs or a woman or the VC—we don't know. His body was found by Vietnamese police."

"Bonnard! He was a fine young man, clean-cut, polite . . ."

"Well, wonderful Corporal Bonnard was found outside a whorehouse with his throat cut, run over by a car. I can't imagine how he managed that feat, unless he stumbled down the stairs of the cathouse, was stabbed at the bottom, then fell in front of a car."

Marshall just stared at him; then terror broke over him like a tide, rushing over his defenses until he was drowning in it. "He was run over?" he choked.

"Emphatically run over, according to the pathologist." Bunker folded his hands in his lap, looking as though he were ready to take a nap. "I'm having it investigated to see if it isn't connected to an accident report we received yesterday."

But Marshall wasn't listening; his ears and thoughts were stopped with horror.

"Run over?" he whispered again, and he began to feel sick as his stomach knotted in the realization of what this meant.

Marshall pushed his plate away. "Bonnard ran over a dog two nights ago, Ellsworth. We were rushing Captain Bishop to the hospital and he hit a dog. I saw a man's face in the window; I've never seen such fury in a human face. *That* man killed Bonnard, Ellsworth. I ordered Bonnard to go on—but it was only a dog."

Bunker closed his eyes. "Orientals *eat* dogs, Brad, they don't have them for pets. I'd be upset if someone ran over my dinner, but I doubt I'd be moved to murder." Bunker shook his head. "No, the report didn't mention a dog, it mentioned a child."

Marshall had played diplomat for twenty years, but he saw what a novice he was to Bunker; the old man had toyed with him effortlessly, had caught him completely off guard, and had sprung the trap without his even knowing he had been the prey.

The elderly diplomat smoothed the table linen before him. "The report stated that a little girl was killed by an American sedan. The father is an influential businessman. He said it was *your* car that ran over his child. He claims it was a hit and run. We were going to investigate, call Corporal Bonnard in for questioning, but . . . he's dead. Quite a coincidence. And since you have diplomatic immunity, it's a moot issue. I suppose we'll make some payment, send our regrets: the usual. That'll be the end of it."

"Oh my God!" Marshall said, rising from his chair. "A child! No—it was a dog, I saw it in the road. I would have stopped if it were a child, but I *saw* the dog."

Bunker nodded his head sympathetically. "Of course you would have stopped if you had seen a child. Unfortunately, *doctors* saw the child. In fact, the child is still in the morgue, pending the results of the investigation."

Marshall sank down in his chair. "Oh, Jesus, no." He looked up to Bunker in anguish. "I would have stopped if I had known it was a child, Ellsworth."

"Of course," Bunker said soothingly.

"We were rushing to the hospital. We thought it was a dog; it was an *accident.*"

Bunker waved his hand in dismissal. "Don't worry. You have diplomatic immunity. Nothing will come of it—we'll take care of it."

Marshall jumped up. "No. I've got to see him. I've got to explain to him. I've got to . . ."

"Offer condolences?" Bunker was no longer sleepy or sympathetic. He sat forward with concentrated focus. "They're too late. The man is beyond forgiving. That's why you have extra security. Bonnard's death isn't a coincidence, of course, but we can't prove anything—there were no witnesses. The man is wealthy and powerful and wants revenge—it's a matter of face. Talking with him will achieve nothing."

"But I *have* to talk to him. I know I can explain. I know I can reason with him."

"Reason with a man who has just murdered your driver? You *are* naive, Brad."

Marshall sat back incredulously. "You want me to just walk away? Forget about it? My God, Ellsworth, I killed that man's child. I have to make amends."

"Amends? With what—money? He doesn't need any. Are you going to bring his child back to life? Just what do you think will satisfy him—your profound regrets, tears? That man wants vengeance, Brad."

"But if I could explain to him that it was an accident . . ."

Bunker reached for his coffee. "I hardly see how that will assuage his grief or help his daughter now. I think you could flagellate yourself through the streets of Saigon and it would not impress him."

"What can I do?"

"Nothing."

"But I *have* to do something—I can't just walk away from this."

Bunker leaned forward. "Brad, the child is dead. That's irrevocable. The father's grief and fury are irrevocable—*nothing* you can do will change that. Since when did you think saying you were sorry would make a difference? You've been reading too many trashy novels, Brad. That man doesn't want sympathy or guilt, he wants revenge—that's why he killed Bonnard. He'd kill you if he had a chance—he'll probably try to kill your children."

"What!"

"It's called eye for eye, Brad—the reparations we were talking about."

"Oh my God. Then I have to talk with him. He *has* to understand."

Bunker shook his head. "I think you have an exaggerated sense of your ability to reason with a man maddened by grief and rage."

Now the full horror hit Marshall. Everything he had done had come to nothing; everything he had touched in Vietnam was ruined. He had been naive and foolish, misguided and stupid. He had meant well, had only wanted to do good—his intentions had been noble, but there had been only accident upon accident, misery stacked upon misery, and now the death of an innocent child.

He bent forward in true pain; his hands gripped the table and he closed his eyes to block out what he had done.

Bunker coughed delicately. "Why don't you let me handle this problem for you."

Marshall shook his head in misery. "You can't. No one can."

The old man's eyes fixed Marshall shrewdly. "I remember you coming to me about a clinic in Cholon. You asked about the possibility of getting orphan children out. I told you the government would never recognize the illegitimate children of whores and GIs. Well, knowing how badly you must feel about this unfortunate incident, I've reconsidered the matter of the clinic."

Marshall looked up distrustfully; Bunker was a friend, but he was staring at him like a sniper who had him in his sights. The old diplomat had been waiting in ambush, and Marshall was out in the open.

With his finger on the trigger, Bunker offered him a reprieve. "Nothing can be done about the accident, Brad; the child is dead, the father inconsolable. You can have no effect on that any longer. But you can save other children—hundreds of them. I can work with you to get an airplane to fly out the children in the clinic. We'll have resistance from State, Naturalization and Immigration, but with White House backing, there won't be a problem."

"The White House will back this? Why?" Marshall asked suspiciously, but with a glimmer of hope.

"To help you. And because it's the right thing."

Marshall shook his head in derision. "Spare me, Ellsworth. Of course I want to help those children; I tried repeatedly to get them out. I'm willing to do almost anything to save them. We're big boys and we've played hardball for years—I understand the game as well as you do. Just tell me what this is all about."

Bunker opened his hands. "All right. There is a man who wants revenge against you. He has already murdered your driver. He would not hesitate to kill you *or* your children, and he is not remotely interested in your regrets or condolences. I will make sure that this man does not bother you. Ever. He will never leave this country. In addition, to mitigate for the loss of that man's child, I will guarantee that a planeload of children is flown out—all the orphans, and the woman who runs the clinic." Bunker closed his hands. "In return, I want a guarantee that you will never mention Trung, his defection, or the invasion plan he was rumored to have."

"I would never do that. This was a confidential mission."

"*I* know that. I know you're honorable, but the White House, perhaps not as honorable as we, *doesn't* know that. They're afraid you'll call a press conference when you return and tell the world that the peace treaty is a sham. Therefore, they want to strike a deal—their cooperation on the orphans for your silence."

"Oh, for Christ's sake," Marshall said in disgust. "Jesus, they're slimy bastards. Do they honestly think I'd do something like that?"

"Brad, Brad," Bunker said mildly. "Remember who you're dealing with. Look at the people in the White House. They're the worst bunch of thugs since the last bunch. Didn't one of them say he'd stomp on his grandmother's heart to get Nixon reelected?" The old man smiled. "Or was that something Johnson said about his own reelection? Or was it Bobby Kennedy? At my age one tends to forget which thug said what, but it's *all* interchangeable, as are the people. There are *no* dirty tricks any of them wouldn't pull to get on top. Or stay there."

Marshall pushed his plate farther away. He felt ill. Catherine had been right; he had been a fool to think he could make a difference, a mindless fool to trust in man's good nature.

Bunker opened his hands. "I'm just the broker, but I recommend you take the deal—you'll never save those children otherwise, and that man could cause immense problems."

Marshall closed his eyes. "Jesus, Jesus."

Bunker took off his wire-rim glasses and rubbed the bridge of his nose as he waited for Marshall to make up his mind.

"I don't have a choice, do I?" Marshall asked at last. "What will you do to that man?"

"I'll make sure he doesn't cause you any problem."

As Marshall looked at him dubiously, Bunker shook his head. "I'm a diplomat, not an assassin, Brad. I'm not going to have him killed, I'll just ensure he doesn't pursue you—I'll have his passport pulled, pressure the Palace—nothing bad will happen to him; God knows, he's suffered enough. We'll just keep a lid on him."

"You guarantee no harm comes to him?"

Bunker raised his hand in oath.

"And you guarantee the plane to fly the children out?"

Bunker raised his hand again. "If you'll guarantee nothing is ever said about Trung."

Marshall considered a second, then nodded.

Bunker slipped on his glasses. "Excellent."

Marshall stood to leave. "Christ. I would do anything to change what happened, Ellsworth."

Bunker dropped his napkin on the table and rose too. "Of course you would, but you can't. You're making the right decision, Brad. Let me take care of this. You are more than making up for the loss of one child by saving all those others."

"No. It doesn't work that way and you know it. A death is a death, and saving a thousand doesn't bring back the one you killed." Marshall drew a deep breath. "But saving those other children will mitigate what I did. God, I'll be glad when this war is over."

"It'll just become another one. There'll be more sorrow and suffering, more soldiers and widows and orphans." The old man smiled faintly. "But more diplomats too. We'll have steady employment." He steered Marshall toward the door. "I'll see you at the next war, Brad."

"Nope. This was my last one, Ellsworth."

"Then I'll see you in heaven; after all, that's where war began."

At the door, Marshall shook hands. "Thank you for helping me with the children."

Bunker nodded. "Those children will be your legacy, Brad—they'll demonstrate that what you did here wasn't in vain."

Thirty minutes later Marshall walked into the clinic to get Sarah and say good-bye to Teresa. They were working side by side on the ward, and Sarah looked up anxiously. "Luke—Captain Bishop—how is he?"

"The same," Marshall answered. "They won't know for a

long time whether he'll make it, or whether there's brain damage."

Teresa, accustomed to so much sadness, turned to the child on the cot before her and said matter-of-factly, "Well, I hope not; he seemed a nice young man." Then, knowing she hadn't fooled either of them, she said earnestly to Sarah, "He's *very* nice."

Marshall took Teresa's arm and drew her aside. "Could I talk to you alone?"

As they walked toward the staff room, Teresa said, "They would make a lovely pair. You should have seen them together. I know he's fierce and loves war, but there's something soft and kind about him too. And your daughter is just wonderful. She wanted to stay here. I had a terrible time convincing her to go back with you. I told her there was suffering everywhere, probably right where she was in America."

Marshall closed the door of the staff room.

"Don't you think they'd make a wonderful couple?"

"I don't think he's going to live."

Teresa closed her eyes, then she shook her head. "Why is love so hard?" She wasn't thinking about it for herself, that was long ago, lost with her youth, which she could hardly remember. She was thinking about it for others, but that seemed an impossibility too. There was no love for the women or children here, no love anywhere she looked. Men didn't want it—they'd rather have a rifle than love, she thought, and even that nice captain would probably choose a football over Sarah.

She looked at Marshall angrily. "Men are so stupid."

He smiled.

"You're patronizing me again!"

"No, I'm not," he said gently. "I've come to get you to leave. You *have* to—the communists are going to take over."

"What do I care about that? Do you think they'll be worse than the French or the Americans? *None* of you cares about the women and children. That's why *I* have to stay with them."

"I *do* care about the children. I'm going to help you save them."

She looked at him suspiciously. "How?"

"A plane is going to fly them to America."

"Are you serious? We've been trying to get these children out for years. I'd given up hope."

"I've already arranged it. But there's a condition. You have to go with them."

"That's blackmail!"

He nodded. "Yes, there's a great deal of that going around these days—an epidemic."

"You're not joking?"

He shook his head.

"I'll have to think about it."

"Why don't we ask Father Dourmant what he thinks?"

"I know what he'd say; he'd tell me to go."

She contemplated several minutes. "All right," she said at last. "If you can get a plane to take these children out, I'll go with them. But I have a condition too."

"What?"

"That I get to come back for more children."

He nodded. "Agreed. But I can't guarantee another plane."

She laughed, then brought her hands to her face in excitement. "I haven't been in America in years; I haven't seen my family since . . . oh, my . . . Are you really serious?"

"I've already discussed it with Ambassador Bunker."

"I can't believe it," she cried. "That'll be so wonderful for these children." Her eyes welled with tears, then she shook her head. "But, you know, the way the war has been going for these poor babies, the plane will probably crash."

Marshall laughed. "Oh, even God couldn't be that perverse."

Then, gathering Sarah, they walked to the door together.

"I'll see you soon," Marshall said.

In the alley he turned to wave, but she had already closed the door, shutting in the women and children from the outside.

At Ton Son Nhut, Marshall turned on the top stair leading into the presidential aircraft for a last look at Vietnam.

Sunlight blazed off the tarmac. All movement was a shimmering mirage in the heat, unreal and otherworldly, the planes like giant insects moving ponderously across a scorched field, and in the distance he saw the sad tableau of Vietnam.

The first advisers had come seventeen years ago, another lifetime, it seemed—history, with names now out of books: Dien Bien Phu, Eisenhower, McCarthy, Khrushchev, Budapest. Even the recent names seemed lost in the refracted haze of the steamy tarmac: Kennedy and Castro, Diem and Cabot Lodge, LBJ, McNamara and Rusk, Tonkin and Green Berets, Con Tien, Khe Sanh, Tet, Buddhists and bonzes. And fifty thousand coffins forklifted onto planes like this one.

He turned and went inside, nodding to the attendants who ushered him to his seat, declining drinks, food, a mint, absently accepting a newspaper.

He settled across the aisle from Sarah, already asleep.

Vietnam was over—all the battles finished, the peace about to be signed, the POWs soon to be returned. Vietnam would be buried in mind and memory; he would not think about it again. He would look to the future. He would save Teresa and the children. He would have time for Chris; he would reconcile with his son.

He rested his head back and closed his eyes on a promising future.

He started to drift asleep, but suddenly on the inner screen of his eyes was a furious face. He jerked forward. It was the face of the man in the car window.

But he had taken care of that. There was nothing to worry about; no one would ever know.

He glanced at the newspaper in his lap to lose the face in the stories of the upcoming conventions and the peace talks. But the face would not go away.

He turned to the inside pages and read a story of five men arrested at the Watergate.

The face began to fade.

"We're cleared for takeoff, sir," an attendant said, checking his seat belt.

Marshall flipped to the entertainment section and even read the television listings.

The plane began to taxi down the runway.

The face disappeared. He took a deep breath. Vietnam

was history—finished, like the man in the window—soon to be forgotten like the little break-in at the Watergate.

He dropped the paper to the floor and closed his eyes to sleep.

After all, what was Vietnam except a little break-in at a country where they all got caught?

Who would remember? Who would care?

CHAPTER 16

Nine months later, Marshall woke one morning as light streamed through the shutters of his McLean home. He squinted against the sun striking his eyelids and looked at his watch. It was seven A.M. He slipped out of bed without waking Catherine, put on a robe, and went downstairs.

He yawned as he passed the dining room, going toward the kitchen, and nearly stumbled when he saw Chris sitting at the table. "What are you doing here?"

Chris looked up from the newspaper and pointed to the bowl of cereal before him. "Reading the sports page. Eating breakfast."

Marshall grabbed the double doors for support. "What's wrong? Why are you here? Why aren't you in school? Jesus, now what?"

Chris put down the paper. "Dad, it's spring break."

"I know! I sent you money. I thought you were going to Catalina, or Capistrano, wherever it is California college students go."

"Some go home to their parents."

"Only those with serious problems," Marshall said, clutching his chest. "And you didn't call to let us know you were coming—my God, this must be catastrophic."

Chris leaned back and put his hands behind his head. "You put on a great show, Dad. You missed your calling—you should have been on the stage instead of a diplomat."

"I should have been *anything* except a diplomat. What are you doing here? Christ, it's seven in the morning. When did you get in? What are you doing!"

"I caught the red-eye and took a cab home. I'm here because it's spring break. I'm having breakfast because I'm hungry. I'm reading the paper because it just arrived. Any more questions? I wish I'd done this well on my biology exam."

Marshall stood in the doorway a moment, then he smiled. Chris looked terrific; he seemed even taller and more fit, an extraordinarily handsome and composed young man with square jaw and light hair.

Marshall shuffled toward the table and pointed to Chris's bowl of cereal. "Didn't you want anything else for breakfast?"

"That's all I know how to make."

"Isn't Hosfa in the kitchen?"

"Who? No, no one was there."

"Shit. Hosfa was yesterday's maid. Your mother is running an underground for aliens through the house."

"Isn't that illegal?"

"Of course it's illegal! I've told your mother a thousand times, but it's like everything else I tell her—or you or your sister for that matter—she doesn't pay attention. And it's stupid besides—none of them lasts more than a few days: she spends more time hiring them than they spend working."

Chris held up the box of cereal before him. "Want some breakfast?"

"No, but I need coffee. Did you make any?"

"Instant," Chris said, handing him a jar, gesturing to a pot of hot water.

"Jesus," Marshall said, going for a cup. "So what are you doing here?"

"How about, 'Instead of going to the beach, I came home to bond with you'?"

"Oh, bullshit," Marshall said, dropping into a chair, stirring coffee. "What's wrong? You flunked out. You wrecked the car."

Chris laughed. "Dad, I came home to be with you; it's time we got close."

"You're serious—that's it?"

"That's it? I think that's a pretty big thing, Dad. No, I didn't flunk out, I didn't wreck the car, no girl is pregnant, nothing is wrong. I just thought I'd come home and hang out with you for a while."

"Hang out?"

Chris grinned. "You know, a father-and-son thing, do guy stuff—drink beer, watch TV, toss the ball around, maybe chase some babes."

Marshall laughed. "You're serious—this is why you came? To be with me?"

Chris nodded. "Yeah. I figured it was time. Ryan's gone. I'm the son, you're the father—all we have is each other. Why put this off?"

Marshall stared at his son for a long minute; he hung his head, then he got out of his chair and went to Chris. Chris stood. They looked at each other, then they hugged.

"Thank you for coming," Marshall said, not letting go, hugging even tighter. "Thank you for forgiving me."

"Thank you for accepting me."

Marshall shook his head. "It was never like that, Chris." Then he smiled. "But you'll be happy to know that after our last talk, I did slash my wrists. And I've been seeing a psychiatrist regularly to find out where I went wrong. He suggested electric shock therapy—for you. You can do it during spring break."

Chris grinned. "It's too late, Dad. Besides, I don't want to change my 'sexual orientation' as we call it today. I'm happy the way I am."

Marshall nodded. "I'll tell you a story you probably don't remember. When you were four, you insisted on wearing a dress your mother bought for Sarah. We tried to dissuade you, but you were insistent, so finally we relented. You went upstairs to change. When you came down, you were radiant—I had never seen you so happy. You skipped about in the dress, dancing around the room."

Marshall shook his head at the memory. "I knew from that day what was going to be. But it was all right, can you understand? I wasn't *happy* about it, but it didn't make any difference—I didn't love you less. And I couldn't have loved you more."

Chris lowered his head. "I remember that dress, Dad—I

was hoping *you* had forgotten." He grinned. "Maybe I did it just to piss you off. Anyway, I never wore a dress again. Maybe it'd been easier if I had—if I'd been a mincing queen. But I wasn't."

"No, you certainly weren't. But was that a reaction—the sports an escape?"

Chris shook his head. "I like sports—*that* was the problem. Ryan was the intellectual; I was the dumb jock. I just happened to like guys. I had to listen to a thousand locker-room jokes about fags, join in all the put-downs so no one would suspect I was queer, and I felt guilty not just because I was a coward, but because I was denying what I felt I shouldn't have to hide. To me it was natural, as natural as throwing a ball. That's why I finally had to get this out—I can't spend the rest of my life in a closet. I am what I am—I'm not apologizing. That's why I was angry with you before. I thought *you* felt I should apologize—that I had done something wrong."

"But you've forgiven me?"

Chris nodded. "I realized you'd been really good about it—you never made an issue out of my sexuality, even though I knew you knew. I don't think you could have done better. The problem was mine—I felt I was disappointing you, but that was *my* insecurity. That's over now. I've decided I don't have a problem, others do. I'm not going to hide anything, but I'm not going to walk around with a chip on my shoulder either. I'm glad we got this all out, because now we can move on to other things. You like girls, I like guys. Why don't we let it go at that?"

Marshall nodded in earnest relief. "Yes. Absolutely. Want a beer?"

Chris hit his father's arm with exaggerated machismo. "Sure, man. Then let's go toss the pigskin, then nail some babes."

"Well, what *would* you like to do while you're here?"

Chris sat back at the table and mixed another bowl of cereal. "I got a week, I'm sure we can come up with something. What do you have planned?"

Marshall grabbed a bowl from the china closet and sat across from him. He picked up the cereal and looked at it.

"I don't think I've had a bowl of Rice Krispies in thirty years. Do they still snap, crackle, and pop?"

Chris munched a mouthful. "I don't know, Dad—I don't listen to my breakfast."

Marshall poured milk and bent over the bowl. "They do," he said happily. "I don't have much planned. I'm supposed to be in court at the end of the week, but I can get a postponement. You want to go somewhere?"

"You mean like fishing or skiing? Nah. Let's just play it day by day here—you pick a day, I'll pick a day. But you go first—I'm beat after the flight."

Marshall spooned cereal into his mouth. "Fine. There's only one thing I have to do today, and I want you to come with me. This is a command performance. You might even enjoy it. There's a possibility the President will be there—it's a great photo opportunity, so he might show. You can meet him, and Kissinger too."

"Sarah would never forgive me. Is Mother going?"

"Actually she is."

"It must really be something for her to show up at the same place with Richard Nixon."

"It *is* special. The only thing I accomplished on my last trip to Vietnam was to get a planeload of children out of the country. They're arriving late this afternoon at Andrews."

Chris's head came up from his cereal with a startled look.

"I went to Vietnam to help end the war and find out about Ryan, but the only good I did was to arrange to fly a planeload of orphans out. They were in a clinic run by an American woman, the most wonderful person in the world—your sister met her. I've worked on it for nine months. You wouldn't believe the crap I've gone through with the State Department and Naturalization and Immigration, but it's all worked out. They're coming in around five, and I want you there."

Chris's jaw dropped. He started to say something, then closed his mouth.

"It'll be a great ceremony, not boring at all," Marshall enthused. "It'll go for about an hour, then Teresa and the children will be taken to a special clinic for a couple days' quarantine, then the children will be sent to foster homes, and Teresa will come here. You'll like her, Chris."

"Dad . . . ," Chris started. He stared at his father but was unable to say anything.

"What's wrong? I'm asking you to go to the airport, not an opera. This isn't a 'cultural' event, Chris—it won't *hurt,* I promise."

Chris stared at him uncertainly. "You . . . you don't know?"

"What?"

Chris looked away, then let out his breath and pushed the newspaper toward his father.

Marshall scanned the front page of the *Washington Post.* There was only one picture—a wide lens shot taken of children inside an airplane. They were being strapped into seats by smiling stewardesses and balloons were everywhere. It was a festive, happy picture.

But above it was the headline "Mercy Flight Crashes on Takeoff," with the subheadline "All on Board Killed, Including 360 Children." The dateline was Saigon, yesterday.

Marshall stared at the paper dumbly. "It can't be," he said in a dull voice.

Chris went to him. "It was on the news last night, Dad. I heard it as I was driving to the airport. I didn't know you had anything to do with it."

"It's not true!" Marshall said, rising from his seat. "Teresa! No!"

He stumbled backward and Chris caught him.

"It can't be."

He struggled away. "No! I don't believe it." He cast about frantically, then threw the newspaper to the floor, then he knocked the cereal off the table.

"Dad!" Chris had never seen his father like this. He was wild, searching for something to latch onto, reaching out for the air, pounding it with his hands.

"No!" he yelled, shaking his head back and forth. "No!"

Finally Chris grabbed him, put his arms around him, and squeezed against the fury bursting from his father. Marshall twisted and strained, but Chris held tightly, and finally Marshall went slack. Chris eased him into the chair.

Marshall's head dropped to the table. "Oh, God. I tried to save them. It's the only thing I did over there. Oh my God, no! Those poor babies."

He looked up in agony. "Teresa," he cried. Then he shook his head and rose. "No, it can't be. No one's called. I would have been informed. The White House would have called. There must be a mistake."

Chris pushed him down in the chair and sat beside him. "Dad, it was on every newscast; I saw pictures on TV during my layover in Chicago. The plane was taking off from Saigon with orphans. There was a band, and a big ceremony, and it started to climb, then it fell from about two thousand feet right after takeoff. There were no survivors. They don't know yet if the plane was overloaded, or there was mechanical failure, just that it went down and the crash was scattered over miles."

Marshall stared at him in disbelief. It can't be, he thought wildly. He and Teresa had joked about this. No god could be so cruel. No, it wasn't possible. He had meant to do good. This was going to be his legacy. This is what he was going to salvage out of Vietnam. This is all that mattered. It *couldn't* end in death and destruction.

The phone rang. Chris picked it up. He listened a moment, then said calmly, "I'm sorry, Ambassador Marshall can't come to the phone. Yes, he's aware of the crash."

There was a pause, then Chris said thank-you and hung up. "That was the White House," he said to his father.

Marshall pushed himself from the table as the terror struck home.

This *was* his legacy.

The phone rang again. Chris listened a moment. "Ambassador Marshall has nothing to say," he said, hanging up, leaving the phone off the hook.

Marshall brought his hands to his face and he sobbed, "This is my fault. I killed them. Oh, God! I can't stand it; I can't live with this."

"No, Dad. You know better than that. This is just . . . what—God? Fate? It has nothing to do with you."

"It has *everything* to do with me," he cried. "I went there. I tried to save them. It was going to be the only thing I accomplished. What's left?"

He was staring into Chris's face. His son was strong, powerful, and decent, and they had finally reconciled. He loved him. Chris and Sarah were all he had left.

Then, suddenly, looking into his son's face, he saw another face—the man in the car window in Saigon.

Marshall jumped up, knocking over the chair.

"What's wrong?" Chris asked.

Marshall backed away. "Oh, Christ! No!"

"What?"

"Oh my God," Marshall said, backing away, raising his hands to ward off the shards of Vietnam as they fell on him, as the full horror hit him like the plane smashing to the earth. "You're next."

Part II

REPARATIONS

CHAPTER 1

Washington, D.C., December 1978

Bradley Marshall sat across from the President of the United States; they were alone in the White House dining room, somber and dark—the chandeliers were not lit and the curtains were drawn—appropriately fitting for the discussion before them, Marshall thought.

Having finished his dinner, he ran his finger around the rim of the empty plate embossed with the presidential seal, then he lifted his glass of apple juice, holding up the crystal to watch apple pulp swirl.

Jesus Christ, he thought to himself, but instead asked the President mildly, "Exactly what is it you want me to contact the Ayatollah Khomeini about?"

"The possibilities of future contact," Jimmy Carter said serenely.

Marshall lowered the goblet. "But we are still backing the Shah of Iran."

"Absolutely."

"Yet I am to meet with the Ayatollah?"

"Yes."

Marshall could not believe that he had just eaten a six-course meal in the private dining room of the President of the United States, sipping apple cider. But everything about the evening and this visit had been bizarre.

Offered the ambassadorship to France last year by Carter, both as reward for past service to Democratic administrations and because an old friend, the French foreign minister, indicated a preference for him, Marshall had accepted gratefully. Sarah and Chris were out of college, Vietnam was lost in the past, and he chafed to get back to diplomatic work. Besides, Catherine wanted to go—she craved respite from whales and trees.

Five years of corporate law practice had numbed him. He was beginning at last to feel his age—fifty-two. His hair was grayer, he was a little thicker around the middle, and he was sure he had shrunk an inch. Washington had dulled him, and he felt Paris would revive him. It had; he felt completely rejuvenated, and now he was even thinking of dyeing his hair.

Previously he had had only a perfunctory meeting with the President, thus he was surprised when Carter summoned him from Paris for a private meeting, and to stay as a guest in the White House. He had expected to meet with the secretary of state also, but he and the President had dined alone.

Until this week, Marshall's role as ambassador had been social and ceremonial. The position was hardly a challenge; he felt anyone who could maneuver a room without falling down could be an ambassador, yet he had to admit that he enjoyed the constant attention and stroking.

But a single meeting with the President had changed that.

The meal had been serious and intense, without humor, but then, the subjects under discussion were hardly jocular: the fall of the Shah of Iran, the return of Islamic fundamentalism, the future of the Mideast.

Marshall wanted to like Jimmy Carter; he knew he *should* like Carter—the man was kind and good and honest, the most sincere, decent man to sit in the Oval Office in his lifetime, a fine, admirable man dedicated to making the world a better place—and utterly unsuited for the job. He was, after all, a peanut farmer from Plains, Georgia, who had brought only good ol' boys as his trusted aides and confidants to Washington where the entire world looked for guidance.

Marshall had served five presidents without trusting any of them—they were all self-serving and lied with breathtaking ease. Kennedy he had liked; certainly he might have become a great president, but his term had been only unfulfilled potential. Johnson was complex and diabolical, all theater, a sellout show even when you wanted to throw tomatoes, but Marshall had liked him even more than he distrusted him. Nixon he had despised; Ford, he could hardly remember.

But Carter was disturbing, for there was a fanaticism about him that made the opinions of others, or even truth, irrelevant. Yet Carter had been genuinely gracious throughout the visit and possessed a keen grasp of world affairs, or at least of their details. At dinner he had discoursed on the Shah, Islam, the complexities of the Mideast, Christians, Moslems, and Jews, and at the end of the meal, he had instructed Marshall to make covert contact with the Ayatollah Khomeini.

"After the Shah exiled Khomeini, he fled to Iraq. Now Saddam Hussein has thrown him out. France has granted him asylum and he's living outside Paris. I want you to contact him."

Marshall drew cider over his tongue as with a fine wine, but a piece of pulp caught between his teeth.

"There are moderates around the Ayatollah with whom we might be able to deal. I want you to open a conduit to Khomeini."

Marshall worked at the apple piece with his tongue, but it would not budge.

"We support the Shah, but he might not survive. We must look to the future. Khomeini might be that future. But we don't want the Shah to get the wrong impression. The situation is delicate."

Marshall gave up on the apple between his teeth. "Mr. President, I first encountered Khomeini when Lyndon Johnson sent me to the Mideast twelve years ago. I found him an intractable man of fanatical convictions. I found no moderates around him. I don't believe there is a 'moderate' Moslem fundamentalist."

Carter smiled. "I am a 'moderate' Christian fundamentalist, Mr. Ambassador. There are Jewish moderates; every religion has them. I am sure you will find them around the Ayatollah; perhaps the Ayatollah is one himself."

Marshall recalled a day in Qom sitting across from the

black-robed Khomeini with glaring eyes, accusing finger, and ranting rhetoric, and he did not remember a moderate, but neither did he see one in the man sitting across from him: he saw a zealot convinced of his rightness—a man not unlike Khomeini, he thought.

Yet Carter had been remarkably successful in personal diplomacy; perhaps only he could have reconciled Egyptians and Israelis. He was, Marshall acknowledged, charismatic in a purifying way, like a Jenn-Air self-cleaning oven. Now he was turning that charisma on Marshall. But it wasn't working; he liked the smile, the friendliness, the intensity—he liked the facade of Jimmy Carter, but not his substance.

Or maybe it was just the apple pulp, he thought; how could he concentrate with the damn thing caught between his teeth?

He said reasonably, "Mr. President, Arabs believe 'a friend of my enemy is my enemy.' We are the Shah's friend, therefore we are the Ayatollah's enemy. Besides, Hussein is his enemy, and many in the CIA, at Defense, and State want us to tilt towards Iraq. But to gain the Ayatollah's friendship, we can't—we must break with the Shah and condemn Hussein."

"We can't do that."

"I understand the *difficulties*, but Arabs view the world in absolutes. They are emotional people who don't reason as we do. We must choose one or the other."

Surely Carter had been advised by the State Department and the CIA of the impossibility of dealing with the Shah and Khomeini at the same time. But charismatic men possessed by purpose seldom listened to advice. That explained why they were dining alone, he realized—everyone else was disassociating himself from the folly.

Carter smiled dazzlingly. "I know you can convey the proper message."

Marshall would have smiled back, except for the apple pulp. "I'm still a little uncertain of this message," he said with tight irony. "Let me see if I have it: I am to tell the Ayatollah that we are 'interested' in him, perhaps might want to be his friend in the event something happens to his hated enemy, who is now our friend."

"You *are* clever," Carter said, teeth gleaming, missing the irony altogether.

Jesus, Marshall thought in exasperation. "Mr. President, that is exactly what we cannot do. In the Mideast, it's a matter of absolutes—there is no middle ground."

"That can't be our policy."

"Then our policy cannot succeed."

Carter smiled indulgently. "Let me assume responsibility for policy, Mr. Ambassador. You just implement it."

God damn! Marshall thought; there is nothing more obtuse than a fanatic. He considered a moment, then tried another tack. "We are just now recovering from Vietnam, Mr. President. Many perceive that we abandoned Vietnam. If we signal we are now abandoning the Shah, others will think we can't be trusted."

"We are *not* abandoning the Shah—we are merely looking at options."

He was not going to get through to this man, Marshall saw. He had a choice—tender his resignation and watch someone else botch the situation or accept and make the best of it—which might only mean avoiding a disaster.

It was, he sighed to himself, the old dilemma—abandon ship and let it sink or risk drowning by trying to bring it to port. Better to stay on board, he decided; he was a good navigator; he was confident he could avoid disaster. Besides, he liked being ambassador. He deserved it—especially after this horseshit, he thought. "All right, Mr. President, I'll do what I can."

After dinner, Marshall fled to his upstairs bedroom to pour a stiff drink from a bottle of Scotch he had smuggled in.

Sipping gratefully, he studied his reflection in the bureau mirror. He *had* shrunk, he decided. And his hair was thinning. He *would* dye it. But he'd better ask Catherine first.

After a second drink, he felt so relaxed and fortified he thought he could manage to talk to his children. Actually that would be a treat for them, getting a call from the White House, so he lifted the phone and gave the White House operator the numbers for Sarah and Chris. "They may not be home," he said.

"We'll find them," the operator said matter-of-factly.

Indeed, the White House operators were justifiably renowned for their ability to locate anyone, and Marshall just hoped they didn't trace Chris to a bathhouse somewhere, or Sarah to an abortion clinic.

Sarah, twenty-six, after Teresa Hawthorne's death, had turned to nursing; now she was living in Berkeley, California, doing social work.

Chris, twenty-four, with a degree in business from Stanford, had moved to New York with someone named Trent. He had a job in international investments with Chase Manhattan, but was considering other "career options."

In a moment, the operator had Sarah on the line.

"Sarah!"

"Dad! What's wrong?"

"Nothing is wrong. Why do you think something is wrong?"

"My God, the White House calls—I thought you were dead. Is Mother all right?"

"Yes, of course. How are you? Where are you?"

"I'm at home. Jesus, Jim answered and almost had a heart attack."

"Who?"

"Jim. The guy I'm living with."

"What happened to Brent?"

"Brent's fine; we're still good friends, but I'm living with Jim. Why did you call?"

"I was showing off. I think I'll cancel the call to Chris."

"Good idea, Dad—God only knows where you'll find him. What are you doing in Washington? I thought you were in Paris. Were you fired?"

"Of course not; I'm staying with President Carter—I thought I'd call everybody I knew. Tell me about your life. Any plans? I mean, marriage to . . . Jim or anything?"

"Marriage?"

"It's a quaint old custom—two people living together have this piece of paper called a marriage certificate, but I suppose it's terribly passé. How about visiting?"

"I'm coming for Christmas—didn't Mom tell you? I'll be there next week."

"No, your mother didn't tell me, but I don't see much of

her these days—I think she's living at Fauchon's. That's great though, we'd love to have you."

"And Jim?"

"He's not worse than Bosco, is he?"

"Don't you ever forget anything?"

"No, I'm your father. Besides, Bosco took ten years off my life. I'll never forget him—it was like having a six-foot, two-hundred-pound erection camped on your doorstep."

There was a pause, then Sarah said, "Bosco's dead, Dad. He was killed two years ago. A truck jackknifed across the highway—he was decapitated."

Marshall fell silent remembering the young, buzz-haired boy who had been so in love with his daughter when she was a teenager, actually a sweet boy, he remembered.

"Dear God," Marshall said; then after a second, "Well, I guess that wraps up this conversation. I'll see you next week."

"You might not recognize me; I had my hair cut."

Any change had to be an improvement, he thought. Over the years, her hair had grown more and more frizzy; the last time he saw her she looked as if she'd been electrocuted. "I'm trying to decide whether to dye *my* hair, Sarah. What do you think?"

"I thought you already were."

"Good-bye, dear." There was a pause, then, "I love you, Sarah."

"Dad, when you say that, it sounds like you're never going to see me again."

"That's always my fear."

As soon as he hung up, the operator told him Chris was on the line.

"Chris?"

There was massive confusion on the other end.

"Chris? Jesus! Chris!"

All he could hear was incredible noise that was either music or the end of the world.

"Dad? Is that you, Dad?"

"Chris! What's going on? I've never heard such a racket. Are you all right?"

"Dad?"

"God damn it! Yes, it's your father. Where the hell are you?"

"Just a minute. Hang on." There was more noise, muffled sounds, then a semblance of privacy. "Dad, is that you? You're at the White House? Holy shit!"

"I just spent a hundred thousand dollars for you to go to Stanford, and that's what I get—'holy shit'?"

"Dad, this is *big*-time. I'm at Studio 54. *Nothing* impresses these people, but they drag me off the dance floor and tell me the White House is calling. Wow!"

"A hundred thousand dollars," Marshall mourned.

"It didn't cost you anywhere near that—I had a baseball scholarship—but Dad, this is terrific. Thanks!"

"Aren't you going to ask me if something is wrong? If I'm dead or something?"

"You sound great. Hey, Dad, this is real status; I mean, I'll always be able to get in here now. You know, the only White House person around here is Hamilton Jordan, but . . . well, you know about him."

"I certainly don't."

"You know who he is, don't you?"

"Of course, Jimmy Carter's aide. You mean, *he* goes to Studio 54? My God, this country is completely out of control."

Chris laughed. "Why did you call, Dad?"

"I guess I was drunk."

"At the White House?"

"Never mind. How's everything?"

"Everything's great, Dad. I'm still with Trent—you know about him, don't you?"

Marshall murmured noncommittally.

"He was on the football team—actually he was a seventh-round pro draft pick, but he turned it down to come to New York. You'll love him."

"I'm sure."

"And I got some big news."

"I don't know if I want to hear about this—I'm not that drunk."

Chris laughed. "Okay. I'll tell you at Christmas. I'm coming to Paris then."

"Why?" Then Marshall laughed. "We'd love to have you. Sarah's coming too. It'll be a real family reunion."

"Sounds gross."

"Well, I don't want to keep you from your friends. Give my regards to Hamilton."

"Say hi to Jimmy for me." Chris paused a moment, then asked very seriously, "Is everything okay, Dad?"

Marshall smiled, thinking of his son worrying about him. "Well, I've been thinking of dyeing my hair. What's your opinion?"

"I thought you'd been doing it for years."

"Jesus! Chris?"

"Yeah, Dad?"

"I love you."

Chris paused again. "I know. I love you too, Dad."

Marshall hung up. That wasn't too bad, he thought; his children seemed all right—they were healthy and employed, seemingly happy, and relatively drug-free, he supposed.

All in all, he and Catherine had done a good job. Everything in his life was going well—he was a blessed man, happy with job and family, in love with his wife, and she still loved him. He was at the top of his career. Yes, Marshall thought, everything was fine. Vietnam was behind him, and the future bright. He *would* dye his hair.

Hiding the Scotch bottle in his suitcase, Marshall prepared to go to bed.

The only irritant in his life was Carter and this Khomeini nonsense.

Twelve years ago, when Johnson sent him as an envoy to the Mideast, Marshall had told him to stay out. "Ten centuries of warfare between Christians, Moslems, and Jews aren't going to be resolved by a battalion of Marines. Caesar Augustus and Richard the Lionhearted couldn't do anything, and neither can you."

That advice was still good, Marshall believed. He brushed his teeth.

The last thing the U.S. should do was get involved with Arabs in the Mideast. Jimmy Carter and America would pay a dear price for that folly, he thought, and a lot of good Christian boys who didn't know Shiite from shiitake from shit would die never knowing.

He climbed into bed and turned off the bedside lamp.

His last thought before sleep was the satisfying one that he was in a position to ensure that this didn't happen.

CHAPTER 2

On the same day, in a suburban neighborhood in Alexandria, Virginia, a few miles from the White House, Wilson Lord concentrated on catching a baseball in the fading light of the front yard of his modest brick rancher. Lance was almost twelve, and he threw a hard fastball. Lord's eyes were not as good as before, his reflexes not as quick—he was fifty-two—and he figured he had only another year of tossing the ball with Lance before his son would be doing *him* the favor of playing catch; then he would put aside his glove forever, for he would allow no one to patronize him.

"Wilson!" Anh, a small graying woman watching her husband and son, called happily from the porch. "You have a phone call."

Calls were rare. Telephones jangled in heaven and hell, but seldom rang in limbo, where Wilson Lord had been sent after his recall from Vietnam six years ago. The Trung affair had torpedoed his career, and he had lain submerged in the Mariana Trench at Langley. Only now was he resurfacing. He had been vindicated about Vietnam; everything he had predicted had come to pass, and he was on his way back from the nether reaches when Jimmy Carter had been elected president with "human rights" as a major foreign-policy concern. The timing had been unfortunate—as if Dracula had come out of the grave at a convention of stake drivers.

Lord's return had been interrupted; brought from the depths, he had yet to be given a major posting, so he had time to play baseball with Lance. He even coached Little League and settled into a happy home life with Anh. Though he ground his teeth at the direction of American foreign policy, the rosin bag on the Little League field absorbed his bitterness.

He handed his mitt and the ball to Anh. She pounded the mitt professionally, then looped the ball into another yard.

"Aw, Mom," Lance moaned, throwing down his mitt.

Lord laughed and went into the house.

"My dear Wilson," came a familiar voice, older, but still strong and ironic. "Could you possibly drop by to visit an old man. Say in about thirty minutes?"

A half hour later Lord was sitting in the library of the man's luxurious, antique-filled brownstone in Georgetown where the loudest noise was the ticking of a Seth Thomas clock. They had not seen each other for years, since the older man's service had been terminated by Carter. The man was tall and thin, fifteen years older than Lord, silver haired, with penetrating eyes and keen mind. A legend who had helped found the OSS, appointed by four presidents to high positions, he had been Lord's benefactor since Korea. He had helped get Lance and Anh out of Vietnam after Lord's recall, but he had not been able to save Lord, or even himself, from Carter and his "handwringers" as he called them.

Nursing a martini, the man came directly to the point as they sat across from one another in worn leather chairs before the fireplace. "Wilson, I need help. Pahlavi is a friend. I like to stand by my friends, though I'm not sure it will do him much good—I'm not sanguine about his future."

Lord thought he was talking about the Shah's chances for survival in Iran; demonstrations had broken out in all the large cities. "I'm less sanguine about the alternatives to him."

"I meant his health; he has cancer. Even if he survives a coup, he won't live long. Khomeini is inevitable—if *he* survives."

"Is he unwell too?" Lord asked wryly.

The man grimaced. "He's old, but not terminally. Apparently clean living has something to recommend it."

"Then he and Jimmy Carter might live forever."

The man pressed his chest in distress. "Please; I'm not that well myself." Then he went on. "Pahlavi has *many* friends; several of us have discussed his plight and tried to place it in larger perspective—the canvas of the Mideast as a whole."

He pointed to Lord's empty glass. Lord declined; he seldom drank and knew his host drank only one martini every night.

"What is the greatest threat to American security, Wilson?"

"The current administration."

"Indeed. Four more years will create irreparable havoc." He said grimly, "Many—you should be able to guess their names—want to prevent this. Most of us are private citizens now, though we look forward to future service when the Republicans return to the White House. That is what we are working towards, and why I am enlisting your help."

He didn't even wait for Lord's acknowledgment. "Iran after the Shah will be a foreign-policy nightmare dwarfing Vietnam; the Mideast will become an inferno incinerating American interests. Jimmy Carter in the White House trying to control it would be like Pinocchio trying to piss out the fires of hell."

Lord nodded. "The communists will take over the Iranian oil fields and get their warm-water port."

"Oh, *Wilson,*" the man said in disappointment. "Are you still hung up on communists? Communism is a hollow shell. There's nothing to fear, and Moslem fanatics are hardly going to align themselves with communist atheists. Communism is terminal; one needn't fear contagion. No one is defecting to Russia. It's like with Japan—it might have a powerful economy, but are people landing on its shores to become *Japanese?* Can you imagine anyone *wanting* to be Japanese?"

Then his eyes lit like fire. "I want you to study the Japs, Wilson. *There's* the danger. Forget the communists and the krauts, they're both bankrupt ideologies—Germans aren't anything for *us* to worry about; they'll implode on their own hatred. But the Japs, ah . . . they're admirably evil, and so *busy.*"

He shook his head in mirth. "And communism? Wilson, communism *was* the bogeyman, but *we* weren't supposed to believe in him. For heaven's sake, do you suppose the popes believed in the devil, immaculate conceptions, and sacred foreskin? How quaint you are. But, Wilson, I didn't bring you from banishment to refight the Cold War. I brought you back to save American interests in the Mideast. Iran."

Lord shook his head. "I'm not a Mideast expert."

"Who is? Certainly not those who live there. That's not important anyway. The handwringers lost Vietnam, now they're going to lose the Mideast. All that nonsense about human rights, and now tears over Savak, the Shah's secret police, as if those mullah fundamentalists won't bring back tortures and horror unknown since the Middle Ages."

He was so agitated he spat into the fire. *"Assholes."* He drained his martini, then went to the bar to mix another. Lord had never seen him so angry, heard him swear, or seen him have a second drink. "Our staunchest ally! Our best friend!" He shook the gin and vermouth violently. "When the Shah falls—"

"Is he going to fall?"

"Falls or dies—in any case, not with us—then we'll face a grave dilemma: find a replacement more popular than Khomeini, or eliminate Khomeini." He returned to his seat and sipped his drink with distaste, holding it up to the light. "I didn't just bruise it, I smashed it; Carter *has* to go—I can't drink wounded martinis for four more years."

"Is there no other solution?"

"Of course," the man said in disgust as he sipped his battered gin. "The one Jimmy found—make an overture to Khomeini, try to work with Islamic fundamentalists. He's doing that right now through an old acquaintance of yours."

"Bradley Marshall," Lord supplied through clenched teeth.

The man nodded. "I thought you'd be interested."

"That bastard," Lord seethed.

"Brad? He's a lovely man; I quite enjoy him. He's cultured and clever, and Catherine is so amusing. Of course, one has to overlook Brad's politics—I mean, trafficking with Jimmy Carter, that is *too* much. But he means well."

"Marshall is meeting with Khomeini?"

"That's what my White House sources tell me. Unfortunately, if anyone can negotiate an understanding between a Baptist Bible-banger and a lunatic Shiite Moslem, it would be Bradley Marshall. We can't have that."

"No, we can't." So the bastard was back. Not just rewarded with an ambassadorship for his perfidies in Asia, the son of a bitch was now going to sabotage his country's interests in another region. "What do you want me to do?" Lord asked furiously.

The man sipped his martini. "When the Shah falls, or his cancer gets worse, he'll need asylum and medical attention. It would be foolish to allow him to enter America, but it *would* be compassionate. Jimmy *is* compassionate; many will press to grant the Shah asylum. I have no doubt he will—inviting hatred, chaos, and retribution in Iran."

Lord frowned. "I see the *outline* in your canvas, but not the details."

"There aren't any yet—merely possibilities, but it doesn't make any difference. All we need is chaos, then let Jimmy handle it."

"A monkey trying to fuck a football."

The man grimaced. "I wouldn't know that analogy—I'm not a sports enthusiast, or into animal sex either. But I am interested in chaos—the greater the better. Create some possibilities in Iran for us, Wilson: instability, revolution, hostages, war with Iraq. Give us something to work with, and Jimmy something to fuck up."

He opened his hands. "There are all kinds of possibilities—one that might solve all our problems is Saddam Hussein. Give him serious thought, Wilson. Hussein is a pragmatic man; he'd never allow principle to interfere with practicality. We can work with him, and he's a bitter enemy of the Ayatollah. He's also the only man in the region who can resist Islamic fundamentalism. All he wants is arms and respectability—hardly unreasonable demands. He may be the key to the future."

The man lifted his martini to Lord. "Ensure Carter's overtures to Khomeini fail."

"Don't worry. I will. With a vengeance. I've been waiting to settle accounts with Marshall. That bastard *owes*."

The man smiled. "I knew you were the man for this." He

set down his drink. "Well, there you are, Wilson. We want you to go out and win this one for the Gipper."

"I beg your pardon?" Lord asked in genuine confusion.

The man frowned. "Maybe I don't have that down right; as I told you, I'm not a sports fan, or a movie fan either, but I think you'll be hearing more of that term."

"Oh," Lord said in understanding. "Ronald Reagan."

The man beamed. "Wouldn't that be lovely?"

"I thought he was stupid," Lord ventured.

"All the *more* lovely. Lazy and dumb—what more could you ask for in a president?"

"Will I be working alone? Autonomously? How much support can I expect?"

The man smiled. "You will be completely autonomous and have all the support you desire. The 'group' I represent has contacts everywhere—the White House, Congress, in business and banking, and within the Agency, of course. Just let me know your needs. I have, however, taken the liberty of getting you one man. He has a rather special talent. Perhaps you've heard of him—Mike Caldwell."

Lord nodded with a smile. "I have."

"Some say he's a younger you. He has a fine reputation in his work; I don't believe he's ever failed. He's arriving in Paris tomorrow."

Then he said sadly, "There is *one* restriction, of course—the usual."

Lord nodded. "To fall on my sword if something goes wrong."

"I'm afraid so." The man sighed. "But you will be taken care of, and your family. You know that. You can trust us."

Lord stood. "I do. Completely."

They shook hands and Lord left the man sipping his martini, staring into the fire, smiling at roasting handwringers.

Lord suppressed his jubilation as he drove home. He was back in the game at last. Even better, he had a real cause to fight for—the Shah, American interests—and a truly worthy opponent, someone he owed: Bradley Marshall.

He could hardly contain his eagerness. But then the reality of what this would entail settled in. He would have to leave Anh and Lance; there would be no more Little League games, and no more lying with Anh for a long while.

But this mission was worth it. And he had carte blanche; he was backed by men of power and influence.

Even before his car pulled into his driveway, his plan was emerging. He would go to Paris immediately; he would stay in a safe house, and he had the best contract man in the Agency working for him—Mike Caldwell was *indeed* known to him.

When he bounded up the steps to the house, Anh knew from the glint in his eye that he was leaving, but she smiled for him—she hadn't seen him this happy in years.

CHAPTER 3

Paris, December 1978

Rain, falling darkly over the cemetery of Père Lachaise, ran in rivulets from the mounds of the newly buried and streamed into the crevices of the old graves. Pools of water formed in the open mausoleums, reflecting the dull sky of a late December afternoon.

The cemetery was deserted, the mourners from the last burial gone hours ago; the only sounds were the rain and the scratching of skeletal limbs of barren trees in the wind.

Beyond the mile of high masonry walls that enclosed the cemetery within the heart of Paris, heavy gusts blew sheets of rain against the pavement. Pedestrians, hunched into the wind with beaten-back umbrellas, trudged past the bleak entrance with no glance or thought to the dead within.

Once the most fashionable burial ground in Paris, the sepulchres were broken into long ago and the tombs sacked. During wars and famines in the last century, the cemetery became a macabre, miniature city of marble and stone for those seeking shelter and warmth. The baroque dwellings of the dead housed the living and reeked of their sweat and waste and, at night, moaned and sighed from the copulations on the sarcophagi.

But in this century the cemetery became fashionable again, a tourist attraction for those interested in funerary architecture or the final resting places of the famous dead, and now a guard stands watch at the entrance of Père Lachaise. On good days visitors wander the paths of elaborate mausoleums and statuary, past stone angels and cherubim, and mourning marble women who watch over martyred poets and tragic composers, and now a chanteuse and even a rock star.

Yet on this dark and forbidding day there was only one tourist, and the young, bored, and cold guard remained within the gatehouse inside the entrance, reading a glossy magazine with pictures of naked women.

Within the cemetery, cats crouched in the sepulchres and peered out with glacial eyes at the rain, and at the solitary man walking under an umbrella, stopping dutifully before each of the graves circled on the map given him by the guard, who would later recall him as an ordinary, middle-aged Japanese tourist in a dark suit.

There was no expression on the man's face; he peered with eyes as cold as the cats' at the plastic flowers strewn before Chopin, and at the pornographic graffiti scrawled above Jim Morrison; nor did he register anything, even irony, at the huge monument to Oscar Wilde with its penis broken off.

Chien Lin Huong's face, broad and powerful, Manchurian, not Japanese, was a mask of indifference as he walked up the Avenue Principale past the mansions for the dead, baroque marble vaults whose bronze doors and grilled gates were ajar, their stained-glass windows smashed, the tombs opened—the fashionable quarter, looted and sacked.

At the end of the avenue loomed the Monument to the Fallen, a huge sculpture of a man and woman, he with bowed head, hers raised, an arm on his shoulder, the other lifted, welcoming him into the chamber of death.

For thirty minutes Huong walked the paths that twisted through the necropolis. Before two tombs connected by bronze hands, a man and wife joined from the grave in a perpetual clasp, he stiffened, and before the grave of a child, flanked by grieving angels, he lingered a long moment.

As it darkened, the mournful statuary seemed to come alive, the wings of the angels dipping in the lengthening shadows, the folds of their marble robes rustling in the wind.

Cats slipped from the tombs to prowl in the crepuscular

light, making a wide arc, following the man walking toward the middle of the cemetery.

Finally, in the center where all paths merged, Huong came to a tiered, horseshoe-shaped columbarium, a vast stone honeycomb of ashes, a looming, incongruous high-rise for fifty thousand dead. With hardly a glance at it, he descended to an underground entrance with deliberate, cautious steps.

At the bottom he stood in a shallow pool of water that had collected before a metal, open-grilled gate. When he swung the gate open, water splashed over his shoes, creating a wavelike effect on a dark sea.

Suddenly an overwhelming rush of pain broke over him, a hurt so great that he clutched the gate for support, for reflected in the pool and in his mind were the dark waters of the South China Sea and the refugee boat, and screams, scream after scream from his wife as they beat and raped her, and from his mother, her head raised to the sky, howling as blood poured from her mouth, a red cavity gushing blood as they ripped out her gold teeth—an old, old woman garbed in rags, fleeing in a boat, clawing at her face, so maddened by pain that when they hurled her into the dark sea she continued to scream until she disappeared into the depths, her mouth open and contorted, her hands not even reaching up to implore for help but groping at her ruptured mouth.

He gripped the gate to keep from slipping to the ground, into madness, as his mother had sunk beneath the waves, leaving no trace on the cold fathoms.

He pulled himself up; he would not let that happen, not when he was so close to the end of his journey. For six years he had pursued Bradley Marshall, since the day Marshall's limousine ran over his daughter and Marshall had left her like an animal, broken and mangled. Nothing mattered to him after that except revenge; all other tragedies and horrors paled beside the loss of his daughter.

Like Job in the story the old priest had told him, he had lost everything. It began with the death of his daughter, but then he was pursued by the South Vietnamese government.

He couldn't understand what was happening as he was incessantly hounded; he was stripped of his holdings in Vietnam and pursued by the authorities.

His passport was confiscated and he couldn't leave the country; his businesses were shut down, his warehouses taken over by the tax officials, and each day brought new summonses and lawsuits. Finally he understood that he was the target of a campaign directed by the Americans to protect the man who had killed his daughter.

When the North Vietnamese came, the persecution continued, but in the confusion after the fall of Saigon, he was able to flee with his wife and mother. They caught a boat on the coast at Vung Tau, bribing their way out with their last possessions, but they were captured by Thai pirates on the third day at sea.

His wife and mother were raped, then the old woman was thrown into the ocean. His wife died the next day as the boat drifted in circles. He had tossed her corpse into the water and waited to die himself, but he had been rescued and brought to Hong Kong.

His family had ties there dating to the early Ch'ing dynasty, two hundred and fifty years ago. He had known he would be safe once he got to Hong Kong, but what good did his money and businesses do him after he had lost everything he loved? What did money matter with his daughter dead, his wife and mother beneath the sea?

He was *not* like Job in the old priest's story. He had placed his faith in the Americans and had lost everything, but he was no stoic sufferer: he wanted revenge—it was all he lived for, but it took him years to forge his rage and grief into a plan that brought him to Paris where Bradley Marshall was.

He saw his opportunity when the United States made its overture to China.

Like all businessmen in Hong Kong, he dealt with the communists; they needed cash, and the businessmen needed China's resources and cheap labor. His own export/import business relied heavily on his ties to the communists; when the United States had recognized China, huge new markets opened, and China was no longer an international pariah. Chinese weaponry was sought throughout the Middle East; it was cheaper than Russia's, and more reliable, but China needed salesmen with capitalistic experience, so they turned to the merchants in Hong Kong as the conduit between

Middle Eastern money and Chinese missiles, clever men who spoke the language of arms sales—English.

Those who also knew French were even more highly regarded, for France was where the sales were made. Chien Lin Huong found an orbital niche in this expanding universe for he spoke both languages.

Through China's efforts, he was granted a Hong Kong passport and went to France on a business visa fronting his export/import firm, but his mission was to contact Libyans, Syrians, and Iraqis desiring Chinese arms.

He had money, influence, and contacts, and at last, proximity to the man who had caused his suffering. He would finally make Bradley Marshall pay. It was not enough to kill his children, inflict pain; he wanted to *see* him suffer. He had to witness Marshall's anguish as Marshall had looked with uncaring eyes on his.

Huong closed the umbrella and stepped through the gate, swinging it shut. The clang reverberated in a cavernous vault, dimly illuminated by recessed lights, then was swallowed in the dankness.

He was in a vast catacomb, an underground hive of the dead, among thousands of small marble cells buried in the walls. The dampness was oppressive, and the acrid smell of decaying flowers overpowering.

Entering the grotto, he stood at the entrance to an underworld. Taking a deep breath, he began down the passage, striking the marble floor with the metal tip of his umbrella. Here and there a candle flickered in the heavy air, rank with rotting flowers, and skeletal mold fingers streaked the walls like Death's last scratchings.

He was here to meet a Sûreté agent who worked liaison with the Americans, the man who had sold him information about Bradley Marshall, but a man he could no longer trust. Greed had overcome him—Huong knew the man was going to blackmail him.

Bracing himself for what he had to do, Huong stabbed his passage down the corridor with the umbrella.

Finally he reached the interior ring of the columbarium. Below was another level with ring upon ring of vaults, an underground colony of the dead, all ash, a cold, dead hell abandoned even by the devils.

He descended the stairs. The bottom level was even darker, and before him a narrow corridor led through concentric circles of vaults.

He had taken only a few steps when a measured voice said in French, "I apologize for this disagreeable meeting place, but we will not be disturbed here."

In the shadows Huong saw a tall man in his late forties who might be here placing flowers before a loved one, except for his utterly cold eyes, and the pistol in his hand.

Huong had not counted on that.

The man withdrew an envelope from his coat and tossed it to the marble floor. "I went to considerable trouble to learn about you, Mr. Huong—yes, I know your name is not Wu Te-chao—I have been in this business too long not to have learned to protect myself, for I know that after I have served your needs, you'll want me eliminated."

But then he put away the pistol with a tight smile. "However, I don't fear you yet; I am still useful; I have learned many new things about your prey—things you want to know and now must pay dearly for."

He nodded toward the envelope. "The pictures and fingerprints of you are clearly identifiable, the passport and visa numbers correct, the biographical sketch accurate. Another envelope with the same information is in my bank vault; a third in my desk drawer. If anything happens to me, Sûreté will have it immediately; the director's office is directly above mine."

The Frenchman smiled without warmth. "Everything is there—about Vietnam, about the boat, everything about your ties to China, your 'business' here in France."

The vault was silent, and the two men motionless.

"You've had an awful journey. I think you are entitled to revenge against Ambassador Marshall—though the Americans won't see it that way of course." His mouth turned in disdain. "They are so narrow, so parochial, but as our allies, I should pass this information to them; I am obliged to help them protect their ambassador."

He shook his head. "I won't. *You* are my client; I'll honor our contract; however, since the risks have grown, I must raise my fee."

Huong stared at him impassively.

"The Americans are concerned. A CIA agent is arriving tomorrow because of this matter, but an older agent already here has made the connection to you; he called me yesterday asking about Chinese businessmen refugeed from Vietnam. It won't be long before he tracks you down. You must hurry; he will learn soon that you are after Marshall's children. That is the information I have today, what you have paid for, as well as for the contacts I got you among the Arabs. That was a bargain, Mr. Huong—the Iraqis and Libyans will make you rich and will be happy to help you get revenge."

He shrugged. "However, further protection from Sûreté—my silence about your dealings with the Arabs—and to keep you informed of what the CIA is doing, that will cost you another hundred thousand francs. Then there is very important information—what you really want: information about Marshall's children. There's been a startling development—the children are coming to Paris soon."

He shook his head sadly. "But the information about their arrival, their movements and security—that has become *very* costly: one million francs."

He picked up the envelope and offered it to Huong; when he did not take it, the Frenchman put it back in his coat. "I must have half the money by noon tomorrow in the usual place, otherwise this envelope goes to the Americans."

He gestured toward the stairs. "We are finished. I'll follow you."

Huong's steps were leaden; he leaned heavily on his umbrella.

The Frenchman was double-crossing him as he had supposed. If he paid a million francs, he would only be blackmailed into paying more. There would be no end to it.

"Don't be troubled," the Frenchman said in an almost friendly voice. "I think you are going to succeed, though it's going to be a terrible blow to the Americans."

He waited as Huong ponderously mounted the stairs. At the top, his legs buckled and he reached to the rail for support.

Steadying himself, he continued on, but then his legs gave and he fell to the floor.

The Frenchman stepped forward. As he bent to help, Huong tipped the spring on his umbrella and a blade sliced out. The man had no time to recoil as Huong drove it into his chest. He stood paralyzed, looking as Huong withdrew the blade, but he was not alive to see it stab into him again.

Huong stood, brushed at his trousers, and looked impassively at the man, then he reached into the Frenchman's coat for the envelope.

He put it in his pocket and wiped the bloody blade against the man's coat.

The Frenchman had overestimated himself. What a ridiculous threat he had made—to turn over information to Sûreté, as if Sûreté would admit one of its agents had been compromised. The man had served his purpose; he no longer needed him after he had put him into contact with the Arabs, and Huong already had an informant in the U.S. embassy—another greedy little man, one with a big-bosomed mistress and an apartment on the Right Bank he couldn't afford.

Outside, he walked heedless of the rain.

That was disturbing news about the CIA; how had the older agent made a connection to him? Probably the greedy little man, he mused, returning the unfeeling gaze of the crouching cats.

But what excellent news about Marshall's children.

He lifted his face, as uncaring as the angels gazing down from the sepulchres. The rain cleansed and refreshed him.

Nothing could stop him now.

He wished he would make all Americans pay, but it would be enough to watch Bradley Marshall suffer.

At the gatehouse, he nodded to the gendarme, opened his umbrella, and walked into the city.

CHAPTER 4

Ron Mead, never a big talker, had hardly spoken on this night shift guarding the massive U.S. embassy adjoining Elysée Palace, just off the Place de la Concorde, in the heart of Paris. Coleman Taylor, his best friend, knew something was bothering him, but had been unable to draw him out during their shift; Mead had been distant and unresponsive.

Preparing to go off duty, Taylor hesitated at his metal locker in the Marines' guard room in the basement of the huge complex. The room was Spartan and functional, with uncomfortable chairs, weights, and a TV set, and they were alone though they could hear others showering, preparing to go on duty.

"You want to talk about it, or you gonna Clint Eastwood it out?"

Mead ignored him.

"Suit yourself, macho man." Taylor slammed his locker shut and started past Mead, then stopped and pointed to the ribbons on Mead's uniform. Among the Marines in the detachment, only Mead had five rows of ribbons; most of the others were too young to have served in Vietnam.

"I keep forgetting which one is the Asshole ribbon, the one you got for being a complete butthole."

Mead considered him, then said evenly, "They're all Asshole ribbons." Then he shrugged. "Okay. I'm just . . . it's Sung."

"I know *that,* man. It's always a fucking woman. What about Sung?"

Mead took his bag from his locker and stood uncertainly. "She's . . . she's too good for me."

"I know *that* too; everybody knows that—you just figuring it out?"

"I'm serious, Cole. I been doing some thinking . . ."

"Bad move, Mead. You're a sergeant for a reason—you ain't a thinker."

"I'm twenty-nine."

"Old. Real old." Taylor was twenty-two.

"You want to hear this or not? . . . Then shut up. Sung's twenty-seven. And she's smart—she knows French and American and gook. She deserves more than being a wife to some dumb Marine sergeant. We been married over ten years. After ten years . . ."

"It's hard to get it up."

"No, it's not that, though it's not like it used to be, it's . . . well, tomorrow I'm going to be Ambassador Marshall's bodyguard and . . ."

"What? They're pulling you off guard? Why?"

Mead shrugged. "I was his bodyguard in Vietnam once, long ago, and Mr. Maynard, the CIA guy, told me that the ambassador needs someone, so he gave me the detail. I start tomorrow. And when I see him, I'm going to ask him to get Sung a job here. She deserves more than me in life."

Taylor shook his head. "Mead, you need a hobby. Give up thinking—take up bowling or something."

"I'm gonna do it. I'm gonna talk to Sung today, and Ambassador Marshall." Mead shut his locker. "I made up my mind."

"How come you decided all this now? I mean, she's been too good for you for ten years. Why this big-top decision all of a sudden?"

"This isn't sudden; I been thinking about it for a long time. I guess getting old sorta makes it more important. I mean, I'm going to be thirty next year. Thirty! There isn't much time left. And when I learned about being Ambassador Marshall's bodyguard—well, that's when I made my decision, because I know he can do something."

Taylor turned, rolled his eyes, and walked off. "See you tomorrow, Ron."

He might be a hero, Taylor thought, but *goddamn,* was he dumb.

Everyone in the detachment knew Mead's story, and everyone liked him. He never pulled rank or traded on the ribbons on his chest. He had rescued younger Marines from bars and fights and sat with them as they sobered up, or came down from drugs, or railed about their women and their lives.

"Been there," he'd say when someone tried to thank him.

Many a night he had been there for Coleman Taylor. Taylor would like to help him now, but he knew there was no talking to Mead when he got something into his head, no matter how fucked up it was. But there was nothing to worry about—Sung could handle him. Mead was like a circus bear—powerful and dangerous, but he just followed along behind her, muzzled, a funny little hat on his head.

Mead *was* like a bear, Taylor thought, and though a big man himself, he would never think of taking on Ron Mead, for lurking beneath Mead's surface was profound ominousness, and there was no doubt in his mind that if Mead were riled, he would tear anyone apart. He would joke with Ron, tease him about being a lifer and growing old, but neither he nor anyone else would push the joke too far. Ron Mead wasn't just six feet three, two hundred ten pounds, lifted more weights than anyone else, ran three miles in sixteen minutes—there was volcanic fury in him that threatened to erupt any minute.

Mead nodded absently to the Marines coming from the shower, his thoughts on what he would tell Sung today. They were going to the zoo; they seldom went anywhere because they couldn't afford it—a sergeant's pay didn't go far in the French economy.

Mead did not venture out often for other reasons—he could feel the animosity the French had for Americans. He felt they looked down on him—his poverty, his shabby car, a clunker Simca, but most of all because of Sung, an Oriental GI wife of whom the French made no attempt to disguise their disdain. He dreaded going out in public with Sung because the French stared at them and were rude, ignoring him because he couldn't speak the language, and viewing her with open contempt as a GI's whore.

He wanted a better life for her. They lived in a poor section of a poor suburb of Paris, drove a dilapidated car, and had no money for restaurants or entertainment. She said she would get a job, but could not get a work visa.

Her life was miserable, he knew; she had no friends, nothing to do, and nowhere to go, but his life was better since he'd rejoined the Marines. He *belonged*. After Embassy School in Washington, he went for special training in security, then a driving course in evasion techniques, and he rose quickly in rank. He had been posted to the consulate in Frankfurt, Germany, then moved to Paris at Ambassador Marshall's request.

They had had a good reunion, talked of their times together in Vietnam, but Mead's contact with him had been limited—he was, after all, merely a guard who saluted dignitaries while Marshall met with presidents. But Mead was content with his life and did not even mind the jests of the younger troops for being a "lifer."

Only Sung bothered him. She deserved better, but as long as she stayed with him, he felt she was doomed to an inferior existence. He was a second-class person, someone who would never be anybody, living in tacky apartments, driving beat-up cars. For him it was all right, but Sung was a better person, held down by him.

That thought had wormed into his mind, and now he couldn't stand it.

He loved her; he owed her his life, but it was true, much of the passion was gone after ten years. He was only twenty-nine, but he didn't want to jump into bed four times a day, not—and this shamed him—with Sung.

But how could she love him? he wondered—a dumb Marine who was never going to be anything else, except older. So after long consideration, having learned he was going to be Marshall's bodyguard, he decided to tell Sung to leave him and find a new life. He had it all planned; he was going to take her to the zoo on his day off and tell her there.

Mead looked at his battered car with disgust, swore at it when the engine failed to catch, then relaxed when it did and drove out of the embassy compound toward home.

The day, like so many in Paris's winter, was cold and grim; the sky was overcast and depressing, but he tried not to let it affect his mood when he bounded up the stairs to his apartment in a tenement building on the outskirts of Paris.

"Sung! Hey, Sung, you ready to go?"

She came from the kitchen, smiling at his eagerness. Her hair was still long, black, and luxuriant, but her appearance had softened over the years. A few added pounds had rounded her angularity; she no longer looked vulnerable, but striking and voluptuous, a grown woman with intelligence and humor, very out of place in the drab setting of the apartment. The furniture was worn and inexpensive, a carryover from their days in the trailer. There was no art or artful objects, and though she had tried to brighten the rooms with fresh flowers and colorful curtains, their poverty and her incongruity in the surroundings could not be hidden.

"Ron, it's a terrible day. Don't you want to stay here? You must be tired. We can go another time."

"It's always a terrible day—we'd never go anywhere if we waited for a nice one."

"Don't you want breakfast first? Coffee?"

"Nah. I ate some doughnuts at the embassy and drank coffee all night. Let's go. Just let me change." He tossed her his wallet. "I got plenty of francs—we can have lunch downtown, some toasted cheese sandwiches; I like those."

"Croque-monsieur."

"Whatever." He always gave her his wallet when they went out because she handled all transactions; he would just point to what he wanted, and she would translate.

He locked the apartment, held the car door open for her, and drove to the zoo, one of the smallest in Europe, located in the center of the city.

He parked in the near-empty lot shortly after ten, and she paid the entrance fee.

"Jesus, that was a lot of money," he said, taking her hand inside the gate.

"They have to feed the animals."

"They must be eating better than me."

"You eat fine," she said hotly. "I make good meals. Yesterday you had pork chops."

He put his arm around her and drew her close. "You know, you have *no* sense of humor anymore. I think you're getting old, Sung."

She smiled. "What do you want to see first?"

"I like the bears."

She nodded. "Yes, you would."

He turned to her. "What does that mean?" he asked anxiously.

"Nothing. They're lovely animals," she said solemnly.

"Dumb?"

"Oh, no." Then she put her arm through his. "You have no sense of humor anymore. I think *you* must be getting old, Ron."

He laughed. "Okay, you win. So what do you like best?"

She thought a moment. "The monkeys."

He shook his head. "They're nasty."

"Monkeys? They're intelligent and funny."

"They're gross, eating bugs off each other's head, and jerking off—I don't want to see it."

They wandered hand in hand, with few visitors except for groups of schoolchildren, who found the tall American and the Oriental woman as interesting as the zoo animals.

Before the elephant house, passing a toilet, Mead said he had to go. Sung walked off to the elephant house as he went toward the bathroom, hesitating to pick out the male figure from the female on the two doors.

"Shit," he said aloud on entering the bathroom and seeing a table with a dish with coins, indicating he had to pay to use the toilet. Frequently a cleaning woman guarded the bathroom, making sure no one left without dropping coins into the plate.

Mead searched his pockets for change, but he didn't have any. He turned to leave, to catch up with Sung, who would give him a franc, but as he left, the cleaning woman entered. Thinking he had used the toilet without paying, she called to him sharply.

Unable to speak a word of French or explain he was going for money, he merely shook his head, prompting an angrier response and a forceful gesture to the coin dish.

"I didn't go!" he said to her.

She started toward him, pointing to his pockets.

"I didn't piss!" he shouted, then turned and ran.

The woman yelled in outrage at the breach of toilet protocol and started after him.

Mead raced toward the elephant house, furiously pursued by the cleaning woman, screaming at him in French. Sung, hearing the commotion, turned to see her husband being chased through the zoo by a stocky, formidable, middle-aged woman.

"Sung! Sung!" Mead cried.

Sung brought her hands to her face and began to laugh.

"Tell her I didn't piss," he said, hiding behind her. "I was coming to get money from you. Tell her. Jesus, give her some money!"

The woman confronted Sung and pointed to Mead, cowering behind her.

"He didn't pay," the woman said, her hands on her hips. "He must pay a franc."

Sun reached into her purse and handed the woman the money, explaining what had happened. The cleaning woman listened, but was not convinced. Casting a reproachful look at Mead, she turned and marched back to her post.

"I hate this fucking country," Mead said, coming from behind Sung.

She giggled. "That was so funny. You were so afraid—I never saw that before."

He looked at her a moment, then took her hand and led her from the elephant house. "Okay, that's it; we gotta talk. There's something I want to tell you."

He brought her to a deserted area by the seals' rock; the animals were inside, and Sung and Mead stood alone by the fence overlooking the large pond.

He glanced at her. She looked at him expectantly, her face kind and warm. She was so beautiful, he thought, but her clothes were worn and her coat threadbare, and she never had money for makeup. She should have been a princess and lived in a palace, but her family had been murdered, and he had found her in a brothel. He turned away in pain. Oh, God, he loved her, he thought, more than anything; he could never love like this again. But she was too good for him, he knew—she deserved better. She would grow old with him; that wouldn't be right. He couldn't help himself; he was just a trailer person. But she wasn't. She still had a chance.

He didn't say anything for a long time, seeming to brace

himself. Finally, he took a deep breath and started his speech. "Remember that time long ago in Vietnam when I asked you to marry me?"

Sung nodded. "Of course. It was the longest speech you ever made. I was very happy."

"So was I. And I've been happy with you all these years. You made my life. I'd be nothing without you."

She smiled, knowing that she was in for another long speech, though it might take him forever to get it out. She even knew what he was going to say; he was, after all, not a complex man, and certainly not a deceitful one. He saw himself as lover, provider, and protector, and indeed he was those things to her, but he was something different too—a precious child, and she loved him for his strengths and weaknesses equally. She was both lover and mother to him, and she never wanted him hurt or in pain.

"You always been good to me, Sung; much better than I deserved."

She waited him out, listening somberly, though wanting to pat him on his head and send him on his way with a cookie.

"I didn't know what I wanted for a long time. I was really fucked up in Arkansas."

He looked to the barren seals' rock. "I guess I'm like the animals here. I can't roam free; I need to be caged, looked after, and fed—thrown some food now and then, paid twice a month, told what to do and where to go, how to dress and what to wear."

He shrugged. "I *need* to be in the Marines, Sung; I'm that kinda person."

She nodded solemnly.

"And I've never going to be anything but a Marine. I mean, someday I'll be a gunnery sergeant or something, but that's about it."

"There is nothing wrong with that, Ron."

"No, not for me. But I'm never gonna have a nice house or decent car. You're never going to be driving in a BMW with me, Sung. You'll be driving a junker always, living in shit places, and never having any money."

"Ron . . ."

"You deserve more. Much more than me. I mean, I can't even go to the fucking toilet without screwing up. You speak

French, and you sure speak better English than me. I hate it when I see these fucking people look down on you. You're a hundred times better than they are, but you got no chance with me. And after here you'd end up back at Lejeune or Pendleton in some dumpy apartment, going to the PX and commissary. Your life should be more than that. You could be *anything.*"

She smiled again. "This is a longer speech than when you asked me to marry you."

"Okay, I'll cut it short. I want you to leave me."

She brought up her hand to stifle a laugh.

"I mean it, I want you to divorce me. It's your only chance to have a good life."

"Ron . . ."

He shook his head. "Look, I finally found myself. I'm okay now. I got my life under control. I'm doing what I want—about the only thing I *can* do. At least I can go to the shitter in the Marines without getting into trouble. I'm not doing drugs and don't drink—not much anyway. I'm squared away. So you can leave me and I'll be all right."

"Ron . . ."

"No! Listen, I got it all figured out. I been thinking a long time, and I made up my mind. I mean, it's not like you love me. I know you *like* me, and, well . . . we're okay together. Better than others, but . . . love? How could you love me? I'm just a fucking dummy. You can *like* a dummy, but you can't love one. And *you* shouldn't."

"Ron . . ."

He waved her silent. "I'm going to be Ambassador Marshall's bodyguard starting tomorrow. I'm gonna talk to him about you. He was the one who let us get married. I'm gonna tell him about how you deserve better than me. I'm gonna ask him to help you get a good job at the embassy, or maybe in Washington. I'm sure he'd do it."

"Ron . . ."

"And you won't have to worry about money. I'll give you everything I make. I'll move back into the barracks. You won't have a lot of money, but you can get by until you make it on your own."

"Now that's enough," she said, pointing at him like an obstreperous child. "I won't listen to any more of this. Of course I'm not going to leave you. What is the matter with you?"

"I told you, you deserve a better life."

"I have a good life," she said emphatically. "I am happy. I do not care about cars or houses. What made you think I did? Where did you get this nonsense in your head? Is this what you do at the embassy at night, dream up foolishness? Why don't you play cards or go get drunk with the other men?"

He drew himself up. "I made up my mind, Sung," he said in a stern voice.

"Well, that's fine for you, but I am not interested. I will decide about my own life, thank you very much. How dare you tell me what to do with my life. *Shame* on you!"

"I'm serious about this, Sung—you're not gonna change my mind. I want you to have a better life. I'm going to talk to Ambassador Marshall about it."

"I don't want to hear any more of this."

Then she got angry, a very rare occurrence, and she stepped back and pointed her finger at him. "You are not to tell me about my life, Ron Mead. I do not know how this got into your head, but get it out, right now. When I am unhappy with my life, I will tell you. But you will not make it up for me. Sometimes you do very silly things. That's all right—you're a man, and women don't expect much from men. You can play your games, shoot your guns, march here and there—you can be a cowboy or a Marine, I don't care, but don't you *dare* tell me what to do with my life. Make a mess of your own if you're bored and don't have anything else to do, but leave mine alone."

"I decided," he said defiantly.

She made a sound of disgust and turned away. "I am going to see the elephants."

"Sung, I meant what I said," he called after her.

"Go look at the monkeys," she said angrily. "You might learn something."

She turned and faced him, more angry than he had ever seen her. "And don't you dare think you can come into my bed anymore."

She stared at him a moment, then she shook her finger at him. "Outrageous!"

With that, she flounced away, leaving him staring after her.

CHAPTER 5

Mike Caldwell jerked out of tortured sleep, instinctively grabbing for the person hitting him, but was pulled back by restraints. He tried to focus: the person hitting him was a beautiful woman, yet he had no recollection of her and did not recognize her uniform—Iranian? Iraqi? But they didn't have women in their military.

Dazed, he glanced about and saw white sheets, but he had no recollection of being in bed either. He had not lain on sheets in months, let alone slept with a woman.

"Sir," the uniformed woman said, "would you like to change your seat?"

Out of the corners of his eyes, he saw he was not in bed, but in a jumbo jet, sitting between two terrified Arab women in white chadors, and the woman before him was a Pan American stewardess. To get any farther from him, the woman in the window seat would have had to crawl out on the wing, and the woman in the aisle seat would have bolted except for the stewardess blocking her path.

"I was having a bad dream," he mumbled in mortification.

"Why don't you move to the back," the stewardess suggested. "There are plenty of seats; you can stretch out—we won't be arriving in Paris for another three hours."

"Yes," Caldwell said gratefully, moving out of his seat quickly, following the stewardess to an empty aisle seat at the rear of the plane, keeping his head down, too embarrassed to meet anyone's eyes.

"I'm really sorry," he apologized. "Was I bad?"

"Oh, yes. You were trying to strangle the woman beside you."

Caldwell dropped into a seat. "I must have been dreaming of my ex-wife."

Jesus, he thought in the bulkhead row, fumbling in his jacket for cigarettes and lighting one with trembling hands, he couldn't handle this assignment. He was too wired—he should be going into a decompression chamber, not to Paris.

Mike Caldwell was thirty-two, six feet two inches, darkly tanned, hair bleached almost white from desert sun, and with broad, clean features—a handsome man, tautly muscular, but too thin, and wound so tightly that he seemed like a spring ready to uncoil. His last months had been spent on the plateaus in northern Iraq, burning by day, freezing at night in rocky crevices, sleeping on a straw pallet, eating bean paste with the Kurds, an ethnic minority persecuted by both Iranians and Iraqis. He thought he had been sent to help them, but soon discovered their fate was of no interest or consequence to the United States. He was there only to gauge how they might be exploited in future upheavals in the region, and to gain the trust of faction leaders in case he later needed to get near them to take them out. His disillusionment had been profound.

Now he was on a Pan American flight from Washington; two days before he had been in Iran. Getting out of there had taken his last reserves; now he was running on empty.

Halfway through the cigarette, he stabbed it out, then immediately lit another.

Langley was right to have pulled him from the field, but why was he on *this* mission? There had been few details in his one-hour briefing in Washington, only that he was to report to Andrew Maynard, but that his real handler was Wilson Abbot Lord. Though little frightened Caldwell, the mere prospect of Lord made him nervous, for in his world, Lord was a mythical figure, a man who had come out of the grave more times than Bela Lugosi. Looking at his trembling hand, he knew he wasn't ready to meet the Phantom.

Langley had to know he was on a precipice, so why not

let him rest? But that wasn't the CIA way. Push the fucker over, see if he lands on his feet—that was Langley's way. They had dropped him over the abyss a year ago, and he was still in free fall.

Iran had been the final blow to his marriage; when he left, Laurie divorced him and got custody of his two daughters, four and five. Though he knew there was little hope of reconciliation, he wanted to go to the States to make a final attempt, but Langley had ordered him to Paris.

Drawing deeply on the cigarette, he turned to gaze out the window. They had announced rain and overcast sky in Paris, yet here it was clear.

If you go high enough, it's always clear sky, he thought.

But he doubted he'd ever get to clear sky in the CIA. After seven years, and three before as a Green Beret, he was what he had always been—an assassin. And if he was going to work for Wilson Lord, this assignment was going to call for his special talent.

He studied the hand holding the cigarette; it was not steady. He didn't want to go to Paris or see Wilson Lord—he wanted to go home; he wanted to see his children. Perhaps it was time to take retirement; he had made good money—maybe he should go to law school and set up practice in a small town in Pennsylvania.

Maybe Laurie would be impressed. Maybe she would run back to him.

He stubbed out the cigarette. Get real, asshole, he said to himself, and to the stewardess passing by, he said loudly, "Scotch."

She brought him two small bottles and a glass of ice. He had not had a drink in three months, yet even the first bottle smoothed the edges of his tension. Opening the second, his eyes fixed on his wedding ring; the gold was scarred and unlustrous.

"You're not paying attention to me," Laurie would often say. "Once you start working, you go into your 'operational mode.' I don't even exist for you."

Despite his protests, it was true, and now he dismissed her again with the second bottle, pulling off the ring easily, for even his fingers were too thin, dropping it into his empty glass, pushing the glass away. A perfect white impression remained on his finger.

He smiled—Langley hadn't made a mistake sending him here, they were counting on his pain and anger, feeding it—they wanted him mean.

On a plane arriving from Washington at the same time, Bradley Marshall was escorted out of the first-class cabin and brought to passport control. As he reached for his black diplomatic passport, a muscular young man elbowed past him roughly.

At a casual glance, the man—tall, blond, perhaps thirty, with a remarkably strong face—might have passed for a young corporate executive, except he looked too good, too fit, and his powerful manner was not of money or position. A second guess might have been of a professional athlete on a promotion to hawk a new line of sportswear, but his appearance was too businesslike, and his alertness more than physical.

Then the man brought out his diplomatic passport, and Marshall knew who he was. He restrained his escort moving to intercept the man and watched Caldwell pass through the gate, then he held up his own passport and walked through.

In the VIP lounge, Andrew Maynard nibbled candy from a dish on a table. Wearing a dirty trench coat, his rain hat still on his head, he looked even more disheveled than usual. After twenty-five years with the CIA, on his last Bob Hope "Thanks for the Memories" assignment in Paris, he no longer cared what he looked like, any more than he cared what people thought.

As he stuffed chocolates into his pocket, a man said, "You're going to get fat; James Bond isn't fat."

Maynard turned to see a tall, imposing Marine officer in dress blues.

Luke Bishop grinned. "Is this what happens to old Marines? Is this going to be my fate—scarfing up free chocolates in airport terminals?"

"I hope so, Major," Maynard said, popping another chocolate into his mouth. He looked haggard, more than his fifty-two years, an ordinary middle-aged man, overworked and tired, but the appearance was a calculated deception, and now he turned a piercing eye on the officer before him. "What are you doing here, Luke?"

"The same thing you are, I suppose—meeting Ambassador Marshall."

"Brad's coming in? I thought he wasn't coming back till Thursday."

"What kind of a spy are you? If you can't even keep track of *our* ambassador, how can you keep up with the bad guys?"

"Our ambassadors *are* the bad guys. What's Brad doing back so early?" Maynard asked in surprise.

Bishop shrugged. "I just got the twix to meet this flight. So here's Joe Aide to meet him. Who are you meeting?"

"Shhhhhh," Maynard whispered. "There may be spies about. I'm here to meet one of ours."

"The embassy's already overrun with you guys; we don't need any more."

Maynard drew himself up indignantly. "Major, just because the ambassador got you a kiss-ass job as his aide, that doesn't give you a right to mock the *true* guardians of truth, justice, and the American way."

"Oh, right," Bishop said in disgust. "My fucking head was almost blown off by one of your assholes."

Maynard scooped up the rest of the chocolates. "I rest my case."

Just then Caldwell entered the VIP lounge, immediately followed by Marshall. Both men approached Maynard. Caldwell held out his hand, but Maynard ignored him and turned to Marshall as Bishop saluted him.

"Thanks for meeting me, Andy," Marshall said, shaking hands. Then he returned to Bishop. "I could have used you a few minutes ago, Luke—some guy with a diplomatic passport almost knocked me down. It's just unbelievable how little respect ambassadors get these days from their own subordinates."

Caldwell turned to the man in back of him, then closed his eyes. "Oh, shit. I beg your pardon, sir."

"Is he some new weapon, Andy?" Marshall asked lightly. "I don't think you've perfected him yet."

"He's our answer to military attachés," Maynard said, introducing Caldwell to Marshall, then to Bishop.

As Bishop and Caldwell appraised one another like stags in a clearing, Marshall and Maynard sensed the incredible animosity emanating from the two, then Marshall put his arm around his oldest friend's shoulder and steered him away.

Maynard turned to Bishop. "Luke, I'll take the ambassador back, you get Mike situated. He's staying at the Hilton. Thanks."

"Rough trade, as my son might say," Marshall observed of Caldwell as they left the lounge. "I don't think he and Luke are going to get along."

"He's here to save your ass," Maynard answered as a phalanx of guards escorted Marshall to his waiting limousine. Marshall went nowhere without guards; Paris was dangerous, and the most tantalizing target was the U.S. ambassador.

Outside the airport, a cordon of gendarmes surrounded his limousine, but even before they could move out of his way, Ron Mead wedged his body between them, knocking them aside, opened the rear door, and saluted.

Marshall smiled in genuine pleasure. "Sergeant Mead," he said warmly.

"Good morning, sir."

"What are *you* doing here?"

"Mr. Maynard said I was going to be your bodyguard, sir. Just like old times."

Marshall looked to Maynard quizzically. "Why do I need a bodyguard?"

"Actually you need several, Brad, but Sergeant Mead assures me he can handle everything," Maynard said.

"I *know* he can. . . . How's your wife, Sergeant?" Marshall asked as he got into the backseat.

"Just fine, sir."

Marshall dropped into the backseat and Mead closed the door, sitting in front beside the driver, assuming his role with such studied seriousness that Marshall smiled.

"Well, bonvenue, Excellency," Maynard said in his inexcusable French as the limousine sped off, heralded by sirens and police cars. "Bon voyage?"

Marshall sank into the seat. "I'm tired, Andy. I want to go home. I need a drink. I had a miserable trip; we'll talk about it later."

As Marshall rested his head back and closed his eyes, Maynard studied his profile; it would look good on money, or a stamp, he thought—strong, confident, imperial. He did not look like a targeted man, just tired. "We need to talk, Brad."

Marshall did not open his eyes. Maynard was going to ask him about his meeting with Carter, and though he wanted to discuss it with him, he did not want to do it now.

Maynard said sternly, "We *have* to talk, Brad."

Marshall yawned. "Later. I've had a hard trip, Andy. I feel like Snow White—I think I drank a poisoned apple."

"Snow White *ate* an apple, Brad."

"She didn't know Jimmy Carter."

Maynard smiled, then settled back also. They had known each other thirty years; he knew Marshall would talk with him.

Marshall kept his eyes closed until he sensed they were in the city. He liked Paris best in winter. The great gray stonework and slate blackened with pollution against the cold, dark sky reminded him of the medieval city, and through the steam rising from the street vendors' carts, he saw an incredibly worn mosaic of life, tiny tiles of human conduct that made the world less significant and easier to bear.

"I think he's going to kill you, Brad, and that'd look terrible on my record."

Startled from reverie, Marshall turned in confusion. "What?"

"It's always a woman who screws things up. This time it was a whore with tits big enough to smother that little shit in PR."

Marshall pulled a pair of glasses from his jacket and turned to look at Maynard. "I'm returning from a meeting with the President of the United States, and you're telling me about some woman with big tits?"

"I'm talking about the man trying to kill you."

Marshall looked over his glasses. "I *did* drink a poisoned apple."

"Caldwell is here because we think someone is trying to kill you; Langley agrees. That's why Sergeant Mead is with you from now on also."

Marshall took off his glasses and put them away, then he brought his gaze to Maynard with an intensity of concentration that Maynard always marveled at. There was a barely perceptible raising of the upper eyelids and a tightening around the corners, then an incredible burst of power from the eye itself that bored laserlike through the object it fixed. Maynard felt as though his thought had been x-rayed, and for this reason he never attempted to deceive Marshall on anything important. He was not sure he could.

The eyes eased and Marshall said amiably, "Andy, someone is *always* trying to kill me. It goes with the job; but if they really want to, you can't protect me. Hell, you people can't even protect yourselves—they're knifing spies at Père Lachaise."

"How did you know that?" Maynard blurted.

Marshall had read it in an intelligence report at the White House. "I keep tabs on the CIA and Sûreté. Somebody has to watch the guardians—lest guards become jailers."

Maynard himself had only sketchy information, and that by chance. He had previously worked with the murdered agent and had contacted him several days ago about a Chinese refugee he had linked to Marshall. A man in public relations, with an expensive mistress and apartment, had been under observation for a long time. When Maynard brought him in for questioning, the man said he had only given innocuous information about Marshall to a Chinese man who was indeed paying him a huge sum, but what was wrong with that?—the information wasn't classified.

Maynard's curiosity had been piqued, and yesterday when he went to see the Sûreté agent, he learned the agent's body had been discovered only hours earlier in Père Lachaise. He had been unable to get anything else out of French intelligence.

Though he had no reason to tie the death to Marshall, instinct told him there was a connection. "I keep forgetting," he said. "Secrets are like the Top Forty, played every hour on the goddamn radio. But you're lucky in this case—I wouldn't have known anything if it hadn't been for that woman. It's always sex, or money for sex."

Maynard pulled a handkerchief from his pocket and blew his nose. "Christ, I'm so goddamn sick of sex I wish I were a eunuch. I have to keep track of everybody's sex life—I have to know who my agents are fucking, who everybody else's agents are fucking, everybody in the embassy, including one hundred Marines, so that somebody's dick doesn't compromise the free world as we know and love it."

"Does Luke know you're keeping tabs on his sex life?" Marshall asked lightly.

In the front seat, Mead grinned. Like all the Marines in the embassy, he knew Major Bishop, and many of the stories about him.

"I have a special detail handling that maniac's sex life. He's your aide, you should talk with him, Brad. I certainly wouldn't let him near your daughter."

Marshall laughed. "Sarah *won't* let him near, and I'm not about to talk to Luke about his sex life. He's a healthy young man, and—"

Maynard raised his hands. "I know, I know, he saved your life, or you wrecked his, or something like that."

Marshall said solemnly, "I trust Luke Bishop as much as I do you and Sergeant Mead, Andy."

"*I* don't try to nail everything that moves."

"You did before you got married; we both did in Korea."

Maynard pointed a finger at Mead. "You hear nothing, you understand? *Nothing.*"

"Sergeant Mead understands the rules, Andy. But don't worry about Luke. We grew up, so will he. Now get on with the threat to my life—you have my undivided attention."

"You're the most important official in Europe. The President listens to you, so everybody else listens to you. You're privy to all state secrets and NATO information. You have a wife and two grown children. Somebody's trying to kill you. Can't you see my position? This would look terrible on my record—I'd never get my pension. He could be with the Russians, the Chinese, the PLO, the Israelis, the Vietnamese, dissident French, the Red Army Faction, the Khmer Rouge, the Greens, the Muppets, a fucking rainbow of nuts—you have no idea how complicated this crap gets."

Maynard pulled at his face tiredly. "Something is very wrong and very dangerous. So work with me; trust me."

Marshall put his hand over his heart. "If it will make you happy, and not incidentally save my life, I will work with you. What do you want to know?"

"I want to know who's out to kill you."

The limousine sped down the Champs-Elysées. Rising above the tree-lined boulevard was the dark domed roof of the Grand Palais. The day was overcast and the city looked metallic, and Marshall, this day, was unmoved by the view. He lowered his gaze, but all he saw was a blurred streak of people, run-on shapes without faces. The people had become a blurred streak in his mind too, and he was no longer sure he believed them basically good, nor did he trust to their better instincts.

Who would want to kill him? Marshall asked himself.

He hadn't thought about that, but now he saw his trip to Washington in a new light. Old CIA hands would be frantic about Carter's perceived sellout of the Shah and wouldn't hesitate to eliminate the man who would make overtures to Khomeini.

"You should have a pretty good idea," Marshall said pointedly. He was glad Maynard was bringing this up—he wanted to talk to Andy about the Shah and Khomeini; he needed help working through the maze, and this was a good lead-in.

"I do. I think it's Vietnam."

Marshall looked perplexed. "Vietnam?" He spoke it like a word from a forgotten lexicon, one strange to the tongue and dim to memory. "What are you talking about?"

"I am talking about the Chinese man."

"What Chinese man? I thought you were going to talk to me about Khomeini."

"Who?"

"The Ayatollah!"

"What the hell do I care about the Ayatollah? I'm worried about the gook who's out to kill you because of Vietnam."

Staring into Maynard's incredulous face, Marshall suddenly realized Maynard didn't know about his meeting with

Carter; he didn't know about the overtures to Khomeini. Maynard had not been briefed about this development.

Playing for time, Marshall took out his glasses again, polished them slowly, then put them on. Why didn't Maynard know, and what is this nonsense about a Chinese man? The only threat would come from the CIA, who wouldn't want him to meet with Khomeini. But if Maynard didn't know, how could he talk to him about this? It would mortify Maynard to learn Langley was keeping him in the dark. Why were they?

"Let's do this slowly," Marshall said. "What Chinese man are you talking about?"

"That's the part I don't know yet, but one from Vietnam."

"Vietnam?" Marshall spoke the word familiarly, and it took shape, mushrooming with frightening speed and darkness, blotting all thought, but Marshall shook it away. He said easily, "Andy, in politics there's no revenge because there's no memory—that's war and crime too: a criminal is the first to forget the crime, and the victims don't want reminders either. What counts is the moment—the past is forgotten. Last year's war is like last night's bingo card—the game's over and the numbers, like the dead, don't mean a thing. I don't know what Chinese man you're talking about. When you say Vietnam, I have no idea what you mean."

Maynard yawned and settled back in the seat. "All right, if you don't want to talk to me, you can talk to Caldwell—I'll get him to beat it out of you."

Caldwell. Suddenly it occurred to Marshall—he had not been notified about the arrival of a new CIA agent. As ambassador, he should have been, but it was strictly accidental that he had learned of Caldwell. Seeing him in his mind, the harsh, almost murderous intensity, it was preposterous to think that man had been sent to help Andy *save* him. And why didn't Maynard know anything about Khomeini?

"I think you know the Chinese man I'm talking about—he killed your driver in Saigon in 1972."

"What?" Marshall said incredulously. Then he reached for Maynard's arm.

"Oh my God," Marshall said, the horror settling over him as he saw that day again, holding Bishop's bleeding head in his lap, the car racing down the street, the collision, then the man running, hands outstretched, hate and agony in his eyes.

The man had gotten out. And now he had come for him.

"Oh, Jesus, Andy. I thought that was over. But he got out. He's come for Sarah and Chris."

Maynard unwrapped a candy from his pocket and popped it into his mouth. "Tell me about it, Brad."

Instead of leaving the lounge, Caldwell dropped down in a chair and motioned to a cocktail waitress. "You don't have to hang around, Major. I'm sure I can find the Hilton."

Bishop sat. They stared at one another harshly, two powerful men confident of their masculinity and prowess, then Caldwell dismissed Bishop with a sneer and craned around for the waitress.

"I'd rather you *not* hang around, Major. I *know* I can find the Hilton. Why don't you go square something away or polish some brass or kiss some ass. I'll be fine."

Bishop grinned. "I *want* to hang around. I haven't met an asshole like you since Vietnam. You remind me of him—*evil* motherfucker."

Caldwell turned. "Careful, Major. All those pretty little ribbons on your uniform won't protect that pretty face. I never did like Marines."

Bishop grinned wider. "So, who do you like, sailors?"

Caldwell sat back to contemplate Bishop. "You might be the only thing that makes this mission interesting, Major—for a couple minutes anyway."

Bishop shrugged. "My guess is that you kill people for a living." He touched the battle ribbons on his uniform. "I didn't get these for baking brownies, so anytime you want to go at it, let me know."

Caldwell leaned across the table so their faces almost touched, and he put his finger on Bishop's ribbons. "You know what my Vietnam experience was? I was a Green Beret who got hooked on killing because my government gave me a rifle and said it was all right. You want to talk about killing, Major? Killing and orgasm, murder and fucking?"

Caldwell's eyes were on fire. "I killed . . . oh, let me calculate—about seventy gooks. At one hundred twenty pounds each, that's four *tons* of gooks. I killed four tons of gooks, and in cathouses, I fucked maybe fifty gook women. Now, at eighty pounds each, that's four thousand pounds; but most I fucked more than once, so let's round it off to four tons. That's my Vietnam experience—I killed eight thousand pounds of male gook and fucked four tons of female gook. I had a hard-on the whole time I was there. Did you?"

Bishop shook his head in boredom. "Nope, I didn't get a hard-on killing people." Then he pressed his face closer, his own eyes on fire. "But I did it."

Just then the waitress appeared. Henna hair fell provocatively over an eye exactly as it did on last year's magazine models, and her hips shifted under a short skirt, but sensing the intense animosity radiating from the two men, she stepped away.

Caldwell glanced up, then eased back in his chair, appraising her. "I suppose you're married," he said in excellent French.

She smiled nervously, showing uneven teeth and a suggestive tongue. "I suppose you're American."

"No. Japanese."

She pointed to his blond hair. "You have a very clever disguise. No, I am not married, but I cannot go out with you—I am engaged. What would you like?"

"Pastis."

She turned to Bishop.

"Coke," he said. "Please."

They watched appreciatively as she walked away, hips rolling for their benefit, then Caldwell gazed about the lounge, scrutinizing and cataloguing. He guessed he was already under observation, and the thought of danger and exposure sent rippling sexual pleasure through his body—he liked danger even better than women.

He turned back to Bishop and they stared at one another until the waitress returned with their drinks. She set Caldwell's before him, along with a glass of water.

"I didn't think being married made a difference in France," he said, splashing water into the liquor, watching it cloud.

"Being married doesn't. Being engaged does."

"Then I'm not too late, just too early." He gestured to Bishop. "He'll pay when we leave."

She left, hips tossing like a distressed ship, and they both grinned in open admiration, their anger dissipated.

"Great ass," Bishop said, stretching out his legs comfortably. Then he turned to Caldwell and held out his hand. "Luke Bishop. Want to try again?"

"Mike Caldwell," he answered with a firm grip. "Yeah; let's start over."

"So where you coming in from?"

"Tehran. Before that I was in Iraq."

"It must be bad; you look ragged."

"Don't get me started on Arabs. I was on a flight from Qom once and a woman threw a can of forbidden hairspray into the toilet. Another woman, trying to fish it out of the shitter, punctured the can and was blown into the back aisle. They had to make an emergency landing in the desert. Iran makes Angkor Wat look like Futurama. There are some very disturbed people there."

Bishop pointed to Caldwell's drink. "What is that? It looks like detergent." He reached for the glass, sniffed apprehensively, then sipped. "Jesus!" He went back to his Coke. "The Shah going to make it?"

"Nope. Khomeini is going to take over."

"I guess you guys really fucked up there."

"Not me, Major. I don't make foreign policy."

Bishop smiled. "I don't either."

Seeing the two men were not going to tear up the lounge to get at one another, the waitress approached more confidently this time.

"Scotch," Caldwell said. "Straight up." He turned to Bishop. "You want another soda pop? . . . Then just Scotch." He pulled a crumpled pack of cigarettes from his jacket, fished out a few broken ones, tossed them in the direction of the ashtray, then lit a badly bent one. "So tell me about yourself, Luke. Whose ass did you kiss to get this job?"

Bishop smiled. "I've known Ambassador Marshall since Vietnam. He had a bad experience with one of his aides once, so when he was posted here, he asked for me."

"He trusts you?"

"He should. Should Andy Maynard trust you?"

Caldwell let out his breath slowly. Bishop had inadvertently scored with that, but Caldwell merely flicked cigarette ash to the floor and said easily, "I don't kiss ass. I live in the real world, Major. I don't have a desk like you do—I don't use pencils and erasers in my work, and kissing ass will only get you cholera."

Bishop smiled. "You just haven't found the right ass to kiss."

"That's because I'm more discriminating than you, Pretty Boy."

Bishop raised a warning hard. "Watch it."

"Ah," Caldwell said, knowing that he'd scored—Bishop was sensitive about being an aide, serving Marshall.

The waitress came with Caldwell's second drink. He sipped it silently, staring over the glass at Bishop. He wasn't sure what his mission was, but he knew if he was working for Wilson Lord, this assignment might call for heavy artillery, and knowing the stakes at risk—Iran and the Middle East—it was conceivable his contract might be Marshall himself. If that was so, then the man he would have to go up against was sitting across from him.

He suddenly smiled as sexual pleasure rippled through him again. "What's the pussy like here?"

Bishop glanced to the white band on Caldwell's finger where a ring should have been. "Plentiful. But I'd put some bronzer on that if I were you. In fact"—he nodded in the direction of the waitress—"you look like you could use quite a few tips. Tons of cathouse cunt don't count here—this is the big leagues."

"Well, I'll be sure to come to you for advice on how to get laid, Lukey." Caldwell stood, dropped a bill on the table, and waited for Bishop. "The Coke was on me."

Bishop followed him out of the lounge, then directed him toward a sedan in the VIP parking lot. They didn't speak for most of the ride down the autoroute, but once the car entered busy traffic, Caldwell turned to Bishop. "The embassy have a gym?"

"In the basement. A good one, all kinds of equipment and free weights."

"Handball court?"

"Racquetball and squash too. You play?"

"Take your pick."

"Handball."

"Tomorrow. Ten A.M."

Bishop shook his head. "I don't want to take advantage of you. Get some rest; I don't want to hear any excuses when I beat you."

The car passed by the Invalides, then the Eiffel Tower, a skeletal colossus looming in ghostly haze over the Champ de Mars. A minute later, the sedan stopped in front of the hotel and Caldwell jumped out. "See you tomorrow. Ten A.M."

Heading into the hotel, Caldwell felt he was going to see a lot of Bishop, and for a reason he didn't linger on, he was looking forward to it.

Bishop watched Caldwell disappear, and a strange feeling came over him also, something he hadn't felt since combat—it was wonderful; yet disturbing too.

CHAPTER 6

Wilson Lord knew he was getting old; he never felt jet lag before—he used to fly through thirteen time zones and not flag a moment, but his eight-hour flight from Washington to Paris had drained him.

Well, he was fifty-two, he thought—not *old,* but some things were better left to younger men—that's why he had Mike Caldwell to do the legwork, to spare his own aged, battered limbs. Legwork and trigger-pulling were for younger men with quick reflexes and sharp eyes; thought and plans were for older men.

His plane had arrived in early evening, but after a delay in getting his luggage and a circuitous journey to the safe house, a nondescript apartment near the Bois de Boulogne, it was nearly nine P.M. before he was settled.

The apartment was a disappointment, more like a dormitory room, a place a younger man could accept, diverted by the pleasures outside, but too Spartan for a man his age. The TV was black-and-white, the bedside radio didn't work, and the instant-coffee maker attached to the wall in the bathroom was a really tacky touch, he thought.

It was altogether depressing, and he had reached the point of tiredness where he knew sleep would not come easily, so he left the building, thinking that in a few more hours exhaustion would hit, then he could sleep through the night and awake accustomed to the time change.

The apartment building was set on a dark street in a residential area not far from Marmottan Museum, too gloomy for his mood tonight, so he caught a cab to bring him to the Latin Quarter. He needed his spirit fed, and there was no safer place to wander in Paris than in this tourist district; besides, he was hungry. He was so accustomed to Anh's cooking that he only wanted Vietnamese food, and the best Vietnamese restaurants in the world were in this crowded area, almost a refugee camp for those who had fled the former French colony, or the war between the Americans and the North.

But he had not taken into account the noise and people. The city jarred his sensibilities; it was too crowded and busy, and the yellow headlights gave him a headache. The French claimed it was softer on the eyes, but they also called snails a delicacy and ate cheese that smelled worse than any diaper Lance had ever dirtied.

Paris was too decadent for his taste, too ornate and feminine, and he had never liked the French—they were frivolous; he preferred the stoicism and subtlety of the Orient.

When the cab dropped him at St.-Michel, he was bustled about by crowds. Feeling aged again, not young enough to smash through them without fear some delinquent might push him to the pavement, he sought refuge down a quieter street in the Quarter and found a relatively deserted restaurant, soothingly quiet and dark. In fact, he was alone, for the others sitting at tables proved to be waiters, who jumped up when he entered.

He ordered a Vietnamese beer and savored it while he glanced at the menu, then he put it down and spoke to the waiter in Vietnamese, asking him to bring whatever the chef had prepared special that night.

He signaled for a second beer, and lulled by the smells coming from the kitchen, he slipped into peaceful relaxation.

He had not been able to think on the flight over, what with a running travelogue from the captain and stewardesses racing carts up and down the aisles, tossing peanuts, drinks, and trays in a veritable feeding frenzy for the passengers.

He *was* getting old, he knew—tired and cranky, and nearsighted too.

He had planned to think on the flight over, form a plan

to prevent Marshall from meeting Khomeini, but there had been too many distractions and he had been unable to put all the seemingly unrelated information into a clear pattern—the Chinese man, the murder of a Sûreté agent, the threat to Marshall.

Before leaving Langley, he read Maynard's report on a suspected threat to Marshall. A Chinese man had bribed an embassy employee for information about Marshall. It could mean anything, Lord realized. No one of Marshall's tenure and experience in government could be without enemies, and the Chinese man could be a foil for any number of terrorist groups who had targeted the American ambassador. Maynard seemed to have it under control, whatever it was. Sending Caldwell to work for him, ostensibly to counteract the threat, was a clever cover. Having Caldwell close to Marshall would enable him to monitor Marshall's movements and keep Lord appraised of any overtures to Khomeini. Marshall would not be able to contact him without Lord knowing, and at the first move, he would intercede.

His ruminations were interrupted when the door opened and more diners entered. He looked at his watch; it was ten P.M.; he had forgotten how late Parisians dined. Soon the small restaurant was filled, and the noise prevented him from thinking.

He paid his bill, was finishing the last of his beer, preparing to leave, when the door opened and a small party crowded into the doorway. There were four men: three Arabs in business suits and an Oriental man. Lord was about to signal that his table was free when he recognized the Chinese man.

Unbelieving, he stared directly at him, but the man did not see him, just glanced at heads, looking for an empty space.

A waiter went toward the party solicitously. Lord knew they would be pointed toward his table, told it would be free momentarily, so he quickly left his seat and went through the beaded curtains in back.

Seeing the table free, the waiter looked startled, but thought the diner must have slipped out while he was serving someone else. He led the party to the table, talking to the familiar-looking man, who was obviously the host, as if he was a regular customer.

It *was* Chien Lin Huong, Lord realized, peering through the beads; there was no doubt of it. He looked older than when Lord had last seen him in Saigon, and he had put on weight, but the strong, powerful features were unmistakable.

A waiter tapped Lord on the shoulder to get by with a tray of food and pointed him in the direction of the toilets, thinking he had come back for that.

"Do you know that man who just took my table?" Lord asked in the prissy, fussy manner he often affected. "I am *very* annoyed."

The waiter glanced toward the table. "It must be a mistake. That is Wu Te-chao; he would never be rude."

"Wu Te-chao," Lord repeated as the waiter disappeared, then he walked into the tiny kitchen, steaming and bustling, and went directly through the back door to the alley without being noticed.

Wu Te-chao; Chien Lin Huong.

Then he remembered that night too, the frantic phone calls, the hysterical woman telling him Huong was at the hospital.

A Chinese man. Someone who threatened Marshall. A murdered Sûreté agent, and Chien Lin Huong hosting a group of Arabs.

Lord shook his head in amazement. The best plans always went awry because of bizarre incidents like this. The unforeseen was utterly predictable, yet he would never have imagined such coincidence or luck.

He was no longer tired and no longer felt old. He needed to walk in solitude and ponder this. On St.-Germain he got a cab and headed back toward his lodgings.

Dropped several blocks from his apartment, he dodged heavy traffic on Boulevard Suchet at Porte de la Muette and headed into the Bois de Boulogne, a huge park with miles of roads and hundreds of paths winding through dense woods.

Though Lord could sit motionless for hours, he did his best thinking as he walked. His languor was deceptive, as his diffident manner hid powerful emotions. Now he needed to move, physically grapple with the myriad complexities and possibilities confronting him.

An unknown Chinese man threatening Bradley Marshall

and the appearance of Chien Lin Huong were neither coincidental nor unrelated.

He chose a road where cars with their yellow lights were mercifully dimmed and he started to walk.

Huong was using an assumed name; obviously he was hiding something. Surely that could be turned to advantage. Huong had been with Arabs. Though Lord didn't know the connection, undoubtedly that could be useful also.

Lord was so intent in thought that he walked past several figures standing alongside the road before he realized what was going on. "Jesus," he muttered to himself as a tight-skirted woman leered at him. He crossed the road to the other side, but found himself walking past garishly made up transvestites.

Cars slowed, and one even stopped beside him. He hurried on and turned left at the next intersection to go deeper into the woods, but cars prowled this road too, and soon he was walking past leather-jacketed hustlers and paired males heading into the bushes.

Jesus Christ, he thought—the only place he could think in this depraved city was on his thin mattress on his metal-framed bed in an austere one-bulb room where only Savonarola could be happy. God damn Mike Caldwell at the Hilton. And God damn Chien Lin Huong sitting in comfort at *his* table in the Latin Quarter.

He retraced his steps so quickly that he was limping by the time he reached the intersection. He stopped to catch his breath, then calmed himself. This would not do, he decided; imprudence and intolerance would lead to mistakes. He was acting like a prickly old man, some silly Prufrock. He had been out of the field too long, had spent too much time at home and at Little League games; he had become unjaded. He should learn something from this; he always gained valuable insight if he took the time and trouble to filter experience through thought.

He took out his glasses, polished them carefully, then put them on to study the carnal scene before him. It was Kabuki theater, he decided, all in slow motion and outlandish costume. Down the road to the left were girls in fake fur and fishnet stockings; down the other were boys in jeans and bomber jackets. Cars traveled both.

Other roads, other places, no doubt lured those with different tastes.

He considered the intersection. What sent a man down one, and another down the other? The result was the same, and the price similar too, he supposed.

He studied the players. There were old whores and young, those for every taste—young boys who wanted to fuck their mothers, and dirty old men who wanted nymphettes. Sneering young males for the guilty at heart, and transvestites for the confused.

Cars slowed to appraise the merchandise, stopped to negotiate a price, and more often than not drove off with the object.

Lord watched the carnival with impassive eye and made no judgment, but he decided that a clever pimp would have both boys and girls in his stable and stock it with furs and leather, whips and chains, and feathers too.

Yes, that was the lesson to be learned: one needed all options available, a wide selection of merchandise, and an object for every taste. This was no new lesson, of course, but its practical application here on the street reinforced its freshness and utility.

Yes, yes, yes, he thought. He needed something for everyone in this game. He had to twist Marshall, Huong, Khomeini, and Caldwell to his purpose, but each would respond to different incentives—perhaps a whip for Marshall, leather for Caldwell, and for Huong, blood.

He turned away and headed out of the Bois. It had been an excellent evening; he had done good work and now he was tired. He would sleep well, he knew, and in the morning he would begin with Caldwell. Then he would turn his attention to Huong. In fact he already had a plan.

When he returned to his apartment, he decided that he liked it after all; it was what he would have chosen when younger. And now he didn't feel very old. He wasn't Prufrock at all, not at all. He *was* like Savonarola, but he had learned a lesson from his bonfire too—fanaticism was lethal to the fanatic in the end. One should always be practical and stock feathers as well as leather.

He dropped onto his thin mattress, closed his eyes, and sank into a purifying slumber.

CHAPTER 7

"My God, Brad, did the plane crash?" Catherine asked, drawing back from his embrace when he entered the foyer of the house, a palatial mansion in the heart of Paris that had served as the American ambassador's residence since the Second World War. Catherine had had it renovated and refurbished to her taste, muted and expensive. The wallpaper had been stripped, the rooms freshly painted in elegant pastels, and cast with deceptive casualness on hardwood floors were Persian carpets that created a harmonious blend of color and design that was rich and warm.

The residence was on several wooded acres surrounded by high, electronically sensored fences and guarded twenty-four hours by French police; at the entrance to the long driveway was a metal gate monitored by Marines.

Catherine, greeting him in the hallway, the staircase behind her, did not bother to hide her surprise at his pale and stricken appearance; he was obviously upset.

Marshall smiled. "Thank you, Catherine. I had a pleasant trip. How kind of you to inquire. And how are you?"

She kissed him lightly, then she let the matter drop for she knew he would tell her what was wrong in his own good time, which would not be long.

He put his arms around her and drew her close. "I forgot how good you feel."

"You are such a satyr, Brad."

"And you are such a nymph. Let's go upstairs and play."

She pushed him away. "When are you going to improve your seduction routine? Nymph! I'm fifty years old and twenty pounds overweight."

"You're gorgeous. Let's fuck."

She laughed, took his hand, and led him to the stairs. "That's better; you talked me into it."

Afterward, he fell asleep. Later they had dinner together, talked about Sarah's and Chris's arrival for the holidays, and he told her of his meeting with Carter and pantomimed his discomfort with the apple pulp.

"He didn't invite you four thousand miles to swig apple juice with him. What did he want?"

"For me to contact the Ayatollah Khomeini. He's worried the Shah might fall."

"As well he should! But Khomeini is worse; he's a fanatic."

"We can deal with him; we all speak the language—power."

She shook her head. "You do *not* speak his language. Islam is a medieval religion based on hate, blood, and suppressing women. Imagine Khomeini in bed."

He held up his hands. "Dear God, spare me. I'm still ill from contemplating Nixon and Kissinger in the sack years ago. Anyway, I don't have a choice—it's a presidential directive."

"Then you're not asking me for advice."

"Actually I am. Do you think I should dye my hair?"

"Should I lose twenty pounds?"

"I love you the way you are."

"Fat?"

"You are not fat, Catherine. You are a mature woman, full and vibrant, a Rubens nymph. I love your body—it suits me perfectly."

She nodded. "Yes. Like your gray hair suits me perfectly."

He laughed and ended the conversation without telling her about the Chinese man, and later in bed, a gray-haired man and a mature woman, they made love again, comfortably, with the good humor of age and familiarity.

At breakfast he did not tell her about the man either; he did not want to frighten her or admit his part in covering up the child's death, and besides, he felt confident Andy Maynard could handle the problem before it grew worse.

When he left the house for his limousine parked in the circle driveway, Sergeant Mead jumped out of the front seat, saluted, and held open the back door. He was in dress blues, and all business. "Good morning, sir," he said briskly.

Marshall had forgotten about his bodyguard, but seeing him so fierce and well meaning, like in Saigon years ago, he smiled happily and patted his shoulder. "Good morning, Sergeant." Then he settled into the backseat and didn't speak again, knowing Mead was now on duty and didn't like to be disturbed with small talk.

When the car pulled into the embassy complex, a huge, modern fortress just off the Champs-Elysées, Mead ushered him through the courtyard to his private elevator that brought them to his top-floor office overlooking the Seine, with a view of the Left Bank, sweeping from the Eiffel Tower upriver to Notre Dame.

As was his mandated routine, he was allowed five minutes privacy in the hushed elegance of his dark leathered, book-lined offices. Only the ticking of an Empire clock broke the silence, its gilded Napoleonic eagle with outstretched wings commanding quiet respect.

The only evidence that it was a working office were the two telephones and an intercom on a Louis XV desk; otherwise the room resembled a library reading room with an eclectic collection of modern paintings that didn't scream for the eyes' attention, but appealed to the reflective mind. There were no photographs of himself with dignitaries, no congratulating certificates, awards, or degrees, no pictures of family, only Oriental art—a small lapis-lazuli horse, netsuke, jade carvings.

When his allotted time was up, his secretary, Helen Sarbanes, brought in his briefing folders. She had been with him ten years, since private law practice. In her late forties, she was short and trim with a jet-black beehive hairdo, a formidable woman with three ex-husbands, carrying her years with style and swagger, camouflaging them with bright, tight clothing and outlandish jewelry.

Today she was wearing a screaming-yellow silk suit with clashing rainbow scarf and earrings the length of stilettos, but no matter how outrageous her outfit, Marshall never mentioned her attire—it was one of the many games they played.

"I need to see Luke," Marshall told her when she finished running over his appointments for the day. He felt Bishop should be appraised of the danger even though the Chinese man probably didn't know he had been in the car that ran over his child. But also, Luke could help him against the man.

"When? The trade meeting will run till noon; you can't cancel lunch with the congressional delegation, and after that you're going to Elysée Palace."

"Just have him stand by; I can duck out of the trade meeting around eleven. I only need to see him for a few minutes."

He picked up the briefing folder on the export/import meeting, but dropped it immediately; he didn't want to think about Plymouths and Renaults. He didn't want to lunch with junketeering congressmen either, and he didn't want to meet with the French president. But Plymouths and Renaults were important for the trade balance, and it was necessary to see the French president to float his "interest" in Khomeini's arrival in Paris. He sighed, picked up the folder, and scanned the figures on Plymouths and Renaults.

Andy Maynard's face was coated with powdered sugar from a sack of doughnuts when Mike Caldwell walked into his office at seven-thirty. He brushed at his mouth and sipped coffee. "What are you doing here so early?" he asked in surprise.

"Isn't this when the workday begins?"

"You could have the day off; I didn't plan for you to work after that flight."

"I got a good sleep. I'm ready to go."

Maynard offered him the sack of doughnuts.

"Those aren't good for you."

"Don't," Maynard said, raising a cautionary hand. "I catch enough shit from my wife and that lunatic Marine."

Caldwell smiled. "Coffee isn't good either; caffeine and sugar spell coronary."

Maynard sailed a folder at him. "Read that. A Sûreté

agent was killed at Père Lachaise two days ago. See if you can tie it to the threat to Marshall." He tossed another folder in Caldwell's direction. "That's what we have on the case so far, except what Marshall told me yesterday. His car ran over a Chinese man's child in Saigon six years ago. Marshall's driver was murdered the next day. Whoever that man is, he's here. Your mission, should you choose to accept it, is to find him and rip out his heart."

"That's it—find one nameless, faceless gook in Paris? Where's the challenge?"

Maynard munched another doughnut. "Now, the bad news is that there's no office space up here; you're stuck in the basement. The good news is that no one will bother you down there; I won't know if you're shooting heroin or snoozing. Any questions?"

Caldwell shook his head. "But I'll probably have a few after I read these."

Maynard watched him leave, then opened his desk drawer and pulled out Caldwell's personnel file again. He could spot a sanitized file when he saw one, and Caldwell's had been vacuumed and bleached.

He reached into the bag, but it was empty. He upended the crumbs into his mouth, then dusted the sugar to the floor.

Yes, he was fat and at the end of his career, but he wasn't *senile*. Only he could have made the connection to the Chinese man and Marshall; only he could have traced the obscure death of Marshall's driver in Saigon and intuited the tie between the Chinese man and the murder of the Sûreté agent. He alone had discovered Bradley Marshall was in great danger—*because* he was old.

What kind of fool did Langley take him for to think Caldwell was here to help him? Caldwell was a contract man, pure and simple, and contract men didn't do paperwork or read files. So why was he here? And what was this bullshit about an Ayatollah? Who cared about a nutty Moslem? And what, after all, was Marshall doing in Washington?

Brad was being kind by trying to protect his feelings, but he knew Langley was keeping him in the dark about something. He fumbled in his drawer and grunted happily when he found a bag of cookies.

Why Caldwell? Andrew Maynard sat tense, hands folded across his belly.

Jesus, he thought when it hit him, he *was* getting old. Caldwell wasn't working for him—that was just a cover: Marshall had been in Washington consulting with Carter about Khomeini. Langley would be paranoid—*more* paranoid, he amended. My God, he thought in glee, the CIA's counterterrorist chief, known notoriously as the Abbot, a thin, frail, alcoholic man who saw moles and conspiracies everywhere, would have gone through the roof; he was probably orbiting Pluto over the possibility of the Shah's fall.

Caldwell was here for that, of course—Langley would do anything to save the Shah.

Jesus, he thought, shaking his head at his stupidity, he had seen the Chinese man as the threat to Marshall, but the real threat was in the basement—Caldwell.

But whom was he working for?

He munched cookies absently, mulling the murderous minds at Langley.

The phone rang and he picked it up, but couldn't speak for the cookies in his mouth. He reached for coffee to wash them down.

"Mike Caldwell, please," a not-unfamiliar voice said, then at the silence, "Mike?"

Maynard knew that voice, but he couldn't place it. One more word and he would though, so he waited, but the phone was hung up abruptly.

Langley would be wild about the fall of the Shah. The Abbot would be ballistic, but *who* would they send to take care of this problem?

The Phantom! He choked on his coffee, spewing it across his desk. They would send Wilson Lord, of course. *That* was the voice on the phone. Jesus Christ, he thought wildly. Wilson Lord was here, and Mike Caldwell was working for him.

Marshall was marked; they would kill him if he made an overture to Khomeini.

Then exhilaration swept him. But they *won't* because he had found them out. He hit his desk in triumph, sending cookie crumbs and coffee over the files. Not only had he pieced together Vietnam and the Chinese man, but the Ayatollah and Wilson Lord.

And they thought he was old and stupid, when all he was, was fat.

He'd show them all. He was going to get the Chinese man and nail Wilson Lord's ass, and Mike Caldwell's too—this was treason.

If he could tie the murder to the Chinese man, he could pressure Sûreté; the French would never admit error—what Nazi collaborators? Vichy where?—but if he presented them with evidence of a compromised agent, they would cooperate.

He'd get the Chinese man, then he'd burn Lord and Caldwell too.

He swept crumbs into the trash can, blotted up the coffee with a handkerchief, and went for his coat, confidence and power surging through him. He felt great, strong and good, an aging Lancelot, somewhat overweight—well, *really* overweight, but ready to take them all on.

Thirty minutes later Maynard pulled his nondescript government-issue sedan into the half-moon parking area before the entrance to Père Lachaise: only hearses were allowed within the cemetery gates.

Inside on the left was a guardhouse attached to the high wall surrounding the cemetery, and leaning in the doorway with folded arms was a young, bored gendarme, his foot absently kicking at fallen leaves.

At Maynard's approach, the gendarme's arm rose mechanically to hold out a map marked with the most famous gravesites, saving the guards from having to explain a thousand times daily the route to the illustrious dead. The youth hated this assignment—in the month he had been here, only one thing had happened, and he had missed it.

The guard he had relieved two days ago told him a body had been found.

The gendarme, a surly youth to begin with, now more irritable because his girlfriend was in her menstrual period and would not let him sleep with her, had said disgustedly, "What do you think they've been burying here—Citroëns?"

No, the other explained: a man was murdered here the afternoon before. Then he related about the swarm of intelligence agents who whisked away the body and swore everyone to secrecy. No doubt they'd return to question him.

But no one did. Not that he had seen anything—that day had been like every other: several burials, a few mourners, some sightseers. And the next was the same, and now today here was another sightseer, a dumpy American in a trench coat, eating a candy bar. He held out the map, then dropped his hand to cup his unrelieved crotch.

Maynard reached into his jacket for his credentials. After examining the photograph with Gallic suspicion, the gendarme handed it back with a shrug.

"Who was on duty here two days ago?"

The youth flinched at Maynard's excruciating French. "I was."

The man's French was an outrage; if it weren't for the credentials, he'd push him out the gate. And what was that white powder on his face? Cocaine? American secret agents were even more depraved than in the movies, and *much* older and fatter.

"I want to know about the Chinese man who was here."

"The one with the camera? I thought he was Japanese. It was too dark for pictures, that's why I remember him."

"Describe him."

"He was old and wore a suit and had an umbrella." What was there to say about an Oriental? "His eyes were slanted."

"How old?"

"Very." His hands opened on the antiquity. "Your age."

Then to the surprise of the gendarme, the drugged fat man stuffed the map into his jacket pocket and returned to his car.

Caldwell was in shorts and T-shirt waiting outside the handball court in the gym when Bishop came down shortly before ten. "I've been waiting," he said without preliminaries.

"You got a glove?"

"I don't use one. You got a ball?"

"In my locker. Give me a couple minutes to change."

When he came out in shorts and T-shirt, also without a glove, Caldwell was on the court, a small cube of a room with a hardwood floor and four walls. Bishop tossed him the ball to slap around for practice, but Caldwell said he was ready.

"Play for serve?" Bishop asked.

"Go ahead, take first serve."

Bishop slammed the ball against the wall with a tremendous echo, caught Caldwell's rebound, and drove it so low it gave no play. He won the next five points with the same speed and ease. "Six to zip. One more is a skunk, Secret Agent Man. I thought you could play this game."

Caldwell just nodded. Bishop smashed the ball with incredible velocity, but Caldwell rifled it into a corner and won the serve, and the next seven points.

Then the game became physical. They slammed into one another, pushed, shoved, hit with their full weight, and drove the other against the walls.

The game was to twenty-one, but had to be won by two points. At the end of an hour they were bruised and hurting, the score tied at forty-six. Unwilling to admit weakness or defeat, they played even harder, smashing violently against one another, throwing themselves to the floor to catch a shot, pummeling and tripping the other. When one got the advantage, the other played even rougher.

After two hours the floor was slick with sweat and spotted with blood, their hands were raw, and the score was tied at seventy-eight.

Leaning against opposite walls, drawing deep breaths, they looked at one another.

"I'll offer you a draw," Bishop said.

"I'll offer *you* the draw."

"How about if we just quit?"

"Done," Caldwell said, heading for the door, saying casually to hide his hurt, "Not a bad game, Lukey."

"I was really off today," Bishop answered with the same faked casualness.

In the locker room they dropped to a bench and didn't speak for several minutes, too tired to move or shower. Finally Bishop stood to strip.

"Shit," Caldwell said. "I didn't bring a towel."

Bishop tossed him an extra from his locker. They headed into the shower, stood under adjacent nozzles, and let water run over them for a long time before they even soaped down. Out of the corners of their eyes they appraised one another.

Bishop saw an incredibly lean, taut body with many scars, some recent, and knife cuts that could only have been torture, or hand-to-hand fighting.

Caldwell saw a man slightly shorter than himself, but packing twenty more pounds of muscle, a very powerful man, and he saw the battle scars—an unmistakable bullet entry in his chest, and numerous shrapnel wounds on his torso and legs.

Drying off, they met each other's eyes frankly, realizing they each faced a man more formidable than first supposed.

"So how's it going?" Bishop asked, toweling his hair. "What do you think of Andy?"

"He looks like he was shot out of a shit gun. I think he's going to have a heart attack or go into insulin shock; all he eats is sugar. Is he diabetic?"

Bishop laughed. "He really pisses me off. He's been a spook forever, but he was a Marine *once*—he ought to know better. Still, he's a great guy."

"The ambassador likes him?"

"They've been friends thirty years. He's the godfather to Marshall's son."

"The queer?"

"Chris," Bishop said coldly.

"Sorry. Chris. What about the daughter?"

"I'm in love with her," Bishop said with a smile, but not joking at all.

"Surely she can do better," Caldwell taunted.

"Oh, she has—lots of times. But I'm still waiting."

"Your heart's on your sleeve, Marine."

"Hey, that's where we wear them."

Bishop put on his uniform, and Caldwell a loose-fitting, dark suit.

"When do you want another game?" Bishop asked as they dressed. "Tomorrow?" He hoped not, for his hand was unbelievably tender.

"I may be too tired," Caldwell answered, unsatisfied with his appearance in the mirror. He looked like a plague victim, he thought, envying Bishop's muscle, but he turned to Luke so there would be no misunderstanding. "Not because of this game—Angie, up in Finance. I turned in my voucher, and . . . there she was."

Bishop checked himself in the mirror. "You *do* need help with women. She's got herpes. And warts."

"I'm not looking for love, just cunt. I'm guessing she has one." Unhappy with his collar, Caldwell hitched his belt to the last notch so that his trousers bunched.

"Yeah, but nasty. Really nasty."

"I don't care. All she wants is dinner and a fuck, and that's all I want, except I could do without dinner. You know what Iran's like? You don't see flesh there; the women are wrapped up like delicatessen ham. It got so bad I was getting hard-ons from the lingerie ads in the Sears catalog; I was beating off like a teenager. Besides, I've got enough penicillin and and tetracycline in me to ward off any virus."

They turned from the mirror to one another at the same time.

Caldwell eyed him appraisingly. "You look great." Then he turned back to the mirror. "I look like shit."

Bishop smiled. "You're in luck; Angie won't care." Then he left the locker room, calling, "Let me know when you want to play again."

"Where have you been?" Helen Sarbanes snapped when Bishop wandered into her office. "He's been looking for you. He wanted to see you at eleven. You're his military aide, you're supposed to be there when he wants you."

"I was in the gym. I told my secretary."

"We *called* the gym. I even sent Sergeant Mead to get you. He said you weren't lifting weights or in the shower. And that slut in your office is not a secretary—*I* am a secretary."

"Sergeant Mead?"

"He's the ambassador's new bodyguard."

"When did that happen? And Candy is a *great* secretary."

"*Lots* of things are happening, Major. If you were ever around, you'd know it."

"I was playing handball, Helen. What does he want? Where is he? And what the fuck are you wearing—I've never *seen* that color before. And those earrings—what are they, bayonets?"

"The ambassador is having lunch with a delegation from Congress, three senators and six representatives. He cannot see you now. I do not know when it will be convenient for him to see you since this afternoon he will be with the President of France. Perhaps you can tell me when it would be convenient for *you* to see him. The color is 'Chinese silk' and the earrings are sterling silver."

"Cut the shit, Helen. Tell me the big news—when's Sarah coming?"

"What on earth do you need to know that for? She loathes you. She thinks you're crazy. We *all* think you're crazy. No decent woman would go out with you."

"I'm in love with her."

"I'm in love with Paul Newman. So what?"

"Come on, Helen. Put in a good word for me."

"I don't know that language, Major. I don't speak barbarian; neither does Sarah."

Bishop reached for the plastic flower in the vase on her desk and handed it to her. "C'mon, Helen. Do me the favor and I'll buy you some real flowers."

She grabbed it back. "I don't *want* real flowers—they're like men, they wilt."

"You haven't known the right men, Helen—some of us don't."

She snorted.

"So when does the ambassador want to see me?"

"Three hours ago. But he'll settle for later. Should he go to the gym, or will you be in your cave tonight if he decides to call?"

"My apartment; I'll be reading a good book."

"Major Bishop, I've had reports on your apartment—there are no books there, certainly no *good* ones. Now get out of here, I have work to do."

Returning to his office down the hall, Bishop examined his hand, swollen and red. He wondered what Marshall wanted; it was rare to be summoned unexpectedly in the middle of the day; his duties were routine and undemanding—usually he coordinated with French military visitors and handled ceremony. He had a secretary, but Helen was right about her—Candy really wasn't much of a secretary—and he had an interpreter, but everyone who had business at the U.S. embassy spoke English. Yet Bishop loved his job and was happy when headquarters told him he had been name-requested by the newly appointed U.S. ambassador to France to serve as his aide. It was a good assignment and would help his career.

Moreover, he *liked* Marshall, and he owed him; Marshall had saved his life—of course he had jeopardized it in the first place, but what after all was he doing as a Marine except pushing life to the edge? But not only had Marshall saved his life, when the Marines had wanted to medically discharge him for his head wound in Saigon, Marshall had interceded to gain him time to recover. After a year on the temporarily disabled list, he had been reinstated on active duty and promoted.

And then there was Marshall's daughter, Sarah.

She had visited him often in the hospital at Bethesda, yet he never got her to consider him as anything except a friend. But another chance was coming up—Sarah was arriving for Christmas. He knew she was living with a professor at Berkeley, but the guy couldn't possibly feel about her the way he did—and besides, the harder things got, the deeper Bishop dug in. She'd come around; he just needed to work at it more.

When he entered his office, his secretary looked up from her paperback book and smiled. She made no pretense of working and wasn't a bit embarrassed by the soft-porn romances she read all day. She was younger than Bishop, divorced, a rather clever woman with long hair of faintly Chinese-silk color who liked Bishop and managed to sleep with him at least once a week.

"Where do you get those books?" Bishop asked as he headed into his office.

"The commissary."

"They have any *good* books there—ones without tits and hunks on the cover?"

Maybe he *would* read a book tonight. He would check the commissary.

And then, he wondered, why did Marshall suddenly have a bodyguard?

Caldwell's right palm was so tender he had to turn the file pages with his left hand.

He was in his basement office far from the gym, down a

corridor he shared with janitors and maintenance. The room was large and sterile, with only a metal desk and swivel chair.

Caldwell slouched at the desk, a cigarette dangling from his lips. Crumpled notepaper littered the floor, and papers from the two files were scattered over the desk. The disorder mirrored his chaotic and intuitive thought.

He ground the cigarette into the desk and got out of his chair. His thought was physical and random, his mind geared to body; lying on his back, hands clasped behind his head, he did sit-ups, flexing like a spring.

Maynard was on to something, but the Chinese man shouldn't pose a difficulty—even an old, fat man ought to be able to handle this now that the threat had been identified.

He buzzed the upstairs secretary to see if he had any messages; he was expecting Wilson Lord to contact him, but there had been no calls. Maybe Lord hadn't arrived yet. He hoped not; he could use some recovery time, and some new clothes—nothing he owned fit any longer, so with no work to do, he left his office to go shopping. He wanted to look as good as Bishop.

At Sûreté headquarters, a deputy director opened his hands in astonishment when Maynard asked for the name of the Chinese suspect in the murder of François Bichot.

"Bichot? A Chinese man? What is this, another American conspiracy theory?"

Maynard reached into his trench-coat pocket for a candy bar.

Are trench coats required? the deputy director wondered. Issued, then never cleaned?

"A Chinese man who lived in Saigon in 1972, and probably there during your 'colonial' period—your file undoubtedly has records. Most likely he fled to Hong Kong after the North's takeover—where else could a Chinese man go, and where else would he have stashed his money? This Chinese man is in Paris and murdered Bichot. We believe this has to do with a plot against our ambassador. If Sûreté is withholding information on a threat to the representative of the United States, my government will be profoundly disturbed. Surely you wouldn't be doing that just to save yourself embarrassment about a compromised agent."

The deputy director sat back. This was working better than he had hoped; he had not counted on the Americans for help with a disturbing problem—eliminating a foreigner legitimately in the country, a Chinese man who had murdered one of their agents. Americans were so rarely helpful; aggressive and boasting, crude and loud, and at every Michelin restaurant—*unavoidable,* and on expense accounts too.

"Such a puzzling case. We are mystified."

"Perhaps I can be of assistance," Maynard answered somberly.

The Frenchman went to a file cabinet and brought a folder to Maynard. The name on the folder was Wu Te-chao.

Wilson Lord woke refreshed and ready to tackle all problems, but he'd been stymied at his first effort; he couldn't find Caldwell—he wasn't at the embassy or his hotel.

But the day picked up when he turned his attention to the riddle of Huong. He returned to the restaurant, bribed the waiter who had identified Huong, and discovered he was a regular diner and had a reservation for the following evening. The waiter even provided a telephone number and a Carte Bleu credit-card receipt.

Bent on revenge, single-minded on avenging his daughter, Huong probably didn't realize he was threatened, but Lord knew that if he had killed the Sûreté agent, Sûreté would not let him live. Huong needed protection. And Lord could use him. How better to stop Marshall from contacting Khomeini than by helping Huong eliminate him?

With two murderous men at his disposal—Huong and Caldwell—how could he fail? All he had to do was turn them to his purposes, and he did not doubt he could do it; they were weak and vulnerable, and he—masterful. The only challenge was Marshall, but he *always* beat Marshall; after all, right was on his side.

CHAPTER 8

As Marshall's police-escorted limousine glided through the ornate gates of Elysée Palace, accelerating quickly and smoothly, he sat back to enjoy the sensation of safely encapsulated motion, his right hand kneading soft leather as he concentrated on the pleasure of propulsion. Speed was youth—primitive, powerful, erotic—and for him explained race-car drivers, pilots, astronauts, and middle-aged men with Porsches, all he would trade his ambassadorship for today after his meeting with the French president—an insufferably arrogant man who had nevertheless immediately caught his casual reference to the arrival of the Ayatollah Khomeini; an almost imperceptible rise of his right eyebrow conveyed his understanding that the United States wanted a meeting, with himself as go-between, for which of course he would gain stature, goodwill, and a favor in return.

Dropping that reference had been the sole purpose of his visit, a ten-second allusion in an hour of tortuous diplomatic blather that would require another hour's work to pound into pudding for the diplomatic pouch that would go back to Washington.

It was a wonder the couriers didn't carry Baggies, he thought.

"Take me home, Marcel," he said to his driver. He would pound the pudding tomorrow. Automobile executives and congressmen together in one day was above and beyond anyone's call to duty, and meeting with the French president put him right up there with Nathan Hale, he thought. He deserved a drink. Besides, there was nothing else he could do at the embassy to establish contact with Khomeini; he had dropped a hint of interest in a meeting—now it was up to the Iranians to initiate one.

There was no more he could do about the threat from Huong either. Andy was taking care of that and would get back to him as soon as he had something, and he could wait until morning to talk to Luke Bishop.

The CIA posed a problem—Mike Caldwell was obviously here to monitor any overture to Khomeini—but until Marshall did, they were not a danger. Nothing might come of that threat at all if the Iranians refused to see him, and in any case, Maynard would help him with that also.

Andy was a knight—aged and overweight, no longer able to get into his armor, but his honor still fit, and he would ride out, a sloppy, belly-bouncing, middle-aged man to joust head-on, facing any enemy, and even now, Marshall felt, Andy was more than a match for Caldwell. Yes, Marshall thought, he and Maynard could handle these problems, but he would bring Bishop in on it just in case.

In the meantime he had Sergeant Mead; no harm could come with him along.

"Pretty boring so far," he noted to Mead in the front seat.

Mead turned. "That suits me, sir. It beats inspections and guard duty, and I never thought I'd get into a French palace."

"Remember the palace in Hue, the day before the Tet Offensive? You saved my life then."

Mead shrugged deprecatingly. "I guess we're about even, sir."

Marshall smiled. Mead seemed even larger than before, but maybe it was because he himself had shrunk, he thought. "No, Sergeant, we are not even, but perhaps we can keep it this boring. How's your wife?"

Mead considered telling him about Sung, but he'd only been working for the ambassador twenty-four hours—this was hardly the time to bring up personal problems, especially coming from the palace of the French president. Besides, he still felt awkward around Marshall; that would pass, he felt, as it had in Saigon, but now he was too nervous with his new duties, and he was having trouble adjusting to a man he remembered ten years younger. Certainly the ambassador wasn't old or infirm, but he *had* changed; not just grayer and a little heavier, he seemed more worn—frailer. Ten years hadn't made him old, just more mortal. Sadder, Mead thought.

"Just fine, sir; everything with Sung is fine."

Marshall nodded. He knew Ron Mead. "Just fine" meant trouble, but he also knew he would never get anything out of him until Mead decided to confide in him.

Marshall reached for a newspaper on the seat and scanned the headlines on the Lafabre scandal, the latest in an interminable series of defense-contract malfeasances, then he put down the paper and stared at the back of his chauffeur's head.

"What about Lafabre, Marcel? Guilty?"

"Anyone that rich has to be guilty, Excellency."

That's probably true, Marshall thought. "Are you a communist, Marcel?"

The driver looked into the rearview mirror with a wary grin. "I like women too much to be a communist, Excellency."

They must teach epigrams in French schools, Marshall thought. "Yes. That's why I'm not much of a democrat."

Marcel laughed. "Powerful men don't have to be anything, Excellency."

"They have to be careful, Marcel."

He folded the paper and dropped it on the floorboard. He *had* been careful in his public career. He had done the best he could, had worked hard and meant well, yet he had caused pain and suffering, the death of that child, and Teresa Hawthorne and the orphans long ago in Saigon.

Yet it was *so* long ago, and he was hardly the major villain in Vietnam, just part of the supporting cast in the tawdry play, his part finished by the time America stumbled off the Vietnamese stage like a desiccated old man fleeing the bed of an insatiable, Goyaesque whore—running to the roof of the charnel house, lifting off in a helicopter, kicking at the survivors: deus ex machina in reverse.

When he was dropped at the residence and bounded up the steps, the front door swung open for him.

"Thank you, André," he said to his valet.

André pressed a sheaf of messages into his hand and murmured, "You have a dinner tonight at eight, Excellency."

He took the papers absently, his mouth crimping in annoyance; he had forgotten about the dinner. But he had to go; given by the Syrian ambassador, it would afford him another opportunity to establish contact with Khomeini. In the muddled minefield of Arab politics, it was impossible to know who was talking with whom at any moment, their suspicion and hatred for one another so great, but for getting a message out, a word whispered in secret was better than a satellite broadcast.

On his way through the living room, he paused at the somber peacefulness of the late afternoon, then dropped into an armchair, tossing the messages onto a table.

Gray winter light streamed through the bay windows of the living room, mingling and dancing with that of the already lighted chandeliers. It was a huge room, warm and comfortable, a blend of Chinese and European furniture, rosewood and mahogany, the floor a parquet of Oriental rugs, and Gobelin tapestries provided a muted, intricate backdrop for celadon porcelains and Ming vases.

His eyes focused through the windows on a row of barren trees whose limbs thrust up like medieval spires. He loved winter. Spring and autumn were too busy; there was too much movement and color, beautiful, but like Bach, too nervous. And summer was too wet, hot, and noisy; it was soft, like Tchaikovsky, a time for women and children. But winter was stripped and bare, a difficult time, a time for men—Mahler.

"Is anything the matter?" Catherine called from the hallway on her way out.

He turned, surprised but happy, and held out his hand for her.

Her sable coat was draped over her shoulders and her hands were working into her gloves; she hesitated, already late, but she went to him, a woman aging well, purposeful and energetic, at peace with herself in middle age. "I didn't know you were coming back."

"Patrick Henry would have packed it in today too."

"How was he?" she asked of the French president.

He waved a dismissive hand.

"Can I get you anything?"

"No, thank you. I was just enjoying the quiet and the trees. It's like a scene from the Middle Ages, isn't it? Dark and grim. Hard."

She looked out the window, saw nothing of the Middle Ages, only some poor cold sparrows pecking futilely in the grass. She frowned.

He patted her hand, amused, for he had seen the sparrows too. "I love you."

She tugged on an earring, contemplating the sparrows. "I *hope* so; I'd hate to be sleeping with a man who didn't." Then she turned. "The children called; they're coming Friday."

"So soon? I talked with them just two days ago—nothing was definite."

"They decided to come for your birthday. But I think there's more to it."

"Dear God, one just shudders at that."

"I think it's good news this time."

He motioned to a chair. "There's a complication, Catherine. I wasn't going to worry you needlessly, but there might be a security problem. Andy's concerned."

"About what? Terrorists?" she asked anxiously.

"It might have something to do with when I was in Vietnam."

"Vietnam? That was years ago."

"It may be nothing; Andy's got a good fix on it. I'll know more tomorrow."

"Well, for God's sake let me know before they come; I'll call them immediately."

"Let's leave it until tomorrow. And there's another thing you should know."

Her hand fell to her breast. "Besides my children being killed? What?"

Marshall smiled. "You should have been on the stage, Catherine."

"You're the actor, Brad, not I."

"Well, tonight we're both going to have to perform."

"At Saud's? An Arab dinner party? We'd have to ride in naked on horseback even to be noticed at his place—it is *so* pretentious. But at least Clarissa won't serve couscous."

"That's what I have to talk to you about, Catherine—Arabs."

She closed her eyes. "Please. There has to be a limit."

Marshall ignored her. "If the Shah falls, Khomeini will replace him. I need to contact him. I'm going to mention this to Saud. There's a chance it could ricochet back to you. Clarissa or someone might mention Khomeini—just play the stupid wife, you're so good at that, say 'Oh, yes, Brad has been talking so much about him lately.' "

She dropped her coat to the floor and leaned forward. "I told you, Brad, that man is dangerous. Why don't you ever listen to me?"

He smiled. "I *do* listen to you, but I *work* for Jimmy Carter."

She swept up her coat grandly. "I have to go. Estelle is hysterical; I'm supposed to comfort her. Claude is having an affair with a Lido stripper. Can you imagine?"

"I certainly can't. What are you going to tell her?"

"Shoot him." She waved from the doorway. "See you tonight. Don't worry, I'll have my insipid wifey look on by party time."

He watched her go toward the kitchen and knew that in a few minutes a maid would be hurling loaves of bread at the birds.

And there was the maid, and Catherine too, pelting birds with bread. He *did* love her. She was kind and good, funny and sexual, loving and passionate. She wept for the poor and comforted the hurt. She fed birds.

Then he frowned. He wished Sarah and Chris weren't coming.

Maynard returned to his office in late afternoon feeling unwell. His stomach was upset and there was uncomfortable pressure in his chest. Probably I'm going to have a heart attack, he thought, but when he stood and stretched, he felt better, and when he lay on his sofa, his discomfort left. Too much coffee and sugar—he would cut back and go on a diet.

Yet with all that caffeine and sugar, he shouldn't feel so

overwhelmingly tired. He sat up: maybe it's called being old and out of shape, he thought—he'd start an exercise program. And as soon as he solved the problem with the Chinese man and took care of Lord and Caldwell, he'd apply for two weeks' leave. He'd take Irene on a trip—the Riviera. At the rate he was going on these cases, he'd wrap them up in a few days. But December was hardly the time to go to the Riviera—maybe they'd go to Greece instead. Yes, he decided, he'd tell Irene that tonight.

He went back to his desk. Sûreté had been more helpful than he had anticipated, but of course they were feeding him information in the hope he'd eliminate their problem—they'd be happy to supply the poison if someone else would administer the dose. All he had to do was warn Wu Te-chao, or Chien Lin Huong as he used to be, that unless he left Marshall alone and fled France, Sûreté would kill him. If that didn't work, he'd turn the problem over to Caldwell—after all, that's what he was here for, theoretically.

Handling Lord and Caldwell shouldn't prove difficult either. Once aware the CIA had targeted him, Marshall could yelp loud enough to Washington to have them back off—after all, alarm systems weren't installed to catch thieves, but merely to scare them off.

Still, he wanted an ally to do his leg and muscle work, and though there were plenty of agents under him, he couldn't be sure who was working for whom, or who had been compromised. There was only one person he could trust completely.

"Luke," he said in surprise when Bishop answered his apartment telephone. "What are you doing home? Did they close down the Folies-Bergère?"

"I'm reading a book, Andy."

"What?"

"The Feminine Mystique."

"Must be a very big book."

"I've already learned lots. You know, I've been making some serious mistakes with women."

"Bishop, *I* could have told you that; but it's not going to help—Sarah thinks you're an asshole, and no book is going to change her opinion. Mine either."

"Is there a purpose to this call? I've got serious reading to do, Mr. Maynard."

"I need a favor, Luke; seriously. The ambassador's in danger. I want to talk to you about it. Can you come in?"

"Be there in ten minutes."

"It's not *that* much of a rush. It's six now, meet me at eight. That will give me time to nail this down, and you to read more of the book and discover what a complete jerk you are."

"I'll be there at eight."

"And, Luke, you don't need to suit up or bring a rifle—this is just to talk."

Wilson Lord was angry, which was not unusual, but it showed, and *that* was unusual. Mike Caldwell had left the embassy in midafternoon, but he wasn't at his hotel.

He was sick of his room; its austerity had worn itself out, and French television was even more insipid than American, which he had thought impossible; the game and talk shows would surely cause some mental malfunction at a key moment in his life.

He wasn't hungry and he had nothing to do—there was nothing he *could* do until he contacted Caldwell. The man might have a formidable reputation, but Lord was not impressed. His life had been spent among "legends" in espionage—*he* was one of them—but they were all terribly flawed. Caldwell's flaw was unreliability.

He looked at his watch; it was nearly seven in the evening; he turned on the TV again and found a channel that was showing a movie. Thank God, he thought.

Then he gasped audibly—it was a Jerry Lewis movie.

He would be brain-dead before his assignment was over. Mike Caldwell was going to pay for this.

CHAPTER 9

Marshall was dressed for dinner and waiting impatiently in the living room when Catherine came in the door. "You're late."

"I'm always late. I'm an ambassador's wife, I make late chic. Estelle took longer than I imagined—she was inconsolable. Stupid woman."

"She's your best friend, Catherine."

"I have lots of stupid friends. So do you."

"What's she going to do about Claude?"

"What *can* she do? If a fifty-year-old man wants to jump into bed with a twenty-year-old stripper, what chance does a fifty-year-old woman have of stopping him?"

"You've managed it. Did you tell her *your* secret—a great body, fantastic sex?"

She just stared at him. "Since when did you think *I* got stupid?" She headed for the stairs. "The secret is guilt—*and* the threat of divorce. I'll be ready in ten minutes."

Exactly ten minutes later she came down the staircase still fastening her organdy cocktail dress, a Venetian lace shawl between her teeth. On the landing she smoothed her dress, draped the shawl over her shoulders, stamped her heels like a flamenco dancer, and struck a pose. "Do I look fat?"

"Should I dye my hair?"

When they got into the limousine, Mead held the door for them; he was again in dress blues and armed with a pistol.

"Good evening, ma'am," he said, rigidly at attention.

Marshall explained that he was going to be his bodyguard.

"Can I hold you personally responsible for my husband's safety, Sergeant?"

"Yes, ma'am."

"And keep him away from Lido strippers?"

"Catherine! Sergeant Mead is a married man."

"What does that mean?" she asked.

"It means he's utterly reliable, like I am."

"Then I want a bodyguard for him too."

Mead laughed.

As the limousine drove toward the Syrian ambassador's residence, Catherine touched up her lipstick. "Anything in particular you want me to say or not say tonight?"

"Just remember about Khomeini, in case anyone asks."

"You're making a mistake, Brad. Claude is bad, all men are bad, but Arabs are *insane*. They're hardly men, Brad—they're still evolving: they're Stone Age adolescents."

"I'll keep it in mind, Catherine."

She blotted her lips and patted her cheeks with rouge. "I'm too old for this. Who cares what a middle-aged woman looks like?"

He snuggled closer in the car, almost too warm from the heater, and warmer against her fur coat. "I do."

"That's because you're still an adolescent too." She pushed him away for fear he'd smudge her makeup. "What did Andy tell you?"

"I haven't seen him. I don't know any more than I did before."

"You better find out fast, Sarah and Chris will be here in a few days."

"Andy can handle this. And I'll talk to Luke; God knows, he can handle it too—he hasn't killed anybody in years; I'm sure he's chomping at the bit."

Then he turned to his wife, and she knew exactly what he was going to say, for they had had this conversation many times. "I wish Sarah would . . . be nicer to Luke."

"She's very nice to Luke," Catherine said, putting away her pocket mirror.

"Why won't she go out with him then?"

"Because Luke is not far from the Stone Age either, Brad."

"I *like* him; he'd make a wonderful son-in-law."

She wiggled to straighten her dress and rearranged her décolleté. "I like Luke too. I consider him almost a son. But I do not see Luke as a son-in-law. And Sarah certainly doesn't see him as a husband."

Marshall turned to glance out the window. Stupid women, he thought.

"What do *you* think of Major Bishop, Sergeant?" Catherine asked Mead.

Mead flushed; all the troops knew of Candy, and Bishop's escapades with female staffers. "Ah . . . he's my superior officer, ma'am."

"Well, *that* certainly answers my question."

At the residence of the Syrian ambassador, just off Place Vendôme in one of the most exclusive areas of Paris, they were formally announced to the assemblage and descended a marble staircase that overlooked a huge reception hall as open and cool as a mosque, shimmering in a sea of formal gowns and glittering jewelry. It was a pleasing sight to Marshall, a familiar milieu.

The room was mutedly lit to flatter aging women, and the classical music by a string quartet unobtrusive. Waiters passed with drinks and hors d'oeuvres. The room shone with crystal and laughter and smelled of expensive perfumes and succulent food. There was banter and repartee, gossip and allusions, reassurances and ego stroking—simple verbal acrobatics that Marshall had mastered long ago, like a gymnast on the parallel bars.

He enjoyed these social occasions. The attentive service and deference were comforting and the conversations untaxing, often amusing. He knew he was playing a game of pomp, ceremony, and self-importance, but he didn't take it seriously; besides, he had a mission tonight, and the subtlety and finesse of diplomatic gamesmanship was a mental challenge—like chess, not significant, but stimulating.

Saud Asari and his much younger English wife, Clarissa, met them at the bottom step. Asari reached for his hand. "Thank Allah you're here. What a dismal affair it's been so far. Now we're saved. You'll make it bright and wonderful. How are you both?"

"Like a battered trawler come to safe harbor, Saud," Marshall said, shaking his hand, kissing Clarissa on both cheeks.

"I don't feel like a trawler," Catherine said.

Asari kissed her hand. Then he kissed it twice more.

"And don't compare me with anything else afloat. Ships and my appearance are not consoling metaphors. Clarissa, you look lovely. Too lovely. I may go home and try again."

"Catherine, you say the cleverest things. I'm so glad you're here. I thought you still might be with Estelle." Clarissa turned to her husband. "Claude is having an affair with a stripper from the Lido."

Asari brought his hands to his face in horror.

"Claude's dead," Catherine said. "We shot him."

"Serves him right," Marshall said. "Like Saud, I was appalled, even though . . . well, you know about Estelle."

"What about Estelle?" Clarissa asked, rising to the bait.

"Shocking indeed." Saud nodded. "She'd be flogged in *my* country."

Clarissa, realizing the men were teasing her, turned to Catherine. "How are the children? Are they coming for Christmas?"

"We hope so," Catherine said.

"It's hard to tell what children will do sometimes," Marshall added.

Asari held up his hands. "I could tell you stories about my children which still curl my hair. Or straighten it, as is the case."

"Well, I'm not the roué you are, Saud. I didn't have eight."

"It was his other wife. Or wives," Clarissa added. "This is before I civilized him."

"You must teach me your secret," Catherine said.

"Catherine's secret would shame a Lido stripper; you should see her fan dance."

"Yes," Asari said to Catherine, "please teach it to Clarissa."

Marshall turned away. "I'm going to mingle and drink. Or maybe just drink if I can avoid mingling. And eat. I hope you've tried to impress us with a lavish buffet."

"Of course. We're third-world overachievers."

"Wonderful. First worlders are notoriously cheap—I don't even go to German parties anymore. And the British . . ."

"Are we still first world?" Clarissa asked. "My mother, who is spending her decrepitude waiting in public-health offices, will be surprised to hear that."

"Catherine wants to know if you're serving couscous, Clarissa."

"I told you, I'm civilizing Saud. If you want couscous, you're going to have to go to the Iraqis, or the Algerians. But I'd recommend a Turkish takeout before either."

Asari waved a finger at his wife. "You can't say these things. We're all Arabs."

Clarissa grabbed Catherine's hand. "Saud says if I ever go to Syria, I'll be hung."

"Flogged," he said. "Both you and Estelle." Then he turned to Marshall. "You know everybody here—the same dreary freeloaders as always. Jarre isn't here yet. The illustrious foreign minister is probably parked around the corner, waiting out your arrival so he can make his appearance. I don't know who's the bigger prima donna, you or Jarre."

"That's easy, he is," Marshall said, moving Asari aside. "I'd like a minute when you get time."

"Oh good, secrets," Asari said. "My party's a success after all."

Marshall and Catherine moved through the room. It was a reception and dinner like a thousand others they had attended. The food was good, the talk diverting, and as Asari predicted, the French foreign minister arrived last, bestowing indulgent greetings.

But he and Marshall were old friends, though they went to lengths to disguise it—a Frenchman was supposed to be distant and mildly repulsed by Americans, so they played their public game to the others in attendance.

When they were alone a moment, Jarre asked quickly, "The President didn't misunderstand today, did he? You intimated a shift in your position on Iran."

Marshall nibbled a shrimp. "Interest. I indicated *interest,* not a shift."

"And you want the proper individuals apprised."

"You see, he's not so stupid after all."

"Yes, he is. And *your* president is also."

"France granted Khomeini asylum, not us."

"It was a humanitarian gesture; we are noted for them," Jarre said, toasting him with a bacon-wrapped scallop. "I thought Arabs didn't eat pork."

"They don't, but pigs aren't *sacred*—they're happy to kill them to serve to others."

Jarre nodded. "I'll convey your 'interest'; I hope Allah looks favorably on your request. I suppose if he doesn't object to butchering pigs, he won't mind dealing with Americans either."

"There's another matter: personal. I may come to you for help, though you might be as impotent in this regard as I would be trying to deal with the CIA."

Jarre popped another scallop into his mouth and chewed thoughtfully. "If you are talking about *our* intelligence service, such as it is, surely a misnomer, then I *would* be impotent. It is a rogue elephant, like your CIA. Governments rise and fall, political parties wane and wax, but they remain fixed, a law unto themselves. I certainly hope you do not need my help with them, because I could not guarantee it."

As Marshall suspected, he would not be able to turn to anyone in the French government for help with the Chinese man. But the matter wasn't pressing—he felt confident Andy Maynard could handle it.

Later, Asari maneuvered Marshall aside. They were the same age and had known each other since Marshall's days as Johnson's Mideast envoy. Asari was a westernized Sunni Moslem who disdained the revival of fundamentalism. If nothing else, its triumph would end his beloved parties.

"You know," Marshall said, "I like couscous. I think Clarissa's being a snob."

"Of course she's a snob—she's British. I married her for it; another example of third-world overachieving. I believe she's upstairs at the moment, purchasing secrets and AWACs from your wife."

"Stupid woman! I told Catherine to *buy* secrets."

"*I'll* sell you some. It would help me pay for this party."

Marshall laughed. "I *know* all yours. That's why we have AWACs."

"Then I'll buy yours. But I probably can't afford them."

"Actually, you might. We may be able to deal, Saud. I'm in the market for a favor."

Asari was surprised; Marshall had never approached him like this. He could not recall a direct appeal for assistance. That was not Marshall's way, but Asari knew it was calculated intimidation. By making a forthright request for a favor, Marshall was raising the stakes: to deny him, and the United States he represented, was foolish.

Asari smiled, and so did Marshall. They both liked this game where the players were expert, and the moves subtle. It was a game for minds capable of intricate nuance.

Asari knew how desperate, and loath, Marshall was to approach him for a favor.

Marshall knew, of course, that Asari was aware of this and therefore made the request overt so that Asari could not refuse him. Marshall was going in as supplicant, but with a bludgeon in hand. "I want to talk with Khomeini, Saud."

Asari was shocked; he had not anticipated anything like this. "Khomeini? The man's a lunatic. You might as well talk to Clarissa's dog."

"Does Clarissa's dog have a following of thirty million Moslems?"

Asari shrugged. "It's not a very charismatic dog; but still, it's got better sense than Khomeini." Asari studied Marshall's calm face. "Are you serious? But what about the Shah? And . . ." He stopped, boggled by the complexities and intricacies. "Brad, this is . . . My government doesn't deal with Khomeini."

He looked at Marshall incredulously. "Do you know what you're asking?" Then he leaned forward and whispered, "Brad, Khomeini is a . . . grenade ready to explode in the Mideast, and the Mideast is . . ."

"Volatile."

Asari stepped back, distancing himself from the problem he saw developing, one that could have profound consequences for his own country. "Does this mean you're abandoning the Shah?"

"Saud, all it means is that I want to talk to Khomeini. I need to contact him. I can hardly send up the Goodyear blimp with the message, so I'm asking you."

"But what does this all mean?" Asari asked in confusion.

Marshall smiled. "Oh, just think, you'll be able to work this over for months—you, the Iraqis, the PLO, the Saudis, the Israelis—why, this intrigue will employ a thousand people for years. Now, will you do it?"

"But what about the deal? What are the terms?"

Marshall shook his head. "You know you don't need a contract. I consider this a major debt; you know I'll pay it."

Asari frowned. "Yes, I know. But you may be asking the impossible; he might not want to talk with you. He refers to your country as 'the Great Satan.' " Asari raised a finger. "Not that he's completely wrong. It's just . . . He *would* hang Clarissa."

Marshall's silence waited him out.

Asari threw up his hands. "You're serious? You really want to meet with him?" He brought his hand to his forehead and murmured to himself, "This is very delicate. I see complications for us all." He fell quiet, then mused to Marshall, "This may not be wise. Meeting with Khomeini could be opening Pandora's box."

Marshall swirled the drink in his hand. "Khomeini may be the key to the future."

"I hope not. He is an evil man, as only men possessed by the divine spirit can be."

"Nevertheless, I need you to float a message. Will you do it, Saud?"

Asari wiped his brow again. "I don't like this, Brad. We are comfortable with the current instability in the Mideast. The place is already enough like an asylum that we don't need a certified, armed lunatic running loose."

Marshall nodded. "I understand, and *you* understand that I would not ask you if I hadn't considered all the ramifications."

Asari gazed about the room, oblivious to the party and his guests. Finally he said, "Nothing may come back, you understand. Khomeini hates America. Don't trust him—or rather, trust exactly what he says; don't try to interpret it."

"That's what Catherine says."

"She's right. Women would be good at dealing with Arabs. There's a feminine, emotional, irrational side to us that women understand."

"Catherine believes she'd be better than men at dealing with everyone."

Asari smiled. "Clarissa too. Perhaps they're right." He fell silent again, then he took a deep breath. "All right, I'll 'float' your request."

Marshall considered him a long moment. "We are friends, aren't we, Saud?"

"Well, we *were,*" Asari said petulantly.

"There are many people who don't want me to meet with Khomeini."

"Indeed. Every sane person on the globe, and Clarissa's dog too."

"It could be dangerous for me, Saud. Perhaps you can see the . . . intricacies."

Asari's eyes narrowed. "Ah. Yes, I do. The Shah's greatest supporter is your own CIA." He nodded in understanding. "It's the danger from behind, the stab in the back, that usually proves fatal, isn't it?"

Marshall nodded. "It would be prudent if no one knows of this."

"Don't worry. If my government learned I was antagonizing the Shah, helping the Americans, and contacting that lunatic Khomeini—they'd hang *me.*"

Marshall gripped Asari's arm in gratitude. "Then let's ensure our survival by keeping this secret. Thank you, Saud." He gazed about pleasantly. "It's a lovely party." Then he leaned closer to Asari. "But I'm worried about Jarre."

"Why?"

"I think he's wearing a bra and panties under his clothes."

Asari nodded solemnly. "I've long suspected it. But you should hear his worries about you."

Bishop rounded the Concorde, passed the brilliantly lit Crillon Hotel, and parked on the cordoned-off street in front of the U.S. embassy. Immediately gendarmes rushed over with machine guns, waving him away, but he held out his identification with the special entitlement of the ambassador's staff, and after verifying it, they allowed him to pass.

The Marine on duty saluted and let him through the electronically sealed doors. "Evening, Major," the guard said in surprise; very few personnel worked at night, mostly communications people, and now and then those rushing to beat a deadline. The ambassador rarely came in after work hours, and his military aide never. Bishop was not known as a man who rode a desk.

"Buzz Mr. Maynard and let him know I'm on my way up."

The vast marble lobby, surprisingly silent—during the day it echoed with sounds of hundreds of people passing through—was soothing and majestic; Bishop stood a moment savoring the quiet, then he bounded up the huge double stairway, pausing at the top to look down. The lobby was deserted, and the full grandeur of the building and its place in American history struck him for the first time.

He was part of history, he thought; minor indeed, a nobody really, but the portraits on the walls of U.S. ambassadors went back to Benjamin Franklin and Thomas Jefferson, and surely they had military aides who did their part. He swelled with pride, and visions of Lafayette, the Revolutionary War, Pershing and World War I, Eisenhower and de Gaulle—he associated history only through wars and generals—Vietnam, Dien Bien Phu, and himself at Khe Sanh. He *belonged* here, he thought, even if his French could only get him drunk and laid. He went up another floor, down several corridors, and knocked on Andy's door.

"Luke, is that you?" Maynard said in wonder at Bishop's appearance. "I didn't know you owned anything besides uniforms."

Bishop was wearing jeans and a sweatshirt. "This is what I always wear, except when I'm here, or fucking."

Maynard's office was large, but so cluttered it seemed small, and bright overhead lights made it seem harsh rather than comfortable. Bishop plopped on the sofa and stretched out, but then he sat up in concern. "You don't look good, Andy, what's wrong?"

"Indigestion; something I ate."

"I'm serious," Bishop said, standing. "Your color is really bad."

"Sit down. I didn't call you here for a medical consult. I want to talk to you about a serious problem."

Maynard was flushed and his breathing irregular, and

Bishop was worried. "Andy, you don't look well. I think we ought to go down to the dispensary. We can talk there."

"I have gas, Bishop, and heartburn. For once, shut up and listen."

Bishop held up his hands, not wanting to agitate him more. "Okay, I'm listening."

"Brad—Ambassador Marshall to you—is in danger. Pay close attention. There are two threats. One is from a Chinese man. When Brad was in Saigon in 1972, his car ran over a child. The father, Chien Lin Huong, is here in Paris—I think to kill Brad, or maybe Sarah and Chris: that would be more like Oriental revenge. He's already killed two people, a Marine corporal who was Brad's driver, Corporal Bonnard, and—"

"What! I knew Bonnard. He saved my life, as much as Ambassador Marshall did. I never knew anything happened to him."

"He was killed in Saigon right after the accident. And a Sûreté agent was killed here a few days ago, a man feeding information to Huong. Huong wants revenge; he's pursued Brad for six years."

"Well, let's fucking nail him!"

Maynard started to laugh, but held his chest in pain, then shook it away. "I knew I'd called the right man. But that's why I have Sergeant Mead baby-sitting Brad—Mead's good; I want you to work with him. I told him to follow Brad wherever he went—especially at night. I don't want him out of Mead's sight. And when this is all done, I want you to decorate that boy or get him special leave so he can take his wife somewhere."

Maynard grimaced, then went on. "The second threat is from *my* company—that's why you're here, not someone in my office. Brad is about to open negotiations with the Ayatollah, who—never mind, you wouldn't understand. The point is that this might seal the fate of the Shah. This is a *very* big thing to many people, Luke. The CIA loves the Shah. The CIA does not want him to fall; they'll do anything to prevent it."

Bishop looked confused. "What about you? You're CIA."

"I don't always buy the Company line, Luke. No dedicated man blindly follows orders or never questions them. Have you always followed orders, Luke?"

To his chagrin, Bishop nodded silently.

"Should you have?"

He dropped his head, remembering in Vietnam the two men who had died because he had not questioned a foolish order. "No," he whispered.

"Did you learn anything?"

"Yes," he said forcefully, looking up to meet Maynard's eyes.

"So did I, Mr. Bishop. A long time ago."

Maynard squirmed uncomfortably in his chair, stood to find relief, but this time the pain did not go away. "Remember Mike Caldwell? The guy you met at the airport."

"Yeah," Bishop said in distraction, now more concerned about Maynard. "We've been to the gym together."

"He's not working for me, Luke—it's a cover. He's working for someone named Wilson Abbot Lord."

Bishop jumped up. "He tried to kill me once. I was in Saigon and he shot me. He's here? Where? I been waiting six years to get that motherfucker. I'll kill him!"

Maynard grinned. "I *did* get the right man," but then his face broke into a horrible grimace and he clutched his chest. He cried out once, then collapsed.

Bishop ran to him. "Andy!"

Maynard lay crumpled on the floor.

"Shit! Oh, shit!" Bishop cried, seeing Maynard's face turning blue. "No, Andy! No!" He put his hand on Maynard's chest, then pounded it with his other fist; he did it twice, but there was no response. He opened Maynard's mouth, put his mouth to his, drew out all his breath, then breathed in. The chest swelled, but Maynard did not breathe. Bishop pounded the chest, then blew into Maynard's mouth again and again.

Finally he ran to the desk and punched the emergency number. "This is Major Bishop, send a medic up to room . . . Fuck! Mr. Maynard's room, on the fourth floor. He's had a heart attack. He's not breathing. ASAP! He's dying."

Then he slammed down the phone and ran back to Maynard, motionless, unbreathing on the floor. Bishop was still pounding on Maynard's chest and breathing into his mouth when three men, one a doctor, ran into the room. They pulled him off and started emergency procedures.

In the distance Bishop could hear a wailing ambulance, but before it pulled into the embassy compound, the doctor stood. "He's dead."

CHAPTER 10

After dinner and one drink in the lounge of the Hilton, a nouveau-blah hotel almost under the shadow of the Eiffel Tower, Caldwell saw a game of seduction was obviously unnecessary. Angie had been all over him in the restaurant and had licked the whipped cream off her dessert in such an obscene display that even the waiter stopped to watch.

"C'mon, let's not waste any more time," Mike said.

Short, brunette, with good features that would have been helped with a more attractive hairstyle, and a softly rounded body that betrayed no interest in jogging or health food, she drew away to study him, debating no more than a few seconds, then smiled. "I'm such an easy lay."

"Is that bad?"

She laughed. "Not for you. Or me either." And that was exactly how Angie Filmore felt about sex and men, both of which she knew a great deal about. After college she got a job with the State Department in Washington, then was posted to Paris.

At twenty-eight, she was happy; she traveled, made good money, could pick and choose among a variety of men, and believed that when the time came to settle down, she would have no trouble. She felt in control of her life, and when dealt a bad card, she merely threw in her hand and asked for a redeal.

Mike Caldwell looked a reasonable hand; he was funnier

than she'd first expected, *didn't* talk about his work and so far hadn't manifested any psychotic behavior, and even seemed comfortable with a knife and fork.

He stood and placed his arm around her waist and led her from the lounge. They kissed hungrily down the corridor. In his room, when he unbuttoned her blouse, she pushed his hand away impatiently and undid it herself.

Suddenly she shoved him away. "This isn't even respectable." She jumped into bed and pulled the sheets to her neck. "I've changed my mind; I'm really not this kind of girl."

He sat on the bed and slowly tugged the sheet back. When he bent to kiss her, she reached her arms around his neck and brought him down to her. He sought to go slowly, but her flesh, her scent—because it had been so long since he had been with a woman, he couldn't hold back. His hand went roughly to her breasts, then between her legs, and he moved on top of her and came as soon as he entered her. He thrust into her long past orgasm, and she watched his face twist in either pain or pleasure, she could not tell.

Finally he opened his eyes sheepishly. "It's been a long time. Sorry."

She put both hands around his neck and brought him down, whispering as their lips met, "Don't be sorry—just make it up to me."

He was, but the phone rang. He took it off the hook and, without breaking concentration, placed it under the bed. Five minutes later a knock came at the door.

"Get out of here," he shouted.

"You have an important phone call. Could you hang up your phone, please."

When he did, it rang within the minute. He and Angie were propped on their sides, entwined, facing one another.

"Mike Caldwell," he answered in a low voice, hunching slowly.

"Mike, I need to see you immediately."

Caldwell did not have to ask who it was; he had never seen or heard Wilson Lord, but the cold authority in the voice had to be his, and instinctively he pulled out of Angie and sat up in the bed.

All the stories about him could not be true, Caldwell

knew, but enough were documented and circulated through the corridors on the second floor at Langley to intimidate any young agent. Lord had known Wild Bill Donovan of the old OSS, and every director of the CIA since, had tangled with everyone, including the Abbot, the seventh-floor legend who terrified everyone. The tales of the Phantom and the Abbot dazzled young agents; they were like warring Titans, but no one wanted to take sides for fear of incurring the wrath of the other.

But here was the Phantom on the phone. "Immediately," Lord said. "Meet me under the Eiffel Tower in ten minutes."

Caldwell hung up and jumped from the bed. "I gotta go."

"Who was that, the President?"

"Worse." He struggled into his trousers, laced up tennis shoes, and put on a windbreaker, and he was out the door without a word to her.

Leaving the hotel, he stopped to light a cigarette, cupping his hands to protect the flame from the sharp wind, and walked briskly toward the park of the Champ de Mars beneath the Eiffel Tower. The cold air was wet and penetrating; it was just after nine, traffic was heavy, and the streets yellow streaks of headlights.

He dreaded this meeting, fearing that he was going to see his father in Lord. Caldwell's father had been domineering and remote, a hard man he had always wanted to please, but never did. Successful and wealthy in business, never once having praised his son, he was killed in a small-plane crash on his way to a construction site in Mike's first year in college.

The park was surprisingly crowded for the late hour, yet he spotted Lord immediately; he was on a bench, watching Caldwell's approach with a gaze neither hostile nor unpleasant, but unnervingly intense. Never having seen a photograph of Lord, Caldwell was surprised at his appearance. He expected someone blunt and brutal, even crude looking, but the man before him was thin, elegantly dressed in a camel-hair overcoat, radiating intellect and determination, and an almost electric charge of tension.

Lord didn't stand when Caldwell walked up, or even acknowledge him.

Caldwell said tentatively, "Mr. Lord?"

"Do you know what I've been doing while waiting for you? Watching a Jerry Lewis movie. That was worse than Korea."

Caldwell saw that he was angry, but also older than he had supposed, his father's age, and he was probably very cold. "I didn't know you'd arrived, sir."

Lord scrunched into himself and nodded toward the Champ de Mars. "There used to be Elysium in the west, at the edge of the world, where the fallen went. And Valhalla was Odin's hall for slain heroes. The Valkyries brought them there. The warriors fought all day and feted at night. Where do they go now? I wonder. Do they come here reincarnated as little boys to fly kites?"

Was Lord drunk? Caldwell wondered. Or was he? He and Angie had had two bottles of wine, but he didn't think it had affected him.

Lord turned laser eyes on Caldwell, and Mike flinched. "I'm told you're very good," Lord said. "Even by that lunatic on the seventh floor."

Caldwell knew he was referring to the Abbot; he smiled nervously—he did not want to get caught in a grudge match between those two. "I've never met him, sir. I was hoping to slip through without anybody noticing me. Especially you and . . ."

"The Mad Monk?"

Caldwell said cautiously, "I heard he had another name."

"He has many, but Mad Monk describes him best—he *is* mad, seeing conspiracies and moles everywhere, and getting more paranoid every year. Absolutely a nut case; they'll carry him out in a straitjacket soon. So stick with me, Mike. I've read your file carefully; I know all about you. It's time you had older guidance. You've been in the field too long—you need a tutor. You're a terrific field agent, but you need to hone the subtleties. Everyone says you're another me. We'll see."

Lord stood and waited for Caldwell to follow him. "How much have you been told about this assignment? Do you know why you're here?"

"I wasn't told anything, sir. Just that I'm working for you."

"Stop with the 'sir'; call me Wilson or Will or WA, something familiar."

Caldwell shook his head trying to keep up, surprised at the older man's quick pace out of the park. "No, sir. I'll stick with Mr. Lord. Your reputation is pretty fearsome."

Lord smiled. "Anyone who has survived as long as I *should* be feared. But I am a nice man—I have a wife, well, two wives, my first wife left me because of my job."

"So did mine."

"I'm sorry, Mike," Lord said, having known that, of course. "But perhaps you'll be lucky like I was and find another good woman. Children?"

"Two."

"I have three." Lord opened his hands. "But I am growing old. I am older than I thought I would ever be. I never thought it would happen. I thought I would always be young and strong." He reached out and touched Caldwell's arm. "But it's nice to see the tradition continue. I see possibilities in you. I don't know whether I'm flattering myself, or insulting you, but I do see a younger self in you."

Caldwell *was* flattered; he had not expected this, never supposed he would like this man or encounter sentiment. His experiences in the Agency had been harsh—no one had ever spoken a kind word to him, nor had he expected one. He felt like a Doberman who had been trained to attack, yet suddenly was being patted and stroked; it was a nice feeling, and he was not immune to kindness any more than the most vicious attack dog.

They walked toward the quay. When there was a break in traffic, they ran across the boulevard to stand by the wall overlooking the Seine. Lord leaned against the quay and stared at the river below, shimmering with a reflection of the city floating on its surface.

Lord turned to him. "You're here because you *feel,* Mike." Again his hand touched Caldwell's arm. "You're different. Like *I* was. You *care.* That's a wonderful thing. It's special, like hearing music or seeing color no one else does. You have a great talent."

Caldwell shook his head in embarrassment.

Lord pointed across the river toward the Trocadéro at the Palace of Chaillot, an austere white stone edifice with low sweeping, curved wings. "What do you think of that architecture? It's cold, flat, and sterile—mock grand; faux Roman; Third Reich grandeur." He turned to Caldwell. "But does it appeal to the fascist in you? Which do you prefer, boots and leather, or all this French-fag decoration?"

Caldwell studied the building; he rather liked it, but supposed he shouldn't.

Lord smiled. "It is not a serious inquiry. It just reminds me of a walk I took the other night in the Bois de Boulogne—everything being a matter of choices and preferences, with none the necessarily correct one. Is the woman going to wait for you tonight?"

Caldwell looked surprised.

"You obviously just came from bed, and you certainly smell of a woman—I assume you were with one, not taking a scented bath by yourself."

Caldwell nodded. "I think she'll wait."

"You were just in Iran, Mike; what are the chances of the Shah surviving?"

Caldwell was having trouble keeping up with the shifts in conversation; they were not random, he knew, but he was unaccustomed to such mental sprinting. "Not good. Iran is a Moslem nation of Shiite fundamentalists—the Shah is trying to drag his people into the modern world when they want to go in the opposite direction."

Lord nodded. "That's Khomeini. A true fanatic, mindlessly, passionately swimming against the current of history. There would be *no* dealing with him, no accommodations, but the administration thinks it can work with him. Those good ol' boys from Bumfuck, Georgia, believe they'll be able to handle him. Hell, they couldn't tell a Moslem from a Martian. 'Billy Bob, who's them little pointy-eared people?' 'Why, thems are Moslems, Bubba; they live next door to the moon.' "

Caldwell laughed. He had never expected humor, and Lord was a great mimic.

"So where does that leave us? Are we just going to kiss off Iran and its oil?"

Caldwell shrugged. "I don't have a solution, sir."

"That won't do. You have to come up with solutions—not even good ones sometimes, just the best *possible* one, or at least not the worst one. Let's start there—the worst. What if Khomeini gets to power with our assistance, if we turn against the Shah? After selling out Vietnam, then abandoning the Shah to a messianic fundamentalist, our credibility in the Mideast would be zero. We *can't* get involved with Khomeini. Vietnam was essentially worthless geography—but Iran, the Mideast? Oil? They count."

Lord leaned forward, his eyes and voice a wizard's spell of intimacy and complicity. "What you are going to do is vitally important, Mike. No one else can do it." His voice dropped, drawing Caldwell even closer. There was almost no distance between them, and Lord's eyes riveted him. "We must stop Marshall from contacting Khomeini."

Lord's head moved like a cobra's, drawing Caldwell, mesmerizing him. "It is our country; it is vital."

His words flicked out like a sorcerer's. "Sometimes we have to do things we don't like, Mike—yet we *know* have to be done."

"Yes, sir," Caldwell said, caught in the trance.

Now Lord closed the distance so their faces nearly touched and his words were whispered to Caldwell. "Our world is not easy, Mike. You know that better than anyone. It's hard and without reward. It hurts, and people don't understand us. We are special, guardians of freedom—the gatekeepers. We keep out the barbarians, though we are barbarians ourselves. But we're heroes too, Mike."

Caldwell swallowed. This was exactly how he felt, and he glowed that someone understood, someone he admired, someone he wanted to admire him.

"I'm fifty-two, Mike," Lord said softly. "Yet I don't feel it, and when I look into a mirror, I'm amazed. I see wrinkles and sagging flesh. It's as if some trick had been played, or a wand waved, turning me into an old man. It must be a hoax, I think, because I don't feel it. I feel young. I still *believe.*" He whispered, "I think I'm you, Mike."

Caldwell stared into his eyes, then turned away. "Jesus, Mr. Lord." He let out his breath, then looked directly at Lord. "You just bought my ass, sir."

Lord put out his hand. "I am very glad to be working with you. It's been a long time since I've had such confidence in anyone. If there's anything I can do for you . . . or anything you might not even think I can do for you . . . let me know."

Caldwell gripped Lord's hand. "Thank you, sir. You don't know how much this means. I needed to know someone like you, sir. I needed some . . . validation in my life."

Lord smiled, then turned, breaking the spell. "How's Andy doing?"

"I didn't know you two were friends."

Lord laughed. "We're not; we despise one another. But we have grown familiar with one another and use each other as bellwethers—whatever he thinks, I think the opposite. He feels the same way."

"I'm worried about him. He doesn't look good; he's overweight and always flushed."

"He's been that way for ten years. How's he doing on the threat to Marshall?"

"He knows who it is; Marshall made the connection to a Chinese man he knew in Saigon. Apparently Marshall's limousine ran over the man's child. I think he's got the case nailed down."

Lord nodded. "Yes, he's always been good; his work is generally sound."

"But I was thinking this Chinese man might be useful. If Marshall poses a serious problem for the Shah, the solution might be the Chinese man. Apparently he's motivated by a blood feud; Marshall could have a great deal to fear from him."

Lord nodded approvingly. "Very good, Mike; you *are* like me. Why do something that you can get someone else to do?"

"The only complication might be Marshall's military aide, a Marine major. They go back a long way, he's fairly savvy for a military man."

Lord did not break stride as he walked up the quay. Though he knew it had to be Luke Bishop, he asked casually, "What's his name?"

When Caldwell confirmed it, Lord shrugged indifferently and handed him a card from his wallet. "That's my number."

At Pont d'Iéna, Lord shook hands. "Next time we'll meet

at the Orangerie. I'll call with the time—answer your phone." Then he headed across the river.

He *was* pleased with Caldwell; Marshall would not reach him as he had others, and Luke Bishop was no match for him. Things were on track, he thought happily, flagging a cab on the other side of the bridge.

Tomorrow he would contact Huong, and tonight he would sleep well. He would murder Jerry Lewis in his dreams.

Caldwell sprinted back to the hotel; Angie was in bed watching TV. She looked at him blankly.

"Mike Caldwell. I was here earlier."

"Oh, yeah, the guy with the—"

"Huge cock," he said, stripping as he crossed the room, diving on top of her.

She pushed him away. "You must have the wrong room. Besides, I'm watching a movie; it's really funny."

He grabbed the remote control and switched it off, then buried himself under the blankets. Later, she was making so much noise he didn't hear the telephone at first, but then he grabbed it quickly.

"Mike Caldwell, please."

"Yeah," he said, putting his hand over Angie's mouth.

"This is the duty officer. The station chief wants you to come in right away. Andrew Maynard died; you need to be briefed immediately."

He hung up and jumped from bed.

"Jesus, now what?" Angie cried.

"I gotta go. I don't think I'll be back this time. I'll give you a call tomorrow."

When Bishop appeared at the residence of the Syrian ambassador, bodyguards would not let him in; despite his credentials, they could not believe a man dressed in blue jeans and a tattered sweatshirt could work for the emissary of the United States, but Mead pushed them out of the way and went inside to find Marshall.

When Marshall appeared, he knew something terrible had happened.

"It's Andy, sir. He's dead. He had a heart attack. It just happened. I was with him. We were talking and . . . he just fell over, and there was nothing I could do." Bishop turned his face aside. "I couldn't save him. I couldn't do anything."

"Oh my God," Marshall said. "Irene. Does she know?"

"No, sir. I notified the CIA chief of station, then I came here."

"Andy, Andy," Marshall moaned, then he walked to a corner of the small garden.

After giving him several minutes alone, Bishop approached. "Andy told me a few things before he died. He said you were in danger. I think we need to talk, sir."

Marshall nodded. "Yes. But not now. I've got to go tell Irene. See me first thing in the morning."

Inside, Marshall slipped up to Catherine. "We have to go; I'll tell you in the car."

They made their good-byes, joking as they went, Marshall asking Saud for a doggie bag so they wouldn't have to go to a Turkish takeout, but everyone knew something had occurred, and all would soon call their embassies to see what had happened, if there was a new crisis, and how it affected them.

In the dispensary, Caldwell and the station chief stood over the sheet-covered corpse. The doctor told them that only an autopsy would reveal the exact cause of death, but from everything he could determine, and from what Major Bishop had described, Andrew Maynard had suffered a massive coronary. "He was a clichéd candidate for one," the physician said, frowning at the cigarette dangling from Caldwell's lips.

"I don't inhale," Caldwell said, flicking ashes to the floor.

When the station chief and Caldwell were alone, the older man pulled the sheet back and gazed at Maynard's face, then he sighed and covered him up. "Secure his office; I don't want anything to leave. Did he get a chance to brief you on the threat to Marshall?"

Caldwell nodded.

"Good. Since Langley sent you, it's your case. Let me know if you need anything. Just keep me informed."

As he left, Caldwell stopped him. "Why was Bishop in his office this late?"

The station chief shrugged. "Marshall, Bishop, and Maynard go back a long way. Bishop is almost a part of Marshall's family, and Andy was Marshall's best friend. They could have been bullshitting, or maybe Andy was filling him in on the threat to Marshall. Ask him—Bishop's no rocket scientist, but he's a straightforward guy—he'll tell you."

In Maynard's office, Caldwell searched the papers on his desk, saw notations on the Chinese man and Sûreté, and his own personnel file under the blotter. Maynard must have guessed he was here on another assignment and confided his suspicions to Bishop. As he had thought, Luke Bishop was going to be his biggest complication.

He pulled out his wallet and dialed Lord's number. A sleepy voice answered.

"Sorry to bother you, but you should know—Andy Maynard is dead. Heart attack in his office. Major Bishop was with him."

There was a long pause, then Lord's voice came with genuine regret. "I'm sorry," he said, hanging up.

Lord lay with his eyes open on the ceiling for a long time. He *was* sorry; he and Andy were exact contemporaries; they had known and fought each other for decades. Andy was a good opponent and a decent man. When men Lord's own age died, no longer unusual, the effect was sobering. But then he started to think. What was Bishop doing with him? Maynard was no fool; he had pieced together the threat to Marshall. He had either identified Huong or soon would and had no doubt seen through Caldwell too.

He nestled under the covers; the heat in the room didn't work either.

He wouldn't have wished it, but Andy's death was good fortune; it would simplify his work. Andy was not an inconsequential foe; he could have helped Marshall.

Now Marshall had no one—he was helpless.

CHAPTER 11

Marshall did not sleep well; he wrenched awake numerous times seeing Maynard's dead face and lay in bed a long while in the morning before shoring the energy to get up; he did not want to face this day. He slapped astringent on his face and soothed reddened eyes with lubricant, chose a tie more colorful than usual, dropped a paisley silk handkerchief in his herringbone-suit pocket, and started downstairs.

The dining room was like a banquet hall, with a table easily capable of seating twenty-four; the centerpiece was a massive floral arrangement of orchids and birds-of-paradise. From the ceiling hung a Baccarat chandelier, and on the walls were tapestries of feasts and hunts. At one end of the room was a long mahogany buffet table on which the staff had set breakfast—sterling chafing dishes with eggs and bacon, fruit, breads, butter and jams, and pitchers with juice, and a large pot of coffee.

Catherine looked up from the paper when he entered the room and went to the buffet table. "I called Chris and Sarah. They want to come for the funeral. Should they? Would they be in danger?"

He took no food, only poured a cup of coffee. He sat at the end of the table beside her and fingered the cup, cobalt blue Limoges, encrusted with gold. "They'd be as safe here as anywhere," he said finally. "They'd have protection; we can't protect them now."

She nodded, staring at the tablecloth. "I'll be with Irene all day."

He set down the cup and stood behind her. Then he kissed her hair. "Call me if there's anything I can do."

When his limousine pulled into the embassy, there was a flurry of excitement, but upstairs was a sanctuary of quiet dignity—no aides rushed about, no one ran up with messages, no one interrupted or detained him.

This morning was as always. For several minutes he sat alone scanning papers, then Helen came in with his briefing folders. He had expected her to wear black today, but she was in a fiery red pantsuit and around her neck were ropes of gold costume jewelry.

He didn't say anything, merely scanned his appointment log—it was blank.

"I didn't commit you to anything today except the trade luncheon—you've ducked it twice before and they called yesterday for confirmation."

Then she wiped her eyes. "I'm so sorry about Andy. You know, we're like a big family here." She blew her nose. "Shit."

Marshall nodded. "Have the CIA arrange a service, but tell them I want to say something."

"Luke's waiting outside; he's taking this as badly as I am. Then there's someone from the CIA to brief you." She handed him Caldwell's file.

"I'll see him after Luke."

When Helen nodded for Bishop to go into Marshall's office, he stopped at her desk. "I thought *black* was for mourning."

"Andy liked red."

"I like nudity—does that mean you're going to come to work naked when I die?"

"Yes. And I'm going to borrow Candy's nipple clips, too."

Bishop shook his head and walked into Marshall's office, centering himself before the desk, so routine and reassuring in his dress blues that Marshall smiled despite his grief. He stood and motioned to the leather chairs on the other side of the room. "Tell me about last night."

"Andy called me around six. He said you were in danger and asked me to come in to talk about it. When I got here, he was looking bad. I told him that, but you know Andy. We talked maybe fifteen minutes, then he just . . . fell over."

"What did you talk about?"

"Andy told me what happened in Saigon. I didn't know Bonnard was killed. He told me about the Chinese man and his child, and how the man is here to kill you, and maybe Sarah and Chris. And he told me about Mike Caldwell, and Wilson Lord."

"Wilson Lord! What about Lord?"

"Andy said Lord's in Paris, running Caldwell. I told him that motherfucker shot me in Saigon. I told him I'd crucify his ass if I found him." Bishop's voice turned vicious. "And I'll get Caldwell, don't worry about that."

Marshall went to the window and stared out on the small park across from the embassy. The crazed man who talked to birds was there as always, and young couples huddled on benches, their hands lost in one another's clothing.

"What did he tell you about the Chinese man?"

"Just what I said."

"No name? No way to find him?"

"He said his name, but I can't remember it, and when I went back to Andy's office, the CIA had secured it."

Marshall turned. "Don't worry about Lord and Caldwell; I can handle them."

Bishop shook his head. "I don't think so, sir. You don't know them. Caldwell is tough. And Lord—well, I never thought anybody could get close enough to shoot me in the head, but he did. His mistake was that he didn't finish the job. *I* will; he *owes*. And Caldwell, I hate that kind of man."

"What kind is that?"

"The kind I might have been—following orders just because they were orders, not thinking. Trusting. A puppet."

What was *wrong* with Sarah? Marshall wondered. Here was the best man she could ever find. "Do you trust anyone, Luke?"

"Yes, sir. But I know the people I trust make mistakes. Like you if you think you can handle Lord and Caldwell. You need me, sir."

Marshall nodded. "What I really need is help with the Chinese man. Andy was right, he wants revenge. I've got to find him. He killed Bonnard, and unless I stop him, he'll get

Sarah and Chris. You don't know this, but you were in the car when Bonnard hit the child. We were rushing you to the hospital. We thought it was a dog; we had no idea it was a child; we only wanted to get you to the hospital."

"What are the chances of Sarah changing her mind about me if I save her life?"

"Save her life and *I'll* drag her to the altar for you."

Bishop stood. "I'll go polish my grenades."

"I was counting on Andy to stop the Chinese man. I don't know anything about him. Now Caldwell has the information. He may not give it to me, but I've *got* to get it."

"I'll get it." Bishop headed for the door. "Just leave it to me."

In Helen's office, Bishop saw Caldwell and went up to him. There was so much tension, so quickly and furiously generated, that Helen gripped her desk; she was sure the two young men, four hundred pounds of muscle, were going to attack one another.

"Thanks for trying to save our man," Caldwell said.

"He was a friend of mine," Bishop answered.

As far as Helen could tell, neither of their lips moved during this exchange, and her hand rested on the button under her desk to summon Sergeant Mead across the hall, knowing that in a minute the two would be flaying at one another.

"Ready for another game," Caldwell said.

"When? Call it."

"Noon."

"You got it."

Then somehow, and Helen was watching carefully, Bishop was gone, without Caldwell's having moved from the doorway or Bishop's having pushed past him. How did men do that? she wondered.

"I'll see if he's ready for you," Helen said to Caldwell, going into Marshall's office. "I thought they were going to kill each other," she told him as she described what had happened.

"They might yet. Show Mr. Caldwell in."

Marshall remembered him from the airport, but the recollection was hazy, so now he freed his mind to see what

Langley was turning out these days—what the new Wilson Abbot Lords looked like.

A man younger, taller, and more physically imposing than he remembered entered with assurance. Blandly correct, Caldwell gave no appearance of a sleepless night. He stood three feet in front of Marshall's desk, polite but not deferential.

"Good morning, sir. Thank you for seeing me right away."

Marshall was surprised at his confident air, unusual in a young man confronting a senior diplomat. Poor Andy, Marshall thought, contemplating Caldwell, so handsome, with blond hair and perfectly straight teeth, so trim and muscular. There's justice—you give them your life, work yourself old, and they replace you with a TV heartthrob type.

So this was the enemy, a soap-opera stud.

"Good morning, Mr. Caldwell. Please sit down. Would you care for coffee?"

"No, thank you, sir. I have the report on last night." He handed it to Marshall.

Marshall put it aside without a glance and rested his elbows on the desk to scrutinize Caldwell, zeroing in on the ill-fitting clothes, lingering long enough to make him uncomfortable. "Why don't you begin by telling me what you think I should know."

"Yes, sir. I'll be working with you on this matter in place of Mr. Maynard."

"*What* matter?" Marshall interjected. "I thought you were here to tell me about Andy's death. Any other 'matter' I would expect to discuss with the station chief."

Marshall's cold manner caught Caldwell off guard, and he realized Marshall did not trust him. Had Andy or Bishop talked to him?

"I beg your pardon," Caldwell said, standing straighter, recovering as from an unexpected jab. "I thought certain things were assumed."

"I assume *nothing* with you people, Mr. Caldwell."

Caldwell struggled to remain pleasant. Briefings were not his forte; he was not accustomed to scrutiny, or being challenged, and now unsure how to proceed, he stood like a boxer, alert, marking time.

Marshall's eyes fixed him with laser intensity. "Mr. Caldwell, Andy Maynard and I knew each other for thirty years. We were Marine lieutenants in Korea together. I am immensely saddened by his death. We grew old together; I had hoped we would grow even older and tell stories of our youth and laugh as we watched younger men replace us, consoling ourselves with the knowledge that we had done the best we could. He was a fine, decent man. Do you have anything to tell me about his death that I don't know, or about the Chinese man who is threatening my life? If not, you're wasting my time."

Caldwell recoiled again.

Marshall leaned forward, eyes burning. "Exactly who are you? And what are you doing here?"

Caldwell fumbled. "I . . . My file is on your desk, sir."

Marshall waved it away. "Don't insult me. I wouldn't believe anything in a CIA file." He tossed it at Caldwell. "Andy didn't believe this shit, and neither do I."

The tension grew ominous. Finally Marshall eased back, having achieved his purpose in unnerving him. "Relax, Mr. Caldwell. You look like an SS commando, bloodless, and what—only thirty-two? Tell me about Andy. Heart attack?"

"We won't know until the autopsy is done, but we're pretty sure. He was old. . . ."

"My age exactly, Mr. Caldwell. So what are you going to do for me in his place? Andy was concerned someone has targeted me. He connected the murderer of a Sûreté agent with the plot, a Chinese man who lived in Saigon in 1972."

"We didn't have an opportunity to talk about that—I just got here, as you know, but I'll go through Mr. Maynard's papers and give you a report as soon as I can."

Marshall's eyes bored into Caldwell. "Why don't you save yourself a lot of time, Mr. Caldwell. Why don't you ask Wilson Abbot Lord about it?"

Caldwell looked so surprised that Marshall shook his head contemptuously. "I know why you're here. You and the man you work for think you know better than the President—the man I represent, on whose orders I am acting. You are about to engage in traitorous activity—let's be very clear about that. I am directing you to cease and desist."

Caldwell merely stared at him, betraying nothing.

"Will you help me find the Chinese man?" Marshall asked.

"I told you I'll have a report as soon as I go over Mr. Maynard's papers."

Marshall shrugged. "Don't come back until then. Good day, sir."

After Caldwell left, Marshall stared at the closed door in deep concentration.

He knew he had come across hard, but that was his intent. He wanted Caldwell to know he was aware of what was going on; that would put him and Lord off guard. But it would gain him only a little time, and he was afraid that was not enough, nor was Luke Bishop a match for them.

As he sat in thought, Helen came in with numerous folders.

"I can't bear to think about Plymouths and Renaults today," he said.

"How about telecommunications or cosmetics?—those people want to see you too. Apparently there's panty-hose disparity: Revlon thinks Chanel is taking unfair trade advantage. The French embassy-workers are about to strike because you haven't authorized a new health package, the Bordeaux people are wild about Gallo imports—I think they have a point here—and the Kraft crowd wants you to do something about Velveeta: France has threatened to ban it as a toxin. You've also got thirty-six invitations to speak, fifty-four requests for interviews, and a hundred people on your appointments list."

"What are the biggest crises?"

"No question—Gallo and Velveeta." She made a thumbs-down. "But there's one *you'll* have to decide. A French pharmaceutical firm with a new birth-control pill has lined up a trade deal with a consortium of condom manufacturers in the States—they'll swap French pills for American condoms. Trojan is behind it. They want your okay so they can start the FDA process."

"A 'consortium of condoms'? This is a joke, right?"

"I would not joke today, Brad."

"Send that one right to the White House for action. And *you* make the decisions for everything else—I'll do whatever you say. Has Catherine called?"

"She's with Irene; Irene doesn't want an autopsy. She knows Andy had a heart attack. She doesn't want his body mutilated."

"Is it in my power to stop an autopsy?"

Helen drew a deep breath. "If the body is handed over to French authorities, they make the decision, but *you* can influence it. If the body stays in the embassy, an autopsy has to be performed because the death was on foreign soil and possibly suspect."

"Call the French authorities, have Andy taken out of here, then get hold of whoever's necessary to stop the autopsy."

"I already did."

Marshall hugged her. "If Catherine divorces me, and you get rid of your current husband, will you marry me?"

"No. I'm looking for a *much* younger man. Someone like that CIA agent—he's gorgeous."

Marshall went back to his desk. "Then do me another favor, Helen. Sarah's coming. Put in a good word to her about Luke. They'd make a great couple."

Helen laughed and left the room. "Forget it. He's insane."

This time Bishop was waiting at the handball court. His hand was so sore he knew the pain would be incredible, but he didn't care. He had been hurt so many times, hurt beyond what morphine and Demerol could numb, that he almost welcomed this pain because he knew that what he inflicted would hurt more than what he suffered.

Caldwell looked just as grim and determined when he came onto the court.

They didn't speak. Bishop tossed him the ball, but instead of practicing with it, Caldwell stepped up to the serving line. "This counts," he said, smashing the ball against the wall. Bishop hit it back; before Caldwell could rebound, Bishop slammed into him, blocking his shot.

"Your serve," Caldwell said, picking himself up.

When he did, Caldwell got it, then caught Bishop in the back of his knee, dropping him to the floor. After that, they made no pretense of rules and, with each shot, escalated their attacks, intent on hurting the other.

After forty minutes, the game was tied at three each, and

both men were limping and hurt. They glared at one another, swelling in animosity, and this time when Bishop served, he dove into Caldwell, who ignored the ball and crashed against him. They fell to the ground, and the game forgotten, slammed knees and fists into one another.

Several men watching the game with mounting anxiety broke into the court and dragged them off each other.

"It's a friendly game," Bishop said through clenched teeth, straining to get at Caldwell.

"Yeah, it's in fun," Caldwell answered, twisting to get away.

"Take a cold shower," said an older man with authority, a very senior staffer. "You just lost the court; get out of here, gentlemen."

They grabbed their towels and headed into the locker room, dropping onto benches far from one another. They cast each other hostile looks, then stripped and went into the showers, keeping a good distance between them.

"You do wear your heart on your sleeve, Luke," Caldwell said under the nozzle, looking for soap in the dish.

Bishop soaped himself angrily. "You bet I do; everything about me is up-front."

"That's fine for you, but *my* job won't let me be that way, and you know it."

"I don't hold your job against you, and I got nothing against your company either. We both work for pretty hard firms," Bishop said, tossing him his bar of soap.

"Then what's the problem?"

"Andy told me things last night that really bothered me."

"Maybe Andy didn't know everything," Caldwell said, soaping himself.

"He knew about you and the man you work for."

Caldwell pitched the soap back to him. "Andy wasn't in on this op, and I can't tell you about it either."

"You don't have to; if it has to do with Wilson Lord, I *know* what it's about."

Caldwell knew he shouldn't let on about Lord, but he asked, "What about him?"

Bishop stepped under Caldwell's shower nozzle. He let water stream down on his head, then he pulled back on his hair and showed Caldwell the surgical scar and skin graft.

"Lord did that. In Saigon, he tried to kill me; I was doing my job, obeying lawful orders. Now he's here to take out Marshall and has you as his hit man. What's my problem? Get real!" Bishop left the shower to towel off.

In a moment Caldwell was beside him. "I don't know anything about that, Luke. I don't know what to say."

"Don't say anything—just listen: nobody's going to get close to me again, and one of us is going to die before anything happens to Ambassador Marshall."

Caldwell went to his locker. He dressed silently and, as he was about to leave, said to Bishop, "I'll think about all this. You know, you're not the *only* dedicated man."

"Then prove it. Tell me about the Chinese man."

Caldwell stopped at the door. "Would that change things between us?"

"No. But it'd be a start."

Caldwell nodded. "I'll see what I can get you."

When Caldwell got back to his office, he was hurting and confused. Marshall had burned him this morning, and Bishop this afternoon, and both knew about Lord.

He wanted to tell Luke of Maynard's notations about the Sûreté agent and Huong, but he couldn't pass anything to him without clearing it with Lord. He worked for Lord, and he knew the Phantom would not approve because Huong could be useful in stopping Marshall from contacting Khomeini.

Bishop talked about loyalty and dedication, but Caldwell's own was no different. They were equally committed, like two gladiators, or guardians at different gates.

Unconsciously he ran his hand over the side of his head. Had Lord shot Bishop? Bishop wouldn't lie about that, he knew, but surely there was more to this. If Lord had done it, there had to have been good reason. Surely.

CHAPTER 12

Marshall was in a trade meeting discussing automobile quotas and tariffs when Helen slipped into the conference room to whisper that he had an urgent call from the Syrian ambassador. He made apologies to the group and went into his office.

"What can I do for you, Saud?"

"Is it convenient to talk?"

"I was in a meeting planning to destabilize the Gulf; it can wait."

"Such a busy, exciting life you have—meetings and murders."

"It wasn't a murder, Saud; Andy Maynard had a heart attack."

"So you say, but the newspapers also reported he was a 'trade official.' We all know what *that* means, though I myself was shocked—I had no idea America had spies."

"No more—he was our last one."

Asari cleared his throat. "I have a client who wants to meet you. We discussed him the other night. But he is eccentric—he doesn't understand how things work."

"Who does?" Marshall asked lightly.

"*I* do. You don't place rude demands on people's time. He says he can meet you today at one for lunch."

Marshall glanced at his watch. "In an hour and a half? I have a luncheon here."

"Of course you do—we *all* plan our lunches—the man's an imbecile to think we can accommodate him. I'm merely passing on the information. Since he's also particular about his food, he's picked the restaurant. Do you want the address?"

"Is it in Paris?"

"Yes, but in no part I've been to. Your security will be hysterical."

"Maybe I won't tell them."

"Oh, good. Another murder for the newspapers—don't wear a tacky tie like your spy did; his picture was terrible, exactly how you'd expect a 'trade official' to look. Anyway, here's the address."

Marshall jotted it down. "My God, what arrondissement is that?"

"I don't think it has one."

"I don't think I can get there in time."

"You could take the metro," Asari said helpfully. "Be sure to buy your token before you get on."

"I'm never going to forgive Jimmy Carter."

"Neither am I. Do you know, he gave me applesauce to drink one night at the White House."

"Apple *cider.*"

"I think it was applesauce it was so thick. It was all in my teeth. I thought I was going to have to go to the dentist. Well, don't count on much to drink today either."

Marshall summoned a deputy to fill in for him, canceled the lunch—now for the third time—then called in his security chief and handed him the address he'd written down.

Floyd Sedwick's appearance never ceased to amaze him, no less than Helen's did. He was not the burly-brawler type, crude, coarse, or even very masculine, Marshall thought. In fact, Floyd Sedwick could more easily have passed for Catherine's hairdresser than the security chief for the U.S. embassy. He was a prim, dapper little man, immaculately groomed, always in suits with carnation boutonnieres, so fussy that had Marshall not seen him in action, watched openmouthed as he tore apart two men twice his size and half his age who had forced themselves upstairs to Marshall's office after they were denied visas downstairs, he would not have taken him seriously.

"This is very delicate, Floyd. I have to go, but no one can know about it."

"Oh, *right.* I'm just going to let you waltz out of here to meet with terrorists. Are we on drugs today, Excellency?"

"I am working on the specific instruction of the President, Floyd. Secrecy is more important than my safety—*no one* can know of this."

Sedwick folded his arms emphatically. "*You* are the ambassador of the United States. *I* am the security chief for the ambassador of the United States. You expect me to let you joyride around Paris? Just what am I supposed to say when your body is found floating facedown in the Seine?"

"Say I snuck out for a quick swim. I'm serious, Floyd; this is an order—I want you to close your eyes when I leave here. But don't worry, I'll have Sergeant Mead—he'll take care of me."

"Mead!" Sedwick fairly screamed. "He's got the brains of a hubcap. You'd be better off taking Helen." Then he pointed toward her office. "Have you *seen* her today?"

"I see her every day, Floyd."

"Christ, she looks like Salome, and yesterday she was Big Bird. And now you're telling me a certified moron, a card-carrying dummy, I mean stupid, Brad—stupid, stupid, stupid!—is going to protect you. What is *wrong* up here?"

"Mead's good, Floyd. Trust me. And none of this is up for negotiation—I am ordering you to let me leave here without being followed."

Sedwick held up his hands. "I had my say. You gave me an order. It's over." He walked toward the door. "To hell with you."

This is more like an asylum than an embassy, Marshall thought; then he summoned Mead across the hall and they left through the back door. In the underground garage, Marshall handed the address to a startled Marcel.

Settling in the backseat as the car left the embassy, Marshall felt excitement swelling as it had years ago in Vietnam; he had forgotten the pleasure danger brought, and how much he liked it.

"Just like old times, isn't it, Sergeant?"

"But what am I supposed to do, sir?" Mead asked. Marshall was treating this like a joke, just as he had in Vietnam, but Mead knew better, and he was growing more and more anxious about this assignment.

"Like in old times—make sure I don't get killed."

Marshall was driven into a poor section in the nether reaches of Paris, overwhelmingly Middle Eastern; the restaurant was in a dilapidated building on a dirty side street. Children played kickball in the street while old men and women watched from tenements where wash hung from railings. The smell was rancid of garbage, and the noise from radios cacophonous.

"Is this in the Michelin guide, Marcel?" Marshall asked when the car pulled up to the restaurant where a tattered sign hung limply. "How many stars?"

As Mead jumped from the car, Marshall restrained him. "Wait here."

Mead looked stricken. This *was* just like old times in Vietnam, but only through bare luck had they survived then. This was even worse, for he feared these unknown enemies more than he had the known ones long ago. "But how can I save you in the car, sir? And who am I supposed to save you from?"

Marshall shook his head. "I don't know; just stay alert."

When Marshall got out, Mead pressed his face to the window anxiously and watched him disappear into the building before him. "Shit!" he said to a very worried Marcel.

Beyond the door, Marshall was struck with the pungent aroma of food, but he was not prepared for what lay inside. Plunging into the dark interior, he entered a restaurant as elegant and formal as any in Paris.

Standing within the threshold, he looked about in surprise, but the maître d' was at his side immediately. "Excellency, you honor us. It is a pleasure to have you with us," and he led Marshall across the carpeted room, safely encapsulated from the outside by heavy damask drapes.

The lighting was dim and intimate, conversations muted, the diners all men, some in business suits, others in white linen robes, served unobtrusively by tuxedoed waiters. No one glanced up as he passed among richly set tables gleaming of silver and crystal.

He had dined before in places like this, extraordinarily

expensive and exclusive restaurants in Riyadh, Bahrain, and Kuwait that catered to sheikhs and moneyed Arabs with Western backgrounds and tastes.

He was brought to a secluded booth in back; the table was set for two, and when he slipped into a seat, a waiter immediately handed him a menu.

"Can I get you something to drink? An aperitif?" the maître d' asked.

"Juice. Orange."

He was in dire need of a drink, but he could not toss down martinis in the presence of the Imam, as unlikely as it was that he would appear in a place such as this. This was not the Ayatollah's style. He could picture himself sitting under an olive tree eating grapes with Khomeini, goats grazing in the background, but he could not see himself sitting across from him in this restaurant swilling gin. He would not show up, Marshall knew.

Probably he was being toyed with, tested for sincerity, he thought. It was all part of the game, he knew. He didn't mind. He picked up the menu and wondered with alarm if he had enough money to pay for this. Did they take American Express?

Suddenly a stocky, middle-aged man appeared at the table. "Ambassador Marshall. May I join you?"

"Am I here to see you?"

The man eased into the seat across from Marshall. "I know you were hoping to meet someone else. I am here to prepare for that." The man held out his hand. "Abbas Nassir."

"Bradley Marshall. You're right, I was hoping to meet the Imam."

A waiter arrived with his juice. Marshall pushed it away. "Martini. Very dry."

"Shaken, not stirred," said the waiter with a knowing smile.

"What? Oh, I don't care what you do with it—hit it with a hammer if you want, just make sure there's lots of gin." Marshall nodded toward Nassir. "Why don't you order for us."

Nassir spoke to the waiter in Persian. When he left, Nassir

said gravely, "We're hoping you can meet the Imam also. You can't understand how difficult this is."

"Yes, I can; that's why I'm drinking martinis."

Nassir smiled. "I forgot how levitous Americans are. I studied in America, at Temple; it was a long time before I got used to the way Americans joked about everything. All of us here—Bani Sadr, Ghotbzadeh, Yazdi—remember those days in America, and laughing. We haven't done much of it since."

"I've heard of these men."

"They will lead our nation when the Imam returns to Iran." Nassir leaned forward. "This *will* happen."

The waiter brought Marshall's martini. He raised it in a noncommittal toast.

Nassir continued worriedly, "But it's going to be *so* difficult. Many of us were schooled in the West—Ghotbzadeh at Georgetown University, and Yazdi at MIT. We know about the world. There are two groups around the Ayatollah, those interested in government and administration who want a better life for our people, and the mullahs whose interests are strictly religious. We are both vying for the Imam's attention."

"Ah, the fabled moderates we hear about."

"In comparison to the mullahs, we are radical liberals. We want good relations with the United States, but many who advise the Ayatollah hate America; you are the Great Satan. A debate rages around the Imam. Some want to work with you, many don't."

The food arrived, a Middle Eastern banquet of lamb and beef mixed with complementing herbs and spices.

"I cannot say that I am your friend," Nassir said. "But I am afraid for Iran if the clerics come to power. That is why we must be careful. We are on the brink—either of entering a new, better world, or retreating into darkness. Everything rests with the Imam."

This was his opening, Marshall knew. The moderates who sought to overthrow the Shah were on an aerial tightrope without a net; below was death and chaos. They might not like the United States or want its help, but they needed it.

Marshall's concern, however, was that America's help

might send them into the abyss even faster, bringing America with them.

His mixed feelings about this mission were growing stronger with each word Nassir spoke. The Shah was doomed, this was patently obvious—the mere fact that a member of the opposition was meeting with the U.S. ambassador foretold it. But to Marshall, Nassir and the others weren't winners either: reason had no role in revolution, especially one inspired by a fanatic like Khomeini. Earnest young men schooled in the West were not going to stop the flood tide of hate the Ayatollah would unleash. Their very moderation would sink them; when word of their willingness to oar with the Great Satan got out, their frail little boat would be scuttled in a sea of blood.

This man was doomed, he felt, like all moderates in Iran, but he could hardly tell Nassir his misgivings, so he chose his words carefully. "My government knows the Shah has made mistakes. We will not interfere if he is overthrown; that is the business of the people of Iran. We will not get involved in your domestic politics."

"That will . . . mollify the Ayatollah."

Marshall leaned forward. "The Ayatollah is not our enemy, nor the mullahs. We support the *people* of Iran; we want to remain *their* friends. I want to relay this to the Imam personally; I must if there is going to be an understanding between my government and any future government in Iran. I have a message from our president."

Nassir stood abruptly. "I will do what I can. Thank you for your time and understanding. I am impressed with your flexibility in meeting me on such short notice."

Nassir shook hands, then disappeared, his food untouched.

Marshall sat back. This was going to be more complex than he had imagined, fraught with more peril for America than he had supposed. Hated by his people, reviled by the mullahs and Western-educated moderates, supported only by the army and Savak, Pahlavi was doomed—for in the end, force and fear were never enough.

As usual, America had backed the wrong horse. It was too late to change the bet, yet it would do no good to shoot the horse either.

America's only hope was with the Ayatollah himself;

nothing could be accomplished through intermediaries. Marshall had to face the Imam and convince him that the Great Satan was only a bumbling archangel who meant well.

Marshall had dealt with John F. Kennedy and LBJ, Richard Nixon and Jimmy Carter; he had dined with royalty and the statesmen of the world; he had listened to consummate liars and joked with mass murderers. He felt he could have discoursed with Plato and Socrates, managed the Last Supper, and not made a fool of himself with Muhammad or the Buddha.

But the Ayatollah Khomeini? That was attempting to reason with the March Hare.

When he left the restaurant, Mead jumped out of the car.

"Everything went fine," Marshall said, getting in the backseat.

Mead was so relieved, and so sure Marshall would never do anything like this again, he decided he wouldn't say anything about this to Major Bishop or Floyd Sedwick. He was so happy nothing had happened that he debated whether to talk to Marshall about Sung, but he seemed preoccupied. He'd talk to him tomorrow, he decided. He had to do it soon because Sung, still angry with him, had made him sleep on the sofa.

Wilson Lord tried to relax. Parisians were the most animated and frenetic of Frenchmen. He had a leisurely *petit déjeuner,* strolled up Avenue Foch, then sat at a café on the Champs-Elysées and had more coffee.

He was depressed at Andy Maynard's death; there were no monuments to spies, no public funerals, and never many mourners; those who lived in obscurity were buried so. How many people would come to his own funeral? Not many, he reckoned, and those only to verify the corpse.

It was shortly before noon, time to make his first contact. At the busy café, he used the public phone and dialed the number given him for Wu Te-chao.

A man answered in French, but Lord recognized Huong's voice and said in Vietnamese, "We missed our last rendezvous, Mr. Huong. I understand why. I am very sorry for your loss."

There was an intake of breath, a move to hang up, then hesitation.

"We should not talk on the phone. Those who are unhappy with a recent demise at Père Lachaise are probably listening in. I hope you are aware of their interest in you, and inability to overlook what happened. We must discuss this matter, and others. I will meet you tonight at ten after your dinner. Wait on the sidewalk until a cab stops for you. Do not be alarmed; you have nothing to fear from me—quite the contrary."

He hung up, knowing Huong's panic, but also that he would be waiting tonight.

He dialed Caldwell's office. There was no answer. Lord glanced at his watch; it was ten past twelve. Did the son of a bitch ever work?

Unable to drink any more coffee, Lord left the café. Sparse Christmas lighting was being strung along the boulevard by bickering electricians, and a few shops offered a miserly *Joyeux Noël*. It certainly wasn't Bloomingdale's, he thought, then realized he had not bought Anh or Lance anything. He would probably not be home for Christmas, and unless he sent packages immediately, they would not arrive in time.

He flagged a cab and told the driver to take him to the Galeries Lafayette. He hated crowds and abhorred shopping, but steeled himself for the ordeal when the cab dropped him before the gigantic department store on Boulevard Haussmann, just in back of the Paris Opera House.

An hour later he reeled out with nothing in his hands, overcome with the odor of perfume from a thousand scent stands, faint from heat, and shaking from rude salesclerks.

He would wire Anh money, he decided.

A woman approached the only available public phone, but he pushed her out of the way and grabbed the receiver. If Caldwell wasn't in, he'd track him down and kill him personally, but to his relief, Mike answered.

"Now!" he said, then slammed down the receiver and glared back at the woman, who muttered an obscenity at him as he walked past toward a line of cabs.

When he entered the Orangerie fifteen minutes later and walked downstairs, Lord felt immediately soothed. The museum was virtually deserted, and Debussy music wafted through all the rooms. He wasn't wild about the Monets—to him they looked exactly what they were: blurry paintings of water lilies by a nearly blind man, yet the muted lighting and somber atmosphere brought the first tranquillity he'd experienced in Paris and erased the madhouse scene of his fruitless shopping foray.

He was savoring the solitude when he saw Caldwell squinting in the darkness to locate him. "Jesus," Mike said, dropping into a seat beside him. "I've been in livelier funeral homes. And this guy can't paint shit. What was he, blind?"

Lord smiled.

Caldwell glanced at the huge murals wrapping the walls. "What did he use for a brush—a broom?"

"They're impressions of his garden at Giverny; he was a very old man when he painted these, and yes, his eyesight was failing. What kind of painting do you like?"

Caldwell thought, then shook his head. "Nothing comes to mind. I guess visually I'm more the centerfold type."

Lord sighed. "Someday I'm going to find a cultured protégé."

"He'll probably be queer," Caldwell said with a grin.

"That might be a blessing too." Then Lord turned burning eyes on Caldwell. "I'm meeting Huong tonight; I'm hoping he can help us. I'm going to need information for 'negotiations.' Marshall's children are arriving soon; I want to know everything about them—their movements, the times, who'll be with them."

Caldwell saw what Lord was up to. He did not like it—women and children should have nothing to do with his work, no more than should taking on a decorated Marine, but he was in no position to question decisions made at Lord's level.

"No problem," he said casually. "But the Major might be a complication. Andy told him last night that I was working for you. Bishop remembers you from Vietnam."

Caldwell looked with what he thought was indifference into Lord's face, but Lord saw that Caldwell was troubled and guessed Bishop had told him about the shooting.

"I'm sure he does. Major Bishop is one of the most dedicated men I've ever encountered, and possibly the most obtuse. Like so many well-meaning men, he leaves a wake of destruction in his path."

Lord pointed to the painting on the wall. "That is a visual depiction of Major Bishop's art—extraordinarily unfocused and crude. Would you like to hear the story?"

"Yes, sir, I would." Caldwell knew he was on a path he had never traveled; he was getting older, the decisions faced more difficult and less clear-cut. He was reaching a crossroads in his life, and soon he would have to decide whether the boundaries he thought existed were real or merely transitory markings on the beach that every tide of an assignment could erase. He hoped Wilson Lord had an answer for him.

Lord settled back and related what had happened in Saigon without embellishment or apology. He told about Marshall's mission, the defector Trung, the battle plan, the events in the church, and the eventual fall of South Vietnam. When he finished, he turned to Caldwell. "What would you have done, Mike?"

Caldwell did not speak for a long time. He hated *Clair de lune*, hated the paintings, and was not happy with himself when he said, "I would have shot him."

"And your eyesight is better than mine. You would not have missed, and Major Bishop would be dead."

That was probably true too, Caldwell thought, and that disturbed him even more.

Lord let him sit in silence another minute, then said softly, "Mike, our world is not an easy one. People are always looking for right and wrong, blacks and whites, but very often everything is gray, and the choices we have to make are all bad. Very little is an either/or proposition; most are ands/buts and maybes. All we can do is make the best choice, then live with our decision."

Caldwell nodded.

"Do you believe in God, Mike?"

Caldwell shook his head. "I don't think so." He turned to Lord. "Do you?"

"I'm old; I grow more detached from everything each day. We live, we die. I find our place in the cosmic order irrelevant. To answer your question, I merely turn the equation around—I find the cosmic order irrelevant to us." Again

Lord pointed to the pictures. "God could have painted those—they're rather undefined, aren't they? Maybe God's blind too. It certainly looks like His brushstrokes were done with a broom."

Lord stood. "The next time we'll meet at Montmartre, on the steps of Sacré-Coeur. I'll call you to give you the time." As he was about to leave, he turned. "Was she waiting for you?"

Caldwell had to think a moment before it registered; he had completely forgotten Angie. "Yes. She was waiting."

Lord frowned. He wanted a man happy with a woman, and a woman happy with a man. He wanted loving families and happy children. He did not see this in Caldwell, and he raised a finger in admonishment, then he saw the futility—he was Mike's age when his own first marriage collapsed. "Montmartre," he said, and left.

Huong tried to be a good host, but his thoughts were wildly distracted. The Arabs with him, however, were so uncomfortable in their surroundings and with the food—an unsavory blend of disagreeable tastes, probably puppy dogs, the staple of the Orient, they knew—and so eager for what Huong offered that they saw only an inscrutable man who didn't seem to hear them, though they guessed this was just Oriental deception.

The Vietnamese waiters, of course, detected profound turbulence in him, but attributed it to gas, indigestion, or the proximity of Arabs, a disturbing and barbaric people who would cause the Buddha himself to squirm in discomfort. What, after all, did these people believe in except bloodshed? Where was tranquillity among these people? Or silence or beauty? And they ate like animals besides; they were worse than Americans, and richer. They were crude and knew only business, and it was common knowledge they were thieves; the table service would have to be inventoried tonight.

With Huong were two Libyans, two Iraqis, and a man with the Palestine Liberation Organization who wanted to buy weapons from China.

The transaction at dinner had taken a startling turn, but Huong had had to struggle to keep focused after the crisis call from Wilson Lord this morning. He had met with these men previously and thought the negotiations neither pressing nor significant, but they indicated their interest was suddenly urgent. There had been a recent development, some new fluctuation in the endlessly fluctuating Mideast.

They saw his inattention and made their case more fervently, finally in the end pleading with him to intercede for weapons, especially missiles. The sums were vastly beyond what had been mentioned before, but all he could think of was Wilson Lord. He was so close to revenge, but now here was a figure from the past who could undo everything. How had he discovered him? What did he mean about Sûreté?

He had to meet him, of course. Lord knew about him, but had always been a friend and had intimated they might help one another now. Could it be so? His experiences since Vietnam had been only of treachery and deception, yet Lord was not part of that world. Huong held out the wild hope that maybe Lord would be an ally again, but he knew he needed something Lord might want if they were to deal.

He turned to the men at the table. Why this sudden change in their position? It might be useful. "I can accommodate your needs, but I must understand those needs."

"The Americans," whispered the PLO representative. "They're making an overture to Khomeini."

The Iraqi nodded. "The Shah is doomed. Khomeini will be in power by spring. Can you understand what that will mean?"

Huong couldn't and didn't care, but he perceived it was a frightening prospect to these men, and verifying this, the Libyan leaned close.

"The Americans are meeting with Khomeini. He is a fanatic who will make war on all of us. He will have the Shah's army and weapons. You must help us."

What little Huong knew of Arab politics, he found boring and stupid, but he knew this mattered to these men, so he nodded sagely. "I will consult with others."

"We need assistance immediately," the PLO representative said.

"Money is no longer a consideration," the Iraqi added.

"We are desperate," the Libyan said. "Khomeini will be a disaster for us."

Who was this Khomeini? Huong wondered. And what had the United States stirred up now? "I will get back with you."

With their business completed, their food untouched, they left the restaurant, and Huong waved an indifferent good-bye to them and started up the street of the crowded Latin Quarter.

A cab pulled to the curb immediately. Huong looked in, saw an older, frailer Wilson Lord; but he had a pleasant look on his face, so Huong got into the cab.

Lord clasped his hand in genuine pleasure; the touch, unexpected and not altogether welcome, nevertheless allayed Huong's fears.

"I am happy to see you, Mr. Huong. I am pleased you are well, though I know the terrible ordeal you've suffered."

Huong sat uncomfortably on the seat as the cab moved through congested traffic. At St.-Michel the taxi turned onto the quay and drove along the Seine, past Sainte-Chapelle and the Palace of Justice, hauntingly lit in the night, their reflections shimmering on the river.

"I was more fortunate than you," Lord said. "My wife and son got out of Vietnam before the communists came, but that has only made me appreciate your grief even more."

Still Huong did not speak; he did not want nor need reminders of what had happened in Vietnam.

Lord was not insensitive; he understood Huong's fear and distrust, so he came directly to the point. "François Bichot was murdered in Père Lachaise; Sûreté will not allow an agent's death to go unavenged, no matter that he was compromised. They think you killed him. Consequently you are marked; they *will* come at you—it is a matter of honor and face. We, the KGB, Mossad, every intelligence service operates the same way."

Huong merely sat on the seat, staring straight ahead.

"I know why you are here. I consider your grievance against Bradley Marshall a private matter. He is, however, aware of your presence in France. He has powerful friends and possibly can have the French authorities move against you. Your position is vulnerable, Mr. Huong. I am here to help you."

Huong turned to study Lord; his gaze was not pleasant, but not hostile either.

"You have no choice but to trust me." Lord told the driver to cross the river at Pont du Carrousel and let them out at the Louvre. "We can talk as we stroll."

When the cab dropped them in the courtyard of the Louvre, they walked under the small Arch of Triumph toward the gardens of the Tuileries.

The night was wet and cold, but they were bundled under heavy coats, and too nervous to feel a chill. "Years ago Bradley Marshall prevented me from getting a man out of Vietnam who might have saved the country and prevented the disasters that happened to you," Lord began. "You and I were going to meet that night to get the defector out of the country—not only did Marshall wreck that, he killed your child. The damage and suffering he caused are immeasurable. We both want revenge against him."

Neither of their eyesights was good in the dark as they moved unsteadily along gravel paths toward the park. "Now Marshall is perpetrating another disaster. He is going to meet with the Ayatollah Khomeini, the Shah of Iran's worst enemy."

Ah, Huong thought in sudden understanding about the Arabs' urgency to secure weapons, and he stopped before a bench outside the gate to the gardens. He bent to see if it was wet, brushed at the seat, and settled onto it. Lord sat beside him.

Around them men moved in the darkness along the paths, weaving in and out of the heavy shrubbery, and Lord realized that they had wandered into another cruising ground, but Huong seemed unperturbed.

"I must stop Marshall from meeting Khomeini. Perhaps we can help one another."

Huong brought his umbrella into his lap; his hand fingered the trigger mechanism for the blade. "Perhaps we can. I may be able to get you information about that meeting."

Lord nodded. "If you can, I will get you whatever information you desire about Marshall and his family, and I promise protection from Sûreté."

"My clients are very agitated by a recent development involving your ambassador."

"That means he has already initiated contact."

Noting Lord's disquiet, Huong felt better and he said reassuringly, "Arabs are as easy to deal with as children. They are utterly predictable; their hate and distrust for one another makes them simple to manipulate."

"If you can get the information about a meeting between Marshall and Khomeini, I will get you what you need."

Huong nodded, but he didn't say anything.

They stared up to the sky; a faint mist wrapped them, and now that their business was completed, they felt the chill in the air. Lord wondered if Huong was thinking about Vietnam, where it was seldom cold; he himself often longed for the tropical climate of days past.

But Huong was not thinking of Vietnam. He was wondering if he could trust Lord; he wished he understood Americans as well as he did Arabs, but Americans were not predictable; they were not like children, but more like animals in rut, and he had made many mistakes dealing with them. Since he could not *feel* their needs and desires, or understand their expectations, he often misjudged them. He had trusted Lord before, and though Lord had given no cause to doubt his word, Huong was not the same man he had been years ago. Nor was Lord, he knew.

"We must arrange for a place to meet. An obvious place where neither of us would be noticed." Lord reflected a moment. "We shall meet at shops. Exclusive ones," he amended, thinking of the hordes at the Galeries Lafayette. "Hermès, on Rue de Rivoli. I shall be buying a scarf. I will call with the time."

Lord stood. "Marshall's children are arriving shortly, and Marshall will be meeting with Khomeini soon. Our business should be completed soon. I urge you to purchase a ticket out of here; you do not want to linger once our transaction is finished."

Lord bowed slightly and then walked off.

Huong watched him disappear, running his hand along the umbrella in his lap.

No, he decided at last; he would not trust Lord. He would trust no one again; he would let nothing interfere with his revenge. He had killed that American soldier who had run over his daughter, had himself stabbed him again and again, and watched him crawl into the street where he was flattened by one of Huong's trucks, had watched the heavy wheels crush his head, and he had gladly murdered the French agent, and he would let nothing stand in the way of seeing Marshall's children murdered.

They *had* to die. There was no justice otherwise; the dead would go unavenged, and America and Bradley Marshall unpunished.

He stood, stabbing the umbrella into the gravel, and he vowed that would not happen.

•

CHAPTER 13

Catherine was at the breakfast table, fortified by coffee and ready for her husband when he came down at seven-thirty. They had returned late the previous night from comforting Irene Maynard and had gone to bed tired and depressed, but Catherine was waiting for him this morning.

"I know something is wrong," she said as he entered the room. "It's time you told me what this has to do with Sarah and Chris." She looked at him levelly. "I called Helen and told her you're going to be late."

He went to the buffet table. "Catherine, I have meetings. GM and Chrysler representatives are here negotiating tariff and quota restrictions. The French workers are screaming about health benefits, and I've canceled a trade luncheon three times. I *have* to go to the embassy."

"You have *nothing* to do except protect our children, and I want to know what's going on. Tell me what happened in Vietnam that put Sarah and Chris in danger."

Marshall took a drink of coffee, then reluctantly explained about the Chinese man.

"You *knew* your car killed his child?" she asked incredulously. "You covered it up?"

He bowed his head. "Yes."

She didn't say anything for a long time, then she shook her head. "My God, Brad, I thought I knew you." Then she got angry. "Sarah and Chris are in danger, and you're worrying about GM representatives? *Damn* you."

She drew a deep breath and folded her napkin. "I'll call the children; they can't come. That Chinese man will kill them. You've got to stop him. Why can't the Secret Service and Floyd handle this?"

"Because they rely on the CIA for information. I can hardly tell them not to trust the CIA because they're out to kill me too. They'd think me paranoid and have me in the bin without shoelaces and sharp instruments. Andy was the only person I could trust."

"What about the French? Jarre would help."

"Yes, but he'd have to turn to Sûreté, and they're in a bind—one of their agents was killed and they don't know how badly he was compromised. And if the Chinese man is a legitimate businessman in the country legally—what can they do?"

"Why not go to Carter and tell him you need help?"

"Because someone in his office is telling the CIA everything. Carter works through his assistants, and *they* can't be trusted. Even if he went to Admiral Turner at the CIA, he'd have to turn to *his* assistants, and probably they're in on this. That's the dilemma with Caldwell and Lord. I could have them recalled, but they'd just send someone else."

"Well, you've *got* to stop him, Brad." She was silent a long moment. "Let's take this step by step. There are two problems—the Chinese man and the CIA. The children are in danger, and you're in danger. Let's take you first. How do you protect yourself from the CIA?"

"No one has lived to write that book, Catherine."

"It may not be difficult—if they don't want you to meet with Khomeini, don't—then the CIA and Lord wouldn't be interested in you."

"The President—"

"Oh, screw him. He's a fanatic too."

"He's a good man, Catherine; he means well."

Her mouth turned in disdain. "No one means ill, Brad—everyone is well-meaning, and the more well-meaning, the more dangerous they are. It's when they want to do things for you—make you free, save your soul—that's when you have to worry. People who *believe* things are frightening."

"There are many things worth believing, Catherine—love, justice . . ."

She grabbed a roll and buttered it furiously. "Men are *so* stupid. Love isn't something you believe in; it's a force. Kindness, love, compassion—those aren't beliefs, they're as elemental as wind—and it doesn't make any difference whether you believe in them or not. *Justice* is a belief; injustice is only someone else's justice. Beliefs are things like the NRA, countries, the Baptist Church, the Republican Party."

He smiled. "You should have been queen."

"Of course I should. Women are much more sensible, but we have to contend with Neanderthal men who love killing—for country or god or sport. That's why *men* are presidents and popes and imams, because a woman wouldn't send her children to die or kill another woman's child. We'd weep and be called weak. Men send children to slaughter and are called bold and courageous."

She shook her head bitterly. "Yet we know our sons—they're like our men, rotten little bastards who love to fight and kill. I'm sure Ryan was very good at it." She pointed a finger at him. "And so are you. Find that Chinese man; stop him."

"How?"

"Kill him if you have to. Hire someone."

"Catherine, I'm a diplomat, not a Mafia don. Do you suppose I can take out an ad in the *Herald Trib?* 'Wanted—Assassin: contact U.S. ambassador. Be discreet.' "

He finished his coffee and stood to go. "Maybe I can deal with them all. If I could meet with the Chinese man, I'm sure I could reason with him. And maybe Caldwell too."

She shook her head. "No, Brad, you won't. You were wrong about Vietnam, Agamemnon sailing off to war, and now you're some idiot Faust if you think you can bargain with devils, even lesser ones. Don't you *understand,* that man is going to kill Sarah and Chris. He's already killed two men and he wants to murder our children because he blames you for *his* daughter's death—you *can't* bargain with him."

He moved to her but she jumped up and backed away. "Don't touch me. Don't come near me. Just get out and let me think."

He stood limp and broken, then he turned. "I'll see you tonight," he mumbled, leaving the room.

He stepped outside, nodding absently to Mead, who saluted as he opened the limousine door. Was she right? Was there no way to stop the Chinese man except by killing him? No! he thought. There *had* to be a way. Reason had to work. What would it say about man if violence was the only answer?

When Marshall arrived at the embassy, Helen told him she'd rescheduled the trade lunch. "But they don't believe it; they have a standing take-out order from Burger King."

Today she wore a short black leather skirt, spike heels, a vaguely see-through white blouse, and huge plastic earrings. The effect was stunning, though bizarre for an ambassador's office.

"Where's Luke?" Marshall asked nonplussed.

"How would I know? He spends less time here than you."

"Get me the papers on the health benefits, I'll sign them."

"Don't you want to read them?"

"No."

"Do you know what you're signing?"

"No, but I suppose the department lawyers have gone over them."

"They have, and they have serious reservations. You're signing a paternity-leave clause—three months' paid leave for women, and for a man if his wife gets pregnant."

"Then there's nothing to worry about; French men don't sleep with their wives."

"They will if they'll get paid three months' leave."

"Just bring the papers, Helen. And find Bishop, and give me a few more minutes alone."

He sat back at his desk and mentally sorted through his problems. Catherine's anger would pass, he knew. He *could* deal with the Chinese man and handle Lord and the CIA too. He wasn't naive, he felt, he was just confident of his abilities. He sat forward and buzzed Helen to start his schedule.

Later in the morning, during a staff meeting, she interrupted him with an urgent call from the Syrian ambassador.

"I can't wait for my country to become a first-world nation," Saud Asari said when Marshall picked up the phone. "Then I can get invited to lunch every day."

"Not again," Marshall moaned.

"Apparently you were a great success yesterday. Same time, same place. Can you make it?"

Marshall glanced at his watch. "I'm afraid so."

"What am I getting out of this?"

"Endless goodwill and the thanks of a grateful nation."

"How about a deal on some missiles?"

"Have Clarissa talk to Catherine—she's handling arms sales now."

Marshall called in Helen. "Cancel the luncheon."

She just stared at him. "You're not serious—I can't cancel a *fourth* time."

"Have Lowell handle it."

"They want to eat with the *ambassador,* not his deputy. There is a reason we have a staggering trade deficit—you are a leading cause of it."

Lord arranged a meeting with an old colleague with Mossad, Israeli intelligence. Amazingly similar in appearance—tall, thin, and silver haired—they looked like prosperous brokers who had stepped out from the bourse to take a coffee break. They met at Fauchon's in midmorning, but when Lord asked what was happening in the Mideast, Chaim Ruben threw up his hands.

"Wilson, there are secrets that are not supposed to be secrets, secrets everyone is supposed to know, secrets no one is supposed to know that everybody knows, secrets only a few parties know, secrets that are dangerous to know, secrets that are deceptions, secrets we spread, secrets you spread—only my mother could understand it all."

"Should I be talking to your mother then?"

"Probably. You know, the best prime minister we ever had was a Jewish mother." Chaim cut a piece of fruit tart. "We thought your ambassador would know better; long ago he advised against involvement in the Mideast. But we are not particularly upset with your government's new shift."

"It is no secret then?"

Chaim swallowed his tart. "My mother and her friends have discussed it endlessly over mah-jongg." He looked at

Lord's untouched cake. "Aren't you going to eat it after all the trouble we went through to get it?"

Chaim shook his head in wonder. "First you look at the desserts, then you select one, then you pay for it, then you go back with your receipt, and only then do they give you the dessert; then you go through the same routine for the coffee. Then there's no place to sit down, and you stand, grazing like a cow over a five-dollar piece of cake and a teaspoon of coffee. Only the Russians could make it more difficult, and they don't have any cake to begin with."

Lord pushed his plate to him.

Chaim cut a piece of Lord's cake with his fork. "You understand that when the Shah falls, Iran will turn on Iraq; with any kind of luck there will be a bloodbath. I am not being callous, but Iranians killing Arabs, Arabs killing Arabs, is preferable to Arabs killing Jews. We are distressed by Hussein's nuclear and chemical buildup, but if he wants to turn that on Shiites and Kurds . . ." He shrugged. "You might not have come to the right person, Wilson. We are not wildly opposed to Khomeini; we see possibilities in him."

He devoured the rest of the cake in two bites.

A meeting later in the day with an Iraqi contact confirmed that everyone knew of America's shift, and all were planning contingencies. Arab nations were turning to the Chinese and French for missiles and nuclear technology, and to the Germans for their proven chemical expertise. The destabilizing of the Mideast was under way, Lord saw, with the U.S. and Bradley Marshall spearheading the crisis.

Lord called Huong, determined to stop it. "Four o'clock."

"I have news."

"So do I," Lord said, for he had found out that Sarah and Chris were arriving tomorrow to attend the memorial service for Andy Maynard.

"What are you looking at?" Helen asked Bishop as he leaned across her desk, staring intently at her blouse.

"I'm trying to see if you're wearing nipple clips. And where'd you get those earrings—Toys 'Я' Us?—they look like Frisbees."

"It's called style. Fashion. Nothing you would know about,

Major Bishop. I'm trying to bring a little pizzazz into the workplace. Now get out and leave me alone. The ambassador is running way behind schedule and he can't see you until the end of the day—at the earliest, and I don't know anything further about Sarah's arrival, so don't bother to ask."

Bishop checked his own office, had no messages as usual, so he went down to the basement to talk to Caldwell. His door was open, and a cup of lukewarm coffee was on his desk, so Bishop assumed he had just stepped out.

The room was windowless and utterly bare except for a desk, a swivel chair, and a metal file cabinet.

Bishop settled into the chair to wait; an hour later Caldwell came in carrying a shopping sack. Though surprised to find Bishop at his desk, Caldwell nodded casually. "What can I do for you?"

"I told you yesterday—tell me about the gook."

Caldwell closed his door and put the sack on the desk. He took off his jacket and let it fall to the floor; he undid his tie and let it drop on top, then he pulled off his shirt and tossed it on the heap, then he shucked his shoes, socks, trousers, and underwear.

Bishop leaned back in the chair. "You should be doing this to music."

Reaching into the sack, Caldwell ripped off the cellophane wrapping of a package and held up a shirt. "Can you believe it? Fifty dollars." He held up a tie. "Twenty-five."

He waved a pair of very skimpy blue briefs on the tip of his finger. "Fifteen."

"You mug a queer?"

"One size fits all it says."

"*You* they'll fit. I have to have mine tailor-made."

"Right, stud." Caldwell slipped them on, arranged himself, and modeled them to Bishop, tousling his blond hair and flexing his muscles. "Straight out of *GQ*. Real turn-on, huh?"

"Depends on who you're trying to turn on." Bishop ran a hand over his own buzzed blond hair. "It doesn't do anything for me, and Angie doesn't care what a guy wears."

Caldwell grinned. "You were right about her. How about Laurie up in the visa section? We're going out tonight."

"She can suck the chrome off a trailer hitch, but you don't need a Givenchy shirt and Gucci tie to score with her either."

"She's just tonight. I'm waiting for Sarah Marshall to show up."

Bishop snapped forward in the chair.

Caldwell laughed. "You are *so* easy, Bishop. I've read her files—she's in a league by herself, or rather *with* everybody else, except you."

Bishop settled back, swallowing his fury. "You have a bad attitude about women."

"I like to fuck them; that's bad?"

"That's all they're good for?"

"No. They're nice to dance with—they follow."

"You got a real problem. You latent queer?"

Caldwell smiled. "Don't try to psych me. Getting off is getting off; women are good for that." He fastened his shirt. "I think it's nice you've fallen in love—too bad you didn't choose someone who doesn't sweat everybody else's sheets."

Luke stood menacingly. "*I* can handle women—you're the one who's divorced."

Mike dodged an imaginary blow. "No glove on that one, Pretty Boy."

Bishop came from behind the desk. "You know what scares me? You. I don't like the way Lord turned you so easily. I don't like you being his hired-gun boy toy."

Caldwell ducked. "No hit."

Bishop moved close and put his hand on Caldwell's buttocks. "Some bad shit is going down, Mike." He squeezed. "I'm worried about you."

Caldwell's eyes flashed warnings.

Bishop reached into Caldwell's briefs, drawing him even nearer. "Your handler, Lord, has mesmerized you."

"Get your hands off me, Bishop," he said threateningly, his body tensing.

Bishop squeezed harder, then pushed him away. "I don't want your ass, Caldwell, but Wilson Lord could have it in a minute. He couldn't get mine, so now he's stroking yours. Watch it—you're gonna get fucked."

Bishop sat on the desk and grinned evilly. "Or is that what you want?"

Caldwell shook his head slowly. "You play a dangerous game, Lukey; I'm surprised you're still alive."

"I plan to *stay* alive. And keep Ambassador Marshall alive too. I'm not going to let you, Lord, or that gook get him."

Caldwell snapped his fingers. "Oh, yeah, that's what you came here for—help with the gook. Guess what, asshole? Fuck off."

Bishop started for the door, shaking his head in disgust. "You can dress in designer clothes, Mike, but inside—you're just an off-the-rack, forty-two-regular piece of shit."

Bishop was walking into his office down the hall from Marshall's when Mead intercepted him; he had been waiting anxiously for him all afternoon.

"Major?" he asked tentatively.

"What?" Bishop said sharply, still angry with Caldwell and frustrated with his inability to learn anything about the Chinese man.

Mead backed away. "Ah, nothing, sir. Sorry to bother you, sir."

Bishop caught himself. "I'm sorry. I was thinking of something else. What can I do for you, Sergeant?"

"It can wait, sir."

"Get in here." Bishop pointed to his office. Even among Marines, not noted for loquacity, Ron Mead was considered a mute. Bishop could not remember a conversation with the sergeant, or even a sentence that had a verb—"Yes, sir," "No, sir," and "Right away, sir" was the extent of his dialogue.

"Sit down," Bishop said as he dropped into his desk chair. Bishop's office was pristine and orderly—his commission, diplomas, medals, citations, awards, all framed and in line, exactly six inches from one another. There was a U.S. flag, a Marine Corps flag, a bronzed football, and a picture of his parents. His office furniture was government issue, metal and uncomfortable, utterly masculine. He loved his office and took great pride that he had a secretary, though he didn't do much work, and she even less.

"What can I do for you?" Bishop asked.

Mead loved the office too; if he ever had one, it would

be just like this, except he wouldn't have any diplomas to put up, and he didn't think he'd display his medals.

They both had Navy Crosses, the nation's second-highest award for valor, but Mead was uncomfortable wearing his—Bishop not at all.

"Well, sir. I wanted to talk about a couple things."

"Let's hear them. You want some coffee? A Coke? My secretary will get it—I need to come up with things for her to do; she doesn't do shit except read books with swooning cunts and half-naked guys on the cover."

Though Mead, like all the Marines in the detachment, knew Bishop's secretary did more than read books, he shook his head. "No, sir. I just wanted to talk about . . . well, the ambassador first, then a personal problem. I don't have anywhere else to go with it."

"Fire away. I'm sure I can fuck up your personal problem worse than you have."

Mead grinned. "I doubt it. You're not married—you've managed to dodge *that* bullet."

"Actually, I wouldn't mind getting hit by that bullet; in fact, I've been trying to step in front of it, Sergeant. But she doesn't have me in her sights."

"You, sir? You're an officer; you went to college."

Bishop smiled. "Some women aren't impressed with a degree in phys. ed. from Oklahoma and a commission in the Marine Corps. I think I aspired beyond myself."

Mead nodded. "That's my problem too."

"Ah," Bishop said, thinking he knew what he was in for—Mead had taken up with a ranking official's wife, not an uncommon incident in embassy life. Unattended, bored diplomatic wives would bunk a Marine and consider it a dalliance while the trooper would fall in love. "Okay, but first tell me about Ambassador Marshall. What's the problem?"

"It's sort of like Vietnam. I was his bodyguard there, and he did some really dumb shit—dangerous. He was always running into scary situations. There were times we just barely made it; we could have been zapped a couple times—we were at Hue when the gooks hit at Tet. And they fired a rocket at his chopper. Jesus, being with him was as bad as a recon patrol in the DMZ. And now he's doing it again. I mean, is this how all ambassadors act?"

Bishop smiled, leaning back in his chair, hands behind his head. "Judging by the ones I've seen, and the bureaucrats here, the most dangerous thing they do is use knives at dinner. But he's different, I know. I could tell you about a night in a church in Saigon, but what's he doing now that scares you?"

"Running off to unsecure areas—like yesterday. He's got no security, just me, and he makes me wait in the car for about an hour. It was like Beirut. Mr. Maynard told me he was in danger, that someone is out to wax him, but I don't even know who, or what, to look out for. And what can I do when he tells me to stay in the car?"

Mead shook his head in agitation. "I know it's not my business to question what he does, and the last time I talked with someone about how I was worried, it was to a CIA guy in Saigon and he ended up trying to kill us both, so maybe this isn't such a good idea."

"What CIA guy?" Bishop asked levelly. "Wilson Lord?"

"That's the motherfucker! How did you know? You wouldn't believe what he did. I was gonna kill him."

"You should have—he's here trying to kill the ambassador again."

Mead rose out of his chair. "What!"

Bishop pointed Mead back to his seat. "I don't know what's going on, but Andy Maynard told me Lord was here and it has to do with an ayatollah, whatever that is, and there's a Chinese man who's after Marshall because of what happened the last time the ambassador was in Vietnam. That's where *I* met Lord, and he tried to kill me too."

Mead's jaw set. "I think it's time we took him down, sir."

"He's got someone here with him."

"Two Marines are more than a match for two CIA assholes," Mead said grimly. "Just tell me what you want done."

Bishop nodded. "I will, as soon as I come up with a plan. In the meantime I want you to do what Andy told you—watch him every minute because he's got two problems—Lord and this Chinese man."

"What Chinese man?"

"That's the part I don't know. But I will. You can count on that; I got a personal reason."

Then he leaned back in his chair again. "So now tell me about *your* personal problem. I've seen your wife; she's beautiful, and everyone says she's terrific. You fucking around on her and got caught?"

Mead shook his head emphatically. "Oh, no, sir. I was gonna talk to the ambassador about it, but he's real busy; that's why I thought I'd better talk to you."

"Why me? You're the one with the beautiful, smart woman, I'm dating sleazes. Well, not all sleazes," he amended, thinking of Candy and several others whom he really did like, but still had no plans to marry. "I should be coming to you for advice."

"No, sir, *I* should be dating sleazes. Sung's too good for me."

Then he told Bishop what had been troubling him.

When he finished, Bishop nodded solemnly because he knew Mead was in earnest, but he could not take this seriously. "Any chance you're selling yourself short, Sergeant? Maybe she has a higher opinion of you than you do. Maybe she sees things in you that you don't. Maybe she loves you for what you are."

"But I'm a nobody, and she's . . . so much better."

"Well, try this—do you want her to marry someone *worse* than you—dumber? Uglier? Sleazier?"

Mead grinned. "No, sir."

"Neither do I, that's why I'm aspiring beyond myself. But since you have what I want, I'm having trouble working up sympathy for you, Mead."

"But she deserves better."

"Maybe she's happy with what she's got. Several years ago, a man told me something wise about women. It was the night Lord almost killed me. This man said that the best women are reformers—they want to make men better. You're telling me that you're not good enough for your wife. Well, maybe that's what she wants—maybe she sees a challenge in you, an asshole she's going to save and make better. Why are you screwing around with her life's mission?"

Mead grinned again. "You think that could be it?"

"I think, Sergeant, that you're messing with something dangerous. You love her. She loves you. It sounds to me like you're trying to fuck up a wet dream. What if she left you? Is there a chance she'd find someone who would love her as much, take as good care of her, treat her as well? Maybe she'd have more *things,* shit you can buy in any store, but maybe she knows she'll never find someone who will love her like you do or treat her as well. Maybe she's happy with what she's got—just like you are."

"You really think that may be it?"

"If she's as smart as you tell me she is, yes, I do."

Mead looked at Bishop with gratitude, then he jumped up happily. "I *never* could have figured that out. I don't know about the woman who won't hook up with you, but *I'm* impressed with your degree and commission."

"But I don't want to marry *you,* Sergeant."

Mead laughed. "Well, if there's anything I can do for you, talk to her or anything, let me know. I *owe* you, sir."

"Just do what I tell you when the time comes to save the ambassador. And for the time being, lie low. Lord doesn't know you're here, and I don't want him to find out. You're going to be the secret weapon. You're going to take him down. Understand?"

Mead stood. "Yes, sir. Thank you, sir."

"And follow the ambassador—*don't* lose him, especially at night."

Mead nodded. "Don't worry, sir. I know how he is—he's always pulling shit to get away from his security, he's already tricked Mr. Sedwick a couple times—but he won't lose me. You can count on that, like I can count on you finding that gook."

Bishop watched him leave. Actually, he had no trouble believing a woman would fall in love with Ron Mead.

Surely then there was hope Sarah Marshall would see *his* merits.

CHAPTER 14

"Again?" Floyd Sedwick asked incredulously when Marshall told him he was leaving and couldn't be followed.

"Nothing happened last time; nothing will happen this time either."

"You sound like some stupid teenager talking about pregnancy—fucking doesn't work that way, and neither does security. You're going to get nailed one of these times."

"I'll have Sergeant Mead with me."

"A goddamn Marine with the IQ of toast isn't going to save your ass. Stale toast. Stale, *burnt* toast."

"I'll take my chances," Marshall said calmly.

"Your chances would be *much* better if you brought Helen. What is she today—Bondage Bambi?"

"I didn't notice."

Sedwick shook his head in disgust. "Is this another order?"

Marshall nodded.

Sedwick smoothed his hair and straightened his suit, then he headed for the door. "You asshole," he said.

Riding to the restaurant, Marshall tried to talk to Mead, but his bodyguard would have nothing to do with it. He sat tense in the front seat, an automatic weapon in his lap.

"You want me to bring you something?" Marshall asked lightly when the limousine pulled up to the restaurant, but Mead's face set only more grimly and he shook his head.

He couldn't believe Marshall had done this again, violating every security code by going to the same place twice. He was a sitting target, and there was nothing Mead could do.

This time Marshall entered the building expectantly, for he had obviously presented the American cause well enough to warrant a second meeting.

He was met at the door with the same deference and led to the same table, but this time a man was waiting and stood as Marshall approached. The man was about his own age, stocky, dapper in an expensive suit, with a colorful silk tie and gleaming Italian shoes. He had numerous rings on his fingers and was smiling broadly.

Marshall put out his hand. "Ayatollah Khomeini, I presume."

The man laughed heartily. "President Carter, how nice of you to join me." He appeared at ease and confident, a man obviously familiar with Americans and their manners. He gestured to a seat, then said to the maître d', "Wine, a nice Chablis," then he winked at Marshall. "Don't tell anyone. It is against my religion; alas, I am a hypocrite."

"At last. Someone I can deal with."

The man laughed again. "Sadeq Ghotbzadeh."

"The famous moderate. Bradley Marshall."

"The famous . . . intermediary. Saud Asari said you can be trusted; unfortunately, I don't trust him—he's an Arab, you know, so how can I trust you?"

"I'm not an Arab."

Ghotbzadeh slapped the table. "Wonderful. Abbas Nassir told me I would enjoy lunching with you—I don't trust him either, but he was right."

"I thought you, Nassir, and Bani Sadr were on the same side."

"We are; but that doesn't mean we trust one another. We trust only the Ayatollah."

Marshall searched for sarcasm or irony, but didn't see any. "Am I ever going to meet him?"

"Ah, wine," Ghotbzadeh said in diversion, greeting the arrival of the waiter. "What would you like to eat—they can prepare anything."

"I'll have what you have."

Ghotbzadeh spoke to the waiter, then interpreted for

Marshall. "A light repast, mostly vegetables. I know Americans don't eat big lunches—at Georgetown I ate only hamburgers. There was a little restaurant that served tiny hamburgers for fifteen cents."

"White Castle, or something like that."

"Yes! I practically lived there. I was a starving student and could only afford hamburgers. How fortuitous you know the place—this bodes well. Nassir was right about you; he thought you could be trusted." Ghotbzadeh shrugged. "But since *he* can't be trusted, I had to see for myself."

He raised his wineglass to Marshall, but then put down the glass as Marshall drank. He seemed likable and sincere, Marshall thought, but almost too forthright and westernized for an Iranian revolutionary, and he confirmed this when he said without preliminaries, "I've fought the Shah for twenty years. In Georgetown they used to call me 'Crazy Sadeq' for my protests against Pahlavi. He is an evil man, Ambassador Marshall, cruel and wicked and corrupt, and he is going to be overthrown."

Ghotbzadeh ran his finger around the rim of his glass. "I lived many years in America, but I never understood why Americans support dictators. Why do you feel more comfortable with tyrants like Marcos and the Shah than revolutionaries like your forefathers?"

Marshall sipped wine. "We are a business-minded people. Democracies are not efficient, nothing can be decided right away, but with a dictator or tyrant, all it takes is his say-so—contracts set up, bases established. We like the efficiency of despotism, as we deplore it on principle. Tyranny is cost-effective."

Ghotbzadeh nodded. "The Shah has been good business for the United States."

"Very. Billions and billions of dollars—oil and munitions. He supplies us with oil, and we sell him arms."

Ghotbzadeh turned solemn. "Americans don't understand us, do they? You have no appreciation of our culture or religion."

Marshall shook his head. "We are a people with little culture or history—how can we appreciate others'? And religion? We haven't a clue what others think or believe. We are globally and historically illiterate—White Castle intellectuals."

Ghotbzadeh smiled. "Yet you are nice people."

"Yes, we are, and the best buys were those White Castle hamburgers. Despite our mistaken politics and misguided policies, we *mean* well. We are, as you say, nice. Our mistakes are not malicious. We are a young nation, our errors those of immaturity."

Ghotbzadeh nodded. "You are a very silly people, insufferable, self-righteous know-it-alls, like little children smugly drawing crayon pictures as they sit on the most incredibly complex Isfahan rug, listening to the music of birds in trees, under a sky Allah gave them." He shrugged. "But nice children. That is why I am here."

It was going to work, Marshall thought; he did not have to seduce this man—Ghotbzadeh needed America; all he wanted was reassurance and someone to trust. Was Carter wiser and more sophisticated than Marshall suspected, sending him on this mission?

Ghotbzadeh waited until their food was set before them. "Pahlavi is going to fall. A tidal wave is rushing over him. The Ayatollah will return before spring."

"Then *your* troubles will begin. Revolutions have the nasty habit of devouring the revolutionaries."

Ghotbzadeh frowned. "Yes, tidal waves are difficult to control. Much hate and violence will be unleashed. But hope and expectations too. And disappointments."

Marshall raised his knife and fork in sympathy. "That's the damnable part of government—you're supposed to *do* something. A cricket can sit on a throne—that's not the trick; the trick is to accomplish good for the people. The Russians and Castro haven't figured that out yet. Conversely, the Shah *has* helped his people; the standard of living in Iran is higher than anywhere in the Mideast."

"He has been a disaster," Ghotbzadeh said emphatically. "We will do better." He chewed his food thoughtfully. "But we know the difficulties; the clerics don't. Even the Ayatollah doesn't appreciate the complexities of 'government.' He's a holy man, not a bureaucrat. Those of us who will manage the government see the problems, foremost of which are the clerics who want to turn Iran into a fundamentalist state."

"Are there really 'moderates' in Iran?"

"You don't know what a radical is until you've met some of the mullahs."

"Khomeini?"

"The Imam is a holy man; he's old, but neither stupid nor senile. You can work with him, but that will require accommodations on your part."

"That is why I am here. I want to tell the Imam that our countries can live together even though we don't believe the same things. I want him to know that those of us with crayons admire intricate art."

Ghotbzadeh nodded appreciatively. "Tell him what you have told me. Convince him of your good intentions. We need you, Mr. Marshall. Unless we establish relations with your government, we will return to the Middle Ages—Shiite against Sunni, Iranian against Arab, endless warfare. We will become a lost people left behind by technology and thought. You are our best hope to bridge the chasm between our countries."

"But I don't want to deceive you; my government is committed to the Shah."

Ghotbzadeh waved a dismissive hand. "We understand politics; we're not naive. We have to listen to Arafat—do you think we believe *him?* You have to back the Shah; we have to condemn you. We will say terrible things about America—most of it will be rhetoric. But as actors in a play, we can wink at one another as we hurl insults and threats, knowing we will be friends and talk business offstage."

Marshall finished his wine. "We understand one another; will the Ayatollah?"

"He is the spiritual descendant of Muhammad—divinely inspired, as infallible as the pope. He has survived eight decades and many enemies. Do not underestimate him, or our devotion to him."

Marshall nodded. "Tell me when he wants to meet with me; I will be there."

"What is the best way to contact you? I'd rather not go through the Syrians—they're Arabs, you know. I fear they are helping the Iraqis."

"Why would they do that? They hate one another."

"Exactly. Saddam Hussein is our implacable foe. When Khomeini comes to power, Hussein will make war on us. We will both be weakened. Who survives? The Syrians. It is all so simple."

He had been right years ago, Marshall saw; America had no business groping blindly through this minefield. Jimmy Carter was treading on live grenades. "Call me at the embassy or my residence. I'll leave a message that I'm expecting a call from CS—Crazy Sadeq. I'll tell them to interrupt whatever I'm doing to take your call."

Ghotbzadeh laughed. "Wonderful. But you must come alone."

"My security people are getting frantic. How about if I bring one man with me?"

Ghotbzadeh raised a cautionary finger. "One man, but unarmed. We will ensure your safety. You must trust us." He shrugged. "But, of course, we cannot trust you."

Marshall smiled. "Of course."

Wilson Lord was jostled along the narrow sidewalk of the Rue de Rivoli by shoppers carrying Christmas bags; when he came to Hermès, he darted through the door, convinced one of the world's most exclusive stores would offer refuge from the mob, but inside he turned back, thinking he had made a mistake—the crowd was as bad as on the sidewalk, and the noise as loud.

He would never find Huong in this madhouse, he thought, especially since the entire clientele looked Oriental.

It was a quarter to four; he had arrived early in the hope of finding something for Anh, but the crowds surging at the counters were too daunting for him. He backed into one counter and bumped into a rack of bangles and bracelets. Since no one was at this counter—the clerks were at another, hauling out bolts of silk scarves for Japanese tourists—he examined the bracelets with mild interest. They were brightly colored inlaid enamel, very pretty he thought: Anh would like them. And the price seemed reasonable—a hundred francs. Yes, he decided, he would buy her one; maybe two.

A clerk, seeing his interest, and because he was an American—a rare sight these post-oil-embargo days—asked if she could help. He pointed to two bracelets and said he would take them. She congratulated him on his taste and asked how he would like to pay.

He knew then he had made a mistake, and taking out his glasses, he winced; he had missed a zero—they were a thousand francs each. "Credit card," he said, too embarrassed to recant his error.

When she disappeared with his credit card and the bracelets, he couldn't decide which annoyed him more—the cost or his failing eyesight, so instead he turned his attention to the Japanese at the scarf counter, remembering what his mentor in Georgetown had advised.

A group of twenty businessmen were at a counter where two salesclerks brought out racks of scarves. One man, apparently the spokesman, rejected them all. The women looked perplexed; they had presented the entire selection. Then the man pointed to one on display, the Hermès signature scarf with the equestrian motif. The clerk nodded, the man nodded, the twenty other Japanese nodded, and they all thrust out their credit cards at once.

Lord's salesclerk returned with his card and a beautifully wrapped, very small package.

"Do they always buy the same scarf?" he asked, nodding toward the Japanese.

She nodded. "Always. We show them the others first to see if one will buy a different scarf, but they never do. All women in Japan must be wrapped in this one scarf, surely a strange sight, wouldn't you think?"

It was a *frightening* vision, Lord thought, not just of clip-clopping Japanese women in Hermès scarves, but of the mindless uniformity and financial power of their men.

Then he saw Huong. "If you had arrived a few minutes earlier, you could have saved me two thousand francs," he said amicably. "But I learned a valuable lesson—never enter one of these stores without my glasses on."

"A better lesson might be to stay out of these stores altogether," Huong said sagely.

Together they moved along the counters, ostensibly looking at merchandise, but Huong came directly to the point.

"Ambassador Marshall has met with the Iranians twice. He had lunch with them today."

God damn, Lord swore to himself, but he asked casually, "Can you find out in advance about their next meeting?"

"Probably. They are eager to please me. But what do you have to share in exchange that would please me?"

Lord fingered a leather handbag; he examined the price—he must be seeing too many zeros this time, he thought; but looking again, he saw he had read the price correctly. "What would you have to put in it after you bought it?" Lord asked in wonder at the staggering cost.

"Trinkets from other men; it is, after all, a woman's handbag."

Lord moved to the next counter. "Marshall's children are arriving tomorrow."

Huong was stunned. "Tomorrow? So soon? I did not expect this."

"They are coming for a memorial service for an old family friend, the godfather to the son. This is coming together very quickly. I think we are ready to enter our final negotiations. I will need your help to stop Marshall and Khomeini, and you will need mine to accomplish your revenge—it is that simple."

"Tomorrow," Huong murmured.

"Tell me when Marshall will meet with Khomeini, and I will tell you about the security for Marshall's children during their stay here."

Huong nodded. "How shall I get in touch with you?"

"I will give you my number. The next time we will meet at Louis Vuitton."

"Why *these* kinds of places?" Huong asked in annoyance.

"Curiosity. I am learning important things."

"At Hermès and Louis Vuitton?"

"Indeed," Lord said, bowing slightly, edging through the crowd of Japanese, who, accustomed to crowds, did not notice him.

When Marshall returned to the embassy, Helen was exasperated. "I've run out of excuses to cover for you. How do I explain that the ambassador can't perform his ambassadorial duties because he's . . . what?"

"Engaged in other ambassadorial duties. Has Luke turned up?"

"Apparently he's taken up residence at the gym—so he says, anyway. He keeps asking about Sarah; he's even more obtuse than I thought."

"Stubborn, Helen; persistent; dedicated—all admirable male traits."

"Stupid is the male trait that most comes to mind. Are you here to work for the afternoon, or just passing through? I know it's none of my business, I'm only your personal secretary, but I could schedule a few things for you if you're going to be in."

"I'll be here the rest of the day. Tell Luke to stop in before I leave."

Marshall spent the remainder of the afternoon in meetings and briefings. Just before five, Bishop knocked on his door.

"You *are* looking in good shape," Marshall said, motioning him to a seat. "Helen has her suspicions that you aren't in the gym all these times she can't find you."

"Well, sir, this morning I was with Mike Caldwell. I'm sure he's working for Lord, and he knows about the Chinese man. I keep hoping he'll tell me, but no luck so far."

"What makes you think you can reach him if he works for Lord?"

Bishop shrugged. "I don't know, I just think he might come through in the end."

Marshall smiled. "Like Sarah will?"

Bishop grinned. "She thinks I'm a Neanderthal, and I was, but no more; I read this book that told me what I'd been doing wrong. I'm a changed man—really enlightened."

"I'll tell her, just in case she doesn't notice when she sees you."

"When is she arriving?"

"I'm not sure; Catherine is trying to delay them. But forget that, Luke—I've got to find that Chinese man, and you've got to help. There's *got* to be a way to find him."

"Nobody's going to hurt Sarah with me around, sir. I'll come up with something."

Marshall nodded; but he knew Bishop was no match for these enemies. He needed another plan.

* * *

At the residence, Marshall went into the living room for a drink.

"Pour me one too," Catherine said from a chair, holding up an empty glass.

He stopped, startled by her presence. The room was unlit and she was sitting in near darkness. "What are you drinking?"

"Harvey Wallbangers. Make it a double."

"Sherry?"

"Fine. Sarah and Chris are coming tomorrow for Andy's service," she said discouragedly. "I couldn't talk them out of it."

He fumbled with the sherry decanter, spilled sherry as he poured, then handed her the glass, dropping into the seat beside her. *"I'll* call them."

She shook her head. "It won't do any good. They want to be here with us." She cradled her glass in her hands. "I'm sorry about this morning, Brad. I shouldn't have said those things, but I'm so worried."

He nodded.

"You have only eighteen hours to stop that Chinese man. What are you going to do? He'll kill them, you *have* to know that. That's how men are, Brad. You are not reasonable, compassionate creatures, and I can't just stand by letting you hope for the best. If the only way to save Sarah and Chris is to shoot that man—I'll do it."

"This is Paris, not Dodge City, Catherine."

"Try to meet with Khomeini and you'll see if this isn't Dodge. You're insane if you think the CIA is going to let you meet with a lunatic Moslem to overthrow the Shah."

She went to fix another drink, then turned. "I've been thinking about this all day, and I've come up with a solution. Go to Wilson Lord, tell him you *won't* meet with Khomeini if he'll help you with the Chinese man."

"Catherine. I am on instructions from my government—one doesn't barter that."

She slammed down the sherry decanter. "You'd *better* if it's the only way to save Sarah and Chris."

He stood. "I will not even discuss this."

"You covered up the death of a child, and *now* you're

going to take the high road of principle and let your own children get killed?"

"Catherine," he said calmly at the doorway. "I cannot change the past; I am sorry for what happened. I am trying not to make another mistake. I am trying to do the best I can."

In his study he didn't turn on the lights but stood at the window gazing out on the back gardens. The trees were bare and the hedgerows thin and anemic; it was late afternoon, darkening already.

Tomorrow, he thought; his children were coming tomorrow. He was out of time.

He had to have help against the Chinese man; Luke would not be able to handle this, but there was no one he could trust with Andy gone and Mike Caldwell in his place.

He stared out on the sparrows that had apparently decided to winter in his garden now that Catherine was trucking in bread for them.

Sparrows were wonderfully comforting; they were always there. When old ones died, new ones took their places, and no one could tell the difference.

Then he raised his head in sudden recognition.

He went to his desk and called the embassy duty officer. "There's a file on my desk, Michael Caldwell—bring it over immediately."

Marshall went back to the window, observing sparrows that would soon be so fat they'd have to walk south if the *boulangeries* went on strike.

Mike Caldwell had taken Andy Maynard's place. Maybe Wilson Lord hadn't turned him yet. Years ago when Lord tried to turn Bishop, Marshall had been able to get through to Luke. Maybe he could do the same with Mike Caldwell.

Perhaps he could beat Wilson Lord at his own game.

Wilson Lord was exhausted. He had given the wrong address to the cabdriver. Well, he had given him the right address, only he had misread it on the map. His eyesight was truly failing, he realized. Now with his glasses on he saw his mistake: Rue de Steinkerque didn't go to Sacré-Coeur—it dead-ended at the bottom of the hill.

Oh my God, he thought; he would have to walk the ten

thousand steps up to Montmartre. He stared up at the gleaming white basilica whose cupolas of Romanesque-Byzantine style towered a mile above him: he couldn't possibly make it, he thought.

Halfway, he paused for breath and looked back. Below was a glorious view of Paris, a golden Oz shimmering in the dark, but he was too tired and irritated to appreciate it, and he was in a hurry; he had told Mike to meet him at eight on the steps of the basilica, but he was not going to get there on time.

This had been a grueling day, most of it on foot. Caldwell was supposed to be the legman, but he'd bet money Caldwell had managed to get a cab to the front door of the church. He plunged on.

Sure enough, out of breath and ten minutes late, he arrived at the church to find Caldwell comfortably stretched out on the steps, watching his approach; apparently he had seen him climb from the bottom.

"That was good exercise," Caldwell said. "I should have done that instead of taking a cab."

Lord was about to fall down, but Caldwell jumped up. "I've never been to Montmartre; let's walk," and he bounded down the church steps and headed for the square.

Lord thought his legs were going to give out, but he was too embarrassed to admit it to the younger man and stumbled after.

At the Place du Tertre, a small square in the center of Montmartre where artists had drawn bad pictures for decades, and tourists gawked and sipped cheap wine at canopied cafés, a large German woman knocked Lord against a caricaturist, who angrily slashed his coat with chalk.

Lord pulled away and turned on Caldwell, dripping sarcasm. "Why don't we sit at one of these quaint little cafés and have a drink. I can't bear to look at any more of these paintings, but those over there on the black velvet might appeal to you—those dogs playing cards and pissing into the Seine. Aren't they cute?"

Seeing that Lord was in a foul mood, Mike followed meekly. It was too cold to sit outside, so they went in, and as they waited for their wine, Lord extended his legs, letting out a sigh of relief. "Any news?" he asked casually.

Caldwell shook his head. "That Marine keeps bugging me; he wants to know about the Chinese man. He's hoping I'll tell him what we know."

"We *may* tell him. Huong could end up a complication—what better way to have him eliminated than by Bishop. But not yet."

The waiter came with wine, and after a sip, Lord felt the liquid soothe throughout his legs. "Huong told me that Marshall has met with the Iranians twice."

"How's he getting out? I know his security people; they're not leaving the building without my knowledge."

"He's not *going* with his security people—the Iranians don't want anything to happen to him. He's their biggest asset. He's single-handedly sabotaging the Shah—he couldn't do a better job unless he stuck a claymore up Pahlavi's ass."

The waiter refilled their glasses. "What would you like to eat?" Lord asked.

Mike shook his head. "I'm having dinner later."

"Ah," Lord said, now noticing Caldwell's spruced-up attire, that he was freshly shaved and smelled of expensive cologne. "Then I won't detain you. Marshall's children are arriving tomorrow. The Chinese man wants revenge; this is not our concern. For certain favors, Huong is getting me information about Marshall's meeting with Khomeini. It will take place sooner rather than later, I think. We will have very short notice, so I want you to be ready. What is your preference?"

"Sir?"

"The distance could be anywhere from fifty yards to five hundred."

"Oh."

"Tell me what you want. I personally like the Israeli."

Caldwell nodded. "Yes, that's good, but the Hungarian model has better accuracy and a sharper scope."

"Done," Lord said, popping a crust of bread into his mouth. "All I want is for you to stand by."

"It's really happening?" Caldwell asked, not in alarm or concern, merely curiosity.

"Our government does some bizarre things, Mike. Look at Vietnam—the North didn't defeat us, they merely outlasted us—we gave up. Our foreign policy is disaster after disaster; our only salvation is that our enemies are more stupid than we are. God help us when we come upon a truly clever, diabolical foe. I shudder to think that somewhere in Asia a little Genghis Khan is growing up, or somewhere in the third world a little Alexander or Caesar or Napoleon is playing with G.I. Joes and Lego atomic bombs."

Lord sipped the last of his wine. "Do you have any reservations about this?"

Caldwell shook his head. "None."

Lord steeled himself to stand; it would take all his willpower to walk out without limping. "You have my number; call if anything develops. I want you available every minute from now on. Stay near a phone. I know there's one by your bedside—answer it, I don't care what you're doing."

Caldwell grinned. "Yes, sir."

"We'll meet at the Rodin Museum next time," Lord said, inwardly bracing for his first step.

"How about the Lido? Or Pigalle? Someplace with women."

"The Rodin, at Hôtel Biron, just across from the Concorde." He reached for his wallet, but Caldwell shook his head and pointed toward Sacré-Coeur. "You can get a taxi there, unless you want to run back down the steps."

"Have a nice evening," Lord said, walking out of the café with a firm stride.

Ron Mead bounded up the stairs of his apartment building and burst in the door.

"Sung! Everything's gonna be all right."

She met him with the same stony expression that had been on her face since their trip to the zoo. "There was nothing *wrong* that needed to be set right."

He grabbed her happily and lifted her from the floor. "You don't have to leave me. I talked with Major Bishop and he set me straight. He said you were staying with me because I was stupid and needed help."

"He's a smarter man than he looks," she said placidly.

He put her down. "Sung, that's not nice. And that's not why you won't leave me. Is it?"

"What *do* you do at work every day?"

He laughed. "Hey, it's hard work coming up with stuff to worry about. But I'll find something else now. I'm sorry I made you mad. You forgive me?"

Her face was inscrutable. "I made you some cookies."

"Yeah?" he asked eagerly. "What kind?"

"What kind do I always make?"

He grinned. "My favorite. Chocolate chip." Then he picked her up again and carried her into the bedroom.

"Dinner will burn."

He nuzzled her neck. "I didn't want any fish heads anyway."

She slapped at him as he tossed her on the bed, but she meant to miss, and she did.

CHAPTER 15

Once again Catherine was waiting for him at the breakfast table; he marveled at her ability to bushwhack him every morning.

He never heard her slip out of bed anymore. When they were young, he was attuned to her every move; she couldn't roll over or shift on the mattress that he wasn't aware of her body, but now she could come and go at will while he slept soundly—it was another sorrowful commentary on aging, he felt.

When Marshall entered the dining room, he threw up his hands in alarm that was not really mock, then he took scrambled eggs and bacon from chafing dishes and poured himself coffee.

"They're arriving on Pan Am at eleven forty-five," Catherine said tersely as he sat across from her. "Are you going to be there?"

"Of course."

Catherine put down her fork. "I mean it, Brad. Will you be there? I'm not telling them you're coming if you're not."

"I'll be there."

"Helen has the information—all you have to do is get in the car."

"I'll be there!"

She watched him evenly. "It isn't necessary—we know

how busy you are; just don't tell us you're going to show, then not make it."

He glanced at his watch. "Catherine, do you know that all wars are started in early morning by bitchy wives? Have you checked your estrogen level lately?"

"Eleven forty-five," she said, sipping coffee.

"Keep them here. I don't want them out no matter what. If they're going to stay in *my* house, they'll follow *my* rules."

"Oh, I'm sure that will work—just tell them that."

"Catherine, they are not safe."

"I *know* that, Brad. I didn't want them to come; I told you that. Now you have only four hours to get that Chinese man."

"I'm taking care of it."

"You'd better. And you can start by being at the airport when they arrive. Eleven forty-five."

At the embassy, Helen greeted him in one of her favorite office outfits, a gold-lamé cocktail dress offset with enamel earrings the size of Christmas ornaments.

"I've cut your schedule to a single meeting with the automotive representatives," she said. "They've given up on having lunch with you; they'll settle for a meeting. I'll interrupt you at eleven so you can get to the airport in time."

She gestured to her own office. "Luke is camped out ready to go with you to the airport. I was almost blinded this morning by his spit-shined shoes and brass. I didn't have the heart to tell him Sarah finds all that ridiculous."

How could she comment on *Bishop's* attire, he wondered, but he merely shook his head. "I know. But I don't understand what he sees in *her.*"

"What do you mean?" Helen asked indignantly. "Sarah is remarkable. She's what women should have been in my day. If there had been more Sarahs, *I'd* be ambassador, and you'd be answering the phone. And Luke would be . . . out of work. Sarah's my mentor in the women's movement. I wouldn't know what to think without her. Why, I might still be married to Jurgen. I was confusing orgasms with . . ."

He closed his eyes. "Dear God, stop."

"I can hardly wait to see her. And Chris—I adore him. He's so sweet. And so gorgeous. Who cares that he's gay?"

"Helen, did you and Catherine rehearse today?"

"You have wonderful children. Be nice to them, especially Chris. After Ryan's death, Chris had to assume another role, heir to the great man. I think he's done very well, Mr. Great Man."

Marshall smiled. "How come you screwed up four marriages if you know men so well?"

"I'm a romantic. Romantics keep believing in men. Sarah tells me it's very stupid. I'll bet *she* doesn't end up with five husbands."

"I'll bet she doesn't end up with *any.*"

"Well, *none* would be better than Luke Bishop," she said, then turned. "I like Luke; he's adorable, and twenty years ago I would have fallen for him myself. But the world has changed; he just hasn't gotten the message."

"I'm not sure I have either." Then thinking of Khomeini, Carter, Lord, and the Chinese man, Marshall added, "Nor am I convinced the world *has* changed."

"Does he know I'm here?" Luke asked Helen when she returned to his desk.

"Yes, but he doesn't need to see you—as lovely looking as you are; I don't think I've ever seen shoes so shiny. Why don't you go find something to do until eleven; he has a couple meetings, but I promise he won't leave without you."

Bishop looked at his watch; it wasn't even nine. He didn't know what to do to make the time pass; he had finished the book and knew, just knew that this time Sarah would see him differently.

"I brought you a present," he said, pulling a small box from the pocket of his dress blues.

She looked at it suspiciously. "*Why* did you buy me a present? Are you trying to bribe me? There is *nothing* you could give me that would convince me to put in a good word for you to Sarah."

Bishop shrugged. "It's just a present; I thought it would go with one of your costumes."

"If these are nipple clips, Major Bishop, I am going to bring a sexual harassment charge against you."

She opened the box. Inside were small brass earrings with

the globe-and-anchor emblem of the Marine Corps, and a small flag lapel pin that Andy Maynard had always worn.

She smiled, then brushed at her eyes. "Thank you. And I have just the outfit to go with them."

She put the box in her purse.

"I was thinking of getting Sarah a pair too. What do you think? Or should I go with the nipple clips I bought her?"

Helen laughed; how could any man over thirty be so stupidly, hopelessly in love? Actually it charmed her, and she said, "Tell me how you and Sarah met." She knew the story as well as he did, but it pleased him so to tell it, and she knew she didn't have anything more important to do this morning than make him happy.

"She was such a bitch," Bishop started, a huge grin on his face.

The trade meeting was mindlessly diverting; Marshall put his brain on autopilot, monitored the conversation, made amusing comments, and did not even have to work at it.

Just before eleven, Helen entered the conference room and whispered, "You should leave now, but a man from the CIA says he needs to see you about Sarah and Chris. His name is Wilson Lord."

It took all Marshall's control to smother his surprise and maintain a bland face. He stood and said evenly, "Gentlemen, please excuse me; something has come up."

He could not believe Lord had the audacity to show up here—in *his* embassy. "Send him in," Marshall said tightly to Helen as he entered through his private door, and he had not even reached his desk when Wilson Lord came in.

They had not seen each other in six years and stood a moment assessing time's ravages, but both were disappointed, and mildly exhilarated—the enemy had not changed much: they each confronted an only slightly older Satan.

Lord took in the luxurious office in a long appraising glance, then said offhandedly, "I'll bet the inner sanctum of hell looks like this."

"No doubt you're going to find out someday."

Lord sat without being asked. He knew he had thrown Marshall off guard with his appearance; he had debated it carefully, but decided to give his enemy one last opportunity to save himself. Perhaps he was getting sentimental in his old age, he thought, nostalgic for the good old days of confrontation, but then, this was a calculated risk that could pay off richly—he held all the high cards. "Shall we get down to it?"

"We? You and I? I was hoping never to see you again. I was hoping you'd sink into that cesspool at Langley, but I keep forgetting how shit floats."

Lord made a tsking sound. "There's no need to get personal. I didn't plan to bring up unpleasant things, like that poor ex-nun you were banging years ago in Saigon, or how you got her and those children out of Vietnam—well, *almost* out of Vietnam: to the end of the runway. Mechanical failure, wasn't it? Just another glitch in the fiasco—no one even to blame, except you for having interfered. That debacle summed up your Vietnam service, didn't it, Excellency? All your good efforts, all that concern, that liberal do-goodery—where did it get those poor orphans and that ex-nun? Incinerated in their seats when their plane crashed."

Marshall's face froze in fury.

"You meant well, of course. You *always* do, but it was a disaster, wasn't it, Brad? They would have been *so* much better if you had never entered their lives."

Lord shook his head. "And what about your other good deed in Vietnam? When you tried to save the defector? Not only did you get him killed, but your driver ran over a little girl. Alas, she had someone to avenge her, unlike the orphans. He murdered your driver. Now he's here for your children. You thought you had it all covered up nicely. Too bad, but it's fitting, isn't it?—all those deaths directly related to you, and now they're on your doorstep."

"*You* caused those deaths—the defector and my driver—because *you* tried to kill Luke Bishop."

Lord crossed his legs comfortably. "Huong doesn't see it that way. He holds you responsible for his daughter's death. You will never convince him otherwise."

Lord smiled wickedly. "You are in trouble, Excellency. Your ship is going down, sinking rapidly. Children first. Got that one, Brad?—Sarah and Chris into the icy waters. You might be a first-class passenger in this world, but in death, the accommodations are all the same, and Huong has booked passage on the Death Boat for your children."

Lord nodded. "You better let me help you. You killed Huong's child. You didn't mean it, but the child is dead, battered into pulp by your limousine."

Lord leaned forward, suddenly vicious. "And thousands more who were abandoned when America sold out Vietnam, loyal allies and friends, including my wife's family, my son's grandparents and relatives. What happened to them is *your* fault."

Then Lord made a diving motion with his hand and sucked in his breath. "Sinking, Excellency—your ship is going down. And Christ do you deserve it. But I'm here to help you. Huong is going to kill your children and you can't stop him. But *I* can. Remember the defector in Saigon? I was blackmailed into giving him up to save my wife and son. Now it's your turn. Except I'm not threatening your children. I want to help—I'm the only one who can. But there's a price—your assistance. I want to meet with the Ayatollah Khomeini."

Marshall laughed. "I'll *bet* you would. And I can predict the result of that meeting—we'd be scraping pieces of him off the moon."

"He is an evil, dangerous man."

"So are you," Marshall said contemptuously.

"I know you're arranging to meet him through those 'moderates' you think you can deal with after the Shah falls." Lord shook his head in disgust. "They're using you—they already have. They know we won't save the Shah. They found out that 'human rights activists' like Jimmy Cracker will abandon him. You've fallen for it again, like you did with the North Vietnamese, like you always will because you are weak. Weakness is not a principle, it is the absence of principles."

"Listening to you discuss principles is like listening to Jack the Ripper discuss women's rights. Spare me," Marshall said scornfully.

Lord made the diving motion with his hand again. "Pay attention, Excellency—your children's lives are in the balance. You are going to meet with Khomeini. In exchange for saving your children, you are going to let me take your place at that meeting."

"I think they'll be able to tell the difference between Bo Peep and the wolf," Marshall said disdainfully.

"You've confused the characters in this play, Miss Peep. The Iranians are the wolves—*they* are the bad guys. Khomeini has to be stopped."

Marshall looked at him with incredulity. "You expect me to help you assassinate him? You must be out of your mind."

Lord smoothed his trousers. "Let's start again: someone wants to kill your children. He will succeed because you are no match for him. You need help—I will help."

"You tried to kill me and Luke Bishop. Now you want to kill the Ayatollah. Are *you* listening? You're insane."

Lord sat forward. "If Khomeini comes to power, millions will die in a holy war. He has to be stopped. This is an opportunity like before Hitler's rise."

"You're being theatrical—paranoid, the zealot's disease."

"Like I was paranoid about the choppers lifting off from the embassy's roof in Saigon? I was *right* then, and I'm right now. Khomeini will be a disaster for America, and Huong wants to kill your children. You better start paying attention to me."

"Never! We have nothing to discuss."

Lord took a deep breath. "I am going to try one last time to get through to you. Your children are going to die, just like your other son did. This is not a game, Brad. Ryan is dead because of Vietnam. Now Sarah's and Chris's lives are on the line. Huong is going to kill them for revenge. In a cosmological sense, it's fair that they die. If Homer or Shakespeare were writing your tatty story, they *would* die. You can't protect them. Sarah and Chris don't stand a chance against the Chinese man. Who do you think will help you, that idiot Marine major?"

Marshall stared at him coldly. "Get out."

"You can't be this stupid. That man is going to murder your children; I'm the only one who can help you."

"Get out!"

Lord shook his head in contempt. "Jesus, you are a fool," he said, slamming the door as he left.

Helen glanced up. She looked like a lounge hostess, Lord thought, but he smiled at her pleasantly, then saw Bishop sitting across the room at the same time Bishop saw him.

Luke jumped up so quickly and with such hostility that Helen cried out in alarm, but Lord went directly to him.

"Why, Major Bishop, how good to see you."

Bishop grabbed his jacket. "I ought to kill you, motherfucker."

Lord didn't step back, merely gazed at his uniform. "Just look at all those decorations. Navy Cross, Silver Star, Bronze Star, *four* Purple Hearts—ah, but one of those is mine, not really hostile fire: you were just in the way." Lord jabbed a finger into Bishop's chest. "As you are again."

Bishop didn't move. "You're dead meat, cocksucker."

Lord turned to Helen. "He's the ambassador's military aide? Such a violent, foul-mouthed young man. No wonder he's not scoring with the ambassador's daughter."

Bishop brought back his fist, but Lord only laughed. "Actually you look quite fine, Major. Even your head—why it looks perfectly normal, when we *know* it isn't."

Then he broke away from Bishop and was gone.

Luke stared after him in fury, then turned to Helen, but she had run into Marshall's office to tell him about this new confrontation.

"My God," she said. "I thought he was going to attack that old man."

Marshall peered over his glasses. "That 'old man' is exactly my age."

"That's the second agent he's almost attacked; what does he have against the CIA?"

"I thought you were a bright woman, Helen." Marshall looked at his watch. "I've missed the flight, haven't I?"

"Yes. Poor Luke; all he's been looking forward to is seeing Sarah. I thought he was going to come in here and drag you out."

Marshall sat back. "Send him in."

Bishop entered so flushed with anger that he didn't center himself or even salute. "I knew he was here. I'm going to kill him. I've been *waiting* to get him."

Marshall pointed to a chair. "Luke; he isn't worth it.

Don't jeopardize your career; you'll be a general someday, unless you give in to that temper of yours."

Chastised, Bishop dropped into the seat. "We missed Sarah," he said mournfully.

He looked so lovelorn and miserable, a strapping man so incongruously abject, that Marshall laughed. "We missed her *airplane,* Luke. She'll be at Andy's memorial service this afternoon. You can see her then."

Bishop brightened. "She will?"

"Yes. But have you found out anything on the Chinese man? His name is Huong—that's the name Lord mentioned."

"I'm working on it."

"There's no time left, Luke."

"Trust me."

Marshall didn't, but he merely waved him off. "We'll see you at four."

When Bishop was gone, Marshall sat back at his desk. Lord was right—he could not count on himself or Bishop to stop the Chinese man. Lord could, but Marshall could never trust him. Mike Caldwell was the last person who could help, but he worked for Lord.

Marshall buzzed Helen. "Get me that agent who was here the day before yesterday."

In a moment Caldwell was on the line.

"I want to talk to you tonight. Are you free for dinner?"

There was a pause, then a cold voice. "Whatever you say, sir."

"Eight at Le Duc. Do you need the address?"

"I'll find it," Caldwell said, hanging up.

Marshall returned to the residence eager to see his children; he was bounding up the staircase when Chris came onto the second-floor landing.

He had filled out even more since Marshall saw him last year; he seemed blonder than he remembered, ruddy and more muscular. He was always surprised at Chris's appearance; his mind pictured a boy, vulnerable and dependent, but the reality was a startling contrast, and it always took him a moment to realize the powerful male before him was his son. They did a mock fight routine, then Marshall threw a bear hug on him.

"Chris! You look terrific. I'm sorry I wasn't at the airport."

Chris smiled with even teeth and strong jaw. "Just as well, the shock wouldn't have done you any good."

"What shock?"

A severe-looking young woman dressed in black, with a flattop and no makeup, came onto the landing.

"Jesus!" Marshall said, releasing Chris to take in his daughter. Though he was stunned by her appearance as always—she never failed to startle him any less than Chris did—his face blanked and his words were carefully articulated in a self-mocking diplomatic air. "Don't you look interesting."

"Like my outfit?"

"No."

"Like my hair?"

"No."

Catherine came from Sarah's bedroom and said with no warmth, obviously still angry, "Missed you at the airport at eleven forty-five, Brad." Then she glanced at her watch. "It's cocktail hour—time for my afternoon Purple Jesus. Shall we drink here on the stairs or go into the salon?"

"Let's go down," Marshall said. "I need a drink too, and I want to hear everything." He raised a cautionary hand. "Well, maybe not everything."

He put his arm around Chris's shoulder and brought Sarah to him. "It's great to see you; I'm very glad you're here, but what did you do to your head, Sarah?"

She laughed. "It's the new look; unisexual, a statement."

"Never mind," he said, leading them downstairs. "I can listen to you *or* your mother harangue me. Your mother already had at me today—yesterday and the day before too; you can have tomorrow."

"When's my turn?" Chris asked.

"You've had the last ten years; it's time you were on *my* side."

In the drawing room, he mixed them drinks and raised his own. "To Andy. I hate it when people speak of the dead as if they still had feelings, but he *would* be happy that you came. He loved you both very much."

"He was always there for me," Chris said.

Sarah studied her glass a moment, then looked at her father. "He bought me an angora sweater when I was twelve, during my really ugly period when I had zits and wore glasses and felt awful about myself. One day he showed up with this soft blue sweater, out of nowhere—it wasn't my birthday or anything. It was the most wonderful thing. It made me feel beautiful."

Marshall nodded toward her hair. "Maybe I'll go buy you one tomorrow. You can wear it on your head if nothing else."

"*He* never made fun of me."

"He never saw you with a flattop. My God, your hair is shorter than Luke's."

"I wondered how long it'd take before you mentioned him." She held up her hand. "I know, I know, he's a lovely person, dedicated, a bulwark of democracy and the American way, but I am *not* here to see him. I am in a loving relationship with Jim Tolson; it may be permanent. I don't want to hear one word about Luke Bishop."

"I never planned to mention his name, and I won't again," Marshall said. "But we do have to talk about a few things. First is the memorial service this afternoon. That's at the chapel in the embassy; it'll last about an hour."

He dropped his head. "Luke will be there, Sarah. I expect you to be civil to him."

"I thought you weren't going to mention him."

"Fathers always lie; they learn it from their children. Then there's the big problem, a Chinese man who wants to kill you."

"Do what?" said Chris.

Marshall poured another drink, then he told them about Huong and what happened in Saigon, and the threat to them.

"You're going to have to be careful. I'm not in danger—*you* are. You're going to have a bodyguard wherever you go. A Sûreté agent has already been killed. I'm meeting with someone tonight I hope will help. All I ask is that you don't do anything dangerous—don't try to get away from your security. Promise?"

"Is this for real?" Chris asked, turning to his mother.

She nodded. "The man's killed two people, a Marine and a Sûreté agent." She looked at her husband severely. "He's a murderer and he wants to kill you both. Your father and I have had long discussions about this. I am *not* satisfied that this is under control or that you are safe."

"You're safe *here,*" Marshall reassured them. "As long as you stay in the house or go nowhere without security, nothing can happen."

"Why did you let us come if someone wants to kill us?" Sarah asked.

"Because you're safer here," Marshall said. "We can't protect you in the States; he could get you there anytime he wanted."

"Then why hasn't he?"

Marshall ran his hand over the armrest and lowered his head. "He watched his own child die. He wants to see me suffer the same thing. He wants to watch. He wants that more than he wants to kill you."

Sarah shook her head. "I don't want to sound self-centered or anything, but just what are you doing to protect us?"

"Yes, Brad," Catherine said. "What *are* you doing?"

"Luke is—"

"Luke!" Catherine cried. "That's who's supposed to save them?"

"And I'm meeting with someone tonight who could take care of this," Marshall said quickly.

Chris, seeing the unusual anger between his parents, said with amelioration, "We'll be all right; neither Sarah nor I has a death wish. We got the message—don't worry about us, we won't leave the house."

Marshall nodded. "Good; now let's drop this. Tell me about your lives. Editing as you see fit, of course."

There was a long pause as Sarah and Chris absorbed the news, then Sarah said, "Let me see. Ah, I have a new puppy."

"Wonderful," Marshall enthused. "What's its name?"

They all laughed.

"Who's Jim Tolson?" Catherine asked.

"He's an associate professor at Berkeley."

"So far so good," Marshall said.

"He's in biochemistry. I'm at the Women's Center doing crisis work—rapes, drugs, abortion counseling, and twice a week I go down to Wino Park in Oakland and—"

"Wino Park?" Chris asked.

"It's where the homeless and addicts go. We have this mobile clinic and drive into the park, and—"

"You'll get murdered!" Marshall said. "What is wrong with you? Why are you doing this?"

"Teresa Hawthorne opened my eyes, Dad. I *love* going there; I feel worthwhile. The crisis center is important, but this means more; the people need me more."

Seeing her father's shock, she smiled. "Anyway, Jim and I just bought a house. And we have a puppy. Chris, your turn—keep it clean."

"I'm doing fine. I found a great guy, Trent, and I finally decided what I want to do—I'm going to med school. I have to go to NYU for zoology and physics, but I've already talked to the dean at Columbia, and he said I can enter next fall."

"That's great, Chris!" Sarah said.

"Yeah. I decided I wanted to help too—maybe not the winos, but others. We were lucky, so I guess we owe a debt."

"What?" Marshall said. "You mean you listened to me, after all? My life hasn't been lived in vain?"

Catherine held her heart. "My son, the doctor."

Marshall looked at them happily. "You mean everything is working out with my children? My daughter, except that her head looks like it got caught in a sawmill, has settled down with a man and a dog in a house, and my son, who has also settled down with a man, is going to medical school—you mean, everything is all right?"

"Well, except that we're going to be murdered tomorrow afternoon, yeah, everything is fine," Chris said.

Marshall waved that away. "Catherine, we've been wonderful parents after all."

Catherine looked at him harshly. "So far, Brad. But you'd better take care of that Chinese man, or it could all be for nothing."

* * *

The service for Andy Maynard was simple and brief. Irene sat in front with her three children beside Marshall and his family. Helen sat in the next pew beside Bishop; she had changed into a simple black dress and wore the earrings he had given her, and the small flag lapel pin.

The CIA station chief and several others spoke, and at the end, Marshall rose. To his surprise, he noticed Wilson Lord and Mike Caldwell at the back of the chapel.

"Irene," he said to Andy's widow, "I knew your husband longer than you did. Andy and I met twenty-eight years ago at Quantico in OCS. I loved him because he was the only person who made me look good on the parade ground. He couldn't march or call cadence worth a damn. And he loved me because I never passed a single inspection and even made him look good."

Marshall shook his head at the memory. "Then we went to Korea, a war few remember, one with no monuments or memorials. I hoped to grow old with Andy. Well, we *did* grow old, but I mean much older. His passing is *my* loss. It is a loss to us *all* because there are few men like Andy—men who understand the fragile balance of our lives in society—who know they can't *tell* their children what to do, but only lead by example, men who are *not* always sure what is right and would never presume to put themselves above their country."

Marshall smiled. "Andy was a spy, a truly noble profession, though there are no monuments to them either, and their names are forgotten. Only poor Nathan Hale is remembered, and he only because he managed a good line at his hanging. But for those who succeed—anonymity, a few accolades, a brief service like this."

Marshall looked directly at Mike Caldwell. "Andy Maynard was a guardian at the gate, a wonderful centurion—noble and brave, kind and decent and honest, merciful and understanding. God grant him rest, and God grant us others like him."

Marshall went to Irene, kissed her cheek, then escorted her from the chapel to a room where there was a reception.

Sitting just behind the families, Luke Bishop did not see

Caldwell and Lord and watched awkwardly as Sarah and Chris left with Maynard's children and Helen.

But Catherine stopped beside him and asked him to escort her to the reception. If Luke was going to save her children—which she had no confidence in—she at least wanted him nearby at all times. "Brad can't be at dinner tonight; can you come?" she asked.

"Yes, ma'am," he answered quickly.

She looked at his uniform. "It's casual; you don't have to dress, Luke."

Holding her arm, he leaned close. "What happened to Sarah's head? Did she have an operation?"

Catherine whispered back, "She joined the Marines. Go get me a drink, Luke—a stiff one."

At the bar Chris came up to him and shook hands. "Luke, you look great."

"So do you. How're tricks?"

It was an old joke between them. Luke and Chris were friends, for Luke was long past caring what people in any combination did with one another in bed. "What's the scoop on Sarah's head? Did she have a lobotomy?"

Chris grinned. "I'm afraid not. If she did, you might have a chance with her, but she's hooked up with some professor at Berkeley. Hey, but I'm available."

Luke laughed. "*I* didn't have a lobotomy either, Chris."

"What's this shit about someone trying to kill us? Is this for real, or just Dad trying to keep us in line?"

"It's for real."

"You mean there really is a guy who wants to kill us?"

"I think so."

"And he's already killed two people?"

Bishop nodded. "But don't worry, I've killed a *lot* more."

Then Sarah approached. "Hi, Luke," she said, pressing her cheek to his. "Nobody likes my hair. Do you?"

Bishop grinned. "*Love* it. Will you go out with me?"

She laughed. "Sure. Since I'm going to be murdered, you'll protect me, won't you?"

"With my life," he pledged.

"What about me?" Chris asked. "Who's going to protect me?"

"Mike Caldwell, the CIA agent over there," Bishop said, pointing across the room. "You'll like him. He's gay."

"Really?" Chris asked, gazing intently.

"Yeah," Bishop said. "He's been coming on to me ever since he arrived."

Caldwell sensed eyes on him and turned at the moment they were all looking at him. He nodded, then moved toward them.

"I told Chris you were going to protect him," Bishop said to Caldwell.

"Sure," Mike said with a smile.

Chris gave him a firm handshake. "Luke says you're gay. That's great; so am I. I think it's important people are honest about their sexuality."

As Caldwell crimsoned, Sarah asked, "Did you know Uncle Andy?"

"Not well," Caldwell stammered. "I understand he was a close family friend."

"Yes," Sarah said, and repeated the story of the angora sweater, then added, "I never told my dad this, but a few years ago, I had a real problem when a woman I admired was killed. It was terrible—she was a wonderful person who had done so much for others. I fell apart because it didn't make any sense and was all wrong."

"When Teresa Hawthorne died," Luke said.

"Yes. I couldn't accept it, and I guess held my dad responsible. Uncle Andy made me see things differently. He told me not to grieve; he said she had done her job—that if I cared about her, I should take up where she had left off. He said the world doesn't work in little spurts, individuals adding something here and there, but in continuity."

Mike nodded. "That was wise."

"It might be his message for you too, Mr. Caldwell," she said. "You could take up where Uncle Andy left off."

"Yeah, you ought to give that serious thought, Mike," Bishop said meaningfully, maneuvering Sarah away.

"Will you really go out with me?" he asked when he got her aside.

She smiled. "Yes, Luke, if I can—Dad is *very* worried about our safety. But don't misconstrue it. I think you're a great guy; you're even fun, but you're like a brother, an addled one; it can never be more than that. I really wish you would find someone your type—I'm not."

"I'm having dinner with you all tonight. We'll go out tomorrow if security allows it. Where would you like to go?"

She looked at him with amusement. "You choose. I am fascinated to see where you'd take me."

"Hey, I'm a changed man. I just read this terrific book. I know why you didn't like me before. I was a jerk. But no more."

Sarah nursed her drink to keep from laughing. "You read a book, Luke?"

"Why does everybody think I'm ignorant? I went to fucking college."

She put her hand on his arm to calm him. "What was the book, Luke?"

"The Feminine Mystique."

"Really? That's a wonderful book—for a starter."

"You think that faculty fuckhead at Berkeley who uses big words and can quote twelve sources knows more than me? He doesn't. You know why? Because they only love what they know, and that's those books and quotes. And you're really stupid if you fall for that, and your hair looks like shit besides. If a guy was interested in that, he'd go out with me. What's wrong with your self-image that you have to deny your sexuality?"

Sarah stepped back in amazement. Then she gripped his arm fondly. "Promise me something, Luke."

"What?"

"Don't read any more books."

Chatting politely with Chris, Caldwell watched Bishop with Sarah. The poor bastard was so obviously in love. Didn't he know that never worked with a woman?

He checked his watch. It was six. Marshall was leaving; no one could possibly have picked up the passing eye contact Marshall made with him, confirming their meeting in a few hours, then Marshall signaled with a faint nod to each member of his family, and they, accustomed to so many years of diplomatic receptions and public life, immediately and smoothly made their way out of the room.

Caldwell watched them leave. He liked what Marshall had said about Maynard, and he liked Sarah and Chris. Before they had been abstractions. Now they were real, and Bishop too. Yet they were all in profound danger. They were prey, and he one of the predators. Before this he had never known any of the people he had killed; it was much easier that way, he decided.

But Lord was right—their world wasn't easy; it was hard and without reward. It hurt and no one could understand them. They were the barbarians at the gate, holding off other barbarians, and their world allowed no sentiment—that would only get them killed, and the gate overrun.

CHAPTER 16

"I'm sorry I can't stay for dinner," Marshall announced to no one in particular in the living room at seven P.M.; Chris was talking with Catherine, and Luke was entranced with Sarah.

"What?" Sarah asked, looking up, then said, "Luke wants to take me out tomorrow night. Is that all right, Dad?"

"Possibly—if you'll agree to be back by ten P.M."

"Oh, it'll probably be a *lot* earlier. Where would we go, Luke?"

"There's a new rifle range that just opened up near the Defense; I thought we'd go there—they have a terrific grenade-toss game. But maybe we could go to a boar-killing contest in Meudon. You get a javelin and whoever kills the biggest boar wins. They know me there—I'm a regular."

"Sarah has all the fun," Chris whined mockingly. "How come you like her better? God knows, I'm better looking and have more hair on my head besides."

"You *already* have a boyfriend," Luke said.

"So does she."

"Yeah, but yours was a pro draft-choice; he might get jealous and beat the shit out of me. Sarah's won't—he's a faculty fatty."

Marshall stood. "I changed my mind, I'm not a bit sorry I'm missing dinner here. Catherine, can't you elevate the conversation?"

"Oh, no," she said. "It's going to get much worse as soon as you leave—then we're going to talk about you."

"Who are you having dinner with?" Chris asked, noting his casual attire.

"A friend of Luke's."

"Where are you eating?" Sarah asked. "Burger World?"

Bishop gave a thumbs-up. "Great fries." Then he turned to Marshall. "You don't mean Mike Caldwell? He's hardly a friend."

"I'm taking your advice," Marshall said. "I'm trying to see if he can't be reached."

"That young man at Andy's service?" Catherine asked. "Forget it; he's got at least two extra Y chromosomes. He makes Luke look like Liberace."

"Are you making fun of me, Mrs. Marshall?" Luke questioned, hurt to think she would pick on him too.

"Absolutely not; it was a compliment. That CIA man reminded me of a cyborg. I'd never let *him* go out with my daughter."

"Sarah's gone out with lots of cyborgs," Chris said.

"You're just jealous," she retorted.

Marshall headed for the door. "I'm out of here."

He called for his car and gave the driver the address.

"Should I call for security?" the man asked. "Your bodyguard isn't here—you told him you wouldn't be going out tonight; Sergeant Mead went home."

"I'm just going to dinner. I'm meeting a more than competent bodyguard there."

Caldwell entered the restaurant shortly before eight. Le Duc was a fashionable intimate restaurant in the St.-Germain district; the interior was art deco, with black lacquered tables and chairs, exotic flowers, and recessed lights and candles reflected in mirrors that wrapped the walls.

When Caldwell gave his name, the maître d' led him to the lounge, explaining that the ambassador had not yet arrived. The bartender handed him a complimentary kir.

Before leaving the office, Caldwell had checked himself in the mirror, tried to look casual, even ruffled his hair, but he saw his unease, for he had never met anyone of Marshall's position head-to-head, and he did not know what the ambassador wanted.

He was downing his second kir when the maître d' led Marshall into the bar.

Caldwell watched him stride across the room, dominating it just by his confidence and poise. He walked directly to Mike and held out his hand. "Thank you for coming."

Caldwell shook hands stiffly. "Your invitations aren't regarded as optional attendance, sir."

Marshall coaxed Caldwell into his seat and sat beside him. "What can I get you?"

"I suppose I should have water," Mike said guardedly.

Marshall smiled and patted his arm. "That's not optional either." His touch was neither heavy nor cloying, but struck exactly between friendliness and formality.

Caldwell pushed the kir away. "Scotch."

Marshall ordered two Scotches and pointed to the kir. "Awful, aren't they—sort of a French wine-cooler."

Never good at small talk, and archly suspicious of Marshall, Caldwell took a large drink when his glass was set before him. "I liked what you said this afternoon. I didn't know Andy Maynard, but you made him sound noble—you made us all sound noble, though I doubt that's how you feel about my profession."

Marshall smiled. "Andy and I burrowed through a few whorehouses in Korea. I have a high regard for *that* profession too—perhaps the only one older than yours."

"Where do diplomats and politicians fit in as a profession?"

"Oh, we're the real whores—and there's no gold in *our* hearts."

"Just a lot of corpses around," Caldwell said, draining his glass.

Marshall watched him closely. "No corpses around you, Michael?"

Caldwell shook his head. "Mr. Ambassador, we're not even in the same league—you're in the pros, and *you* don't have to pull the trigger."

The maître d' informed Marshall that his table was ready, and they followed him to an isolated corner in back where the waiter and sommelier were waiting.

"Whose account shall we put this on?" Marshall asked as he sat. "I invited you, but it might look good on your account—they'll think you've pumped me for information."

"Then let's put it on mine. I can use all the help I can get."

"By all means—I'd love to stick this one on Wilson Lord." Marshall turned to the wine steward. "We'll start with Le Montrachet, 1975. Is that all right with you, Mike?"

Caldwell shrugged. "If the light's good, I can tell red wine from white. I take it Le Montrachet is expensive."

Marshall's eyes lit. "I can't think of a more expensive one. Lord will be apoplectic." He settled comfortably and broke off a piece of roll.

The sommelier came with the wine and poured a little into Marshall's glass; he tasted, then raised his glass. "To your profession, and Andy Maynard."

Caldwell nodded guardedly and drank.

Marshall opened his menu. He chose foie gras, sole, and lamb. Caldwell, after asking the waiter several questions, chose foie gras, turbot, and duck.

"Your French is excellent," Marshall said. "You're a fine linguist."

"It'll be something to fall back on if I don't have a future with the Agency."

Marshall swirled wine in his glass then sipped, drawing it over his tongue without sound. "Oh, you have a *fine* future with the Agency—you're nouveau Wilson Lord."

The foie gras was placed before them. Marshall cut a piece and savored it on his tongue, then he changed the subject and, during the fish course, drew Caldwell out on different subjects and listened with interest, desperate to turn him, employing all his powers of seduction.

Caldwell understood this, and though he had relaxed, he was not off guard.

The sommelier poured the last of the bottle.

"Shall we stay with the burgundy or go to a Bordeaux?" Marshall asked.

Mike shrugged.

Marshall said to the sommelier, "We'll have a Lafite, a good year, but not to overwhelm the lamb," then to Caldwell, "Lord will be wild."

With the second bottle, as Marshall pressed more familiarly, Caldwell still did not mellow, and Marshall began to sense that he might fail. But that had never happened, so he intensified his campaign.

Marshall set down his glass and looked intently at Caldwell. "My oldest son died ten years ago; he was a Green Beret like you."

Caldwell nodded. "I know."

"My daughter is a strong woman and I love her very much."

Caldwell waited.

"And Chris is a strong, decent man, but now they face a terrible problem because of me. They're vulnerable because they don't know how evil men can be—Huong, Lord. You."

The meal was over and Caldwell understood they had arrived where Marshall had been leading. Marshall's hand smoothed the tablecloth and brushed crumbs to the floor. "Do you *like* killing, Mike?"

Caldwell saw in the slight movement of the hand, the effortless erasure, where the man had been, and what he had witnessed—not just wars, but government policies—Chile, Ethiopia, Lebanon, Africa, Latin America, Vietnam, swept away like the bread crumbs. He had seen cruel men, sat across from murderers, and Caldwell realized that Marshall recognized one in him.

There was no point in deception. They were in depths he had never been, with neither bottom nor shore in sight. It was like swimming naked in a cold, moonlit sea, exhilarating and frightening, so he did not bother with subterfuge.

"It's not the *killing*. That's anticlimactic. It's what leads up to it."

"Foreplay."

"Yes. I love *fucking*—but the act, not the release. Killing is like orgasm, but what feels so good, what *hurts* so good, is before." Caldwell spoke slowly, the first time he had talked about his work. "In the beginning I thought I was a maniac, but then I saw killing was common, all men can do it—I just happen to be good at it."

Caldwell's face was handsome, smooth and agreeable. The eyes, as part of the face, looked friendly and open, but by themselves were gelid. Even after all the alcohol, they remained separate and isolated.

Marshall sipped the last of his wine. "You are going to be asked to kill me. I don't want you to do that. But I can use your talents."

He signaled the waiter. When Caldwell reached for his wallet, Marshall shook his head. "Absolutely not. I'm not going to *guarantee* termination over two bottles of wine."

He left money on the table and stood. "Come, let's settle this outside."

Marshall held the restaurant door for Caldwell. They stepped into a rush of noise and noxious air. The traffic was heavy despite the hour, and pedestrians crowded the sidewalks—drunks and lovers and freaks heading into the Latin Quarter.

"I'm too old for that—fire-eaters and sword swallowers, mimes and midgets," Marshall said, buttoning his overcoat. "Let's cross to the Louvre; we'll do the scenic."

They had gone only a block when Caldwell felt they were being followed, but he couldn't be certain. If they were, the man was very good, but he'd know for sure when they got to the bridge.

"My children are in danger," Marshall said, breaking Caldwell's concentration.

"I know—your car ran over a child, and the father wants revenge."

"I never saw the child. Another faceless victim, I suppose."

He stopped on Pont Royal and stared upriver toward the Ile where Saint Louis erected Sainte-Chapelle to shelter the crown of thorns stolen from the Venetians in 1239.

Towering before him, its reflection glimmering across the Seine, was the Conciergerie, its torture chamber called "the babbler" where a little boy had once paced, the dauphin waiting for his mother, Marie Antoinette.

To his left were the apartments of Richelieu, who believed he could not afford to be good—the ultimate diplomat, whose intrigues made and enslaved a nation.

Behind him, at the Concorde, was the obelisk stolen from Egypt, rising not as high as a single mast of any ship sunk at Trafalgar. And beyond was the Arc de Triomphe where the Unknown Soldier lay in rot, above whom, on the walls, scratched like obscene graffiti, were the names of 558 generals.

Wherever Marshall looked, he saw monuments to folly and madness.

He gestured across the river to a huge dome. "The Invalides—a warehouse of sarcophagi—Napoleon, Foch, Duroc. Before us, an arch of triumph; around us, obelisks and statues—all in pursuit of power and glory, in this case monuments to a dumpy little man with a tiny penis. Go to Berlin and see the ruin *that* atrophied little penis wrought."

Marshall sighed. "History isn't even biography, it's just psychology and anatomy we fashion into meaning. My children's lives aren't caught up in anything grandiose—a man trying to kill them for an *accident* I caused."

He put his hand on Caldwell's arm. "But Wilson Lord is trying to turn this into a grand issue of Mideast politics and national interest. Don't let him confuse my mission with my children. I represent the President of the United States. He has asked me to talk with Khomeini. It is not for Wilson Lord or you to question that."

Caldwell removed Marshall's hand. *"Yes,* it is. It would be easy if I only did what I was ordered to do, if everything was black-and-white, if there were but two doors—the lady or the tiger—but there are lots of doors, endless passages and corridors leading to more doors, and mirrors and mirror images of more doors. Finally you just choose one."

Caldwell glanced casually about him, then started across the bridge toward the Louvre. At the end of the bridge, he turned quickly, but there was no one there. Yet he knew they were being followed. He was positive, a gut feeling that had saved his life a hundred times, but he saw no one. None of Marshall's security could be this good—Floyd's men could never fool him, so this had to be someone hired by the Chinese man, or the man himself. Yet where was he?

On the Pont Solférino, of course, and he had probably already crossed and was waiting for them. The man *was* good, Caldwell realized, a charge of excitement racing through him.

They walked into the Louvre's courtyard. "I want you to

save my children. Help me." Marshall placed his hand on Caldwell again. "I need you."

"A hired gun—you want me to kill the Chinese man."

"No. I only want to talk to him. I want to beg him to leave my children alone."

Caldwell laughed harshly. "You're rationalizing. If it came down to having to kill the Chinese man to save your children, you'd have me do it. Why don't you go to Lord with that proposition?"

"He's already come to me with it. He offered to save my children if I would let him kill Khomeini."

Caldwell supposed Marshall said this to shock him, but he merely shrugged. "That sounds like a reasonable bargain—your children for Khomeini."

"I can't do that."

"Right," Caldwell said contemptuously. "You can have *me* kill the Chinese man to save your children; you can let me dirty my hands—but soil *yours?* That would be messy and violate your principles. The Chinese man threatens you and your family, so you'd eliminate him. Khomeini endangers the entire Mideast, but because *your* reputation and principles are involved, he can't be touched. What a hypocrite. I think Lord has this right—help us, and we'll help you. You want us to kill? Then help us kill."

"Surely you can see the difference," Marshall pleaded. "I'm asking you for something personal—my children; Lord is asking you for an abstraction—country, ideas."

Caldwell shook his head again. "I'm a hired gun. There are lots of us—all those who serve the 'public welfare and safety.' We're the pit bulls guarding the perimeters—the cop risking his ass for a few bucks a year, the soldier out on the lines. We're expendable." He shrugged. "I can handle that—it's just that sometimes it's not easy being the guard dog when people like you, our owners, keep changing the rules and the enemies. You pat us and stroke us, say 'good dog' as you send us out to kill new threats to you. Now you're telling me the enemy isn't Khomeini but a Chinese man."

Caldwell said unpleasantly, "The Chinese man is *your* enemy, not mine. If you need help, get Luke Bishop."

"Killing is *your* specialty."

"It's Luke's too—he's probably killed more men than I have."

Marshall was stunned. "You won't help me?"

"Not unless you're willing to do something in return. I'm on *Lord's* side."

Marshall pleaded, "Then give Luke the information about the Chinese man. You know where he is. I *must* talk with him."

Caldwell turned away. "You wasted your time tonight. But I'll give you a little return on the cost of your dinner—the man who wants to kill your children is good, better even than I thought. I'd be very worried if I were you; I'd reconsider Lord's offer." He didn't tell Marshall about the man following them because despite his constant vigil, he hadn't been able to pick him up in the shadows or darkness. He *could* have hallucinated it, but he doubted it. Yet if the man was out there as he felt he was, that man was accomplished and dangerous. He scanned for him again, saw nothing, then he nodded curtly to Marshall and left.

Marshall watched Caldwell cross back over the river. He had never failed against Wilson Lord; he knew that this time he had.

When Caldwell got back to his hotel, he called Lord to tell him about the dinner, and about the man following them.

"You're sure about it?" Lord asked.

"I'm so *unsure* that I'm sure—does that make sense?"

"Absolutely; that's how we survive. But Huong has unlimited resources; he could hire the best."

"Then Marshall's children are going to die."

So the man of principle had no principles after all; as if he hadn't known that, Lord thought. What a sleaze Marshall was—his high road veered into shortcuts through gutters and back alleys like everybody else's. "Well, that changes things. I'll take care of this in the morning. I'll talk with him again. Have a good sleep, Mike. See you tomorrow."

Lord scrunched under the covers, wriggling his toes, drifting back to sleep with a smile on his face. Tomorrow he would give Marshall what he needed to save his children—Caldwell. All it would cost was Khomeini.

CHAPTER 17

For a long while Marshall sat on a bench in the back garden of the residence. The night was cold and moonless and his mood near despair. Caldwell was not going to help; Marshall was alone, and out of time. Finally he went inside. Upstairs, passing Sarah's room, he saw light streaming under the doorway.

She was in bed reading and looked up when he stuck his head in the door. "It's been a while since you came to tuck me in, Dad."

"I've been afraid of who I'd find. What are you reading?"

She held up the book. "*The Ball-Breakers Guide;* it's a new how-to book published by the Women's Center."

"You don't need it."

"I was underlining passages for Mother."

"She doesn't need it either." He went to the bed and sat on the edge.

"You don't look good, Dad; apparently the dinner wasn't a success."

He sighed. "It wasn't. You would have thought enough horror happened in Vietnam that it didn't need to follow us here."

"That's not how horror works. When you think you've seen the worst, it's only the surface."

"Dear God. What *are* you seeing in Oakland?"

She put down her book and brought her knees to her

chest. "What do I see in Oakland? Battered women and abused children, torture you would think possible only in some primitive society—disease, neglect, suffering no different from what was in Teresa's clinic in Saigon. Men are very cruel, Dad."

"Is that why you see Luke as a serial killer?"

"For a name you were never going to mention, Luke pops up a lot." She smiled. "Actually, I like him. He's rather cute in a prehistoric way."

"You could do worse. You *have* done worse."

She laughed. "Dad, I am not going to marry a Marine; or fuck one."

Marshall plugged his ears.

Sarah ran her hand over her hair. "The reason I can't get serious about Luke is because of you, just like this haircut is, Dad. It's pretty simple psychology: I'm trying to get over being a woman in a man's world, a daughter in a powerful man's house."

"What are you talking about? You make me sound like the Marquis de Sade. I am a nice person."

"Yes, you are. So imagine what cruel men do to women."

"How is your stupid hair my fault, and what do I have to do with you and Luke?" he asked in exasperation. "And what cruelty? What powerful-man nonsense? Your mother is a powerful woman—she runs this house and has been far more cruel to me than I've been to her, by the way."

"Mother had no chance in life to be an ambassador, only an ambassador's wife. Women were chattels thirty years ago. I didn't want to grow up like her, an appendage—certainly not Luke Bishop's, and that's what Luke wants and needs. I want to be my *own* person. I want to be like you."

"I don't have a flattop."

She laughed. "Dad, the best feminists are made with the loving hand of a father. You didn't want me to be a cheerleader; I didn't become one. But I had to lay all the football players to realize I didn't want to be a football player either."

"Now I remember why I didn't tuck you in."

She touched his lips. "Shhh, you'll learn something. I wanted to be *me,* but I had to find out what I could *be.* I like who I am—a woman. A woman is always a woman, Dad.

Little girls are *born* women. But boys aren't born men, even little men—they're androgynous creatures who have to learn how to be men, have the roles acted out for them, like puppies have to learn to lift their leg to pee against a tree. Girls don't have to learn how to be women, but I had to learn what I could *become* as a woman."

He smiled, then reached for her hand. "I always wanted a strong, powerful daughter. Lear would never have expected his *sons* to love him—he knew they would usurp him. It was his daughters' love he wanted. As I wanted yours. I didn't expect your brothers to love me. I knew their wives would probably love me more."

He dropped his head. "Hell, maybe one of Chris's boyfriends will love me."

She laughed. "You are *such* an old fraud. Don't you *ever* give up?"

He looked up sheepishly. "I never could fool you. But you know I loved you."

She nodded. "I never doubted it. Your love made me strong."

He kissed her hands. "Oh, Sarah, I loved you all so much. Do you know what was the most unhappy day of my life?"

"When Ryan died," she said softly.

He shook his head. "The day you got your first pair of glasses. You were only seven when you complained the teacher wrote too small. I was crushed, but you were pleased when we took you to the optometrist. You happily picked out different frames and tried them on. I put up a good front, joked, tried to make the best of it, but inside . . ."

He touched her eyes. "It was such a *mortal* thing. It was a defect, a flaw not your fault. I wanted you to see unaided, unmarred. I wanted you to be perfect."

He was silent a long minute. "I saw death in those glasses. It was the first time I realized you all were mortal and would die someday. I even remember there was a smell to everything that day—everything stank. And always afterwards when you wore your glasses, I felt cold."

He shook his head. "Ryan's death was a nightmare I had dreamed many times before. When it happened, it was waking to find I wasn't dreaming. That's why I'm afraid now; I couldn't stand it if anything happened to you or Chris."

"You don't need to worry about us, we can take care of ourselves—you taught us."

"How can you say that? I didn't even teach Chris how to pee against a tree—he's still squatting down."

"Oh, for *Christ's* sake! You are *such* a ham."

He looked at her from the corners of his eyes and smiled, then he stood. "You're right, I am. But the funny thing is that everyone takes me seriously. They see me as a proper, intelligent man of serious intent, when I'm not."

He kissed her cheek. "I love you."

She hugged him. "I love you too, Dad. But I am other things than a daughter. Someday I'll be a wife and a mother. Lear never understood that—he demanded too much of his daughters. Good night, Dad. Would you turn out the light, please."

He flipped off the light switch and stood a moment in the doorway. Cordelia, he thought. They killed her. He closed his eyes tightly and whispered, "Good night."

Passing Chris's open door, he stuck his head in. "It's past your bedtime. Go to bed—you'll never grow up," he said in a mock-stern voice to a son taller than himself.

Chris, wearing only his pajama bottoms, turned from his desk and feigned petulance. "I thought you were going to walk by, ignoring me as usual."

Marshall stood awkwardly a moment, then gestured to the desk. "Writing letters? How come you never wrote your parents?"

"You probably didn't want to know what I was doing."

Marshall nodded. "That's probably true. Being in the dark has a lot to be said for it. People talk about senility as a dread fate, but I'm looking forward to it."

Marshall sat in the desk chair across from his son and tried to keep a straight face. "So who's the lucky guy? Tell me about Trent."

Chris laughed. "He's terrific; he convinced me to go to med school. We've known each other two years. He turned down the pros to be a broker; you'll like him."

"I'm sure I will. Your sister says I'm responsible for her flattop. Am I responsible for Trent too?"

"We talked about this before," Chris said with a slight edge. "I don't look at it as a thing someone has to take responsibility for, or excuse because of genes or hormones. Guilt is not an issue for me, Dad."

Marshall nodded. "At last, something I don't have to take blame for."

"In Trent's case, you might be able to take the credit."

"Dear God," Marshall said, bringing his hands to his ears.

"I'm serious. You know what's been the hardest part of being homosexual?"

Marshall's mouth dropped open. "Is this really happening?"

"Finding someone."

Marshall smiled. "It's no different being a heterosexual, Chris."

"Oh, yes, it is. Boy-girl, that's the natural pair-up. Boy-boy?" Chris shook his head. "There are plenty of guys around, obvious homosexuals, but I'm not attracted to them. I want someone like Luke, but the Lukes like girls, or else they're so repressed they can't admit they're attracted to men. It takes a lot of power and confidence to admit you're different. There's so much hatred and discrimination—people who *really* want to harm you, people who think God's a queer basher too. Trent's like Luke, macho and physical. If I wasn't the same way, I wouldn't appeal to him. We're alike. If I'd grown up a sissy, I'd be doomed in all my relationships. By making me strong, you ensured I'd find someone strong. So, you see, you *are* responsible for Trent."

Marshall still couldn't find words. "Well."

Chris sat back on the bed. "Maybe I'll get a puppy so we can have something safe to talk about. Or how about the tree? We decorated it while you were gone."

Marshall shook his head. "I didn't see it; I didn't go into the living room."

There was an awkward silence, and Chris sensed his distress. "Are you okay, Dad? Are you in danger?"

"No! You and Sarah are. That's why I'm a basket case."

"Dad, give us some credit—we can take care of ourselves."

"But you can't—"

"I don't want to hear what I can and can't do, Dad. I don't want to be patronized. I don't want someone 'taking care' of me. No one 'took care' of Ryan."

"Ryan's *dead.*"

"I'd rather be dead too than have others take care of me. I don't want the CIA or Luke protecting me. I can take care of myself; I have so far in my life."

"This man has killed people!"

"Dad," Chris said coldly. "I decided long ago not to live in a closet. And I'm not going to live in fear either."

"*Do* you understand there's great danger?"

"Yes; we're not stupid, and we don't want to get killed. We'll do what you say. But is that going to be enough?"

Marshall recoiled. Then he gripped his shoulders tightly and his jaw set. "Yes," he said through clenched teeth. If Caldwell wouldn't help him, he'd find another way. If violence was the only answer, if he could save his children only by killing Huong, then he would do it. He would do it himself, he realized. But how was he going to find him?

In his own bedroom, Catherine was mercifully asleep, and he crawled under the covers quietly. But he tossed most of the night. Finally at six, he slipped out of bed and went downstairs, startling the morning staff, who hadn't started breakfast. He got coffee from the kitchen and went into the living room, confronting an eight-foot Christmas tree.

He was finishing his coffee when Catherine came in. "What are you doing up?"

"Thinking," he answered dully.

She cocked her head at the tree, then went to right an off-centered angel. "About what at this time of morning?"

"My prostate. That's next—getting up in the middle of the night to piss. Burning pain. Cancer. Death."

"Oh, for God's sake," she said, but smiled; she loved his morose act—it was always amusing, and mercifully brief, and it only occurred just before he made a major decision.

"Soon I won't have any more testosterone; my hips and breasts will sag. I'll look like your mother."

"Charming, Brad. What about your teeth? They're going to fall out too."

"And my brain cells are dying. Soon they'll say, 'Here he is, His Excellency, The Banana.' " He sighed. "Don't let me drool, Catherine. When it happens, put me out of it."

A toy soldier was out of position; she moved him, then moved him again, and stepped back to look. "Don't worry,

I will. I may even find another man—a young one with perfect teeth, tight hips, and no brain at all."

"Dear God, then what? I don't mind dying, I just don't want anything beyond."

She gave up on the soldier. "This is getting tedious. So what about the Chinese man? Did you find someone to kill him?"

"Catherine, how can you say something like that? My God, you're standing in front of a Christmas tree; that's a sacrilege! This is a holy time of year."

"To save my children, Brad, *I'd* kill him, and I couldn't care less about the time of year."

"You sound like Lady Macbeth."

"And you're acting like some decrepit Hamlet. Stop thinking and *do* what you have to."

"Kill somebody."

"Yes, damn it, if that's the only way. Am I supposed to have sympathy for this Chinese man who wants to murder my children?"

"I keep hoping for another way out, Catherine."

"You can't reason with lunatics—Chinese or Moslem; Christians or the CIA." She turned away. "And it isn't like you haven't killed someone before, Brad."

He looked up at her in shock. "My God, you *are* like Lady Macbeth."

Her face was grim and uncompromising. "I'm hungry. Do you want breakfast?"

He shook his head.

After she left, he stared at the tree for a long time. Each ornament had meaning; each had been carefully selected—a silk camel from China, a tiny cradle from East Germany—or they had been made by the children: a plum-colored snowflake from Ryan's purple period in kindergarten; Sarah's little Easter bunny, which she insisted be included because she would be lonely otherwise; and Chris's eleven-point star, because he loved cutting out points, saying at four with great disdain, "*Anybody* can make a star with five points."

And there was his own favorite—a carved wooden king from Spain, looking neither wise nor holy, but baffled and slightly mad—Lear in Bethlehem, probably true to life, for what kind of king would venture out on a winter's night to chase after a star? One soon to be deposed, most likely.

The soldier was still wrong, he saw, staring at the little musketeer in blue pants and red tunic; Catherine had not got him right. But what was a soldier doing on a Christmas tree? A herald for those gambling beneath the cross on Calvary, he supposed—tree to cross, adoration to crucifixion, all appropriate after all.

He stood; enough—his moroseness had become tiresome even to him. He *was* acting the fool; Catherine was right. No more! He would do what was necessary to save his children.

Confidence flowed into him. Anyone could ride the crest of a wave—mastering the rapids, shoals, and reefs was the hard part. Any sailor could navigate a calm sea; the trick was to weather typhoons and hurricanes. He *had* been Hamlet; now he would be Caesar.

He called for his car and arrived at his office thirty minutes before Helen.

When she came in, wearing neon green leotards and a matching blouse, she was not pleased. Very territorial about the office, she did not regard it as his. "You're going to have to come in a *lot* earlier than seven to catch up on all your work," she said.

"I could get a lot more done if I had a secretary who didn't stroll in at midmorning. I need to work—no calls unless they're from CS, Crazy Sadeq."

She stared at him. "How about the President and secretary of state?"

"Well, of course them, Helen. And get me Luke."

He turned to the papers on his desk, losing himself in work until his back began to hurt and he stood to relieve the pain.

He went to the window and looked across to the park. A young couple caught his attention. The boy's face was bent into the girl's, kissing her, and she responded, hands inside his coat. Others moved out of their way as the couple lurched forward, absorbed in one another.

Hungered. That was the word. They hungered for each other so badly they wanted to get into each other's skin. Finally they stumbled, caught one another, laughed, then resumed, hands and mouths seeking again.

Why can't that last? he wondered.

His hand massaged his aching back. Age. Age with its cares and worries and back pains. The young know only their bodies and a few sprouts of knowledge; love is blind, and deaf and dumb besides. Then the flesh sags, becomes more burden than discovery, and the sprouts become a thicket of brambles and weeds—philosophy, religion, politics.

A youth leaps with life and energy, runs, kicks cans, but men think and worry and plan. Men hold on to life, hug the earth as if afraid they'll fall off.

Even Wilson Lord didn't hunger; he just believed. Perhaps that's what beliefs were, Marshall thought—hunger gone awry, youth aged.

Helen buzzed him on the intercom. "You have a phone call, from a Mr. Crazy. And I've got Clarabell the Clown on hold."

He picked up the phone. "Bradley Marshall."

"Tomorrow for lunch, say around one?"

"I don't see the point in another lunch," Marshall said guardedly.

"You'll be met at the restaurant, then brought somewhere else. Your host is ascetic, perhaps some grapes and figs, so you might want to eat beforehand."

"I'll be there." Then Marshall hung up and went back to the window.

What did he know of the Mideast and Islam? Even less than he had about the Orient where he had been at the hub of negotiations after America's army had been drawn into the quicksand, sucked in as the missionaries had been before them, swallowed like babbling Christianity because of Western arrogance.

Now it was happening again. He was about to meet an imam, depose a shah, carve up a subcontinent where men murdered one another for the subtlest interpretation of the Koran, an obscure inflection of a single prayer.

For what? Oil? Money, stocks, commodities, transfers?

Out the window he saw a happy couple, a man his own age, a father, and a young woman, his daughter. They kissed.

Marshall turned in chagrin; they were not father and daughter: it was an unseemly liaison of an old man and a young girl. He was watching sex, lust—not the hunger of youth, but the gluttony of a fat man who had missed lunch.

And he suddenly realized that he wasn't meeting with the Imam because America needed oil; America's hunger wasn't that of a starving man. It wasn't oil or money behind his mission. It was the simple tale of the playground, the reason he had fought for grades, girls, commission, why he had punished his body, run miles—hurt.

He hadn't done it for money. Neither had Galahad or Lancelot. Or Arthur or Attila. Or Christ or Khan, Buddha or Bonaparte, Hitler or Hegel. They would not have sold their destinies for money or oil, any more than Luke Bishop would. Or even Wilson Lord.

Helen Sarbanes entered. "Luke's here, but I told him you might be busy with one of your cartoon friends."

Marshall turned to her. "Helen, what are men interested in?"

She laughed, held out her fingers about six inches, expanded them, them brought them in. "We're not talking complexity, just millimeters."

"Thank you, Helen. Have him come in."

He returned to his post at the window. Yes, it was the lesson of the playground, and later, the bar, bedroom, and boardroom—not money or oil, but cock. Women didn't envy penises—men did. Each wanted the biggest and best, and America, with the biggest and best, wanted to keep it that way.

Men were no different from animals lifting their legs, marking territory, scratching up the dirt behind them. A peacock had plumes, and an orangutan a fireball ass to attract the female, but they strutted their butts for other males. Wars were not fought for money any more than sandboxes were; national interest was only marking and scratching.

Vietnam had not been about self-determination; it had been a leg-raising exercise, and now he was going to spearhead another marking-and-scratching exercise in the most improbable place, among the most improbable people. He was on a mission for a Christian president, meeting with an ayatollah to solve ten centuries of warfare between Christians, Moslems, and Jews. No wonder Wilson Lord was apoplectic, he thought.

Bishop positioned himself in front of the desk. Marshall turned from the window and motioned him to a chair. "Tomorrow at one P.M. I have a meeting with the Ayatollah Khomeini. I'm taking Sergeant Mead because it could be dangerous."

"Then you should take *me.*"

"Luke, this isn't *John Wayne Meets the Imam*—I want you to find Huong. You've got to. I'm desperate. I didn't get anywhere with Caldwell last night. He won't help unless I set up Khomeini to be killed. I can't do that."

"I told you, sir; leave it to me; that Chinaman is a dead gook."

"You and Catherine should have been at the O.K. Corral. I don't want him killed, I just want to talk to him."

"Trust me—we have a deal: if I save Sarah, you'll make her marry me."

"She doesn't *want* to marry you, Luke."

"She just doesn't know the real me."

"Luke, forget Sarah, find Huong. And get out of that uniform—I may as well have Babar looking for him. Do you own a coat and tie?"

"Jesus, sir! Of course I own a coat and tie. I'm a regular person."

"No, you're not."

Seeing Bishop flinch, Marshall said softly, "That's *good,* Luke." Then he stared at Luke curiously. "You *would* kill him, wouldn't you."

"In a nanosecond."

Marshall sat back. "Why? You don't like Caldwell because he'll follow orders blindly. Aren't you the same?"

Bishop shook his head. "I'm not doing this on orders; I'm doing this for other reasons. There's a difference between being told to guard a gate and *wanting* to guard a gate. Caldwell's doing a job; I've got a higher calling."

Bishop saluted and walked out.

Marshall stared after him. There were so many centurions at so many different gates, he thought—good, decent men willing to sacrifice themselves for a cause. He shook his head sadly. The world hadn't changed at all, and as long as there were Luke Bishops, it never would.

Then he frowned. But was that altogether bad?

He buzzed Helen and told her to send in Mead. A minute later the sergeant stood rigidly before Marshall's desk.

"I'm going to need you tomorrow around noon. It could be dangerous."

"Yes, sir."

Marshall shook his head. "Why am I telling you this? It wouldn't make any difference to you, would it?"

Mead smiled faintly. "No, sir."

"You haven't been happy about our trips to the restaurant, have you?"

Mead did not smile. "No, sir."

"Well, it won't happen again, and tomorrow should be the last time you'll have to provide any security for me."

"Yes, sir."

Marshall tried to keep from smiling; Mead was always so serious, and he made Marcel Marceau seem like a talk-show host. "By the way, how are things these days?"

"Great, sir."

"Before they were only 'fine.' You sure everything's all right?"

"They're great, sir. Major Bishop set me straight. He's . . . well, he's great too. I sure hope he gets that woman he's after. She must be one dumb woman if she's turning him down. Something must really be wrong with her."

"Mmm. Go home, Sergeant. Get a good night's sleep. And don't wear a uniform tomorrow. Do you have a coat and tie?"

"Ah, no, sir, but I could borrow one."

From whom, Marshall wondered—Frankenstein?—but he said mildly, "Casual would be fine, Sergeant. The idea is not to look threatening, just to save my ass."

The gray December sky was deceptive, for it was not cold and there was no wind. It was such a mild day that Mike Caldwell took off his jacket and slung it over his shoulder as he left the embassy in midmorning, heading on foot toward the Tuileries.

He needed air; he hadn't spent this much time indoors in

years, and besides, he was moved by Paris—the city was alive to him because he had read Victor Hugo and Alexandre Dumas as a boy. He dreamed of growing up to be d'Artagnan, and his boyhood throbbed with *vicomtes* and dukes and musketeers, hunchbacks and cardinals, kings and damsels.

He wanted to be d'Artagnan, but ended up a Green Beret, and then a CIA agent.

He crossed the busy Concorde and walked along the quay. He loved the mansard roofs of the buildings along the river and the majesty of the Louvre; he could even picture Richelieu sweeping imperially through his apartments, his crimson robes brushing along polished parquet floors, and he lingered, gazing at the dilapidated Gare d'Orsay on the Left Bank, then looked upstream to the Ile and the Conciergerie, and beyond, to Notre Dame where the hunchback had wept for Esmeralda.

Finally he entered the Tuileries. He had come at a good time—mothers were with small children, boys sailed boats on the fountains, and lovers strolled gravel paths, oblivious to the world, as ridiculous pigeons strutted and puffed at their feet.

He sat on a bench. A flock of pigeons assembled, parading before him, waggling tail feathers. Males bobbed and cooed and puffed up before females, who ignored them.

Caldwell watched one, either blind or mad, that had gone into its seduction ritual before his outstretched foot. He kicked at it, yet in a moment the pigeon was back.

"Give it a rest," he said, kicking at it again.

But he's not the schizoid one, Caldwell thought. The pigeon had just confused foot and female—*he* was the killer. Surely something was wrong with him, confusing murder with duty. D'Artagnan wouldn't. Was he insane? A psychopath? Forget duty, honor, country—he was a murderer, a serial killer for a cause, and he liked it. Given the choice of killing or fucking—he would kill. He could relive that a thousand times while he could hardly recall a single intercourse. Killing was to be a god. Gods murdered—that's what they did best, and they murdered everyone in the end.

If gods could be brought to justice, we would hang them, Caldwell thought. And if gods were mass murderers, how could they hold him accountable for a few deaths?

Yet he *was* troubled, and it all had to do with Bishop and Marshall. Lord was right about this mission—Khomeini had to be stopped and he had no compunctions about killing him. Yet Marshall was right too; he *didn't* need a civics lesson to understand that it was wrong to subvert the policy of the President of the United States. Would d'Artagnan?

But Luke Bishop bothered him most. Why? he wondered.

The pigeon was back in an elaborate seduction of his right foot. Caldwell looked about, saw nobody watching, then connected solidly with his left foot and sent the bird twenty yards into the trees.

He was angry, for it had come to him clearly—he understood why he was so bothered: *Luke* was d'Artagnan; he was only Rochefort, the cardinal's spy.

CHAPTER 18

"Good morning," Lord said to Helen Sarbanes when he entered Marshall's office. He blanched slightly at her outfit; she looked like an aerobics instructor. Wasn't there a dress code? he wondered, but he asked lightly, "Where's the pit bull?"

She smiled pleasantly; she found him attractive, a thin, elegant man supremely confident, but with a sense of danger and decadence about him, an appealing, unwholesome sensuality. She also admired the way he had handled Bishop yesterday; he hadn't been intimidated at all and made him look the perfect fool he was. "Probably at the gym, or pining after the ambassador's daughter."

"Ah, youth. So much energy. Such hope. Such an ass. Would you please tell the ambassador I'd like to see him for a few minutes; it will be very brief."

He was in an excellent mood. Huong had called with the news that Khomeini and Marshall were meeting tomorrow. Huong would tell him all the details at one, and at three Lord would finalize plans with Caldwell. However, to spare himself all the logistical problems, he would give Marshall one last chance to save himself and his children. It was very generous of him, he decided, especially now that Marshall's help made no difference to the outcome.

Lord entered confidently and sat in the brown leather chair before Marshall's desk. He pointed to the drapes behind Marshall. "They're getting shoddy, Brad. You should have them replaced. But thank you for seeing me, though this is strictly in your best interests."

"I'm sure," Marshall said dryly. "Your altruism is so widely regarded."

"As noted as your principles. I'm here to offer the deal you wanted last night."

"It didn't take Caldwell long to get back to you."

"He *works* for me."

"And for whom do you work? Any names I might find familiar?"

"How about the United States? Democracy?"

"Please, I'll get sick."

Lord leaned back in the chair. "Well, fair's fair. I was nauseated last night when Mike told me what you asked him to do—the man of principles seeking a hired gun. However, I'm here to accept your offer."

"It's been withdrawn."

"Found your principles again, have you? Elusive things, aren't they? Better lose them again if you want to save your children. Mike can do that—I'll give him to you."

"You *do* sound like Lucifer, bartering lives, offering temptations."

"Oh, the imagery is too grand, Brad—you're no Christ; this is a minor drama. Let's keep focused—I'll swap your children for Khomeini."

Marshall shook his head in derision. "You expect me to deal with you? What have you promised Huong? Does he know you're here betraying him?"

"Huong is nothing. Khomeini is important. Stay focused, Brad. We're talking about Sarah and Chris. Do you want to save them or not? This is your last opportunity."

Marshall laughed. "Where will you go next? What will be your counteroffer to Huong when you betray me?"

"Your answer is . . ."

"Get lost."

Lord crossed his legs. "Jesus, you're a fool, and so *pompous,*" he marveled.

"Because I won't murder two people?"

Lord smiled. "Last night you were negotiating to murder

one—what's another? Obviously I'm missing some subtlety here."

"Was this all you had to discuss? I'm busy."

Lord stood. "I feel like Pilate, washing my hands."

"Don't bother, you'll never get them clean."

Lord nodded. "Well, I'm sorry this didn't work out. I really have nothing against your children. I'm a father too."

"Yes, I know. But then so was Caligula. Good day."

Lord smiled, nodding toward the drapes. "Actually there's a lot in here that should be replaced. The carpet is worn. And you, Brad—you're woefully out-of-date too."

My God! Wilson Lord thought when he entered Louis Vuitton, the exclusive luggage shop two blocks from the Arc de Triomphe—they must herd the Japanese from store to store like moneyed sheep. Once again, except for the clerks, he was the only non-Oriental.

He had taken the precaution of putting on his glasses, but glancing about, he did not see Huong. All he saw were Japanese making staggering purchases—at one table several men had piled a little Fuji of purses, wallets, and accessories, while at another, a clerk was writing an order for at least twenty suitcases.

A salesclerk approached him.

"I thought Louis Vuitton had a shop in Tokyo," he said to her.

"We do, but even with the customs duty they pay when they go back, it's much cheaper to buy here than there."

"There's a lesson in that."

The woman smiled. "Yes. Live in Paris, not Tokyo."

I must go to Japan, he thought to himself; the Ginza must be a bizarre sight—asshole to belly button in Hermès scarves and Louis Vuitton handbags.

Just then he noticed Huong enter the store, making his way past much smaller Japanese. He looked rich and powerful, and very disdainful.

"I'm early," he said to Lord. "I hoped to save you some money."

"I can't afford anything in here."

"Then why come?"

"It's fascinating, a cultural experience like a museum."

They entered the showroom and moved from counter to counter.

"I was able to get the information you want," Huong said. "The Arabs despise one another so much they're happy to betray and murder for free—money isn't a consideration." He nodded toward the Japanese. "They're quite unlike these greedy little people."

"The information you have is reliable?"

"They wouldn't deceive me because they want weapons, and they wish to be rid of the man you want to eliminate. You will be doing them a favor."

"Which brings us to the favor you want from me."

Lord nodded to the salesclerk as they moved past her, appearing to browse at a display of steamer trunks that Lord hazarded cost as much as some yachts.

"You will need help from your Arab friends, but they should be happy to assist. Marshall's family has tickets at the Garnier for *The Nutcracker* Friday. If they go, I'll arrange to have their car unguarded. That will be simple, for like the Japanese, Americans are also greedy. Security is *never* what it should be. Your friends will do . . . whatever is necessary so that when the family leaves in the automobile, *your* family will be avenged."

"I can trust you?"

"With Khomeini dead, Islamic Jihad will jump to take credit for murdering the American ambassador's family in revenge. But others will claim responsibility also, those wanting to ingratiate themselves with Iran, or just lunatic groups looking to make a name for themselves—their thirst for blood is unbelievable, but their abilities limited. In any case, the result will be chaos, which is my goal."

Huong pulled an envelope from his jacket. "The information you want is in here; they even provided a map for the location of the meeting."

Lord put the envelope in his pocket. "This concludes our business. We shall not meet again. I urge you to make arrangements to leave France."

Lord glanced at his watch; it was time for his next rendezvous. He shook hands with Huong, cast a final look at the Japanese sack of Louis Vuitton, and left the store.

* * *

Lord arrived by cab at Hôtel Biron on the Left Bank at two-thirty; he walked the grounds of the museum, studied the sculptures in the outside gallery, and lingered many minutes before the massive *Burghers of Calais*. He was standing before *The Gates of Hell*, a bronze cavalcade of damnation and suffering, when Caldwell came up to him.

"Is there symbolism in this?" Mike asked good-naturedly.

"We've already decided there isn't a god, so why are you worried about hell?"

"I'm not. But if there is, it looks exciting—lots of naked, writhing women too."

"Oh, I'm sure hell will be far more entertaining than heaven, with *lots* more flesh. You'll have a good time."

"You too?"

"I'll be able to chat with old friends. Shall we go in?"

Inside the museum, Lord handed him the envelope. "I'll make all arrangements; it looks like a perfect place. The meeting is set for one; we'll be ready long before then."

Caldwell took the envelope, but something caught his attention and he walked to a sculpture on the first floor. "Jesus. Now *this* is art."

Though the museum was crowded, everyone seemed to give wide berth to the work before Caldwell, and when Lord moved beside him, he saw why and nearly leapt back himself. But instead he put on his glasses—it *couldn't* be what he thought it was.

Yet it was, and he felt particularly foolish with his glasses on examining the vagina of a spread-eagled woman's torso.

Caldwell stepped closer.

"Don't put your *nose* in it," Lord said, looking about in mortification.

"That's terrific," Caldwell enthused. "I wonder who modeled for it?"

"Probably his mistress, Camille Claudel," Lord said, moving away quickly.

"This is pornographic; you'd never find cunt like this in an American museum."

"The French have a more mature approach than Americans; very evidently so if you're any standard."

Caldwell examined the base. *"Iris, Messenger of the*

Gods," he read. He turned to Lord. "Maybe heaven wouldn't be so bad, after all."

But Lord was heading for the stairs; he followed after.

"I need to know if Marshall's family is going to the opera house Friday night."

On the second floor, Caldwell stopped before a life-size nude sculpture of Balzac. "That's disgusting. He's a ton of lard. Did he *pose* for that?"

Lord nodded. "Yes. Rodin tried many times to do something with Balzac's body, unsuccessfully as you see. These are studies. Finally he just threw a cloak over him."

Caldwell turned. "Friday night? I'll find out from Luke. He might be with them."

"At the opera? I doubt it."

"Love can make you do strange things—for Iris downstairs, *I'd* go to the opera. But why will his family go Friday if something happens to him tomorrow?"

"It's called a contingency plan. If Marshall's family is murdered for his meeting with Khomeini, how would Carter explain it? Who *could* explain it? Was it Shiite revenge for Khomeini's murder? Sunni revenge for overtures to Khomeini? Savak? A *fatwah* by some lunatic mullah? A PLO rogue unit? Who could possibly figure out that nonsense? Even they themselves can't. The goal is chaos, Mike—not a difficult end to achieve in the Mideast."

Caldwell nodded. "What time do you want to meet tomorrow?"

"Six. I'll pick you up in front of your hotel. We'll have the entire morning to set this up. Bring something warm to wear."

Lord started for the stairs. "And get a good night's sleep."

"We can't stay locked up here the entire time," Chris said when Marshall returned to the residence, pursuing his father into the living room, followed by Sarah.

"We went over this last night," Marshall said, pouring a Scotch, offering the bottle to Chris, who declined. "I told you that you were in danger."

Sarah grabbed the bottle and mixed a drink as her father watched in alarm. "I didn't come to Paris to sit in my room," she said. "I'll even go out with Luke—you said maybe I could."

"I'm going crazy," Chris added. "I'd rather get shot than spend another day in here. It's Christmas; there are all kinds of parties going on. I know a lot of people in Paris. I want out. What am I supposed to tell my friends—I'm on restriction? I'm twenty-four!"

"Didn't I get through to you yesterday? You are in danger! Someone wants to kill you. What is wrong with you both?"

"You said we could go out if we had security; get us some security then," Chris said, taking the Scotch bottle from his sister, pouring himself a drink.

Catherine came into the room. "Oh, good, drinking. Drinking and picking on your father—my two favorite activities."

"What would you like, Catherine?"

"A Moonride."

"Dear God, what's that?"

"Vodka, gin, and tequila."

He poured her sherry, the only thing she drank.

"Mom, tell Dad to let us out," Chris said. "At least to go shopping; Au Printemps ought to be safe."

"Why don't you exercise? You're getting fat," Marshall said.

"I am not."

"Then read. You're getting stupid."

"He's always been stupid," Sarah said. "He'll always *be* stupid—reading won't help, any more than it has Luke."

"Luke reads?" Chris asked in amazement.

"Stop picking on him," Marshall said. "And all right, you can go out with him Friday."

"What about me?" Chris asked.

"You're not his type."

"I mean out on my own. If Sarah's going out, I want out too. It's not fair—you always favor her. You've always loved her the most."

"Of course; she's more lovable."

"C'mon, Dad," Chris said. "I need to get out of here. I won't do anything dangerous. Just let me go shopping; I need to buy Christmas presents."

"Have you no fucking understanding of what I've been telling you?" Marshall exploded.

Catherine nursed her drink and said wickedly, "Haven't taken care of that Chinese man yet, have you, Brad? I thought you were going to do that."

"I am! But I can't have Sarah and Chris running around Paris until I do."

"How about a play or ballet or the opera?" Sarah asked. "Surely there are safe places for us to go, as long as we have security."

"No," Marshall said. "Not until I can stop the Chinese man."

Catherine mused over her glass. "Why not the Opera House? I have box seats Friday for *The Nutcracker.* The Garnier is hardly Ford's Theater. Surely you could arrange security for us, Brad. We'd go directly to the ballet and come directly back, and there would be guards with us all the time."

"I don't like it."

"I'm not wild about it either, Brad, but the children are right—they can't stay locked up here forever, or until you take care of that Chinese man—whichever comes first. I'm sure Floyd can provide adequate protection at the Garnier for a couple hours. If he can't, then all this is hopeless anyway."

Marshall considered as he swirled his drink. "All right," he said at last.

"I can't picture Luke at *The Nutcracker,"* Sarah said. "But I like the idea. How about it, Chris?"

"Christ, I'd go anywhere to get out of here."

"Done," Marshall said. "Friday night at the Paris Opera—you three, Luke, and Floyd's security men. I'll tell Luke tomorrow."

CHAPTER 19

Marshall hoped to get out of the house before encountering Catherine, but she was waiting for him again at the breakfast table. The orchids were gone from the table, replaced by a huge centerpiece of pale pink poinsettias that blended perfectly with the tapestries on the walls, and in all the windows were candles framed by holly wreaths.

"I'm furious with you," Catherine said. "You're meeting Khomeini today."

"How did you know?" he asked in surprise.

"We've been married thirty years."

"Yes, but I can't see through you."

"You're more transparent. You haven't mentioned him in days, therefore you must be meeting with him. How dangerous will this be?"

"Not very; besides, I'll have my bodyguard with me."

"Can he protect you from the CIA? Aren't you worried about them?"

"Of course I am, but I don't have a choice. I can't refuse a presidential request. Do you want me to resign?"

"If it's a matter of life and death, I do—I'm too old to find another man."

"I thought you were going to get a young one with good teeth, tight hips, and no brain. Paris is filled with handsome models like that—you could call up Pierre Cardin for one."

"I mean to settle down with; I'm worn out training you—

I couldn't possibly manage another husband. I don't *want* another husband."

"Then you've forgiven me for the Chinese man?"

"Of course not, and I expect you to have that solved by tomorrow night when we go to the ballet. And I *mean* that, Brad."

When Helen entered his office after his five minutes of solitude, wearing a white nurse's outfit, complete with cap, highlighted with white rhinestone go-go boots, it took all his aplomb to ignore her. "Get me Luke and Floyd."

"Should I cancel everything today?" she asked, realizing something was happening.

He nodded. "But pretend I'm keeping all appointments."

"What about the funeral for the prime minister? The Foreign Ministry needs to know if you're going."

"Another prime minister died? My God, if I went to the funeral of every Fourth Republic prime minister, I might as well bring a sleeping bag to Notre Dame."

"We'll call that a no-show then," she said, leaving the room.

When Sedwick came in, he was still staring at the door behind him. "You have *got* to do something about that woman."

"Who?"

"Cher Nightingale! Who do you think? Where does she *get* her clothes? She's crossed over the line, Brad."

"I don't know what you're talking about, Floyd. I called you in to tell you that I need to disappear again today, but this will be for the last time."

"You mean this time they're finally going to kill you?"

"I mean that this will finish my business for the President. But I want you to increase the security on my family."

"I already have; there's a five-man detail assigned to them at all times. Andy and I talked about the threat to Sarah and Chris. He was worried and we discussed security for them while they're here. They're covered, and I've put a special guard on your car. Nothing's going to happen to them."

"Would they be safe if they went to the Opera House tomorrow night?"

Sedwick considered, then nodded. "I can handle that, as long as they go there and return to the residence without any side trips."

"Okay, set that up then."

"But what about you, Brad? I can protect your family, but I can't guarantee *your* safety if you're trusting Plant Life to save you."

Marshall smiled. "Sergeant Mead has saved my life many times, Floyd."

"You're a fucking idiot," Sedwick said, leaving the room.

Bishop came in a few minutes later wearing sweat pants and a T-shirt.

"I told you to wear a coat and tie."

"I was on my way to work out."

"Again? You're supposed to find Huong—is he in the *gym?*"

Bishop smiled. "You should trust me more. I'm working on a plan."

Marshall merely shook his head; he could not take Bishop seriously. "Check on Sergeant Mead before you go. I told him to dress casual—God only knows what *he's* wearing, probably a loincloth. And you can go out with Sarah tomorrow. What are you going to wear?"

"A loincloth."

"You can't, not to the Opera House."

"The where?"

"You're taking her to *The Nutcracker.*"

"The opera? *The Nutcracker?* On a date?" Bishop asked incredulously.

"Yes. You, Catherine, Chris, and Floyd's security."

"Jesus. You're not taking any chances on me scoring with your daughter."

"Oh, I think Sarah can take care of herself."

"How come everybody has to go along? Why so many chaperons?"

"Take it or leave it."

"I'll take it, but how about if we go to dinner alone first, then meet everyone at the Opera? She doesn't need Floyd's security if she's with me."

Marshall considered. "Ask *her,* but one last thing before you go. See if you can't track down Caldwell. Maybe you could set up a meeting with him—I'd feel better knowing where he is today."

"I'm seeing him at one this afternoon."

"You are?"

"We have a match on—it's a long-running thing."

"Good," Marshall said in relief. "Then I don't need to worry about the CIA?"

Bishop shook his head. "Nope."

Wilson Lord was cold. Though the sun had miraculously appeared for the first time since he had arrived in Paris, its tantalizing promise delivered such faint warmth that he seemed more chilled now than when they had moved into place before sunup.

He and Caldwell were on a hill overlooking a plain twenty miles south of Paris. They had approached from a back road and pulled their car off to the side, leaving the hood open, with a white cloth hanging from the antenna; then they crossed a wheat field and climbed the hill.

"It can't be this good," Caldwell said when he saw the view, for even in the dark he could make out the grove five hundred yards below. As the sun rose, however, the vista proved even better—an approaching vehicle could be seen a mile away. The grove was in a clearing off the side of a dirt road, a natural rest stop—the perfect place for a picnic, surrounded by mustard and wheat fields.

They walked down the slope to the trees and stared back at the hill. It was too close and steep for anyone in the clearing to see the top.

"They'll come from different directions," Caldwell guessed. "The only problem will be if Khomeini's people do a security sweep, but I doubt it. These people are religious fanatics, not pros."

Lord shrugged. "It won't make a difference; the idea is chaos. Killing Khomeini or Marshall doesn't matter. All we have to do is prevent the meeting. If the Iranians discover us, they'll think Carter tried to set up Khomeini; they'd never trust America again." He smiled. "We can't lose."

"What if the Iranians don't show?"

"Then *we'll* shoot Marshall. How will that be explained? What was the U.S. ambassador doing out here? Word will slip out that he was on a secret mission to sell out the Shah. Islamic Jihad or another nut group will take credit for the assassination."

"What's the worst-case scenario?"

Lord considered. "There is none," he said at last.

"So we win whether we hit or miss."

"Yes. But we're good shots, and the target is easy."

They returned to the hill, sighted in with their rifles, and were ready by nine A.M. Caldwell wrapped himself in his parka and lay back; he was asleep within minutes as Lord shivered beside him.

Ron Mead was nervous, not about his duties today or that the ambassador had told him it might be dangerous, but about his clothes. He didn't know what *casual* meant to an ambassador, and he had fretted all last night and this morning. Finally Sung had dressed him.

"You look fine," she said after outfitting him in a blue polo shirt, cotton slacks, and a windbreaker that she had made a special trip to the PX to buy.

"I look *stupid.* Who dresses like this?"

"Everybody. You said casual, this is *casual."*

"How do you know?"

"I have eyes; I read magazines—I see the ads. Ron, you look fine."

But he was not reassured, and all morning he fretted at his desk. He felt profoundly uncomfortable with his shirt tucked into his trousers, a black belt hitched around his waist. He never wore a belt, and his only casual pants were jeans.

At eleven, Bishop entered his little cubicle across the hall from Marshall's suite. Bishop was wearing a coat and tie, and they both looked at one another in surprise.

"Hey, you look great," Bishop said. "Nice shirt."

"Really, sir?"

"Yeah. Ralph Lauren, right?"

"I . . . I guess."

"Nice-looking trousers too."

"Are you making fun of me, sir?"

Bishop shook his head. "No, you look great—casual."

"I was kinda worried. Actually Sung dressed me. I felt like a fucking monkey."

"She did a good job. Relax. You worried about today? I'm here to give you a pep talk if you need one—you know, officer to snuffy, 'go get 'em' kind of thing."

Mead smiled. "I'm okay, sir—mostly I was worried about my shirt. I mean, it's got a little horse on it—who'd wear something like that?"

"It's called a polo shirt, Sergeant."

"It's fucking stupid! Why not have a little clown with a balloon on it?"

Just then Helen walked into the room looking disturbed, but seeing them, she stopped. "Have the Marines gotten rid of uniforms?" She directed an unbelieving gaze at Bishop's coat and tie. "What happened to you?"

"This is the real me—Luke Bishop, the Clark Kent of Marines."

She rolled her eyes and turned to Mead. "Sergeant. We just got a phone call from a hospital in Neuilly."

Mead jumped up. "Sung!"

"We don't have any details, just that she's there."

"What happened? Jesus! I just left her." He looked about frantically, then whirled to Bishop. "I gotta go to her."

Helen handed him a piece of paper. "This is the address of the hospital. They wouldn't give me any information over the phone, merely asked for . . . the closest relative."

"Oh, Jesus," Mead cried. Then he turned to Bishop furiously. "You know who did this? That motherfucker Lord. He knows I'm the ambassador's bodyguard, and he's trying to stop me from being with him. If he hurt Sung . . ."

Helen stepped back at the transformation before her. She had never seen such fury.

Bishop stepped up to Mead, calm and assured. "Sergeant, take it easy. Look at me."

Mead's eyes were wild, but Bishop stared him down. "Go see about your wife."

"But the ambassador . . . He told me . . . I . . ."

"That's an order, Sergeant. You won't help the ambassador the way you are. I'll cover for you. Go see your wife. Take it easy. I'll get a car to take you to the hospital."

Mead stared at the paper in his hand, then shook his head

in agony. "I can't stand it if anything happened to her. Oh, Sung," he started to moan.

Bishop turned to Helen. "Can you get a staff car for Sergeant Mead?"

"It'll be downstairs by the time he gets there," she said, rushing out.

"Come with me, Sergeant," Bishop said, taking him by the elbow. "Everything's going to be all right."

"Oh, shit, oh, shit," Mead cried. Then he pulled on his shirt. "She got this for me."

Twenty minutes later, Bishop entered Marshall's office.

"Helen told me about Sergeant Mead's wife. Could this have anything to do with the meeting?"

"Yes, sir, you know it could. That's the first thing Mead thought of. But don't worry, I'll be with you. And I'm even dressed for the part."

Marshall considered him a long minute, then he nodded. "Yes. You are, and it's a very nice tie."

"Dior. Forty fucking dollars. But worth it; it's gotten me laid twice."

"A tie?"

"Women are strange. I learned that in San Diego. Some women go for a uniform, some for a business suit, some like a hard body, some like books and professors."

Marshall sat back in amusement. "You're telling me something. What?"

"Sarah can like me. I can change into anything, wear anything, but it's all bullshit—a uniform or a Dior tie. I'm the good guy. She can't do better. She'll figure it out as soon as she gets past all the crap in her own life."

Marshall looked at him with genuine fondness. "Tell that to *her.* She thinks I'm the obstacle in her life."

Bishop nodded. "You are. Mine too. You're the one we have to hurdle to make our own lives work. Then *our* kids will have to overcome the obstacles we make. Then their kids will have to do the same." He smiled. "I don't want my kid to be a dumb Marine; I want him to do better. And his kid better than that. All I have to do is set a standard. Then my kid will get to a higher plane. And his kid to an even higher one."

"You really think about that?" Marshall asked in amazement.

Bishop nodded. "Oh, yes, sir. I didn't beat my brains out at Quantico for *me.* I didn't go to war for *me.* I see things way in the future. I mean, what would be the point of life if there wasn't something better to come out of you?"

Marshall smiled and stood. "Terrific lines. They go with the tie."

Marshall led him out the back door of his office down to the underground garage. "Lunch," he said to his chauffeur. "The usual place, Marcel."

The American-made car, huge and even more cumbersome because of reinforced metal plating and bulletproof glass, lumbered out of the garage and was immediately swallowed in the traffic of the Concorde.

Mead rushed into the hospital on the outskirts of Paris, pushing roughly past those in his way. It had taken nearly thirty minutes to get here and he was wild.

At admissions, a nurse sitting behind a glassed-in booth did not look up when he stood before her. He pounded on the glass with his fist. "Where's my wife?" he shouted.

The woman jumped, then went back to the form she was filling out.

Mead smashed the glass so hard the woman leapt out of her chair.

"Where's my wife? Sung Mead," he yelled, hitting the glass again.

The nurse pushed a button, and within seconds white-coated attendants ran from the emergency room. The nurse pointed at Mead, and the men tried to grab him, but he hurled them across the corridor, slamming them against the wall.

Two elderly ladies waiting in line screamed and fled the hospital, and a man in a wheelchair raced away down the hall.

The attendants picked themselves up and moved cautiously toward Mead, but he held up his hands threateningly. "Don't fuck with me. My wife's here. It's an emergency."

By now other attendants and a doctor had come onto the

corridor. The doctor waved the others back. "What is the problem?" he asked in English.

"My wife's here. I want to know what's wrong with her. I want to see her. Now!"

"What is her name?"

"Mead. Sung Mead. I got a message she was here." He held out the paper to the doctor.

Approaching cautiously, the doctor took the paper, saw the embossed eagle on the stationery from the office of the U.S. ambassador, and looked up at Mead curiously. "You work at the American embassy?"

"I'm Ambassador Marshall's bodyguard. I want to see my wife!"

The doctor spoke to the nurse. In a moment he turned to Mead. He was polite and reassuring. "There must be a mistake. We have no record of your wife. She is not here."

"But I got the message."

"I can see it. But your wife has not been admitted, or even received treatment here. Perhaps they got the wrong hospital."

"You're sure she's not here?"

The doctor smiled. "Sometimes patients die, but we don't misplace them. Maybe you should call your embassy." He handed the desk phone to Mead.

Mead debated a moment, then he dialed his home number. It was busy. He slammed the phone down, turned, and ran out of the hospital. "Take me home," he said to the driver, giving him the address.

Twenty minutes later, shortly after twelve, Mead ran up the stairs of his apartment. Bursting in, he found Sung vacuuming the living room. "What are you doing here?" he shouted, almost beside himself. He ran to the phone. It was off the hook. "Why'd you do that?" he yelled.

"Major Bishop told me to. Why are you home?"

"Major Bishop?"

She nodded. "He said someone had gotten hold of the embassy directory and was making obscene phone calls to wives while their husbands were at work. He said they wanted him to call only certain numbers that had a tap on them so they could trace him."

"That son of a bitch!"

"Major Bishop?"

"Motherfucker! God *damn* him." Mead glanced at his watch. "The ambassador's already gone. I was supposed to go with him. Major Bishop tricked me into thinking you were at the hospital and had you take the phone off the hook. Bastard!"

"Why did he do that, Ron?"

"So he could go instead of me."

"Maybe he has a reason."

Mead's face set furiously. "It better be a good one."

Sung smiled. "Well, you still look nice in your shirt and pants."

He ripped off the shirt and went into the bedroom to change back into his uniform.

"Relax," Marshall said to Bishop in the backseat of his limousine when it pulled up before the restaurant. He felt Luke's body steel at the danger. "Just do what they say when we get inside. Don't resist or cause trouble."

Bishop merely set his jaw. Marshall sensed another person beside him, no longer the love-maddened male, but a brutal man who had survived combat twice.

"You don't need to wait, Marcel," Marshall said, getting out of the car.

The maître d' greeted him as before, then led them to the back, but this time into the kitchen where two burly men pointed them toward a wall. Marshall braced against it as they searched him, then it was Bishop's turn, but he faced them, spreading his arms and legs. When they were satisfied, they motioned Marshall and Bishop out the back door where a car was waiting in the alley.

Marshall settled into the backseat, cramped between Bishop and a bodyguard. The other guard sat up front with the driver, and Marshall saw a shoulder holster and pistol bulging beneath his jacket, and Uzis under the seat.

It's a mad world when holy men travel with armed escorts, he thought. Or perhaps holy men are getting wiser—if Christ had had armed guards rather than sleeping apostles, he would not have ended on the cross, and if Gandhi had had these men, he could have finished his days in futile negotiations between Hindus and Moslems, not dead from an assassin's bullet. Perhaps the Ayatollah was cleverer than he supposed—that he had lived nearly eighty years was a tribute to more than his diet and circulation, Marshall felt.

He gazed out the window as the car sped down the autoroute past Orly, then he looked to the guards and Bishop; they sat so intense they could have been stone—or molded plastic, he thought, a child's toy soldiers.

The car turned off the toll route and raced down roads that grew more narrow, until finally it turned onto a dirt road.

From the hill Lord and Caldwell watched the little blip of dust rise in the distance. They scrunched into the ground, their rifles beside them.

Lord was having trouble with his glasses; he had to take them off frequently to wipe them because they fogged up from his breath in the chilly air.

The car slowed and pulled into the clearing. The bodyguards got out, searched the grove, then returned, holding the door for Bishop and Marshall, pointing them toward the grove. Then the two guards got back in the car and rolled down the windows to watch.

"What's Bishop doing here?" Lord whispered in alarm.

"I expected it," Caldwell said. "But he's harmless—he couldn't be armed."

While Bishop glanced about alert and on guard, Marshall sat on a stump, then reached down for pebbles and tossed them absently against tree trunks.

Bishop squatted on his haunches, his gaze sweeping the ground, then he moved into the clearing and bent over.

"What's he doing?" Lord demanded, wiping at his glasses.

Bishop's hand smoothed the ground, drew an outline, then he turned toward the hill, cocking his head. He moved closer and traced another outline.

"He sees footprints," Caldwell said. "He's marking them."

"What is he, a fucking Indian?" Lord snarled.

"He's good," Caldwell said in calm approval.

Bishop stood and looked to the top of the hill. Lord drew in his breath sharply.

"He can't see us," Caldwell said, but he did not like the

way Bishop kept staring, turning to the clearing, then back again toward the hill.

Suddenly the sun, momentarily hidden by a cloud, burst from behind it, showering light. Bishop blinked, blinded by the sun's reflection off something metal at the top of the hill.

Caldwell and Lord pulled their rifles away, but Bishop called to Marshall and pointed directly at them. As he ran toward the hill, the guards shouted. One jumped from the car with a gun, but Bishop started up the slope.

Bishop knew Caldwell was up there, and he was so outraged it did not occur to him to be afraid.

Just then, a trail of dust rose on the horizon.

The guards called more sharply. Bishop turned, saw the car in the distance, then moved up the hill with more determination, adrenaline pumping like in combat.

"Bastard," Lord hissed furiously.

Caldwell nodded in calm admiration. "Gutsy fucker," and he was thinking of d'Artagnan, who would do exactly this.

Both guards and the driver were shouting. Marshall called also, but Bishop was charging up the slope.

The car closed, only a hundred yards from the clearing now.

"A minute," Lord said wildly. "All we need is another minute."

Bishop stumbled, then catching himself continued to climb on all fours. Below, a black Mercedes sedan pulled into the clearing. Three guards jumped out. They saw a man on the hill and shouted to the other guards aiming rifles at Bishop.

Finally the rear door opened, revealing a black-shrouded, bearded figure.

But there was no time left. Bishop was on the crest of the hill; a few more steps and he would see them.

"Shoot him," Lord said desperately.

Caldwell brought his rifle into his shoulder.

"Now!" Lord ordered.

Caldwell sighted. It was such an easy target, a man only yards away; the bullet would explode his head or rip a hole through his heart. He touched the trigger and drew back on the flange.

Lord held his breath and glanced to the clearing. Marshall had stepped forward to greet the Imam.

Then the rifle beside him exploded.

Bishop went down, tumbling over and over.

Before Lord could sight into the clearing, guards pushed the shrouded figure back into the car and slammed the door, and the driver threw the vehicle into reverse.

Marshall dropped to the ground as his guards fired at the top of the hill.

Then Marshall jumped up and ran toward Bishop, hurtling down the hill, but before he got to him, Bishop somersaulted onto his feet and dove on top of Marshall, rolling him into the grove.

The guards continued to fire blindly, but by then Caldwell and Lord were already down the other side, racing toward their car.

"Are you all right?" Bishop shouted.

"Yes," Marshall gasped, looking for blood on Bishop but not seeing any. "I thought you were hit."

"I did too," Bishop said, feeling his arms and shoulders, sure there was a wound somewhere.

Then they both collapsed against trees, out of breath and overwhelmed.

The guards came into the grove and stood over them with rifles.

Marshall said soothingly in Persian between breaths, "Allah Akbar. God is great. We were lucky."

The two stared at him.

"Major Bishop just saved the Imam's life; if he hadn't gone up that hill, they would have shot us."

"Who were 'they'?" one of the guards demanded.

"I didn't get a look," Bishop said. "All I saw was the flash; I didn't know whether I was hit or fell, but the next thing I remembered was the bottom of the hill."

The guards were not sure what to do, or even if Marshall and Bishop had been part of a plot to assassinate the Ayatollah. Sensing their confusion and indecision, Marshall rose confidently. "Take me back," he said, then reached out to the tree again for support. "Jesus, Luke, I think you broke my back."

Bishop brushed at his trousers and jacket.

The guards debated; they had no instructions for this contingency. Finally one went to help Marshall: "Allah Akbar."

In the car Marshall and Bishop did not speak. Marshall feigned nonchalance, but it was a facade between poles of relief and anger: no one had been hurt, but his mission was a failure. There would never be contact with Khomeini now; he had not just failed, but doomed any future ties with Iran after the Shah fell.

"Drop me at Orly," he said to the driver. "I can get a taxi there; it wouldn't be wise for you to bring me to the embassy."

Ten minutes later, Marshall and Bishop got out at the passenger drop. When they settled into the taxi seat, Marshall turned to Bishop. "He could have hit you if he had wanted."

Bishop nodded.

"He *would* have killed Sergeant Mead, wouldn't he?"

Again Bishop nodded.

Marshall looked at his watch. It was shortly after one. "This was what you were talking about—your long-standing game?"

"Yes. And it isn't over."

CHAPTER 20

"You *meant* to miss," Lord accused as soon as he caught his breath when they returned to the car; he was angry, but not very.

"You told me a miss was as good as a hit," Caldwell answered complacently from behind the wheel, steering the car down the dirt road toward the autoroute. "What would have been the point in killing Bishop?"

Lord closed his eyes, resting back against the headrest. "Are you getting sentimental on me? You didn't want to kill a decorated Marine? It offended some sense of decency? He's a naïf."

Caldwell smiled out the window. "So was d'Artagnan. If it had *meant* anything, I would have shot him. But as soon as Bishop started up that hill, it was all over—there was no hope of getting Khomeini or Marshall. The bastard has balls, I'll give him that."

Lord settled into his seat comfortably, his breath and temper returned. "Jesus, Marshall is lucky. But it doesn't matter. Khomeini will never meet with a representative of America after this."

Lord had accomplished his mission, he knew; he had sown the seeds of chaos. Now it was up to others to nurture it into a foreign-policy nightmare Jimmy Carter could never control. Maybe it was even better this way, he mused, for now there were no bodies, no smoking guns, no one who even knew for sure what had happened, and when the debacle occurred, there would be no one to blame. Caldwell's sentiment might have worked for the best.

Lord turned to him. "What happened to d'Artagnan, by the way? Didn't that woman kill him? I certainly hope so."

Caldwell shook his head. "That was another story. D'Artagnan had a long life. He and Rochefort, the cardinal's spy, fought many times—always to a draw."

"I don't like draws, Mike. I'm prepared to forgive your lapse today on one condition only—you never do it again. I'll allow sentimentality *once.* You've used yours. Now your career is in the balance. I don't like threatening people, but I want to make this absolutely clear—you will do *exactly* what I tell you from now on. I am working for people with extraordinary influence and power—they will be around long after Carter and Admiral Turner are gone. Do *not* question what I tell you. Understand?"

Caldwell met his eyes. He had reached the line at last, and it was only a mark in the sand after all. The decision was much easier than he had expected; actually he was disappointed how little he had to debate. He nodded to Lord. "Yes, sir, I understand."

When Marshall returned to his office, he went to a cabinet and poured a tumbler of Scotch. Christ; how was he going to explain this to Carter? he wondered. He himself wasn't sure what had happened. What could he prove, and who would believe it?

He was sipping Scotch when Helen knocked and entered. She looked at her watch. "Happy hour already?"

"It's either this or an ambulance. No more phone calls."

"Not even Mr. Crazy?"

"Especially Mr. Crazy."

"What about the President?"

He threw the drink down his throat. "*Especially* the President."

Helen glanced at the paper in her hand. "How about . . . Fu Manchu?"

Marshall poured another drink.

"A Chinese man called; he said you would know who he

was. He said he would call back. He sounded *very* strange, like someone you'd want to talk with."

Marshall put down his glass and said evenly, "Yes. I'll take that call; thank you, Helen."

So here it was, Marshall thought. The uncertainty was over, the conflict was out in the open. He went to his desk and sat. As a child he had been taught that one paid for one's sins—one was rewarded or punished according to one's deeds. It was a mathematical equation, life's acts recorded as pluses or minuses, the final sum settled by a scrupulous god. But as he grew older, saw war and horror, suffering that transcended any geometry, he put away the childish calculations of divinity.

He no longer feared God, but *chance,* a roulette of horror that could not be explained by science, mathematics, or religion. He was always waiting for the ball to drop into his life. It had once before, with Ryan's death, and now he waited for it again. He knew every terror—accidents, drunken drivers, madmen, disease—and looked each in the face every time he thought of Sarah and Chris. Always in his mind was the fear that tragedy would befall them, and it would be *his* fault.

Helen buzzed him on the intercom. "Mr. Huong is on the line."

Marshall drew a deep breath as he picked up the phone. "Yes."

A confident voice said in slightly accented English, "I will meet you tomorrow night. Can you think of the most appropriate place, Excellency?"

Marshall did not answer.

"Probably you cannot. Are you familiar with the Deportation Memorial?"

"I am. On the Ile-de-France, just in back of Notre Dame."

"Perhaps you have attended commemorative ceremonies there."

"No," Marshall said. "It does not figure significantly in French memory."

"I didn't imagine so. It would be so much easier if everything were forgotten, wouldn't it? Except there are all those *bodies.* And their survivors. Ten o'clock tomorrow night. Alone."

Marshall held the dead phone until a recorded message told him to hang up.

When Bishop returned to his office, Mead was behind the door and slammed it shut after he entered. Bishop whirled, then relaxed.

"I've never hit an officer before," Mead said threateningly.

"Now wouldn't be a good time to start, Sergeant," Bishop said, taking off his jacket to change back into his uniform.

"Why'd you do that to me, sir? You had no right."

"I know, but it was the only thing I could think of to get you out of the way. You wouldn't have obeyed my order because you were on a higher order from the ambassador. I'm sorry I caused you to worry about your wife—that was shitty."

Mead shook his head. "*That's* what saved you, Major. I was so worried, and so pissed at you, that on the way back to rip you apart, I saw you'd been right about Sung and me. I was stupid to have thought about leaving her—I couldn't have stood that. Thinking that something had happened to her made me see that. You helped me before, Major, but now we're even. Don't fuck with my head again. *Sir.*"

Bishop held out his hand. "Deal. I'll level with you from now on. But this time I had to trick you; Lord and Caldwell were waiting for Marshall and Khomeini. They would have shot you."

"Why didn't they shoot you?"

"Lord would have—he *did* before. But I didn't think Caldwell could—it was just a gut feeling. You know how it is in combat—sometimes you have to go with a hunch. I thought that in the final second, he wouldn't do it. And he didn't."

"Then everything's finished? It's all over with?"

"Oh, no; now Ambassador Marshall needs us more than ever. Someone is going to try to kill him and his family in the next couple days. All he has is us. But this time it's not just us against Lord and Caldwell—there's a Chinese man. He killed one Marine, and a Sûreté agent; this is going to be a lot tougher."

"Do you have a plan?"

Bishop shook his head. "Not yet, but I will tomorrow. I think that's when they're going to try to get his family."

"Just tell me what you want me to do."

Caldwell's door was open and he was waiting, feet propped on his desk, when Bishop appeared in the doorway at five. "I've been waiting for you, Lukey."

Bishop closed the door. "I can't decide whether to kill you or thank you."

"Thank me. You won't have another chance."

"There won't *be* another chance, Mike."

"That depends on you. Don't get in the way again. I won't give you another break."

Bishop turned for the door. "I won't count on one."

Caldwell stopped him. "Luke, you counted on me pulling that shot. It was gutsy, and I admire what you did, but understand something—we're playing hardball from now on."

"It's the only way I know how to play, Mike."

"It could be a rough game, Lukey."

Bishop went to the door. "You're on."

"There's good news and bad news, Sarah; which do you want first?" Marshall asked when they sat down for dinner in the huge dining room lit only by candles.

"Since it's Sarah, let's hear the bad news," Chris said.

"Let's say grace first," Catherine said.

Sarah looked startled. "Jesus, is the news *that* bad?"

Catherine bowed her head. "Thank you, Lord, for all our blessings. For food, for health, for each other."

Chris grabbed his glass of wine. "What is this crap, Mother? We've never said grace."

"I'm trying something new—maybe *prayer* will work."

"I'll give you the good news first—I promised Luke you'd have dinner with him tomorrow."

Sarah bowed her head. "We better say grace again, Mother; the last one didn't work. Jesus! If Luke Bishop is the good news, what's the *bad* news?"

"The Chinese man called a short while ago; I'm going to meet him tomorrow night."

There was complete silence.

"Obviously prayer doesn't work at all," Catherine said;

then she slammed down her glass. "That is *insane.* For God's sake, Brad, don't."

"It'll be all right. And I don't see any other way."

"You're not going alone, are you?" Chris asked.

"He doesn't want to hurt me. He wants you and Sarah—that's why I have to meet with him face-to-face. I know I can deal with him."

"Well, take someone with you," Catherine said. "Talk to Floyd. Or take Luke."

"Luke is going to be with you. Besides, I have to go alone or he won't meet with me. He's not stupid—he's picked a perfectly isolated place. He'll know if someone is with me. This is going to work; I know it."

Marshall looked to them reassuringly, but he only saw fear in their eyes.

Huong wrenched awake in the middle of the night. Dull pain gripped his stomach as he lay in bed; he had lived with pain since the death of his daughter, but this was different, not the pain of loss, but of *fear,* and not personal fear, for he did not care about himself any longer, but fear that he would fail, that everything he had worked and suffered for would be lost.

He had come so far, had suffered so much, was so close.

Many times, Huong had read the story of Job, which the old priest had told him long ago, searching for meaning, but he never found the one that was taught. In the Bible, after all his losses, Job was restored and rewarded.

But *his* daughter was not going to be returned to life. Or his wife. Or mother. He didn't care about money or possessions. Did Job care about cattle and sheep?

He wanted what could not be restored, so instead he wanted revenge, not against God, but against the mortal man who had caused his grief. He wanted eye for eye. Was the denial of this to be his final punishment and humiliation, God's last cruel joke?

The nightmare that woke him, the pain that gouged his soul, was that he would fail.

Huong sat up and brought his legs over the side of the bed. No! He would not fail.

Everything was arranged. Lord had confirmed that Marshall's family was going to the Opera and their car would be unattended for the Iraqi to attach a triggering device that would set off the explosion when it passed a car parked a short distance away. Money bought most anything, killing or couture, and what it didn't buy, other coin—hate or jealousy—could.

Huong lay back and took a deep breath. His pain ebbed. He would avenge his daughter, his wife, and his mother. They would finally rest in peace.

He closed his eyes. He was not Job; he did not want to be Job. He did not want to forgive nor be forgiven. He wanted revenge. And he would have it tomorrow.

In a moment he was asleep, and this time there was no nightmare; his daughter was not dead in the street, there was no boat, no screams from his wife and mother, and he saw a clear blue ocean with a smooth surface.

He slept peacefully for the first time in years.

CHAPTER 21

"Catherine, why don't you sleep in some morning," Marshall said when he came downstairs for breakfast. "Surely you could use the sleep, and *I* could use the peace."

"I think it says a lot for a marriage when a man and wife breakfast together after thirty years."

He went to the side table for eggs and bacon and poured coffee. "Your breakfasting with me has nothing to do with devotion. It merely provides you with an opportunity to hammer me before anyone else."

"Nonsense; I am interested in your welfare, and you need reminding of things."

"What this morning?"

"That you are a fool to meet with the Chinese man. He is a murderer and he wants to kill our children."

"That could have waited until dinner."

"I plan to bring it up then too. You *are* insane to do this. Really, Brad! Was I wrong about Khomeini and the CIA?"

"We went over this last night, Catherine. The man doesn't plan to harm me. I *have* to meet him. I can't have him murdered—what is wrong with you? I'm sure we can resolve our problem when we get together."

"You are sounding very pompous, and vastly underestimating the danger."

"The danger is to Sarah and Chris, but tonight they'll be at the ballet with Luke and Floyd's men—they'll be safe. If

I can't reason with him, then I'll talk with Jarre, and if that doesn't work, I'll consider other means."

"Why don't you kill him if you have the opportunity; it may be your only chance. You could take a gun and shoot him."

He stared at her. "Jesus Christ, Catherine. Are you serious?"

"Yes, damn it, I am. If that man plans to murder your children, you *should* kill him."

"I can reason with him," he said firmly.

"Like you were able to reason with Wilson Lord and the CIA? Aren't you still worried about them?"

He shook his head. "They accomplished what they wanted; I imagine both Lord and Caldwell are already out of the country. Their goal was to stop me from meeting with Khomeini; they succeeded—I'll never hear from Khomeini or his people again."

"Brad—"

"Catherine! I am not Macbeth, but the representative of the United States government, and I am not going to gun down a man in cold blood no matter how much you harangue me, so just stop it."

Catherine's chair crashed to the floor as she furiously left the room.

In his office, after his customary five minutes, one of which he devoted to speculating what Helen would have on today, she entered with his briefing papers and appointments log, wearing a long floral Laura Ashley dress with a high Victorian collar and lace bib, and on her feet were rounded patent-leather Mary Jane shoes.

"It's a full day, mostly ceremonial—lots of chitchat and photo ops. The White House called during the night. The President wants to talk to you at two-fifty. I've set aside one and a half minutes."

"One and a half minutes?"

"He's not famous for small talk, Brad." Helen glanced at her notes. "The only other thing is for you to decide on tomorrow night. There's a reception at the Grand Palais—the American surrealists exhibit you're supposed to open, then a dinner at St. James for the benefactors: GM or Three M, or maybe it's M&M's, I forget."

"What American surrealists? Never mind, I don't want to know. Let Catherine decide."

The day passed quickly; he had a working lunch with his senior staff, then held a series of short meetings. Knowing the President's schedule was to the minute, he returned to his office at two forty-five for Carter's call. He hated the scramble phone; there was an annoying time delay that caused conversation overlaps, and the voices sounded mechanical, without inflections or emphasis, but it was secure and allowed them to talk freely.

The call came at exactly two-fifty. "Bradley," an eerie voice said.

"Good morning, Mr. President."

"I understand you were not successful in contacting the individual we discussed."

That was an understatement, Marshall thought, but said, "We had a brief encounter but were interrupted. Further contact is going to be difficult, if not impossible. Paranoid might best describe his reaction to what occurred, though it might be justified."

"What are you telling me?"

"I am telling you that my failure might be understood if one considered the parties who did not want contact to occur—with particular emphasis on a certain party headquartered geographically closer to you than to me."

"I understand."

Marshall could almost see the frozen smile, the lips pursing in annoyance.

"I want you to try again."

"I would have a better chance of success if you signaled that the administration was distancing itself from Baghdad."

"That won't be necessary; I'm sure you'll succeed otherwise. Good-bye, Bradley," said the voice through teeth that could bite the phone in half.

Marshall looked at his watch. One minute and eleven seconds.

Jesus, he thought, then buzzed Helen to call the Syrian ambassador. Saud Asari was his only contact to the Ayatollah's people.

Within moments, Asari was on the line, his voice strained and tense. "That was quick; those AWACs certainly work. Did you call to offer me asylum or to say good-bye?"

"You've been recalled?"

"Asked to return for 'consultations.' You know what *that* means." Asari didn't bother to disguise his anxiety.

"Is this because of our conversation?"

"The word is that your people tried to assassinate him, but he was spared by Allah. What happened benefited him; it was a disaster for reason and moderation, and I am going to be the first to suffer because I put you in contact with him."

Indeed Marshall knew what "consultations" meant—in Asari's case, probably a firing squad. This was an unforeseen side effect of his overture to Khomeini. By merely touching a brush to the Mideast canvas, the picture had been ruined, and his dabbling had brought the fall of his friend. "I owe you a favor, Saud."

"What good would it do? My children are in Damascus. If I don't return, they'll have to pay the penalty."

"You are forgetting our influence. We could bring pressure to prevent that."

"You would do this for me?"

"We're having a reception tomorrow night at the Grand Palais—some horrifying exhibit that will confirm everyone's belief that we have no aesthetic sense. You will love it. Bring Clarissa. Six P.M. I'll take care of you from there. If we announce that you are going to the U.S. for emergency medical treatment for a life-threatening illness, or perhaps to have a sex-change operation, it will soon be forgotten in future Mideastern upheavals."

"A sex-change operation?"

"Jarre is having one too."

There was a pause. "Thank you; I'll see you tomorrow night."

Marshall buzzed Helen again. "Get me the secretary of state. A one-minute phone call from the President usually requires hours of follow-up calls."

Two hours was what it took; it was five before Marshall finished the arrangements for getting Asari to the United States. He hadn't touched the paperwork on his desk, but the afternoon had passed quickly, taking his mind off meeting Huong tonight.

"How come I haven't seen Luke today?" he asked Helen as he prepared to leave.

"He has a date with Sarah tonight; I'm sure he's been primping."

"Primping what? He doesn't have any hair to comb."

"Sarah doesn't either. I suppose now I'll have to get mine cut too."

"You're fired if you do."

When he returned to the residence, his family and Luke were in the living room. He went to the bar and poured a Scotch. "Anything for anyone? Another Moonride, Catherine?"

"I'm on the wagon today. We all are."

"I'm not."

"You *should* be. Wouldn't it help to be sober when someone is trying to kill you?"

He turned to Luke in slacks and a sport coat on the sofa beside Sarah. "What a nice tie. Does it have a lucky past too?"

Bishop grinned. "We were just waiting until you got here."

"Are you sure you haven't changed your mind, Dad?" Sarah asked "It's not too late—you can still forbid me to go. I'll mind."

"Yeah, then I can go out with Luke," Chris said.

"His chances with you are *much* better than they are with me."

Sarah kissed both her parents, then went out the door with Bishop.

"They make a lovely couple," Marshall said after them.

"They look like two Marines. Or two dykes," Chris said.

"I'll have a drink after all," Catherine said. "Make it a Kneewalker."

"I've never gone out with someone with a flattop," Bishop said to Sarah as he drove his Citroën out the residence gate. It was just before six, but completely dark; the night was not cold, and faint mist refracted the light of the city into a million particles.

She leaned against the passenger door to study him. "Well, you're the first psychopath I've been out with." She reconsidered. "Actually, maybe not, but they weren't *paid* for it—it wasn't their *job.*"

"I don't get paid much."

"Oh, I think you'd do it for free, Luke. But I have to admit, a Deux Chevaux isn't the car I thought you'd own; I was expecting a red Corvette with zebra-skin seats and a garter hanging from the rearview mirror."

"You see, you don't know me at all. You have a stereotype image of me, some crazed killer without brains or sensitivity. I am a *very* sensitive guy."

"Right. And you kill people with love and tenderness."

"The world isn't a nice place, Sarah. Some people, like your dad, float above it on cloud-level nine: doors are opened for them, security arranged, appointments made, passages cleared. They talk. But that's not the real world—a lot has to happen before these people get to talk and decide things for the rest of us."

He accelerated onto the boulevard and headed toward the center of the city. "It's like electricity—there's more to it than flipping the switch."

"Or a toilet—there's more than pulling the handle."

He smiled. "Now we're talking *my* job—national sanitation engineer."

"Somebody's got to do it, right?"

"You better hope so. You better pray those guys you sneer at keep joining the Marines, and army, and police forces—someday you might need them."

"I've heard that fascist line before. But there will always be psychopaths, good *and* bad ones. They're not in it for glory or money. You're not."

"Nope. It's a way to meet girls; like this."

"Then you better find a new career, Luke."

"But I *like* my job."

The car traveled down the Right Bank, past the Louvre, and the Conciergerie. He crossed the Seine at Notre Dame and pointed to the cathedral. "It's just a calling—like football or the priesthood. It sounds stupid, but I had to do something for my country, and since nobody asked me to be ambassador, I had to find something else. I'm like a warrior bee—my job is to protect the hive, sting and die."

He hit his head. "Dumb, I know, but I guess we serve a purpose."

She stared at him for a long minute framed in the window against the cathedral. "You'd die to protect me, wouldn't you? You would have long ago in Saigon. Dad says you almost got killed yesterday saving him."

She frowned at the thought. Jim said he loved her—but would *he* die for her? Would he have saved her father? "This isn't a joke, is it, Luke? Someone is trying to kill Chris and me."

"I think so."

"And here you are in the middle of it—warrior bee to the rescue. Are you afraid?"

He shook his head. "I've seen too much death to be afraid of it. It's like the dark, inevitable. You can't keep your eyes open forever, so you might as well trust and go to sleep. What's the choice? Are you afraid?"

She looked back to the Right Bank, a beckoning carnival of night. "You know, I tried not to be afraid of the dark, but I always was."

"The dark comes every night," he said gently.

"I was afraid every night."

"Did it do any good?"

She stared at him levelly. "It prepared me for nights like this."

"You're going to be all right. I'm not going to let anything happen."

"What *is* it about you? I am not your type, Luke."

He grinned. "You're exactly my type—well, you with longer hair."

There was little traffic on the Left Bank; shops and galleries were closed, but the night life would not start for hours, so he had no trouble finding a parking place. He jumped out to open the door for her, but before he could, she was on the sidewalk.

"I'll give you a choice of places to eat—there's a great Thai restaurant a couple blocks that way, or an excellent Japanese one in the other direction. If those don't appeal to you, we can hit the freak show at Le Procope. The food sucks, but the ambience is great, and the red upholstery is what you'd expect to find in a Corvette with a garter belt."

She stared at him. "You've rehearsed this, right? Otherwise I'd have to consider that I might have been wrong about you."

"I told you—you can't see beyond the stereotype." He put his arm around her. "What's your preference?"

She smiled. "You haven't done anything wrong yet—you choose."

"Japanese. They need the business—it's a new place run by some young guys and they're not doing well; the French eat all kinds of strange shit, but they get squeamish about sushi."

She stopped on the sidewalk and turned to him. "You *did* rehearse."

He laughed. "Sarah, I know how I come across to you, and I know I should have been putting on some act so you'd think differently of me, but I can't *be* anything I'm not, so I never bothered. I'm not stupid, and I've gone out with a couple women before—I understand that a guy shouldn't put his heart on the floor for a woman to stomp on, but with you . . . well, I fell in love long ago, and I never saw any reason to hide it. I just hoped that sooner or later you'd see me for what I really am."

When they got to the restaurant, Bishop was greeted familiarly; he bowed and said good evening in Japanese.

"Can you handle the sushi, or would you rather have cooked fare?"

"I'll have what you order."

"I don't order. They just bring me what they're specializing in that day."

"That's fine with me. How often do you come here?"

He told the owner to bring enough for two and ordered beer. "A couple times a week, usually for lunch, but at least one night. I eat out a lot; I'm not much of a cook."

"Are your girlfriends sushi eaters? I'll bet they're more the meat type."

He pointed admonishingly. "You're stereotyping me again."

"Not in this case; I've heard about your girlfriends."

"I don't have a girlfriend, Sarah. I've been waiting for

you. Everybody I've gone out with has just been marking time."

"You're right, Luke—you *shouldn't* say these things to a woman."

"Why? Should I lie? Play a role you might like and fall for? Act uninterested?"

He poured beer for her, then gave her the bottle to pour for him, explaining it was a form of Japanese politeness. Then he raised his glass to her. "You're a smart woman, Sarah, liberated and funny, beautiful and worldly, you do good work, you help people, you're kind and generous—am I supposed to pretend I don't think you're terrific? You're everything I'd want a woman to be. I know I've aspired beyond myself, but I can't help it. I just hope someday you'll see beyond the false image you have of me. I know I'm no genius, won't live in a mansion or drive a Rolls, but I have some pretty decent attributes."

She raised her eyebrows.

He smiled. "That too, but kind and loyal and loving besides."

She laughed, then said seriously, "I never doubted that, Luke. No one who knows you could question your loyalty. Or kindness either."

He dropped his head. "Aw."

A platter of raw fish was put before them, along with two plates and chopsticks.

She shook her head. "I guess my problem *has* been that I saw you as shallow, but I still don't understand some things."

"What?"

"Like the Marines, all your macho posturing, all your *loyalty*. How do you justify it to yourself?"

"With a bunch of old clichés—duty, honor, courage. But if you're so smart, what's the real reason?"

"The same one that sent my brother to Vietnam—the one Ryan died for: a *sense* of duty, honor, and courage. There's a big difference—nature versus nurture."

Bishop popped raw tuna into his mouth. "This is *way* above me."

"It doesn't matter. As much as men drive me insane, I

know there's fundamental decency about you. I suppose it's irrelevant whether it's innate or tribal custom."

"You have a higher opinion of men than I do. As much as women drive me nuts, I think they're more decent."

"We are. But then, I wouldn't be risking my life for people. I wouldn't fight for my 'buddies' or sisters—flag or country. That's *nature,* because if women fought and sacrificed themselves for the stupid things men do, the species would end quickly."

"Good thing I'm going to save you, not Denise—she's one of Floyd's people."

She laughed. "Maybe I can take care of myself."

He studied her a moment. "Maybe." He ordered two more beers and they tried the different fish. "That's squid. And this one is eel," he said.

"I'll pass on that."

"No, try it—you might find you have a misconception about eel too."

They talked lightly for another twenty minutes as they ate, and when they finished the platter, Bishop looked at his watch, then called for the check. "It's seven-thirty. We have to leave. I'd rather go somewhere alone with you, but I told your folks I'd bring you to the Opera House."

She smiled. "I had a very nice time, Luke. Thank you for dinner."

"Can we do it again?"

She considered. "Yes. But you must understand, I'm serious about Jim."

He held her chair. "I'm sure he's a great guy."

When they left the restaurant, she suddenly shivered. "Is my dad safe, tonight?"

"I assume he knows what he's doing; it isn't up to me to question what he does. My job is to protect you."

She took his arm and they walked back toward the car. "Do you really think someone will try to kill me?"

"Yes," Bishop said evenly. "But don't worry, I'll jump in front of the bullet."

"Is that what it will be?"

He shrugged. "I have no idea. We'll just play it by ear."

"You mean you don't have a plan?"

"I have many. I'll have to improvise. It's like football: you might want to throw into the end zone, but everyone's covered, so you run up the middle."

"You are not comforting me with idiot sports analogies."

"I wish Denise were here to explain this better." He smiled. "Trust me."

She stared into his eyes. "I hate to admit something so sexist, but I'd trust a lot of guys with my life, men I'd never even think of going to bed with."

Bishop laughed. "You've got a real gentle way about you, like Lizzie Borden."

"I've gone out with a lot of guys who would have jumped in front of a bullet for me, not because I was beautiful, but because it was in their *ethic,* a tribal custom to protect their woman, even if he was a real loser. I suppose there's honor even among losers."

"Are you trying to tell me something?"

When they reached the car, she faced him. "I am telling you that I trust you for the same reason I trusted my brother. Any girl could have trusted Ryan."

He put his arm around her gently. "That's the nicest thing anyone ever said to me."

They were parked along the Quay St.-Michel overlooking the Seine. Across the river was Notre Dame and the Palace of Justice illuminated in the haze.

She looked into his eyes and could see her reflection, and she saw his face moving closer, blocking both church and court, and her mouth parted slightly as his lips pressed to hers ever so gently, more gently than she had ever remembered a kiss. His hands lightly drew her nearer as his mouth opened, but it was her tongue seeking his, and still he was so gentle, and then finally she pushed him away.

"I *knew* you would kiss great," she said.

"I never kissed like that before." He pulled her back, closing her eyes with his lips, then kissing her neck.

She pushed him away. "Stop it. This isn't even our first date."

"You mean there's a chance?" He asked it so hopefully that she laughed.

"Luke, if I ever need help, you'd be the first man I'd go to."

"Remember that. I won't forget you said it."

She nodded seriously. "I won't either. If it doesn't work with Jim, I'll be back."

"Then I'll see you soon; I know you're going to change your mind about me."

"How do you know?"

He just smiled. He couldn't tell her because it was all indistinct in his mind; it had to do with Elysium, but he could never explain that.

Bishop believed in Elysium; it was a place where men fought and drank and did manly things, but women were there too, women to love and honor, and children also. It was a place where everyone lived happily ever after. And Bishop knew, he just knew, it was a place you could get to on this earth.

He opened her door. "Thanks for giving me a chance. You won't regret it."

"You don't think I'd regret being a Marine officer's wife?"

"Why would you? You could still do good work. There are lots of battered Marine wives you could help."

"I'm sure, but I don't want to be one of them."

"Do you think I'd ever hit a woman? Someone I loved?" When she didn't answer, he said, "How about if I gave up the Marines—would that make a difference?"

"You'd *do* that?"

"If that was the only way you'd take me seriously, yes."

"But what would you *do?"*

He grinned. "Oh, I'm sure there are other ways to serve my country—other ways to kill people for a living."

She smiled as she settled into the seat, thinking seriously about him for the first time, but when he got in the car, her face betrayed nothing of course.

CHAPTER 22

When Bishop pulled into an illegal parking space in back of the Garnier Opera House, he saw Marshall's limousine behind a chain-link security fence. Getting out of his car, Bishop jumped the fence and walked around the limousine.

"Where's Marcel?" he asked Sarah behind him. "And Floyd's men? There's supposed to be someone with the car at all times; it should never be unattended." He tried the doors; they were locked, as well as the hood and trunk, but he was still unhappy.

"Don't you *ever* go off duty?" she asked. "The car's safe; no one can get in, and the area's well lit. Maybe Marcel went for coffee. What can happen? I'm sure everything is all right." She pulled on his arm. "We have to go; they won't seat us if we're late."

"This isn't right. I don't like it."

"But Dad isn't even here," she said reasonably.

Bishop turned to her with a look in his eyes that she had seen only once before, that day in Saigon when he had brought her to Teresa's clinic—absolutely single-minded and resolute. He said slowly, "Right," then he took her hand. "Let's go to the ballet."

They joined an immense crowd streaming into the Opera House and went up the grand staircase. In the bar and lounges, waiters with trays of champagne moved among tuxedoed men and women in evening gowns. Marble floors, gleaming chandeliers, and mirrors created radiant brightness, and the sounds of popping corks, clinking glasses, and laughter gave the rooms a warm glow of celebration.

Chris saw them enter the lounge and waved them over. "Behave yourself?" he asked when Bishop and Sarah joined him and Catherine.

"Absolutely," Bishop answered, coming to an approximation of attention and bowing, heels nearly clicking. "Good evening, Mrs. Marshall."

She smiled at the ceremony he always performed for her.

"Don't you love it when he does that?" Chris asked. "Do they teach that at embassy school?"

"As a matter of fact, they do," Luke said, clicking and bowing again.

Sarah kissed her mother and her brother. "We had a lovely dinner. I learned some fascinating things about Luke."

"She learned I was terrifically sensitive and she'll marry me as soon as she dumps her professor."

Catherine grabbed Chris's arm. "Go get me a tray of drinks," she said.

"There's no need, Mother; Luke is *wildly* exaggerating."

Chris put his arm around his sister. "Sarah?"

She turned to him.

Chris smiled. "Think about it."

The lights were dimmed, signaling the audience to take their seats.

Catherine turned to Bishop and said pointedly, "I'm worried about Brad. Don't you think you should be with him tonight? It's not too late. He's still at home."

Bishop shook his head. "Ambassador Marshall told me to stay with you."

"It's called 'duty' and 'loyalty,' " Sarah said. "Luke has them in *abundance.*"

"I'm curious about the car though," Bishop said, turning to Chris. "Did Marcel drive tonight?"

Chris shook his head. "There was another driver; one I've never seen."

"Were Floyd's security men with you?"

"Yes, several of them," Catherine said. "They brought us to the door. Is something wrong?"

"They're not with the car now."

Sarah put her arm in his. "Luke is just trying to get out of seeing the performance. Take his other arm, Mother."

"That's not it. Something isn't right. Maybe I should check again. It'll only take a minute. I'll be right back."

Chris gripped his shoulder. "Nice try, Marine, but you're going to this ballet. If I have to watch this shit, you do too. Check at intermission."

Bishop debated. He looked to Sarah, then relented. "All right." He followed them to their seats, but first he searched the box.

Sarah tugged on his jacket. "Relax! See that chandelier? It weighs six tons. Look at the ceiling. Aren't the paintings wonderful? Chagall did them."

Bishop glanced up without interest. "They look like cartoons." Then he leaned out of the box to view below.

"Sit down!" Sarah hissed. "That's the orchestra pit, not a machine-gun nest."

The lights went out and the audience applauded the conductor's approach to the podium. He bowed to the audience, lifted his baton, and the overture began.

At eight-thirty, Marshall summoned André to his office. "Lend me your coat and hat and your car."

"But, Excellency . . . ," his valet began.

"I'm a good driver, André; I'll get your car back safely. I just need to step out for a while, and no one can know."

"They'll recognize you as you go out the gate," André pointed out sensibly.

"But then it'll be too late—I'll be gone," Marshall said in satisfaction.

André did not share Marshall's pleasure at outwitting his security, but he nodded in compliance and handed him his car keys; then he brought his coat and hat. It was of a quality as good as his own, Marshall noted; maybe better, he reconsidered, checking the label.

At nine he went out to the garage in back where the staff parked. André's Renault was a much flashier model than he would have expected of his valet, and though Marshall hadn't driven a stick shift in years, he maneuvered the car up the driveway to the security gate without trouble.

Seeing the familiar car, the guard opened the electronic gates, then recognizing Marshall, he ran out of the booth, but Marshall merely waved and drove off.

He had given himself plenty of time because he had never driven in Paris and was unsure of directions, or if he'd find a place to park anywhere near the cathedral, but he found a spot on the Ile de la Cité by the flower market, not far from Notre Dame.

The earlier light rain had turned into a wet mist. He buttoned his overcoat and walked toward the massive edifice, its Gothic towers a haunting specter in the dark. Water dripped from the mouths of gargoyles into the street. Sheltered marble saints and martyrs peered from crooks and niches, and the huge bronze doors sealed the cathedral from temporal intrusion.

He stared at the acid-eaten figures carved seven hundred years ago, and dead a thousand before that, then he noticed a large rat crouching in the gutter before the church. The rat raised its head and bared its teeth at his approach.

Marshall moved closer. The rat snarled, then turned and ran toward the river.

He walked to the gutter and saw a broken egg, its yolk mingling with rainwater, streaming toward the drain, the gnawed embryo slick with oil from cars, swirling as it disappeared into the sewer.

He looked up. Directly in front of him was the Portal of the Last Judgment. On the tympanum was carved the Resurrection; above was the Weighing of Souls, the saved being led to heaven, the damned to hell.

It was inevitable that he was here, he knew. It was true, after all: one did pay for one's sins and misdeeds—the calculations were meticulously kept.

He looked at his watch; it was ten before the hour.

He walked to the gate on the side of the cathedral. Looking through he saw a gravel path leading past the flying buttresses to John XXIII Square, and beyond to the Square of the Ile-de-France where the Deportation Memorial stood at the tip.

He pushed on the metal gate and went in. He did not notice a man watching him from the shadows.

* * *

At intermission, the boxes emptied. "Isn't it wonderful?" Sarah said.

Bishop nodded as he followed them to the lounge. "It's okay," he allowed grudgingly. "I've never been to an opera before."

Chris smiled. "It's a ballet."

"Never been to one of those either."

"And aren't those mice cute," Sarah taunted.

"I like the prince," Luke said. "He reminds me of me."

"If you could dance like that, I *might* marry you."

"I'll start lessons tomorrow. I'd look great in those tights, but I'd need a bigger cup." Then he checked his pocket for his ticket stub. "I'm going to look at the car. I'll be right back."

"Want me to go with you?" Chris asked.

"No. You stay here; don't any of you leave without me."

Bishop walked out of the lounge, down the staircase, and passed through the doors. A dense crowd was on the steps smoking cigarettes and cigars. He bounded down the stairs and walked around the Opera House toward Marshall's limousine.

The area was deserted; the lights in the lot were out and Marshall's limousine was barely visible in the darkness.

Bishop stared for a long time, then he stepped over the chain and went to the car.

"You *are* good," Caldwell said in admiration from the shadows. He had a pistol in his hand and Bishop saw its silencer. "Dedicated and loyal. A real fucking hero. I *knew* you were going to show up, just like at the hill—the U.S. Marines to the rescue. I'd have been disappointed if you hadn't come; in fact, you would have really fucked things up if you hadn't. Put your hands out where I can see them and come here."

Bishop lifted his hands and stepped toward him. "You're not going to do this."

Caldwell smiled with utterly cold eyes.

Bishop shook his head. "I don't believe it, Mike. You're not going to hurt Marshall's family—Jesus Christ, you're talking innocent people, two women and a kid."

"Save the psychology, Luke—I have a job to do."

Bishop stood before him. Caldwell pressed the pistol against his temple. Bishop didn't move or flinch.

"Aren't you going to ask me about this? I mean, like in the movies—you get me to tell you what it's all about, then miraculously save the day?"

Bishop shrugged. "Hey, do what you have to do. I been shot in the head before."

Caldwell laughed harshly. "You *are* something else."

"All right then, tell me the plan while I come up with some miracle way to get out of this. But I'm warning you, I might—you know how movies end."

Caldwell pressed the barrel harder against Bishop's head. "The plan's simple—shoot you, stuff your body in the trunk, then go inside and inform Mrs. Marshall that something happened to the ambassador and you had to leave. Then I'll escort them to the car, which will drive them back to the embassy—or rather, down the boulevard where an unfortunate accident will occur."

"Oh, bullshit," Bishop said in disgust. "No one's going to buy that crap."

"Who cares? The idea, as Wilson Lord puts it, is to create chaos. This will work *real* well." He cocked the trigger on the pistol and started to pull on the trigger flange. "Come up with the miracle yet?"

Bishop nodded. "Yeah. I have. Want to hear it?"

"Sure. Let's see if it's as good as the one I would have come up with if my ass were in your shoes."

Marshall stood on the Square of the Ile-de-France.

The upstream point of the island was deserted. In back of him loomed the Cathedral, and before him was a view of the entire east end of Paris, including Ile St.-Louis, its lights shimmering in reflection on the river. A few yards away on the tip was the secluded memorial to the deported Jews in World War II and the tomb of the Unknown Deportee.

Marshall drew himself up and walked to the marble monument, then descended the stairs to a platform area.

A man was sitting on a marble bench staring across the river, his back to Marshall; he wore an overcoat and held an umbrella in his lap.

"Mr. Huong?"

The man merely raised his head. Marshall stepped closer, then sat beside him. He followed the man's gaze to the brightly lit top floor of a building on the Left Bank.

"Have you eaten there?" Huong asked flatly.

"Tour d'Argent? Yes."

"Did you ever contemplate the view from there to here?"

"No."

"I suppose not." Huong turned to him with an expression so severe that his eyes burned like coals. "Those who dine in a place like that would never dwell on a place like this. They would eat their sumptuous meal and drink their fine wine, see the bright lights of the city and marvel at its beauty with no thought to any suffering they had caused."

"We should have met long ago."

Huong's eyes hooded. "Indeed, but you seemed in a rush that day."

"I didn't know what happened; I had no idea. I am sorry; I seek forgiveness."

"Your condolences are too late. Forgiveness is no longer possible."

Marshall looked to the urns surrounding him, then he took a deep breath. "I came alone. This is between us. I am here to plead for my children. I will do anything."

"I imagine you would. There is nothing I would not do to have my child back."

Marshall's hands pressed together in his lap. "What happened was an accident."

Huong's lips barely parted. "Death is not divided into chambers; the accidentally dead are no closer to the living than the intentionally dead. My daughter is as dead under the wheels of your limousine as if you had shot her in the heart. Or had her napalmed."

"I meant her no harm. You must distinguish between an accidental death and an intentional one."

"The unalterable fact is the death, not the intent. Perhaps it wasn't your intent to kill her, but you did. Then you covered it up and tried to ruin me—you *did* ruin me. I was hounded by the government for years because of you. They took everything I had, and I could not even leave because they took my passport too—all this done to protect you. You never once thought of me or my suffering."

Marshall did not speak for a moment, then he sighed. "I am prepared to accept the consequences."

Huong said with finality, "It must be your children for mine."

Marshall stared into the cold eyes. "That is not justice, that is murder, worse than any crime I committed. You would not avenge your daughter, but dishonor her."

Huong shook his head in disdain. "You are a clever man, Excellency. You murder with logic and reason."

Then Huong leaned into Marshall's face and said furiously, "How can you speak of honor and dishonor? I can't even recite the grievances against you, nor number the dead in Vietnam who cry out for vengeance, those who have no one to avenge them—anonymous women and children, the aged, a mountain of corpses for whom no one cares or remembers—the blameless dead for whom there will never be a monument."

Huong gestured to the memorial around him. "Your country killed a million innocents, but you don't remember. Even the Germans have memorials for the Jews they murdered—but where is the memorial for the millions *America* killed?"

Huong's words slashed as his metal-tipped umbrella stabbed the ground. "Your country is so steeped in blood and violence that it can't be moved by a single innocent death. You demand horror and tragedy, sensational deaths, a river of blood."

He gripped the umbrella tightly. "But horror and tragedy are individual, and *holocaust* is just a word for many individual murders. Your country committed horror on such a grand scale that a single existence lost meaning in the overall horror; there was so much murder and killing that one death crying for vengeance could not be heard among the cries and screams of all the dying. But *I* heard, and I never forgot."

Huong shook his head furiously. "Do not speak to me of justice—you don't know what it means. You cannot speak of justice and honor because you have forgotten what crime is." His eyes were gelid. "You killed my wife and mother."

"That is not true!"

"As I said, you have forgotten what crime is."

"What crime? What are you talking about?"

"I am talking about your participation in the 'peace.'"

"I did everything I could to end the war."

Huong slammed the umbrella against the bench between them. "No, you did everything to extricate your country. You gave no thought to those who remained. You abandoned us. Your war ended when the helicopters lifted off from the embassy, its crewmen kicking at those begging for deliverance. But the war did *not* end. The suffering went on, the mountain of corpses grew steeper."

Huong gripped the umbrella, brought it back into his lap, and said softly, "My wife, my mother. They died trying to flee. I watched my wife raped again and again. They beat her to death. They ripped the gold teeth from my mother's mouth and threw her into the sea."

His eyes froze Marshall. "I watched. There was nothing I could do."

Marshall whispered, "I had nothing to do with that. I am not responsible. You don't understand."

"I understand. You came to Vietnam and murdered its people. Then you abandoned the survivors. You gave no thought to them. You betrayed them, kicked at them as they pleaded for help, then turned your back on those who fled in boats, consigning them to horrible deaths." Huong brought up his hands. "Even now I cannot speak of what happened on that boat when the Thais came. They raped the women, turned them into dogs—even my mother."

His voice choked. "My mother—an old old woman. And they beat the men and sodomized the boys. They took the younger girls and strong youths into slavery and set us adrift without even an oar. Then in two days, more Thais came."

Huong shook his head in sad wonder. "You ask what crime? Your greatest crime is having to ask. Oh, I know, you and your country flailed away at the tragedy of Vietnam. You finally remembered the dead and those who suffered. But all you remembered was *your* tragedy. *Your* suffering. And when you erect a monument someday, it will be for *your* dead. All you will do is vindicate yourselves. You will have learned no lesson, only made others pay to help you forget."

Huong opened his hands to the tomb before him, then he brought his hands together and held them out to Marshall.

"A dewdrop can reflect the universe; in it one can see the stars. You seek the reflection of the world in the ocean, in ideas and events, policies and power; you search for meaning in the sea. I find it in a drop of rain."

His hands closed. "My daughter is dead. You killed her. Now *your* children must die. That is the only way people such as you learn. I wish I could teach your country that. Oh, I would love to see America suffer—you are so smug, so self-righteous, so egocentric. You fight wars for your advantage, then see only *your* suffering, *your* dead, *your* misery. You treat others as if they were not even human."

He pointed at Marshall hatefully. "You murdered my family. You took everything I had. I suffered like Job. Now your suffering begins."

Huong looked at his watch. "They will die in minutes; there is nothing you can do."

Marshall jumped up. "No!" It couldn't be, Marshall thought. Sarah was with Bishop; they were safe at the ballet.

Huong nodded in satisfaction. "I have planned it so carefully. The performance is ending now. Even with a few curtain calls, the audience should be leaving the theater. Perhaps the car is picking them up in front now."

"What are you talking about?"

"The car was parked in back of the Garnier and left unattended. A signal device was attached to it. When the car travels down Avenue de l'Opéra, the signal will set off explosives in a parked car. Even your limousine could not survive the blast. Everyone in that car will die."

"I don't believe you."

Huong shook his head. "It doesn't matter." He looked at his watch again. "You have no time left. Any moment you will hear the explosion. You will hear them all die. I wish you could hear their screams. I wish you could watch it as I saw you murder my daughter. Her name was Ai-ling." He bent forward in crippling sorrow. "Ai-ling. You killed her."

Marshall recoiled. Huong was mad; he *couldn't* reason with him. He had to get away. "You bastard!" he shouted, reaching out for him, but Huong flipped the trigger on the handle of his umbrella and the blade slashed out, ripping Marshall's overcoat.

Marshall looked down at the knife pressed against him, then into Huong's murderous eyes.

"Sit down, Excellency. You are going to listen with me for that explosion."

But Marshall stepped closer; he felt the tip of the blade against his skin. *"This* has been your life's work—to murder innocent children? That's your legacy, your tribute to your daughter? And *you* talk to me of justice, honor, decency, crimes? How dare you talk to me, you who murdered the French agent, and my driver, an innocent boy who had a life to live, parents who loved him. Was his life nothing to your daughter's? Nor my children's lives? Nothing matters except *your* revenge?"

Marshall shook his head in disgust, looking down at the blade pressing against him. "You talk of Job?" he mocked. "Job was a man of love and devotion, kindness and sacrifice. You would have him raise his fist to God, curse Him, tear down His temples, trample His image, murder His priests."

Marshall laughed scornfully. "For what purpose, Mr. Huong?"

Huong's lips curled and Marshall leaned into the umbrella as Huong pushed it harder against him.

"This is what you have done for your daughter? This is how you honor your wife and mother, by killing children, sacrificing innocent blood?"

Marshall shook his head. "If there is life after death, I do not think your mother wants to look into the eyes of my wife, nor will your daughter feel better bathed in the blood of mine. I do not think they will want to share eternity with those you murdered. You alone can revel in the blood of my son, and you can wash yourself in mine too."

Behind him came clapping hands that echoed in the enclosure. Marshall whirled to see Wilson Lord standing behind them.

"That was very good, Brad. You should have been onstage. Ah, but you are—what is politics but theater on a grand scale, and for *real."*

Lord bowed slightly to Huong and approached them.

"Is everything accomplished?" Huong asked.

"Yes. It all went smoothly."

Lord reached into his jacket and, with an unhesitating motion, pulled out a pistol and shot Huong in the center of his forehead.

The silencer muffled the sound; the only noise was the clattering of the umbrella striking marble, and the dull thud of Huong's body dropping to the ground.

Marshall recoiled, then he knelt beside Huong. Seeing the bullet hole, he looked up at Lord with incredulity.

"He's dead, I trust? My eyesight is terrible, but even *I* shouldn't miss at this range."

"No. You didn't miss." Marshall rose to his feet. He looked at Lord questioningly. "It's not true what he said, is it?"

"Actually, I'm not sure; it *might* be. If it is, it's your fault. I tried to talk with you, but you wouldn't listen, so I had to work with Huong. He had contacts among the Arabs. They told him about your meeting with Khomeini for the weapons he promised them, and he told me. But I had to help him in return—he wanted information about your family. I told him they were going to the ballet tonight. Islamic Jihad was probably able to plant the bombing device; if it works, they'll take credit for killing your wife and children. Isn't it amazing they'd actually *brag* about something like that? Mike Caldwell was there to ensure everything went all right because that idiot major might stumble in the way again. But I don't know what happened. I can only guess."

Lord smiled. "Caldwell and Bishop are . . . not altogether predictable. They are young, so you can't be certain they'll succeed even when you know exactly what they're going to do. Nor can you be sure if they'll come to the right decision—the one you want them to make. Youth is *so* erratic."

Marshall just stared at Lord, unable to comprehend what he was hearing.

"Poor Huong. He thought I wanted him to lure you here so that I could kill you, but it was *Huong* I wanted. He couldn't live knowing what he does. Not that it makes any difference—his life was over when his family was killed, and after he got revenge, he had no desire or reason to live. I'm sure he died a happy man."

"You're insane," Marshall said in disbelief.

"Not at all," Lord answered smoothly, directing the pistol

at him. "In fact, I'm *amazed* at my saneness—quite a feat in the midst of all this lunacy: you and Jimmy sabotaging U.S. interests in the Mideast, toppling the Shah, meeting with Khomeini, Huong dealing arms to fanatical Arabs."

Lord gestured to Huong. "We couldn't have him and the Chinese selling missiles and weapons to lunatics. He had to be stopped, especially since he knew everything about Khomeini. He was blinded by revenge; he couldn't even understand that Sûreté might be upset that he murdered one of their agents. Now Sûreté owes me a favor."

Lord smiled. "No, Brad, I am eminently rational. You see, I never planned to harm you. And I've been thinking of some way to spare you, but I can't come up with one. You know too much. I'm afraid you're going to be bitter about this. You'll probably tell everybody what happened."

"Yes. I *will* tell everyone."

"Well, we can't have that. I'm really sorry; I'd grown rather fond of you over the years. Do you want to beg for your life? Promise you'll never say a word about all this?"

Marshall stared him in the eyes. "No."

"Alas, I knew it. You didn't disappoint me. It's too bad you won't be able to read about all this tomorrow. I wonder how they're going to play this—U.S. ambassador and Chinese arms merchant found dead together. What do you suppose they'll make of it? I don't imagine anyone will ever put it all together. It will be just one more unsolved mystery about Vietnam."

Lord cocked the trigger. "Can *you* come up with a way to save yourself that won't cause me difficulties?"

Suddenly a powerful grip on Lord's arm raised the pistol and another hand struck his throat and pulled back, forcing him down, and then the pistol was aimed at his own head.

"Pull the trigger, motherfucker," Mead hissed, pressing against Lord's windpipe.

Marshall fell backward against the bench.

"I been waiting for this," Mead snarled. "Pull the trigger."

Lord couldn't breathe. The pain was intense, but he couldn't break the grip.

"I want to see your brains on the marble," Mead said through clenched teeth, crushing the throat. "Pull the trigger."

Marshall jumped up. "No! Stop it!"

Mead looked up, gorged with fury. "He *owes.*"

"Mead, no. Stop! That's an order."

Lord's eyes bulged and his finger drew back reflexively against the trigger, but then Mead raised Lord's arm and smashed it down against the marble, breaking the hand, sending the pistol clattering across the marble.

Lord collapsed. Mead put his foot on his throat and stepped down.

"I said stop!" Marshall shouted, pulling Mead off.

Mead backed away, heaving furiously, as Marshall grabbed the pistol.

Lord struggled up, holding on to his throat, trying to breathe.

"Shoot him," Mead urged. "Everyone will think they killed each other."

Marshall shook his head. "Get out," he said to Lord.

Lord caught his breath, then cast a contemptuous look at them both and walked up the stairs with all the dignity he could muster.

"Sarah, Chris—are they all right?" Marshall asked.

Mead watched Lord disappear, then he turned to Marshall with a look of censure. "Major Bishop wouldn't let anything happen to them, sir. And there hasn't been any explosion."

Marshall sank onto the bench.

Mead examined Huong's wound, then went to Marshall. "Major Bishop knew Caldwell and Lord were up to something, so he told me to follow you tonight. I been watching you every night. I was there when you went walking with Caldwell."

"You've been following me?"

Mead smiled. "I know how you operate, sir. I was with you in Vietnam when you'd pull your disappearing act all the time. I figured you'd drive a car out the front gate; I talked to André about it. If you *didn't* do it, if you called a cab or came up with another trick, he was going to let the guard know, and he'd relay it to me."

"You knew all along? *Everybody* did?"

"Well, yes, sir. I mean, it's our job to take care of you—no matter how hard you make it."

"Then I owe you my life again? You and Luke both?"

But Mead didn't answer, merely reached down for Marshall and tugged gently.

"We better get out of here, sir."

Marshall glanced a final time at Huong's body. "Do you have any idea what this was all about, Sergeant?"

Mead looked at Huong's body sprawled on the marble before the tomb of the Unknown Deportee. Beyond was the river, glistening with the lights of the city.

"I think it was about Vietnam, sir."

Marshall nodded with a sigh. "But now it's over; Vietnam is over."

Mead stared at him. His face reflected a curious mix of sorrow and dismay. Then his features smoothed and Marshall was looking at the classic warrior, proud, noble, and timeless.

"No, sir," the Marine said to the diplomat. "It won't ever be over. Even after we're all dead it won't be over."

Then they turned and went up the steps.

Caldwell and Bishop faced each other in the dark lot. Bishop had just explained his miracle plan when Caldwell smiled, then laid his pistol on the ground. "Amazing, Lukey. That's *exactly* what I had in mind, but I wasn't sure *you'd* come up with it. I would have felt better if I could have explained all this to you, then seen your grateful surprise when I spared your ass, but this way is fine too."

"You mean you never planned to shoot me?" Bishop asked doubtfully.

Caldwell laughed. "Did you really think I would?"

Bishop nodded. "To be honest, I thought you might this time."

"Then what you did is even more impressive. But I'm impressed with myself too—I fooled you. And you actually thought I'd let the ambassador's family get killed?"

Bishop nodded again.

"God, I *am* good. For Christ's sake, what kind of maniacs do you think we are?"

"Well, there's Wilson Lord . . ."

Caldwell shook his head. "You know, I doubt he expected me to go through with this. I don't think he *wanted* me to. I think he was counting on this to happen. He figured you and I would end up doing this. I think he orchestrated the whole thing. He knew Islamic Jihad would be able to sabotage the car, but sent me out here to ensure Marshall's family *didn't* get killed; he probably guessed you'd stumble into the way again. He has a healthy respect for your knack to fuck up things. He was also counting on me to come up with another plan if you didn't show. He's not as bad as you believe, Luke."

"Oh, yes, he is."

"No. You see everything like in the movies—good guys and bad guys—but Lord isn't all bad, and your man, Marshall, isn't all good. They're just like us."

Bishop grinned. "I'm all good."

"Right," Caldwell said, then he glanced at his watch. "Okay, we have to wrap this up. We'll fake this 'encounter.' I'll be out here sabotaging the car when you discover me in the act. We fight, you beat me, I run off, and you save the day." Caldwell shook his head angrily. "This really pisses me off though."

"Can't we pretend to fight, and you just run off?"

Caldwell shook his head. "I'm on orders to let this car get bombed, even if Lord really doesn't want me to do it, so we have to make this look real to save my ass, and Lord's too. Islamic Jihad is expecting this to happen; when it doesn't, they're going to be suspicious, so this has to look authentic for them to buy it. Besides, if I'm going to come out looking like a loser, you're going to suffer. Now let's get on with it. You want to go first?"

"Oh, yeah."

Caldwell braced himself as Bishop took a terrific swing, then fell backward, rocked by the blow. "Shit!" Then Caldwell stepped forward and landed a solid punch against Bishop's jaw.

Bishop spat blood. "Prick," and he swung again.

They came together, locked, then butted heads until they both fell away.

"Holy fuck!" Bishop cried, holding his head.

"I *said* this had to look good. You're going to send me into the hospital, but I'm going to do *serious* damage to you, Bishop. No one will buy this unless we both end up wrecked."

Caldwell jabbed Bishop twice, knocking him backward.

"You know what pisses me off most? Once again, it'll be the fucking Marines who end up the good guys, when it's me, the CIA, who's the real good guy." He crossed with his left and splintered Bishop's teeth.

Bishop held his mouth, then charged. "Okay. This is for Mrs. Marshall," and he blackened Caldwell's eye.

Caldwell slammed back with a brutal cross to the nose.

Bishop recoiled. "This is for Chris," and he hit Caldwell so hard he slammed him against the wall, dropping him to the ground, then he stomped on his chest.

Caldwell curled up. "I think you broke a couple ribs. *Don't* hit me for Sarah." He held out his hand feebly. "Help me up. I'll stagger off and get a cab."

Bishop reached down.

Caldwell grabbed it and flipped him. Bishop crashed onto his back and Caldwell smashed his face with his fists. "That's for Rochefort," he said, rolling off him.

Bishop moaned, "Who?"

Caldwell kicked him in the sides. "That's for Richelieu."

Bishop doubled over. "Who the fuck are these people?"

Caldwell brushed at his clothes. "Heroes." He squinted at Bishop through swollen eyes and grinned through broken teeth. "Hey, *good* game. Let's do it again sometime."

Then he limped off, struggled over the chain, and disappeared down the street.

Bishop lay for a moment, then sat up, spitting blood.

Finally he pulled himself up and went back to the Opera House. He showed his ticket stub to startled ushers and slipped into the box long after the performance had resumed. Only when the ballet ended and the lights went on did they see Bishop's bloody face and torn clothes. His right eye was swollen shut and his left blackened.

Sarah brought her hands to her mouth, but Bishop smiled through cut lips and jagged teeth. "I was getting bored—it started to drag in the middle so I thought I'd go out and pick a fight with someone."

He struggled out of his chair, dropped to the floor, then pulled himself up. "Ready to go? There's been a change in plans. We'll be going home in my car."

He reached into his trouser pocket and handed his keys to Sarah. "I can't see real well; you drive."

CHAPTER 23

Several months later, on a cold, sunny February day in Washington, Wilson Lord sat before a fireplace in the library of a home in Georgetown.

"My dear Wilson," his host enthused from his leather chair, "you exceeded our expectations. Congratulations."

"It didn't work *quite* as I wanted," Lord said in a hoarse voice, nodding toward his bandaged hand.

"It never does," the elderly man commiserated. "I can't tell you how many disappointments I've had over the years, but in this case, everything worked marvelously. The Gripper, or is it the Gipper?—and what does that *mean*, anyway?—couldn't be more pleased. Well, not him, of course—his grasp of international intricacies is somewhat limited—but those about him, they appreciate your work. Someday in the near future, my dear Wilson, your work will be rewarded." He poked at the fire sorrowfully. "Alas, in the meantime, you will have to go to—"

"Limbo. I know it well."

"I'm afraid so. I suppose Bradley is behind this. You have a bitter enemy there. What happened between you two?" He waved the poker. "Never mind, I don't want to know. But no one else knows either—he hasn't spoken of the matter, never mentioned it to Jimmy or that"—his voice dripped scorn—"admiral at Langley, so I suppose your stay in limbo won't be long. The Shah has fallen, Iran is in chaos . . ."

The old man closed his eyes, shivering with pleasure. "Can't you just see it—the dying Shah brought to America for compassionate medical treatment, outrage in Teheran, riots, maybe even hostages. Carter is finished—the fool, thinking the world was just a peanut patch he could husk."

He cocked his head. "Is that what one does to peanuts? No, one *shells* them." He shook his head. "I'm getting old. I can't keep anything—Gippers or peanuts—straight anymore."

Then he leaned forward and patted Lord's arm. "We owe you, Wilson, and believe me, we never forget our friends. Your day is coming. I think you're going to be in Baghdad soon. You'll do wonderful things for us there."

"Baghdad?"

Lord's mentor nodded. "That's where the future is. We're going to be bogged down there for decades—you'll have steady employment. The zanies there will keep us busy for years. We'll be able to stir that mad pot to a froth anytime we wish. I *love* Arabs. Of course the *real* future is in Japan, but we want to reward you, not punish you, and besides, they won't show their ugly little heads until later. Have you followed my advice, by the way—about the little Nippers, I mean?"

Lord nodded. "Yes. I've been observing them carefully. They're frightening."

The old man shook his head. "No, Wilson. Horrifying. The Japs are *horrifying*. Think of the Trojan War and that horse. The Japanese are my nightmare. I keep seeing this . . . what *was* that movie, the one with the monster?"

"Godzilla?"

"Yes, exactly. Well, I dream they've sent us this Godzilla creature, like the Trojan horse, and when we're all asleep, or zombied out watching their TVs, a secret door will open on the monster, and thousands of little Japs will rush out and chain us up like the Lilliputians did to what's his name. God, I *am* getting old. What *was* his name?"

"Gulliver," Lord answered absently, envisioning a horde of Japanese beating Gulliver with Louis Vuitton handbags, tying him down with Hermès scarves.

"Of course." The old man shook his finger in admonishment. "Oh, be careful of the Japanese, Wilson. I won't live long enough to fight them, but someone will have to. And do you know *why* they're so dangerous?"

Lord knew he was not expected to answer, so he merely waited.

"It's not because they haven't learned from history—it's because they don't even *teach* it."

The old man smiled. "You're such a good audience. And such a good learner. But enough is enough; let's have lunch. I promise I'll stop pontificating. I really must, you know. It's such an old-man type of thing, so boring and tedious. But then, the next administration is going to be nothing but old men, so I'll fit right in. Oh, God, what dreary meetings there will be, a bunch of old men trying to tutor a fool. But the frightening part is that the fool is older than we are."

They went in to lunch, and when they finished, Lord returned home.

His day *was* coming, he knew. After Paris, he had been sent to his mole hole down the Corridor of the Damned in Langley, but Marshall had not orchestrated it; Lord had arranged it himself. Seeing the looming disaster in the Mideast, Lord wanted refuge. The fallout from Iran was going to rain destruction on many careers, but the Lost Corridor offered safe haven until he got to Baghdad, where indeed the future lay.

He would wait in Langley until his patrons gained power at the next election. He would switch off his systems and enter a state of suspended animation. He would be back, he knew. But for now he would have time for Anh and Lance. This would be a wonderful time. He pulled into his driveway. Lance was in the front yard with his mitt.

"Hey, Dad," he shouted. "Want to play a little *one-arm* catch?"

Yes, Lord decided happily, he had plenty of time; this spring he would coach baseball—his hand would have healed by then.

That same day, Bradley Marshall was finishing lunch in the White House with a troubled President.

"I'm getting conflicting advice, Brad," Jimmy Carter said. "What do *you* think I should do about the Shah?"

Marshall put down his glass of apple cider and said emphatically, "Nothing."

"But he's ill. Many are advising me to let him in for medical treatment."

"I would be cautious of those who offer that advice."

"I want to do the right thing," Carter said earnestly. "I want peace and understanding. I want to breach the differences and animosities. If I could get Egypt and Israel to come together, why can't I do it with Khomeini?"

"Because Khomeini is an Islamic fundamentalist from the tenth century. He is bitter and cruel, small and intransigent. You will not be able to reason with him."

"What should I do?"

"Close the embassy in Teheran and get everyone out." Marshall was silent a moment, staring out onto the snow-covered Rose Garden. "Ten years ago I undertook a mission to Vietnam for President Johnson. It was a failure. We didn't know anything about Vietnam, its culture or history, and made a great mistake getting involved. We have paid a dear price for our ignorance and hubris."

He locked eyes on Carter. "We know nothing about the Mideast or the Moslem world. Don't make the same mistake; don't involve us in Iran or Iraq. We must stop these incursions into places we know nothing about; we must stop thinking we know best for everyone when we can't even take care of our *own* problems. It's time to tend to them. Long ago, Lyndon Johnson had a program to help the poor, but he made war in a faraway place and forgot about ignorance and poverty, sending our own uneducated poor to that faraway place. That war is over, and Johnson is dead, but there is *still* ignorance and poverty. Don't send our youth to another faraway place—educate them first, eliminate their poverty first."

Marshall leaned forward. "Let me tell you a story. I have a military aide, a wonderful young man who is in love with my daughter, but my daughter does not love him; at least right now she doesn't, and nothing he can do—including saving her life—will change her mind. I grieve for him. I *want* him to succeed, but there is nothing I can do. I cannot force them together. I hope she changes her mind, but it is *her* decision."

"What if she never changes her mind?"

"Then it will be her loss." Marshall smiled. "But maybe not—maybe it isn't meant to be; maybe she will find someone else. Surely he will. Still, there is nothing *I* can do."

Marshall dropped his napkin on the table. "So it is with Iran—back away, give it some time—let them decide what to do. Maybe they'll change their minds. But again, maybe they won't. It's their decision. We'll survive. Just like Luke will."

He stood and pushed back his chair. "After twenty years in government, I've learned that America isn't good at telling time; frequently we use the wrong instruments. We keep checking our watches, when we really should be looking at the calendar."

Then he bowed slightly and left the room.

Outside the White House, he took a deep breath of cold February air.

A Secret Service agent held his limousine door open. "Home," Marshall said.

As the car rounded the Lincoln Memorial and headed across the bridge, Marshall saw the eternal flame of John F. Kennedy's grave flickering on the hillside of Arlington National Cemetery. Kennedy was dead fifteen years now, and cemeteries all over the country had filled with young men killed in that faraway war. Vietnam had not gone away, nor had the memory of JFK.

The old diplomat had been right about reparations—the bill always comes due in the end: someone has to pay for the mistakes and errors and wrongs.

Well, you just pay it, Marshall thought to himself, then try not to run up another bill.

He gazed at the eternal flame, whipping so violently in the wind that he feared it might go out.

Then he smiled. It *had* gone out, several times, he remembered. They just relit it.

They could always do that—there was always hope—as long as one still had the fire.